The Way We PLAY

USA TODAY BESTSELLING AUTHOR

TIA LOUISE

Playlist

"Particle Man" - They Might Be Giants
"Supermodel" - RuPaul
"Square One" - Tom Petty
"Show Me Love" - Robin S
"Mr. Brightside" - The Killers
"HOT TO GO" - Chappell Roan
"Fantasy" - Mariah Carey
"Hot Hot Hot" - Buster Poindexter
"Apple" - Charli xcx
"Fortnight" - Taylor Swift, Post Malone
"Thank U" - Alanis Morissette
"New Attitude" - Patti LaBelle
"Man on the Moon" - Megan Moroney
"Country Girl (Shake it For Me)" - Luke Bryan
"Return to Sender" - Elvis
"All I Want Is You" - U2
"Spice Up Your Life" - Spice Girls
"Birdhouse in Your Soul" - They Might Be Giants

For the book girlies who prefer their Heroes tall,
dark, broody, and wounded.
And really good in bed.

"Perfect is the enemy of good."
—Voltaire

Prologue

Zane

Twelve years ago

"THINK FAST!" THE FOOTBALL FLIES AT MY FACE, BUT I CATCH IT before it bounces off my nose.

I level my gaze on my youngest brother Hendrix, who recently turned eighteen. "Don't do that."

His blue eyes sparkle, and a grin splits his cheeks. "Or what?"

"I'd hate to have to kick your ass on Thanksgiving Day right here in front of those girls."

A pair of teenage girls have stopped walking to watch us, and he gives them a wink and a wave. "Happy Thanksgiving, ladies!"

The girls laugh and wave, and I suspect they know him from school, where he's both a senior and the starting running back on the football team. To be fair, everyone knows my brothers and me in this small town, and any time we start playing, people stop to watch.

"Don't taunt the kicker, dumbass." My other younger

brother Garrett grabs him around the shoulders, attempting a headlock. "What makes you think they're looking at you? You're so ugly, the doctor slapped the wrong end."

Hendrix does a quick twist, escaping our oversized brother's grip. "Get off me, sasquatch. You're so ugly, the cat ran away."

"The cat did run away."

"That's why!"

"Lame." Garrett shakes his head as Dylan, our baby sister jumps onto his back, which is quite a feat, considering she's an entire foot shorter than he is.

"I'm on Grizz's team!" she calls out, riding piggy-back out to the waterfront park a few blocks from our house.

It's the first time we've all been together for the holiday in a few years. Our oldest brother Jack is in Texas now, making a name for himself as the starting quarterback for the Mustangs. Garrett is building his reputation in Tuscaloosa, and I'm headed to Baltimore as the starting kicker.

It might also be the last time we're together for a while, since Hendrix got an offer from the University of Southern California and Dylan has auditioned for the American Ballet Company in New York. We're all just waiting for that acceptance letter in the mail.

Our parents would be proud, and thinking of them looking down on us makes me nostalgic for the days when they'd be here watching us, Mom playfully scolding and laughing.

We lost them almost four years ago, and I always feel it during the big holidays.

"Hendrix, go long!" Jack shouts.

He takes off like a gazelle, and Garrett stands beside me, watching with Dylan on his back.

"He runs the way you dance." I glance at our baby sister.

Her dark hair is in a high ponytail and her amber eyes sparkle with happiness. She's always happy when we're all together. Losing our parents hit us hard, but I know Dylan lost the most when we buried our mom.

Dylan was Mom's favorite, but ultimately, we all spoiled our only sister. After four failed attempts, Mom finally got her wish of having a little girl, but with Hendrix only eighteen months old, she was pretty overwhelmed.

She handed Dylan to me in the hospital, and it was all hands on deck.

I'd never seen a baby with such big, dark eyes. She was so little, and her expression was so serious. I didn't know what to do. Mom told me to read to her, and as time passed, it became our thing.

Dylan would sit on my lap and listen so intently. We started with a book about pooping, because Mom said it would help her learn to go potty, then we graduated to books about dancing mice.

When she was four, Dylan announced she was going to be a ballerina just like Angelina, and she started ballet. She was quiet like me, but she worked long and hard to make her dream a reality—just like Jack and Garrett and Hendrix.

I wasn't like them. I didn't sleep with my head on a football as my pillow. I didn't watch every single game all weekend long. I liked the game, but I liked other things, too.

Still, when Dad told me to be a kicker, I said okay. Looking back, I realize Mom probably played a hand in that directive.

Now we're all poised for success, aided in no small party by the fame of our football-star father. Walking out to the field now, I can still see Mom on the porch laughing and cheering us on.

She loved her sons, even if they were wild animals, and she loved her only daughter, the light of her life.

"How was that?" Hendrix passes the ball to Jack, clear on the other side of the park, and I think of all of us, he was the most obsessed, the most like our dad. "Jack and I are going to clean the field with you two."

"I'm playing, too!" Dylan skips sideways, holding Garrett's arm.

"You cover Zane, and I'll take Butt Face over here." Garrett nods at our brother.

Jack catches the pass easily, and the four of us line up facing each other with Jack a few feet behind Hendrix waiting for the snap.

"You're so fat, you have your own weather system." Garrett loves to trash talk on the line.

"You're so fat…" Hendrix falters, and Garrett straightens waiting.

"What?"

"You're fat."

"Bruh, your burn game is embarrassing. We gotta work on it before you leave for LA."

"Yeah, but my *ballgame* is strong. Watch me!" Hendrix makes the snap and shoots straight forward like a rocket.

Garrett's on him, and I cut to the left, getting out of the clump before turning back to where Jack is looking for who's open. Obviously, it's me. Garrett is the best lineman I know, and Dylan's a shrimp.

What I don't expect is for her to be keeping pace with me, tracking my moves like a real cornerback. Jack makes the pass, and I reach out, swiping it right out of her hands.

"Dang it!" Dylan jumps up and down with the graceful style of a ballerina.

"Way to hustle." I pass the ball to Jack before patting her shoulder.

"Seven-zero!" Hendrix yells, all fired up. "Nice try, Swan Lake!"

"Don't be hasslin' my girl!" Garrett lifts Dylan off her feet in a hug. "That was a good run, Dee!"

We're back at the line, and this time Jack plays QB for Garrett and Dylan, who takes off running as fast as our younger brother. Hendrix is right on her heels, reaching easily over her head to steal the pass.

She gives him a shove, and he laughs, yelling, "Illegal contact!"

"I was the receiver!" She pushes him again, and he laughs more, running to the center of the field before Garrett stops him.

Dylan's arms are crossed, and she's pouty on her way back to the lineup.

"Don't hate the player, hate the game!" Hendrix does a shuffle step, which makes her sulk more.

"Just because you're all a foot taller than I am."

We line up again, and I'm inclined to give Dylan a break, since she's working so hard. Hendrix knows me too well, and insists I cover Garrett this time.

It's how we spend the rest of the afternoon. Until the sun slowly makes its way to the horizon, and the chill in the air grows a touch more distinct. It never gets too cold this far south.

More people have stopped to watch us, clapping and cheering as each side runs it in for the score. Everyone in this small town knew our dad, and they know we're continuing his legacy. I guess it is a little thrill to see us play, even if it's just for fun.

With one goal separating us, our youngest siblings won't stop until we have a clear winner. Garrett manages to keep Hendrix at bay long enough for Dylan to complete a pass and run it in, and she does a little pirouette in the end zone.

"Excessive celebration—call it back!" Hendrix yells, and Dylan flips him the bird, which makes everyone laugh.

"Looks like y'all need one more player to even things out." Dylan's dance partner Craig runs onto the field.

"It's my boy, Cray!" Garrett immediately grabs him in a bear hug. "Get out here, so we can win this thing!"

I don't bother pointing out Jack, Hendrix, and I make two and a half pro players versus their one college athlete and two dancers.

"We call Jack!" Hendrix yells, and our oldest brother shakes his head, looking down.

"Pretty sure that was always the plan, Einstein," Garrett quips.

"Last play," Jack calls. "It's sudden-death overtime."

As the oldest, Jack slid easily into Dad's role. He has both the patience and the natural leadership qualities that make him a good team captain.

While I tend to be more of a loner, Jack steps up and checks on everybody, makes sure we're all okay and gives us advice if we need it.

Hanging back, I watch our small clan laughing and rough-housing as they approach the line, and I think we've made it. I think we're going to be okay.

Just goes to show what I know.

We line up for the snap, and Hendrix and Dylan are practically nose to nose. "Don't go soft on me, Zane."

I shake my head at his ferocity. "It's only a game."

The snap is made, and Jack falls back, his eyes scanning Garret hulking over Hendrix and Dylan skipping around me.

Craig makes a beeline for him, and he's forced to throw it. My eyes are on the brown pigskin spiraling like a bullet straight to me. It's a perfect pass, and I seem to be wide open. Dylan's not in my sights as I reach for the ball.

It's higher than I expected, forcing me to jump. Hendrix yells, but I've got it. The only problem is I'm a kicker, not a runner, and I'm not used to calculating how fast I'm moving. As I'm flying through the air, I realize I'm going to hit the ground hard. *Shit.*

Clutching the ball to my chest, my muscles tense as I brace for impact. It all happens so fast, yet so slow at the same time. I feel her small body under mine. My chest seizes, and I try to twist away from her.

It's too late, and all my weight comes down hard on my little sister. Throwing out my arm, I try to fight my velocity, but at six-two, I can't stop it. She screams, and I lose the ball, doing everything I can not to hurt her.

We hit and bounce, and I hear the crunch of bone. Another scream, and I know without looking I've broken something that can't be fixed.

I'm on my feet fast when we stop moving, but Dylan doesn't get up. She rolls to the side, holding her leg, her foot bent unnaturally.

Her cries echo in my ears, and it's not just the physical pain. This injury changes everything, but not only for Dylan.

It's the first in a series of breaks that will change my life.

Chapter 1

Zane

"**G**IVE ME YOUR HAND, AND I'LL HELP YOU." I PLACE MY HAND OVER Benji Maxwell's small one and guide the plastic brush in smooth circles along the horse's side.

We repeat the process gently, moving the brush slowly along the shiny, chocolate-brown coat, over powerful muscles until the tension eases from the boy's shoulders.

His brow is furrowed, and his eyes are focused on our motion. I'll give him a few more strokes, then I'll let him do it by himself.

The old thoroughbred blows air through his nostrils, and his large head hangs over the door of the stall. It's early morning at Second Chance Stables on the outskirts of Newhope, Alabama, and dust hangs in a beam of sunlight streaming through the door. It's warm for the first day of November.

"You're a natural with these kids, Zane." The owner Gloria Fruit stops at the door, cupping her arm around the horse's neck. "I wouldn't object if you decided to hang around here full time."

She's dressed in knee-length shorteralls and a black tank,

and her mousey brown hair is in a ponytail under a tattered baseball cap.

Beat-up, dusty work boots complete her outfit, and her dark eyes crinkle at the corners with her smile. I've never seen Gloria dressed up or wearing makeup as long as I've known her.

"Look, Ms. Fruit." Benji's voice is focused. "I'm doing it."

He doesn't get too excited, but the last time I was here, he held his palm under Shiloh's velvety nose. When his mother saw him looking into the horse's huge eyes, she started to cry.

I cleared my throat and did my best not to draw attention to them. I'm not licensed in equine therapy, but I help Gloria with her students if they arrive before she does.

"You *are* doing it, Benji." Gloria's voice is low and encouraging. "That's very good."

The horse lifts his head, exhaling a playful snort, and I move my hand to the boy's shoulder.

"He's nodding because he likes it," she laughs.

Gloria is at least fifteen years older than me, and she opened this ranch on the outskirts of town while I was still in college.

Her obscenely rich parents couldn't figure out why their only daughter was more interested in broken-down thorough-breds than debutante parties and dating the most eligible bachelors in their circle.

They'd taken her to Churchill Downs, hoping she'd meet the son of one of their friends there, but instead she'd spent the weekend hanging out with a female veterinarian, who opened her eyes to several things, including the number of former race-horses headed to the slaughterhouse due to overuse or injury.

As soon as she got home, in her characteristic, take-charge fashion, she convinced her parents to buy the old polo club, which she turned into a shelter for the animals.

Then when she learned about equine therapy, she took it a step further by getting licensed and inviting local parents to bring their kids here to ride and care for the older, gentler horses and only charging what they could afford to pay. Even if that meant they participated for free.

People like Gloria give me hope for mankind.

"Good Morning, Mr. Bradford." Sandra steps up beside Gloria, letting out a little whistle. "Out here at the crack of dawn, looking like a snack in those jeans."

Sandra never misses a chance to flirt with me, like all the old ladies in our small town on the coast. The only difference is I know Sandra's genuinely teasing.

Still, I don't engage. "Benji's mom said he woke up asking to feed the pretty horses."

"Pretty horses, eh?" Gloria's brows rise. "I'd call that progress."

"You sure she was talking about the horses?"

"Leave him alone, Sandra. You know Zane doesn't like flirting, and I need him here."

My smile is tight, because she's not lying. I don't have much patience for frivolity, but I do have a sense of humor, as dry as it might be.

"I'm not going anywhere." I step back to open the door of Shiloh's stall.

"That's a relief." Sandra winks. "This town needs more tall, dark, and broody former football players with chiseled jawlines and a love of books and special-needs children."

"I've got to get to Miss Gina's." A wince tightens my smile when I step wrong, and a spasm grabs my lower back.

Concern lines Gloria's face. "That old injury acting up again?"

Shaking my head, I take a halting step. "Miss Gina had me moving potted trees around yesterday. They were a lot heavier than they looked."

"Oh, and don't forget, he takes care of rich, old blind ladies," Sandra calls after me.

"Miss Gina's some tough competition." Gloria elbows her partner before taking my place in the stall beside Benji and

Shiloh. "But I'm willing to share as long as Zane keeps my mornings covered."

Gloria is not a morning person, something we established up front.

I take the morning shift, welcome any therapy kids who show up early, keep things running until she appears, then I head back to Montrose, the small town north of Newhope where I'm a glorified handyman for Miss Gina Rosario, who lives alone in her historic mansion on the bluffs.

Miss Gina is the last of a very wealthy family, one of the founding families of our town, and thanks to Dylan's obsession with her massive, Italian-style estate, we've become friends. Dylan is also the reason I started working for her after her octogenarian groundskeeper retired.

"See you tomorrow." I give them a brief wave.

The doors are off my old Jeep Wrangler, and the wind swirls around me as I head back up the scenic drive to town. Live oak trees stretch heavy limbs over the two-lane road, creating a shady tunnel, and my mind travels back in time.

Our parents moved us here because our mom loved being near the ocean, and our dad liked the friendly people. He said it was a place he felt at home. By contrast, I've always been an alien in the middle of a family of extroverted siblings.

Jack is the most like me, but Garrett started talking and never stopped. I've never known anyone with a personality as big as his body, and he's massive.

My siblings got it honest from our dad, but Mom understood me.

She told me it was okay to be alone, to read, to walk away from the noise when the house got too busy. Sometimes she'd walk with me along the bay. We'd watch the waves rippling on the quiet shore. We'd stop and watch the turtles sunning on logs.

We'd watch the huge silver and black egrets slowly spread their wings wide and lift off the ground like massive gliders over the water.

Mom said I reminded her of her father, but I didn't understand. Weren't girls supposed to grow up and marry men like their dads? I'd read that somewhere. She said not to believe everything I read.

As always in November, my thoughts go to that Thanksgiving-Day football game, and my shoulders tense. We were having fun, goofing off, but every time, I beat myself up for not being smarter.

Dylan shouldn't have been out there. She was too small to be on that field with all of us towering over her. It's a rough game, and to make matters worse, she was as competitive as Garrett and Hendrix.

When Jack passed me the ball, I didn't even see her right beside me. She shouldn't have been able to keep up with me, but she was so strong. She had worked so hard.

I can still hear the crunch of bone when we hit the ground. I can still hear her cries of pain and loss.

They were the same cries I made when I was caught under a three-hundred-pound lineman in the fake field goal play that ended my football career.

When I broke Dylan, ending her dreams of dancing forever, I said I'd never forgive myself. I couldn't forget the look on her face when the doctor told her she could still dance, but going *en pointe* or completing the elaborate jumps and fouettés she had to do as a professional were now impossible.

Lying in my own hospital bed in Baltimore twelve years later, her soulful brown eyes fighting tears were all I could see when the doctor told me my career as a kicker was done.

Dylan says she never held what happened against me, but I knew it was only a matter of time before karma evened the score. It hurt, but nothing hurt as much as that Thanksgiving Day.

I didn't lose a dream, but I did lose the only thing I knew how to do.

The sound of dance music wafts through the front door

of our house when I pull into the gravel driveway and put the Jeep in park. I'd only planned to stop by and pick up my tools, but Jack's truck is parked out front with several boxes stacked in the bed.

Rachel's brother Edward has a small one in his arms, and he's frowning as he carries it into the house.

The tightness in my shoulders hasn't eased from my un-welcome trip down memory lane, and I'm still limping when I follow him inside to where the music is playing louder. It's some kind of dance song with trumpets and voices shouting like a cheer.

"Why are we moving all our things in here if we're only staying a few days?" Edward's tone is flat.

I've only met the kid one other time at Halloween, when he and his sister stopped by the house during trick or treating.

Rachel had just returned from an emergency trip to Birmingham with her brother in tow and nowhere to put him. Dylan offered to let them stay with us in our big family home until they could find their own place.

It's only Dylan, me, and Dylan's fiancé Logan Murphy here now. I didn't want Rachel sleeping across the hall from me, but I've given up on arguing with my little sister.

When her dancing dreams ended, she pivoted to running our family restaurant Cooters & Shooters and helping or find-ing help for anyone and everyone in need.

"We're not moving everything—just the things we need until we find our own place." Rachel appears in the hallway and my stomach tightens.

She's really pretty, and she has an annoying habit of asking questions and offering to help fix everything. It's bad enough when Dylan does it, but Rachel is new and new is irritating.

"We don't need all these books." Edward looks into the box, and Rachel lifts out a tattered, black paperback with pale hands holding an apple and *Twilight* on the cover. "*Au contraire, mon frere*—books are life!"

"Are you speaking French?" His nose curls, and I notice he doesn't meet her gaze.

I hadn't picked up on that when they stopped by at Halloween. I only noticed he talked quickly, as if he were an actor in an old-timey gangster movie. He'd called himself Eddie Nashville.

Rachel said he had gotten into some kind of trouble at school, and her grandmother couldn't keep him anymore. Naturally, my little sister swooped in for the rescue.

"Zane! What are you doing here?" Rachel startles, taking a step back.

Her green eyes blink wide, and her cheeks flush. She looks down at her tank top and leggings before looking up at me again, her blonde ponytail bouncing.

"I live here." My jaw is tight, and I'm not interested in her hair or her body or her bright green eyes.

"Yes, but I thought you'd left for the day."

"I need to pick up my tool kit."

Her face lights, and I can tell she's about to say something I won't like.

"Perfect timing! Give me just a minute to shower, and I'll ride with you to Miss Gina's."

"I'm not staying that long."

"Good, because I don't need that long!" she sings out, dashing up the stairs. "We've been moving all morning, so I just need to get the sticky off me. I'll be right back."

Shifting my weight causes me to wince, and thankfully she doesn't notice. I tear my eyes off her round ass bouncing as she jogs up the stairs. I swallow a groan, wishing I didn't have to follow her to get what I need.

"What is this music?" I gingerly take the stairs, doing my best not to give any indication my back is aching.

The last thing I need is her to offer free massage therapy again. As Miss Gina's new nurse slash assistant, we're basically co-workers, and I do my best to avoid being around when they're doing things like yoga or water aerobics. Rachel has more curves than I want to think about.

"It's RuPaul!" she calls out before slamming the bathroom door. "Drag queen music is the best! It's about surviving and being strong and optimistic."

"Does it have to be so loud?" I shout from across the hall as I pick up my canvas tool bag.

"She's always loud," Edward grumbles.

"She's come to the right place."

Today he's wearing a threadbare They Might Be Giants T-shirt, and I notice he's quietly humming to himself.

"I like your shirt."

He looks down. "Their songs are like little stories. Like 'Particle Man,' critics try to make it about science versus religion, but John Linnell said it's strictly about the characters in a literal sense."

My eyebrows rise. "And John Linnell is?"

"The songwriter."

"I guess he'd know." My brow furrows when I notice an unusual, smoky-herbal scent. "Is something burning?"

"Sage. Rachel says it clears negative energy and promotes healing."

"Sounds like bull sh–*pit* to me."

"*Schpit*." He repeats the word frowning. "I'm not familiar with that word."

I do a quick sweep of his size and weight. He's skinny, but he's as tall as Rachel, and I understand why his grandmother would be concerned if he has started to have episodes or fight, although to be honest, he doesn't seem like the fighting type.

"I misspoke. I think burning sage is bull spit."

Hesitating, I lift a framed photograph off the dresser and my jaw tightens. Talk about bullshit.

It's a man whose face I haven't seen in a long time. Not since I was a boy, and my parents decided to open a restaurant on the bay. A man who caused a lot of pain and disappointment for my parents, and someone I never want to see again.

"Why do you have this picture?" I can't keep the anger out of my tone.

Edward takes a step away from me. "That's Papa."

My brow furrows. "Your father?"

I don't know how much Edward can be trusted with the facts, and I look across the hall to the bathroom.

I'm not sure when I notice Rachel's loud singing of RuPaul's song "Supermodel" stop, but at that moment, a dull thud sounds from the other side of the door.

"Stay here." I order, hustling across the hall.

"Rachel?" I bang on the door, but only the noise of the shower responds. "Rachel, are you okay?"

I knock harder, but again, it's only silence. My jaw tightens, and I look down, listening to the spray of water as a cold realization filters through me. She's in trouble.

"Rachel!" I try again, shouting louder and banging my hand against the wood.

I don't want to do this, but I don't have a choice. Grabbing the handle, I hit the wooden barrier with my shoulder. The door shudders, and I do it again. It only takes once more before the door yields, flying open.

Staggering into the small, steamy room, I see Rachel on her knees in the shower. She's holding one of the silver bars we installed to help me after my injury.

Her eyes are closed, and her shoulders heave like she's having difficulty breathing.

"Rachel?" I grab a towel, opening the door and stepping into the spray.

I'm worried she has a physical condition I don't know about—how could I know? We only started working together a few months ago, and we don't talk about our personal lives. I didn't even know she had a twelve-year-old brother until a week ago.

"Edward, bring me a glass of juice!" I shout.

I'm pretty sure he's able to do that, even if he's only been in our kitchen a few times.

"Rachel?" Reaching out, I turn off the water, and my lips tighten as I drape the towel over her naked body, doing my best not to look at her.

She has a beautiful body—ivory skin, perfect, large breasts and a small waist. I swallow hard not wanting to find her sexy as hell, but *damn*. Rachel looks good in clothes. She looks like a fantasy naked.

"I'm okay," she whispers. "Dizzy… Need a minute."

Relief twists my chest, and I guide her onto her butt with the towel placed over her front, up to her chin.

Chapter 2

Rachel

'M NAKED.

I'm sitting on the floor of the shower naked with Zane Bradford on his knees in front of me soaking wet and looking like an angry god.

A hot and sexy angry god.

Thankfully, a soaking-wet towel covers my body—a towel that he put there. I'm too dizzy to be humiliated… *yet.*

His dark brown hair is wet around his square jaw, making it appear almost black, and his pale blue eyes are so intense. His hand touches my cheek, and my eyes follow the lines of ink in the sleeve covering his muscular right arm.

Most prominent is a tattoo of the taijitu or yin-yang symbol, only it's not the traditional curved one. It's the one with black and white lines. *Taijitu symbolizes the two opposing forces in nature.*

"Rachel?" He holds a glass of orange juice to my lips. "Drink this."

The blood pulses in my veins. I can feel it thump-thump-thumping in my limbs, and I know what happened. We'd been running up and down the stairs all day, unloading the truck, and I only ate a piece of toast for breakfast.

As I was standing in the hot shower, my hands started to shake, but I didn't want to make Zane wait. I really was afraid he'd leave without me.

Blinking slowly, I wrap an arm over my waist as I try to sit up straighter. The water is off at least, and Edward is at the door not looking at me.

"If you're okay, I'll go back to my room." My brother doesn't handle excitement very well.

"Are you diabetic?" Concern laced with anger is in Zane's voice.

"Hypoglycemic. I didn't eat enough breakfast, and all the running up and down the stairs then the heat of the shower must've made my blood sugar drop."

I sip more of the juice. It helps, but now my stomach is weak. I'm nauseated, and I wish I hadn't gotten so distracted.

"I should've…" My voice breaks off, and I shake my head.

I should've grabbed a grape Jolly Rancher off my nightstand. That little hit of sugar was all I needed.

"I don't think you hit your head." Zane grips my chin between his finger and thumb, forcing my eyes to his. "Your pupils aren't dilated."

"I didn't hit my head." The last thing I remember is singing along with RuPaul when my knees buckled. "I'm lucky that bar was there."

I nod at the silver rod on the side of the shower, and his lips tighten. "We installed it when I came home."

Right. They would've installed it when he came back here after his injury—he wouldn't have been able to put weight on his leg for a while.

Not long after I got here, in an attempt to understand his grumpy demeanor, I watched the video replay of the hit on YouTube. I'd heard the story of how he'd tried to fake a field goal, but I didn't expect what I saw on that video.

He spun left, and a lineman the size of a refrigerator came down on him so hard, it looked for a minute like he might not get up. I actually gasped out loud, and my heart dropped to my stomach. Even though I knew he'd made it through, it was horrifying, and the cry of pain he'd made brought tears to my eyes.

His foot was broken so badly, he's lucky he can still walk. It ended his career as a professional kicker, sending him back here, far away from the parties and the flashing lights and the celebrity.

Understandably, he's closed off and distant, right? Still, I'd like to be friends. We work together, and now we're practically roommates, being right across the hall from each other.

Shifting around, I move the towel to cover more of my body. "Thank you… for helping me."

He stands, turning to get a fresh towel out of the cabinet, which he uses to dry himself. "You're a guest in our home."

It's a curt reply that sucks all the warmth out of his act of kindness, but I've been practicing positive meditations, overcoming negativity.

I give him a neutral smile. "Still, you did a good thing."

He glances at me. "You shouldn't be alone in case it happens again."

"I know how to manage it. I was just distracted." I'm still sitting on the floor holding the glass.

I don't say *by him*, because I'm not distracted by Zane Bradford. I was trying to hurry so he'd give me a ride to work. That's all.

"Are you okay now?" He gives me a pointed look, and my throat tightens.

"I'm fine. Trust me, I've been dealing with this for a long time."

Zane's lips tighten as if he'll say something. Instead, he simply nods.

Nodding seems to be his response to everything.

"Are you going to work today?"

"Yes!" I hold the bar to help myself stand, then I stop when

I realize I'm about to give him the full-Monty view of my vag. "If you'll give me five minutes, I'll be dressed and ready to go."

"I have to change out of these wet clothes, so take ten."

"In that case, I'll put on some lip gloss."

He shakes his head. "Miss Gina is blind, so it won't matter."

My lips twist, and I attempt to lighten the mood. "Who said it's for Miss Gina?"

His tone turns impatient. "Are you able to stand?"

"Not with you in here."

A fresh pinch of annoyance tightens his attractive features. "I'm right across the hall if you need help."

He leaves, and I finish off the juice. I started having trouble with low blood sugar when I started having my periods, but I've learned to manage it. I'm pretty embarrassed this happened, but everything falling on me in the last week has been a lot— from the surprise of taking care of my brother to the question of where we'll live.

Still, I have to be more responsible. Edward needs me to take care of myself, and the last thing I need is a lecture from meanie Zane Bradford.

I wring out the towel and hang it on a hook inside the shower then I grab a dry one from the cabinet. I'll have to do a load of laundry to help with this mess I've made. My hair is wet, and water is all over the floor.

Taking a minute, I clean it all up before I dash across the hall to get dressed, securing my damp hair in two braids on the sides of my head. I pull on leggings and an oversized, light-green sweatshirt, then I swipe up my bag and motion for Edward to follow me.

"It's 'take your sibling to work' day." His brow furrows, and I point to the Kindle on the dresser. "Bring that so you'll have something to read. You have your phone, and I'll find something constructive for you to do."

He's twelve, not two, and he can sit quietly while I work

during the day. He's been doing it for a while now, ever since I had to pull him out of school, which was a total shitshow.

They talk about mainstreaming kids like him, but if he's bullied and fights back, they insist he be medicated. Edward has never had a problem at school, but it didn't matter to his new teacher. That "leader" only cared that my brother behave like every other kid in the class.

Scrubbing my fingers over my brow, I swallow the lump in my throat. I was supposed to start working with Miss Gina in August, but getting him settled delayed everything.

Gran finally told me to go ahead and come here and pursue my life, but when the fight happened, I had to go back and get him. Our grandmother has a good heart, but she's old-school. When she called to say she was going to have to medicate him or move him to a group home, I panicked and raced back to Birmingham.

Now our entire future is uncertain.

When I took this job as Miss Gina's nurse, it really did feel like my life was finally taking a turn for the good. I had my own room in a mansion on the bluffs overlooking a beautiful bay. I was taking care of a sweet old blind lady, who wasn't demanding in the least and gave me as much free time as I needed.

It was all going great—if you don't count Zane Bradford, the super hot and grumpy handyman who took one look at me and decided he'd rather be enemies than friends. I didn't need him—I made friends with his little sister Dylan and the staff at her hilariously wild family restaurant Cooters & Shooters.

Dylan is nothing like her brother. When she found out what happened with Edward, she insisted we stay here in her family home. She even offered to help me get him enrolled at the school here—if that's what I decide to do.

We hustle down the stairs to where Zane is sliding his feet into his work boots. His dark hair is still damp, but he's in his uniform of jeans, a gray T-shirt, and a plaid flannel overshirt rolled up at the sleeves. He has a dark scruff on his cheeks, and sometimes he adds a baseball cap to make me drool.

Straightening, his heart-stopping blue eyes fix on me for a second. He lifts his chin and heads out the door. Exhaling heavily, I follow.

The wind blows loud around us as we drive north along the bay. If I had to guess, I'd say he keeps the doors off his Jeep so he doesn't have to do things like have a conversation with his passengers.

Edward is in the back seat with the hood of his sweatshirt pulled over his shaggy, blond head. The strings are tied tight under his neck, so it creates almost a cocoon. I'm sure he doesn't like the wind, but bless his heart, he's learned to cope with a lot in his twelve years on this planet.

When we finally arrive at the house, Zane exits the vehicle without a word. He reaches into the back of the Jeep for his bag, but he doesn't get far before he takes a halting stop. He tries so hard to hide the muscle spasms, but I've been trained in sports medicine and physical therapy.

"My massage offer remains open." I reach behind my seat for my backpack and to help my brother out of the Jeep. "I saw that video of your injury, and I'm sure you still have trauma in your hip and lower back."

"No thanks." It's a flat reply, and I decide to try a teasing olive branch.

"It's only fair now that you've seen me naked that I get to see you naked."

His voice turns stern. "I didn't *see you naked*. I didn't have a choice."

"You mean you didn't look?" I squint one eye at him. "I don't believe you."

His square jaw flexes attractively, and his dark brow lowers. "Is your father Jayden Wells?"

Wow. I didn't expect that comeback. My stomach pits at the mention of my father's name. It's like a slap, and my chin pulls back reflexively.

"Why… what?"

"He saw Papa's picture in your room." Edward's quiet voice comes from behind my shoulder.

Shit. Gran put Jayden's picture in my things, and I was trying to decide if I was going to shove it in a drawer or throw it in the garbage. I'm leaning hard to the latter option.

Straightening my shoulders, I lift my chin. "Do you know him?"

Zane's eyes flare. I wouldn't be surprised if smoke came from his nostrils. "I was only a boy when your *papa* swindled my dad out of the downpayment on a restaurant they had planned to open together. He pulled out of the contract, leaving my parents holding the bag."

My throat tightens, and embarrassment rises behind my ears. I'm quite familiar with my father's selfish behavior, and I'm sure he'd have some narcissistic reason why he wasn't to blame for whatever pain he caused. Yep, garbage.

"If it makes a difference, he doesn't treat his own family any better. I've worked hard to distance myself from him, and now that we're here, I plan to make my own—"

"I'm not interested in your plans or why you're here." Zane's jaw is tight, and the embarrassment in my neck moves to my chest. "Just stay on your side of the house, and I'll stay on mine."

My lips tighten. While I want to assure him I'm nothing like my father, I don't appreciate the way he's slapping a label on me I don't deserve. He doesn't know anything about me, and I'm ready to make the point emphatically.

I'm prepared to tell him he's being a prejudiced jerk, but Edward sways behind me, softly humming "Particle Man." He doesn't react well to tension or raised voices, and I have to let it go for now.

So I look down, swallowing my desire to fight, and simply say, "Understood."

Zane walks away, and my eyes drift from his broad shoulders down his strong back to his perfectly square ass in those jeans. I've never had an opponent, much less one who could be a male model.

My father ruined a lot of things for me, but I didn't expect him to follow me to this beautiful place where I thought I'd have a chance at having my own life.

Now I'm back at square one, and I sure could use some drag queen music right now.

"I'm sorry I had to leave so abruptly." I lift Miss Gina's brown cashmere scarf off the back of the chair and drape it over her shoulders.

She's wearing soft white pants and a loose, long-sleeved shirt. A floppy, beige canvas hat is in her hands. She lifts it and plops it onto her head.

"You don't have to apologize. Family first. I was worried about you, though. I hope everything is okay."

My shoulders drop, which thankfully she can't see. "I need a mantra for when life gives you everything you ever wanted, then takes it all back just like that."

"My sister loves mantras." Edward pipes up from behind me, and the old woman's brows shoot up.

"Who is this?" She leans forward as if she'll look at him, and her straight, gray hair falls forward on her jaw.

"Miss Gina, meet my younger brother Edward. He's twelve." I move my hand between them, even if it's only for Edward's benefit.

"Well, hello, Edward!" Her smile beams, and her blue eyes blink as she looks towards the horizon.

My brother turns to look behind him, confused. "What are you looking at?"

"Miss Gina is blind, Edward." My voice is low, but it only makes her laugh.

"You'll get used to me!" She stretches out her hand, which he shakes so briefly, I'm not sure it counts. "I'm pleased to meet you. I've heard you have a lot of personality."

"You have?" I look from her to him confused. "Who told you about Edward?"

"Dylan was here last week. She said you have a brother named Eddie Nashville, and he's quite a character." Her voice is warm and genuine.

Still, heat creeps up the back of my neck. "Oh."

"That's my stage name." Edward says it like everyone has a stage name, *duh*. "I'm not famous for anything yet, but when I am, it's what I'll use."

"I like it, and I like your approach." She stands slowly. "It's good to be prepared, and Eddie Nashville has style. It reminds me of Paul Newman in *The Color of Money*."

"I don't know who that is."

"I have a job for you, Eddie." The old woman puts her hand on his forearm, giving it a brief pat, almost like she knows not to crowd him.

"Okay." He doesn't pull away.

In fact, he actually seems comfortable with Miss G, which I've learned is her superpower. Less than five minutes in her presence, and everyone is at ease.

"My cat Sky has been living under my deck for the past few weeks. I think she has a litter of kittens there." The two of them walk slowly in the direction of the ornate glass doors leading out to the patio. "I can't see, of course, so I need your help. Would you check, and if she has, count them for me and make sure none of them are hurt or injured. I want to know what to tell the vet when I call him."

"A mother cat will take care of her kittens." Edward's tone is certain, as if he's already studied the situation. "People think they're rescuing kittens, but it's actually worse to take them from their mother if they're well-groomed and healthy."

"Oh, I don't want to separate them. I just want to be sure they get their shots." She leans closer. "And I'd like to have Sky fixed. This is her second litter in a year, and we barely found homes for the last ones."

"It's far less traumatic to neuter a male cat than spay a female."

I have no idea where my brother gets his information, but he's usually right.

"I agree." Miss Gina nods. "However, I don't know who or where said male cat is located, and we have to stop this."

Edward's lips purse. "I see your problem. I'll let you know what I find out."

"Thank you, Eddie. I can tell already you're going to be a wonderful addition to my household!"

He takes off, and Miss Gina stretches her slender hand in my direction. "Rachel, your brother is adorable. You must have so much fun together."

I almost laugh. "I never really thought of it that way."

"You're joking! Why not? He's so intelligent!"

Taking her hand, I walk with her through the French doors onto her back patio where two pear trees stand in enormous, cerulean blue ceramic pots, and pink bougainvillea grows in twisting vines over an arch erected behind a wrought-iron bench.

Her patio is immaculately landscaped, with square beds between flagstone paths. She even had a raised, wooden platform constructed for my massage therapy table, complete with full-length beige-linen curtains for privacy.

It's all so elegant and beautiful, and she can't see a bit of it.

"I guess, since he was born, I've spent all my time trying to figure out how to take care of him. *Fun* was never part of the equation."

The old woman's brow furrows, and concern deepens her voice. "Isn't childcare something for your mother to work out?"

A sad little half-smile pulls the side of my lips. "It should've been."

Miss Gina holds my hand. "Tell me what happened."

I exhale a brief laugh, thinking how if she were anyone else in the world, this question might seem intrusive. As it is…

"She never wanted another child. My father insisted, and when he found out Edward was a boy, he was obsessed." My lips tighten. "Then when Edward was diagnosed, he lost interest. That left me."

Miss Gina stops walking and turns to pull me into a hug, holding me close to her body for several seconds. "My goodness, Rachel. That's the saddest thing I've heard in a while."

My memory travels back to baby Edward lying in his crib quietly crying, and no one going to check on him. I remember myself at sixteen with posters of my favorite boy bands on the walls, putting on makeup while I watched YouTube videos, and hearing him fuss until I'd finally go to his room, pick him up, and carry him to mine.

"He was actually pretty easy as a baby." I lift one of the pink bougainvillea flowers on the vine, turning it in my fingers. "I didn't have a car or a boyfriend or anything else to do, so I'd hold him or change him or give him a bottle."

"You're a warm soul." Miss Gina holds my arm, and we walk again. "I'm so lucky to have you here."

"We'll see about that, I guess. Now that I have all this extra baggage."

"A brother is hardly baggage. More like an unexpected gift."

She has no idea how unexpected. "I mean, I know it isn't what you expected."

"At my old age, I've learned the best thing I can do is stay flexible—so I don't break." She pats my hand. "And you're staying at the Bradford house? I told Dylan she and that handsome Logan could come and spend the night in the bungalow here if things get too crowded. I like having friends around at night."

"I'm sorry I can't fulfill that part of our arrangement. Trust me, I really wish I could stay with you here."

"Don't worry. I've seen it time and time again—life always seems to put people together in the way they're supposed to fit. It will all work out. You'll see."

My lips twitch, and I shrug. "I hope you're right."

"Now, speaking of flexibility, I think I have a yoga class scheduled?"

"Yes, you do." I take her hand, leading her to the outdoor space overlooking the bay.

We spend the next hour moving through flows, working on balance and flexibility. It's a relaxing class focused on breathing and light core work. We finish, seated in the lotus position with our hands in prayer pose.

"Namaste," I say quietly as my brother approaches.

"You have five kittens, two pure black, two tuxedos, and this one," Edward announces, walking over to where we sit. "He looks like a Russian Blue, but his head is shaped like a Chartreux. Although, Sky is Siamese, so he's more likely Russian Blue."

Edward places a fuzzy gray kitten in her hands, and Miss Gina exhales an affectionate laugh. "I don't like to complain, but I do wish I could see a Russian blue kitten. Describe him to me, Eddie!"

My brother's expression is as serious as if she's a queen and he's her loyal subject. "He's pure gray, and you can feel his thick coat, almost like a pelt. He has phantom rings on his tail, and when the light hits him, he appears to have a silver halo."

"My goodness!" Miss Gina's eyes widen. "He sounds magical."

My jaw is on the ground. "How do you know all these cat facts?"

"PetMD has an extensive online database." Edward's brow furrows. "I've put out a bowl of food and plenty of water for Sky, since they're all still nursing. I didn't see any signs of a male cat anywhere."

"He's off living his best life, no doubt." I don't miss the touch of humor in her voice. "You've done very well, Eddie. I'll call Dr. Moore at the Eastern Shore Animal Clinic and let him know what all you've discovered."

"The mother is very friendly."

"Yes, Sky is a good mamma. Her kittens grow up to be good cats. Maybe Dylan would like one—what do you think, Rachel? It can keep mice away from the restaurant."

I think I'm annoyed that Sky sounds like a better mother than ours ever was, but I don't say that part out loud. "I'll ask her."

"Are you okay?"

It's impossible to get anything past Miss Gina, even blind, so I force a smile into my tone. "Of course! I'll let you know what she says."

It's five when we're all finished and loading into the Jeep. I have no idea what Zane did today, and to be honest, as appreciative as I am to him of helping me in the shower this morning, I'm still irritated at him for speaking to us the way he did.

Miss Gina walks with us to the edge of the driveway, and I give her a hug while Edward goes ahead of us to the Jeep.

"I fixed the broken window on the greenhouse, and I'll take a look at the elevator tomorrow." Zane puts a hand in his pocket and looks down, annoyance lining his face as he waits for me.

My eyes narrow, and I glance ahead to where my brother is already sitting in the backseat with his hoodie over his head and ears and the strings pulled tight under his chin as if in preparation.

We're far enough away that my tone won't upset him, and I reach out, putting my hand on Zane's arm to stop him.

"You said your piece this morning. Now I have something to say to you."

He turns, putting his hands on his hips as he faces me, which stretches his gray T-shirt attractively across his broad chest. "Go ahead."

His brow lowers, and the scruff on his square jaw moves with the flex of his muscle. It doesn't matter how handsome he is. I won't be distracted this time.

"I spent the first half of my life with a man who was cruel and unpredictable, and I'm not spending another minute of it the same way."

His low voice is gruff. "No one's asking you to."

"I'm building my own life now, and I'm my own person. Understand?"

He only nods, but it's enough for me.

Lifting my chin, I turn on the ball of my foot and walk straight to the Jeep, climbing in without looking back. I hear the crunch of his boots on gravel, and I look away, out the passenger's side of the Jeep.

For once, I'm equally happy the doors are off, because the last thing I care to hear is the sound of his voice.

What I do hear before he cranks the engine is the sound of Miss Gina's delighted laugh.

Chapter 3

Zane

RACHEL WELLS IS HER OWN WOMAN.

I'm walking beside a tall, brown horse with my hand on his shoulder. A teenage boy sits upright, stock still in the saddle, watching silently as we circle the stadium.

The horse's muscles ripple under his shiny black-brown coat, and his spindly legs lift in practiced steps, trained for racing around a track.

My mind keeps traveling back to Rachel standing in Miss Gina's driveway with her blonde hair in those two braids, that sweatshirt falling off one shoulder, and her green eyes flashing with defiance like an angry pixie.

She's Jayden Wells's daughter.

It's pretty much all I need to know.

It doesn't matter how bright her eyes shine or how much she helps Miss Gina. Or how sexy her body is, those breasts, narrow waist, bare pussy… *shit.*

I clear my throat, quickly adjusting my jeans as I turn the horse.

I've fought to keep that image out of my mind. She was having a problem, for chrissakes. Am I going to hell for being aroused? Ultimately she was okay, and I can't help it if she's a fucking centerfold.

I also can't help that her father is a lying, double-crossing, untrustworthy asshole.

He'd sit on our back porch with my parents, looking out at the bay and making big plans to turn the old home with the tin roof and wrap-around porch into a destination restaurant. I was only seven, but I can still hear him laughing full-throated when my dad suggested the name.

He seemed like their friend for a long time, until he ghosted.

"Howdy, handsome. That sure is a serious look on your face." Sandra joins us on the other side of the horse, placing her hand on his side. "Good morning, Mark."

"Good morning, Ms. Hightower." The boy's voice is high-pitched, right on the verge of dropping, and his eyes don't leave the horse's mane.

"Something on your mind?" Sandra peeps at me over the horse's back.

"I'm good." The last thing I need is Sandra and Gloria in my business. "Just planning my day."

We make the turn and start back to the stalls as the boy counts the horse's steps under his breath.

I started working here when I came back after my injury. The therapist said it would help me process my feelings, since I found talk therapy annoying. I didn't like rehashing what happened. I didn't like talking about losing a football career I'd just started to love.

Time passed, and I was able to relax. Then, when I got off the crutches and could move around more easily, I saw how far I'd come, and I asked Gloria if she needed extra help.

I like the equine therapy kids. I don't mind their stoic demeanors or confusion about how to show emotions. I like that they're not bullshitters. They're straight-shooters, not afraid to say what they really think.

You don't have to watch your back around them. Whatever they're thinking comes right out of their mouths—at least the highly functional ones. The ones who work with me.

We're back at the stall, and Sandra squints an eye up at me as she helps the kid off the horse's back. "You're not planning to leave us, are you?"

Another student is right behind Mark. She walks him to the door, pausing to rest her arm on it, waiting for my answer.

"Just the opposite, actually. I have a kid who might be a good fit here. I'm pretty sure he's on the spectrum, but it's mild. He could help when I'm not around."

She nods, pushing out her lips. "Those kinds of decisions are up to Gloria, but we can talk to him."

I look down, passing a hand over the back of my neck and wondering why I'm sticking it out for this kid. Why is Edward different from Rachel?

"If you want, come by the restaurant tonight. He'll be there with his sister Rachel."

"Oh, is that the new girl working with Miss Gina?" Her voice rises. "I've heard she's really cute."

"I wouldn't know." I step to the center of the horse to check the billet strap.

"But you see her every day at work, don't you? I heard she's a yoga instructor." Her tone turns conspiratorial. "Yoga instructors are *very* flexible from what I understand."

Heat rises hot around my collar—because I'm annoyed or possibly even angry. "She sticks to her side of the house, and I stay on mine."

My voice is sharper than I intend, but Sandra isn't deterred. Her brows rise, and I can feel her grinning even if I can't see her. "Okay, okay. I'll see if Gloria wants to make the drive to town. Maybe we'll see you both at the ole Coot-Shoot."

I give the horse a pat before leaving the stall. "See you later."

She mutters something under her breath about overreactions, but I don't stop.

It's Thursday, so I go straight from the stables to the small, former weather-alert station Logan bought and is turning into a sports-radio hub. He's been putting in long hours to get it up to speed, and on Thursdays, the two of us have a show where we discuss the marquee games each week.

Some days we do interviews, and today we're chatting with Hendrix and Garrett over Zoom. It always ends up with more content than we can use in a ninety-minute program.

Walking into the small, white-painted, cinder-block building, I'm still irritated by my interaction with Sandra. I didn't bring up the subject of Edward to have a discussion of Rachel's flexibility. In fact, I've done my best not to think about her at all since our conversation on Monday.

It's been annoyingly difficult.

Sometimes when she looks at me, her neck and chest go all pink. I'm not sure why, because she isn't afraid at all to stand her ground when we're forced to interact. It makes me think about things I pretty much put on the back-burner after my accident.

Things like how soft her skin is and how the early-morning sun shining through the open door of the Jeep makes her cheeks look like velvet as we drive to Miss Gina's. My throat tightens and I think about sliding my nose along her jaw, inhaling her clean scent of honeysuckle, the body wash she leaves in our shared bathroom.

It's been a battle in my mind since I burst through the door to save her, when I tore my eyes away from her soft, full breasts slick with water.

Exhaling a low growl, I fight these thoughts. She was ill, and I'm a sick bastard for thinking of her perfect breasts. Fuck, but she has really great tits.

As I requested, for the last three days she's kept to her side of the house—both at Miss Gina's and at our place—and I've kept to mine. Still, I wonder what they're doing.

Dylan hasn't noticed a thing, but school's back in session, which means she's running back and forth between teaching ballet classes at the high school, helping Jack with his six-year-old daughter Kimmie Joy, managing the restaurant, and making time for Logan.

Logan doesn't notice anything outside of my little sister and this station, which is pretty typical male.

Since he bought WNFO last year, he's been consumed with making it the hottest sports radio channel in his dad's media empire.

I've never met Kellan Murphy, but from what I've heard and observed in the behavior of my future brother-in-law, he's an impossible man to please.

Luckily, our dad left us pretty well connected in the football world, and Jack kept the tradition going when he was the star quarterback in Houston. He retired at the top of his game, and now that he's the head coach at the high school, there's a legion of fans still interested in what he's doing and who's playing for him.

Any time we have a slow night, we can always pull Jack in for a conversation that pulls in big numbers. Logan retired with a record-setting reputation, and even though I was pretty much a loner in the league, I still have a few friends who make interesting interview subjects.

Logan's in the booth wearing a pair of headphones when I enter, and he signals for me to wait. He fit right into our clan, and after sitting up one night, shooting the shit about the future of the game and how it's impacting players, we got the idea for this talk show. I let him take the lead, since he's got the broadcasting degree.

"Ready?" He meets me at the door to the small studio, slapping me on the shoulder. "The guys are calling in in five. What do you think about recording these chats and putting them on a YouTube channel? A lot of podcasters are doing that now, and it might bring in a new audience—and a new revenue stream."

"Sounds good to me." I follow him into the room where a round table holds two very expensive microphones. "We'd have to find somebody to produce it."

I sit in one of the office chairs and pick up the black headset. The guys will appear in a split screen on the giant television hanging on the wall in front of us.

"Maybe an intern?" Logan picks up his headset and puts it around his neck. "Maybe Allie could help us find a high school kid who needs college credit?"

Allie is the librarian at the high school. She's also a single-mom, who works at our family restaurant in the summer and is another of Dylan's many best friends.

"She's usually at the restaurant for Dare night."

A few years back, Dylan became obsessed with hot peppers. Now, every Thursday night, she prepares a free "Dare Dish" for customers to try using one of the hottest peppers on the Scoville scale. It's turned into a big party night with "hot" themed dance music and lights and dancing.

I wouldn't know anything about hot peppers if it wasn't for her, but I've become a fan—unlike Logan, who steers clear of all fiery foods.

The television flickers, and I pull on my headset in time for Garrett to appear on the big screen.

"Thunder and Lightning," he calls playfully, leaning back in his chair. "How's it hanging?"

Logan's nickname when he played ball was Lightning. I'm not sure how I got branded as Thunder, but since we started doing the show, it stuck.

"You ready to get your ass whipped tonight?" Hendrix appears on the screen, already teasing his older brother.

At six-four, Garrett is the biggest one of us, but Hendrix is a fast six-foot. Jack and I fall right in the middle at six-two each. Dylan's a shrimp, and she stopped watching the games after our dad died of what we're pretty certain was chronic traumatic encephalopathy. It was never confirmed, but all the symptoms were there.

Now she keeps a steady drumbeat of trying to get us all to retire.

"Keep telling yourself that," Garrett quips back.

Garrett's an offensive lineman, so he and Hendrix are never on the field at the same time, much to Dylan's relief.

"Ricky Berke's been making waves this season." Logan's smooth voice keeps us on track. "How's he fitting in as the newest member of the Pirates offense?"

After Logan retired, his old rival transferred into Logan's position, playing closely with Garrett.

"He's no Logan Murphy." Garrett adjusts the ball cap over his short brown hair.

"I hear you're still calling him The Dick," Hendrix laughs, rocking in his chair. "I'm sure that's great for team building."

His blue eyes sparkle and Garrett shakes his head, looking over his shoulder. I'm thinking of this group on video. Despite the shit his dad gives him, Logan has good instincts. He's barely making ends meet as it is, but a YouTube channel could change that.

"He's got a lot of maturing to do." Garrett's voice is serious, and I study my middle brother.

He was the youngest long enough that he never lost that teasing, playful manner, but now I think he might be growing up. He's getting to that point we all do, where he's thinking about the future and how many years he has left in him.

Logan keeps our conversation focused on the game, despite the nonstop teasing between my two brothers. We discuss last week's highlights, and it feels like we've just sat down when the ninety-minute bell sounds.

We all make our final comments, then Logan switches off the recording. The guys stay on screen a bit longer. Garrett is usually an hour ahead of us in New York, but today he's on the

West Coast with our brother for the game. It's not even lunch-time in LA.

"What's Dylan making for tonight's Dare dish?" He shifts in his chair.

"Is she still doing those?" Hendrix stands, stretching his arms side to side.

"Roasted chile de árbol salsa." Logan taps a few buttons on the control panel.

"Of which you will have none," Garrett teases. "Man, I wish I was there to try it. It sounds delicious."

"It sounds like you're retiring—is that true?" Hendrix leans into his camera.

Logan's eyes flicker up to his friend's face on the screen. "You're retiring?"

"No!" Garrett hits the word hard enough to make us all exchange a glance. "I'm not. It's just, it's different now that you're gone. The other guys all have families. I don't like being the old man at the club, but what else am I going to do?"

Hell, I know that feeling from my own forced retirement two years ago. I was fucking lost, depressed, pissed—but I try to encourage him.

"There's actually a lot more to do around here than you realize." It's not a lie.

"You sound like Dylan." Garrett squints his hazel eyes at me. "Tell me what you're doing around there with Rachel. When are you getting your head out of your ass and asking her on a date?"

"What the fuck?" My chin pulls back. "Rachel's my co-worker, and I was trying to ease *your* mind."

Fool me once.

"Miss Gina won't care if you date her. Hell, if I know that old lady, she's already figuring out ways to put you two together."

He's not wrong, and my jaw tightens. "Worry about your own love life." I stand too fast, and a jab of pain shoots through my hip, forcing a growl from my throat.

"I heard Rachel has a degree in sports medicine." Garrett's

not letting it drop. "I bet she'd be glad to give you a personalized massage, put her hands on that ass. You got a pretty decent ass, bro."

Logan leans forward, covering his grin with his hand.

"No." My tone is flat.

"You're not getting any younger, and she's right there."

"Don't listen to him, Zee," Hendrix interrupts. "You have fun while you can."

"Who are you talking to?" Garrett's voice is pure sarcasm. "That has *never* been Zane's style. Hell, have you even dated anybody since you got home?"

He looks at me, and I take off the headphones.

"You're all so ready to play house," Hendrix continues. "I don't get it. There's plenty of time for all that when you're old."

"Spoken like a true thirty-year-old player."

"I'm not a player. I'm just not into marriage and babies and poop."

"I can't wait to meet the girl who knocks you on your ass," Garrett quips. "I'll get one of the old ladies to cross-stitch those famous last words on a pillow."

"And I'll sleep on it comfortably." Hendrix points at the screen.

"Bye." I flick my wrist in a wave. "Y'all be safe out there tonight."

"Love ya, Zee!" Hendrix yells, but I'm gone.

Nothing annoys me more than my siblings hovering over me, or worse, trying to meddle in my love life. Ever since my injury, I've been dodging their "helpful" suggestions—more like meddling. It's part of the reason I lost my cool with Rachel the first day we met.

I don't need help, and I don't like hovering. I'm not interested in being anyone's project, especially not hers. Finding out about her dad was the final straw I needed.

Stalking to my Jeep, I consider I could've told them who her dad is. Although, to be honest, only Garrett might remember the name. Logan wasn't around, and Hendrix was only a baby.

Maybe it was the way she responded when I told her what he did. I won't be surprised if she's the same as her dad, but I don't spread rumors or talk out of school.

It's a lesson I wish my siblings would learn, but their small-town minds are dead set on interfering in my business. I'm not giving them any more ammo.

Chapter 4

Rachel

"Lift your arms up, down, now cross, cross." It's a semi-cool Thursday afternoon, and I'm standing in the shallow end of a heated, jade-blue swimming pool guiding Miss Gina through gentle water aerobics.

"I feel like a balloon." Miss Gina's voice is tinged with humor as we bob up and down flapping our arms just below the surface of the water.

"The movement is good for your circulation and balance, and there's virtually no stress on your joints." I'm facing her in the water, my braids twisted up on my head in a bun.

"It's good for my constitution, too." Her lips twist like she's sharing a secret.

"Same," I deadpan.

"If you have pooping problems, they only get worse as you get older."

I snort a laugh through my nose. Nothing is off-limits at this house.

"We can try adding magnesium to your diet."

"Magnesium." She exhales as she says the word. "Lord, you'd think it's the cure for everything these days—insomnia, heart disease, constipation, anxiety…"

"It is sort of a miracle mineral. Let's go in a circle." I hold her wrinkly hands in the water as we slide our feet and hop. "A lot of our minerals have been stripped out of the soil by factory farming."

"You sound like one of those health nuts."

"Sorry, I'll stop. But if you want to know, just ask me."

"I want to know about this music. It's fun." We change directions, and she adds a twisty motion to her bounce, humming along to "Show Me Love" by Robin S.

I exhale a laugh. "My dad says it's ridiculous, but it makes me happy."

"It's very empowering." She shakes her finger along with the beat and joins in. "Say what you want…"

I laugh more. "You're manifesting devotion."

"With your heart in your hands." She nods. "I like it."

"No, kitty, don't eat the charging cords." Edward appears at the side of the pool, scooping up the little gray kitten chewing on my phone cord. "I think this would be a good one to take to the restaurant. He's more of a loner than the others, and he likes people."

My brother holds the kitten under his chin. He's wearing his usual They Might Be Giants T-shirt and jeans, and I wonder if he ever notices I have three versions of that same shirt I switch out and wash every week.

"Dylan asked us to pick the cutest one." I drift to the side of the pool. "I think he qualifies."

"Dr. Moore said they're at least six weeks old, so we can get him fixed in a few weeks."

"Good work, Eddie!" Miss Gina smiles up in my brother's direction. "You're such a helpful addition to the group."

My brother looks down at the kitten who is now swiping the lapel on his jean jacket between its paws and biting it. I don't know, but I think I see a hint of a smile cross his lips before he nods and walks away. It warms my eyes.

I clear the emotion from my throat as I grab a long, foam noodle, turning to her again. "Thank you for being so kind to him."

"It's a pleasure to be kind to kind people." Miss Gina is still bouncing and dancing to the music. "I want you to find what you're looking for, too."

Wrinkling my nose, I blink away my sentimental tears. "What might that be?"

"Hm…" The old lady arches an eyebrow. "Love and devotion?"

I shake my head and hand her the noodle. "I'm fine for now, but it's time for you to do your knee lifts."

"Oh, no," she fake-cries. "Not leg day!"

We both laugh, and I glance around the empty garden. Zane doesn't work on Thursdays because he records the radio show with Logan. I have no reason to miss his surly butt lurking around, ignoring me, but the thought of him tingles in my mind.

"This looks delicious." I lean forward on the large, stainless-steel work table beside Dylan in the kitchen at Cooters & Shooters as she blends a giant pot of roasted chile de árbol salsa in an industrial-sized blender.

The scent of onions, tomatoes, and garlic fills the air as I suck on a grape Jolly Rancher, which creates a funky flavor combination in my mouth.

We came straight here from Miss Gina's, so I'm still in my bikini top and leggings with a long-sleeved wrap-sweater. I've taken out the braids, so my hair hangs in kinky waves down my back.

"Chile de árbol is spicy, but not as hot as Habanero." Dylan tosses a handful of diced white onions into the blender along with the tomatoes and peppers. "It's right on the edge of hot and medium on the Scoville scale."

"Chili peppers have three times more Vitamin C than oranges." Edward is at my side.

He pulled a black, long-sleeved hoodie over his tee, and he's holding the little gray kitten under his chin.

"It's true." Dylan smiles at him. "They can help you lose weight and reduce blood pressure, too."

"Some people think peppers cause stomach upset, but it's actually the opposite." My brother only needs a little encouragement to turn into a walking encyclopedia. "Capsaicin increases the good bacteria in your gut."

"That does it, you're hired!" Dylan laughs. "I'll have you walk around singing the praises of my peppers to our customers."

"I can be the guinea pig and taste them." I don't know the facts, but I do love a hot pepper. "I've never met a pepper I won't try!"

"Be sure to wash your hands with the coconut oil." Craig taps my shoulder as he passes on his way to the dishwasher. "You don't want any of that stuff in your eyes or your nose… or your coochie."

"That can make for some potentially embarrassing situations." Dylan cuts her eyes at him, and Craig snorts, lifting the lid off the dishwasher and taking out several large, silver bowls.

"Especially if you're busted helping your fiancé clean it off his—"

"Craig Schiffer!" Dylan's voice goes loud, and he waves a hand.

"Nevermind!"

They're laughing and having so much fun, and I can't help remembering what Zane said about my father leaving their parents holding the bag on this place. It weighs heavily in my chest, but it looks like things worked out for them.

Still, I wonder if Dylan knows, and if she doesn't know, I

wonder if she'd still be my friend. But how could she not know if Zane does?

"Is that my kitten?" Dylan lifts her chin at Edward, and he nods.

"He looks like a Russian Blue, but it would be impossible for him to be a pure breed." He holds out the little guy. "Miss Gina doesn't know the father cat."

"Where's Miss Gina this evening?" Dylan turns to me.

"Home." I shrug. "I asked her if she wanted to join us tonight, but she said she was exhausted from leg day."

"Aunt Deedaaaay!" Jack's daughter's voice echoes through the restaurant just before she bursts into the kitchen. "Daddy said I can have a special treat today, because I didn't drop a stick all week!"

Kimmie Joy is a blue-eyed, curly brown-haired ball of loud energy.

Dylan's frown mirrors mine. "What does it mean to drop a stick?"

"It means I didn't walk in a straight line or I didn't stop talking during reading circle or I didn't wash my hands after bathroom break or I didn't take my tray to the window after lunch or I didn't—"

"Jeez Louise, Peanut!" Craig walks over to where Kimmie is counting off on her fingers, scooping her up and onto his hip. "That's a lot of don'ts."

She puts her small hand on his shoulder, eyes round. "First grade is a lot harder than kindergarten, Uncle Craig."

Dylan pulls her lips between her teeth, fighting a laugh before patting her little back. "I bet Uncle Craig can find you a treat."

"A kitten!" she cries, wiggling to get down. "Can I have a kitten, too? What's his name?"

"He doesn't have a name." Edward motions at Dylan. "Your aunt has to name him."

"Nope!" Craig cuts in. "Dylan is not allowed to name pets. She'll call him *mushroom* or *quinoa* or some other type of food."

"I wouldn't name him either of those things!" Dylan cries. "Why don't you take him out back, and I'll let you two come up with a name for him."

Edward nods, dutifully obeying Dylan's orders. Kimmie hops along beside him, reaching up to touch any part of the kitten she can reach through his arms.

"Can I hold the kitten, Eddie?" Her high voice is loud, but to his credit, my brother seems to be patient with her.

"He's really sweet." Dylan tilts her head, smiling as she watches them go. "What have you decided about school?"

My throat tightens. "I don't know. I'm so nervous after his last incident, and middle school can be rough."

"Shew, tell me about it."

"Where's my Danger Girl?" We're interrupted by two handsome giants entering the room.

Logan enters first, looking like he stepped off the pages of a men's magazine. He's a jock, but his wealthy background is all over him, from the dark jeans to the expensive-looking navy sweater covering his broad shoulders and muscular arms.

He walks straight to where Dylan is still mixing and blending the salsa, and wraps her long ponytail around his fist, giving it a gentle tug. Her head tilts back, and he covers her mouth with his.

My stomach tightens, and I look down at my hands. I've never had a serious boyfriend, and I can't imagine having one so proud and possessive, he'd walk right up and kiss me in front of God and everybody.

Warmth expands my insides, and I bet I'd like it, though. I think about Miss Gina's words about love and devotion.

Zane grabs a chip off the counter, seeming not to notice as he passes them. He doesn't even look in my direction as he continues to the refrigerator.

His dark hair hangs in perfectly messy waves around his

collar, and he's in his uniform of jeans, a T-shirt, and a rolled-sleeve plaid shirt on top.

If Zane were my boyfriend, I'd slide my hands up his chest and push that shirt down his arms. I've seen him working in only a T-shirt a few times, and his body is incredible.

Clearing my throat, I stand up and turn to prop my lower back against the silver worktable I've been leaning on. Zane Bradford is not my friend. He's my enemy, remember?

"Have I told you how beautiful you are today?" Logan's voice is pure honey.

"The coconut oil is over there." Craig's loud voice interrupts their love-fest, and Dylan snorts a laugh through her nose.

"Okay, okay." She rises on her tiptoes to kiss her fiancé once more. "Love you, now let me finish. The Dare crowd will be demanding hot peppers in less than an hour."

"I'll let you finish." A naughty smile curls Logan's lips, and he gives her another quick kiss. "Is Allie here? I need to talk to her about hiring an intern at the station."

"I think she's checking the pool tables." Dylan nods in the direction of the main dining hall, and he starts that way.

Chewing my lip, I watch as Zane goes to the hall leading to the back door where Edward and Kimmie are sitting outside with the kitten. He opens the screen door, stepping out, and while Craig and Dylan discuss tonight's pepper warning, I drift quietly behind him.

"Silver!" Kimmie calls out.

"That's a horse's name." Edward dismisses her suggestion.

As soon as she sees Zane, she's on her feet holding up her hands to him. He doesn't even hesitate before lifting her onto his hip, and she puts her curly brown head on his shoulder.

"Eddie doesn't like any of my names, Uncle Zee." Her voice is pouty. "And Daddy said I could have a treat because I didn't drop a single stick all week."

"Tell me what you've got." His low voice is serious, and he pats her back with one of his large hands.

He's so sweet with her, I'm pretty sure my ovaries explode. I remember Dylan saying when she was little, Zane would read books to her. They're five years apart, and I imagine him as a ten-year-old taking care of his little sister. *Swoon.*

"I said Sprinkles, and Eddie said no. Then I said Sparkles, and he said no *again!*" Her little voice rises.

"I'm detecting a theme here." A gentle tease is in her uncle's tone.

"Sprinkles are colorful and sparkles are orange," Edward explains.

"So I said Silver, and he still said no!" Her head shoots up, and she gestures with her arms like my brother is being *so impossible.*

I can relate to her frustration.

"Silver is the Lone Ranger's horse, and he's white."

"Uncle Zane rides horses!" Kimmie announces, and my brow arches. *New information.*

"How do you feel about Smokey?"

Zane doesn't push. He just lays the name out there gently, letting them decide what they think. I've never heard him talk this way to anyone, and it's like I'm getting a peek behind his grumpy curtain.

"I like it." Edward nods. "It's not a horse, and it's not a party favor. Kim, meet Smokey."

"Kim?" The little girl's nose wrinkles, but she changes her mind just as fast. "You can call me Kim! It sounds like a grown-up lady."

"I expect it's your real name, since Kimmie is clearly a nickname." My brother's logic is sound if potentially incorrect.

"Can I hold Smokey now, Edward?"

She stretches out her arms, and my brother hesitates. "He'll probably scratch and try to bite you, and his teeth are like needles."

"I know!" She bounces on her toes, curling her fingers, and he relents, putting the kitten in her arms.

She immediately clutches him to her chest, swaying side to side. "I love you, Smokey! We're going to have so much fun together. You'll see, we'll be best friends!"

The kitten struggles, but Zane puts his hand on my brother's shoulder. "Speaking of horses, how would you feel about working with them?"

Edward's brow furrows. "I've never ridden a horse, but I've read about them. They're believed to have an empathic connection with humans. They tap into our need for safety and connection."

Zane's brow arches. "Have you heard of equine therapy?"

"Yes." My brother blinks like he's retrieving the information. "It's an emerging realm of treatment for depression, PTSD, neurodivergence, among other things."

Zane exhales a laugh. "How do you know so much about everything?"

I wonder the same thing all the time.

"I read," Edward says without a hint of irony. "Readers are leaders."

A snort exhales from my nose, and Zane straightens, turning to where I'm standing at the screen door.

"Sorry!" I open it slowly. "I was just coming to check on the kids."

Zane's eyes move from mine to my mouth to my neck, where they seem to freeze and not drift any lower.

He clears his throat, turning away from me. "I was just telling your brother, I work at Second Chance Farms most mornings. It's a shelter for old thoroughbreds, and they also provide equine therapy for kids his age and up."

"Really?" I blink up at him, and when our eyes meet, his stunning blue ones have returned to their usual look for me—impenetrable.

"If Edward would like to join me, the owner said he's welcome. I think he might get a lot out of it. All the kids do."

My chest warms, and I don't care if I annoy him or if he

hates me or whatever he says. The fact that he wants to help my brother goes a long way in my book.

"I think that would be wonderful. What do you think, Eddie? Would you like to help Zane with the horses?" I say it slower than is probably necessary, but I can't help being careful with him.

My brother shrugs, and he's watching Kimmie now holding the kitten over her head as she dances with him. "I could give it a try."

Loud music cranks up inside the restaurant, and I hear Allie's voice on the mic announcing the warning for tonight's spicy dish. Zane lifts his chin, taking a step to the side.

"Sounds like they're getting started." He continues like he'll walk all the way around the restaurant just to avoid walking past me here at the back door.

"You can go this way." I step outside, holding the door open for him. "I'll round up these guys, and we'll meet you inside."

He doesn't even look at me as he jogs up the steps and into the kitchen. His square jaw is set, and his shoulders are so broad. A whiff of sandalwood and cedar, soap and his scent drifts past, and it's a flash of heat from my neck to my toes.

It's over as fast as it happened, and I exhale a sigh, looking down at Edward, who's frowning at Kimmie now rocking Smokey back and forth in her arms.

"She's going to make him vomit."

"Come inside with me and get some of Dylan's salsa."

Pushing off his knees, he rises, entering the kitchen at once. That just leaves Kimmie.

"Don't you want some salsa, KJ?" I call after her.

"Peppers burn my mouth." She's rocking the little gray cat in her arms, gazing at him rapturously. "I want to play with Smokey."

My brow furrows, and I hear the stomp of boots on wood. "Oh! It's 'HOT TO GO!' I love that song. Don't you want to see the girls dance? We can dance, too."

Her head tilts to the side, and she listens to the singing. "Okay!"

She puts Smokey on the grass, and he immediately dashes under the building.

I grab her hand, helping her up the steps. "Do you know the words?"

"It's just spelling."

"Do you know the dance?" Her eyes light, and she nods quickly.

"Let's do it then!" We run into the restaurant, and when we get there, everybody's on their feet waving their arms. Kimmie goes straight to Craig, and in a sweep, she's on the bar.

Chapter 5

Zane

MY SISTER IS BEHIND A LONG TABLE SERVING UP CHIPS AND SALSA AS fast as she can with Allie right beside her. Craig is on top of the bar in a blond wig with a line of waitresses behind him, twisting their hips and curling their arms over their heads to spell out the letters to the loud blast of the music.

"It's the perfect song for a hot pepper night." I recognize that sassy voice strolling up behind me the minute I hear it.

"Sandra." I turn around, reaching out to shake her and Gloria's hands. "You made it. I'm glad—you'll get to meet Eddie."

The two ladies are dressed in their no-nonsense jorts as always. It's exactly what I need to get the sight of Rachel's perfect tits barely covered by a tiny bikini top out of my head. *Christ*.

I had to get away from her when I walked into the kitchen and saw her leaning forward on that table.

"This salsa is amazing!" Sandra crunches a chip and immediately shoves another one into her mouth. "Your sister made this?"

"Dylan loves hot peppers."

"We should've made this trip sooner." Gloria's eyes are on the nubile waitresses in Daisy Dukes, dancing on the bar and waving their arms. "I had no idea all of this was going on."

"It's probably a health-code violation." I exhale a low chuckle, thinking of my sister's ongoing complaints about the *Coyote Ugly*-inspired dance party that breaks out every Thursday night along with the hot peppers.

"I'm not complaining if you're not!" Sandra slaps my shoulder.

I shake my head, because it's impossible to talk over the music. I've gotten to where I hardly notice until someone new arrives. Glancing to the front, I see Dylan has served up the last salsa basket. Now she's sipping a beer as she leans back against Logan's chest watching the party.

His arms are around her, and joy is all over her face. It makes me think of what Garrett said today about being alone and how long it's been since I had my arms around someone. It makes me think of Rachel, and her bright green eyes and occasional smile.

I don't give her much reason to smile at me. What would it be like if she did? My stomach burns, and I focus on my brothers meddling in my business.

"Your sister should go to culinary school," Sandra shouts in my ear. "Are you going to eat that?"

I shake my head, handing her my serving of chips and salsa. "My brother says the same thing."

Dylan loves making food and watching people eat it, but she says doing it for a living would steal the joy. She could be right, but our regular cook Thomas doesn't seem to have lost any joy making the best burgers in three states.

Thomas has been with us since we opened the restaurant. He used to play with our dad, and he's got the game on in the kitchen on his little black-and-white television. It's also on the big screens above the bar—over Dylan's head where she can't see them, I also notice.

She hates watching us play.

Or I guess, Garrett and Hendrix play.

Beside her, Allie dances with her son Austin. He's a sophomore now, and he's on Jack's high school football team as QB-2. Her eyes keep flickering to Coach Jack who's ignoring all the commotion as he watches Garrett and Hendrix on the big screens with his arms crossed.

Allie's good people. A single mom from New Orleans, she moved to our neck of the woods three years ago with Austin to be the school librarian and to get away from her drug-dealer ex-husband.

Her ex is now doing time at Angola, and I watch as she pushes a dark wave of hair behind her ear. Her cheeks flush when Jack steps forward for a fresh beer, and I think my brother might be the most clueless person I know.

Just then, Kimmie Joy races in, and Craig pulls her up onto his hip on the bar. They immediately stretch out their arms doing choreography everyone seems to know. Eddie is here, Kimmie is here, and dammit, I scan the entire room looking for Rachel.

She's standing near the back wall holding a paper tray and shoving a chip laden with hot salsa into her mouth. A tall, lanky guy stands over her with his arm propped above her head, and my throat tightens.

It's Sam Allen. He's five years younger than me, the same age as Dylan, who I happen to know is the same age as Rachel. His light brown hair is long in the front, hanging over his eyes like some dumb skater boy, and he's clearly flirting.

I think he works in animal control. He smiles, leaning closer, and I want to push him into the bay. *What the fuck?*

The driving, cheerleader music starts to fade, and Gloria's voice is easier to hear. "I was just thinking it might be fun to host a pool tournament here, like as a fundraiser for the farm?"

My brow furrows. "The farm needs money?"

"Not really. But it would be a great way to raise awareness, and any money we earn could be used for scholarships or to cover our current students who can't pay."

I'm nodding before she finishes speaking. "It's a great idea. I'll talk to Dylan, but I'm sure she'll be onboard."

"Sounds like a win all the way around." Sandra clinks the neck of her Corona against mine.

They continue brainstorming the details while I fight to keep my eyes from returning to where Sam is leering at Rachel. His gaze slides down her neck, and my fist clenches.

Gloria is going on about giving the kids forms so they can get sponsors. She's saying how it could be like a walk-a-thon where they secure a certain amount of money per pocket.

Sandra thinks this is a great idea, but I'm getting more annoyed by the second.

Rachel licks a drop of salsa off her lips, laughing, and her chin lifts as she says something to Sam. He grins, reaching down to wipe her chin with his thumb, and a low growl vibrates in my throat. She lifts her hair off her shoulder, and her back arches. The movement lifts her perfect breasts higher, and that fucking bikini top moves beneath the thin, wrap sweater she's wearing.

Her nipples are pointed, and Sam's practically drooling on her body.

"Excuse me." My tone is abrupt as I walk away from my friends in the direction of Rachel and Sam the slobbering jerk.

I hear Sandra's voice say something behind me, but my vision has tunneled. As I get closer to the two of them, I can hear their conversation.

"It's a fun song. I just don't know it very well." Rachel's voice is sweet, and as the song ends, Craig is already cueing up a new one.

"Fantasy" by Mariah Carey starts, and Rachel squeals, jumping up and down with her arms over her head.

"I love this song!" She twists her hips, moving in time with the music. "That's my jam!"

I swear, Sam's tongue rolls out like one of those cartoon

wolves, and I want to wrap it around his neck and strangle him with it.

"You're pretty enough to be on the bar dancing." His voice is thick, and I can practically see the semi in his pants.

I want to punch it.

"Thanks." Rachel blinks away embarrassed. "But I don't work here, so…"

She blinks in my direction, and when our eyes meet, she jumps slightly, lowering her beer and stepping away from Sam.

"Zane?" It's a breathless laugh, possibly nervous. "Hey."

"Hi, Zane!" Sam steps forward, extending a hand. "I haven't seen you since you got home. I wanted to tell you I watched all your games, and that injury was—"

"Thanks." I don't even look at him. "Sorry to interrupt, but would you come with me? I have someone I'd like you to meet."

"Oh." She looks from me to Sam. "I guess… Do you mind, Sam?"

"No way! No problem." He nods. "Can I get your number before you go?"

Now I really want to punch him in the junk.

"Hurry before they leave." I place my hand on her elbow.

I'm not gripping her, but she can feel the pressure of my touch. I'm sure it confuses her as much as it confuses me. *What the fuck am I doing? Why am I so pissed?* I don't have time for these questions.

I guide her away before she can respond to Sam's request, but halfway across the dining hall, she jerks her arm out of my grip.

"What are you doing?" she snaps.

I like that she's mad. I need her to be mad so I can get my head out of my ass.

"Gloria is here." I don't look at her. "She owns the stables where I work. I thought you might want to meet her since she runs the equine therapy program."

"Oh." Her tone changes at once. "I'd love to meet her. Of course. Please."

I lead her across the dining hall where everyone is dancing to Mariah Carey to where Gloria and Sandra are standing side by side bopping along.

They're not great dancers, but I can tell they're having fun. Every so often they lean into each other and say something.

Sandra's eyebrow arches when I approach with Rachel, and I don't have to ask what she's thinking.

"Gloria, Sandra, this is Edward's older sister Rachel." I gesture between them. "Rachel, Gloria owns Second Chance Stables and runs the equine therapy program there."

"It's so nice to meet you." Rachel reaches out to clasp Gloria's hand in both of hers. "I've read about equine therapy, and I think it would help Edward so much."

"Is he special needs?" Gloria frowns, and I realize I only told Sandra about his situation.

"Very mildly," Rachel answers quickly. "He had a little incident in Birmingham… At school. Some boys were making fun of him, and I think… I think he punched one of them in the nose. He was suspended, and they wanted to put him on medication. So I brought him here. I'm kind-of home-schooling him for now, but I know he needs to be in school. I'm working on that part."

She seems nervous, and her voice grows more apologetic with every new piece of information she provides. It's all new to me, and as she unfolds their story, protective anger surges hotter in my chest.

"Edward's not a fighter." My tone is sharp, and Rachel blinks up at me confused.

"No, he's not." She watches me like she doesn't understand me at all.

I'm not sure I understand, but I don't like hearing about her fighting for her brother all by herself. It shifts something in my chest. It makes me want to help her, protect her, and we don't have that kind of relationship.

We don't have a relationship.

Gloria puts her other hand over Rachel's still holding hers. "I think you made the right call, and I'm sure he'll find what he needs at our ranch. I'll work with him."

"You're so kind." Rachel's voice breaks, and I have to look away from the two of them.

I look around the room, and I notice Sam is waiting where we left him. I guess he's wondering if I'll bring her back or let her go to him.

He can get lost, because I'm not doing either.

She and Gloria finish their conversation, and when she starts to return, I catch her arm. "Do you know where Edward is?"

The burn in my chest has nothing to do with worrying about a twelve-year-old boy. Edward would be fine in Newport if he were six. He's simply the first thing my caveman mind grabs in its attempt to keep her from going back to Sam.

"He was in the kitchen with Thomas last I checked." Her eyes blink wider. "Did something happen?"

"No." My tone is flat. "But Thomas is watching the game."

"You don't think he's—" She starts when her brother walks up to where we're standing.

Her shoulders drop, and the relief that floods her features almost makes me feel guilty. Until I see Sam watching her.

"I'd like to go." Edward's voice is tense, and if I had to guess, I'd think he's reached his limit on noise and celebration for the night.

"I'm ready, too. I have to work tomorrow." Rachel blinks around the room. "I need to pay my bill—"

"I'll take care of it." My hand is on her shoulder again, and my eyes remain above her neck.

She shakes her head. "I can't let you pay for us."

"What did you have? The Dare Dish is free, and you had what? One beer?"

She tilts the longneck in her hand, pressing her lips together. "I had two."

"I'm sure we won't miss two beers, and there's food at the house if you want to eat something." I'm not sure how hypoglycemia works, but there's sugar in beer. She should be okay. "I'll walk you back."

"Okay." Her shoulders drop as she relents.

I pause to say goodnight to Sandra and Gloria. I motion in Edward's direction, and the two of them understand right away. This type of party is not ideal for anyone with sensitivity issues.

Edward's body is tense as we walk the short distance from the restaurant on the bay to my family's sprawling home on the bluff. The farther we go, the more he relaxes.

"I'm sorry." Rachel's voice is gentle. "You know, you can always leave if it's too much—I'll understand."

He nods, watching his feet as he walks. "I didn't want you to worry."

"Oh…" It's laced with guilt, and I don't know why I take that as my cue to jump in.

"I'm glad you were there to meet Gloria and Sandra. They're not always at the stables when I get there. It's usually pretty early."

He nods. "I've heard you. I'm always awake at that time."

"In that case, you can ride with me."

We reach the house, and I lead them to the kitchen. "If you're hungry, we've got plenty of leftovers or sandwich stuff."

"Thomas made me a hamburger." Edward's tone is flat.

"He did?" Rachel's brows shoot up. "I didn't know. I'll pay for it."

"Stop." I hold up a hand. "Thomas makes us all hamburgers all the time. Ground beef is not that expensive."

"I'm not taking advantage of your generosity, especially considering you don't like me at all."

Her jab makes me want to argue. Instead, I only say, "You're not."

Frowning, she puts a hand on her hip. "Who are you, and what did you do with the Zane Bradford I know?"

It's a fair question, and it's one I've been asking myself.

I don't have an answer, so I grab a water bottle out of the fridge and start for the stairs. "Goodnight."

She makes a noise like she'll stop me, but I don't give her the chance. I don't want to talk to her anymore. I don't want to look at her standing in my kitchen with her blonde hair hanging in crimped waves over her breasts.

I need to take a shower and get my head straight.

Standing under the spray, I brace a hand against the wall and all I can see is her sexy body moving to the music, her blond hair swaying and that bikini top sliding to the side almost revealing a rosy nipple.

My cock hardens, and my hand lowers to cover it as I allow the images to flood my mind. Her soft body sitting on my lap, lifting her full breasts to my mouth…

How long has it been? Garrett's question is in my ears. My hand slides over my tip, and I rest my forehead against my fist on the shower wall as my hips begin to rock. I imagine sliding my thumb along her jaw. I imagine tracing my tongue along the seam of her full lips. I imagine her bouncing as I fuck her, and I groan.

I picture turning her body so her back is to my chest, lifting her leg and sliding deep into her wet heat. I hear her voice as soft pants, desperate whimpers. I want my hands all over her, lifting, clutching, squeezing.

My hand moves faster, jerking as I picture it, up and over my tip. I can see our bodies rocking together, melting into one as her fingers thread in the side of my hair as she says my name.

"Fuck," I groan as the orgasm grows tighter in my pelvis.

I've been living like a monk for too long, and no matter how I try to distance her, Rachel is a walking, breathing temptation.

My hips jerk, and my mind narrows. Her soft voice is in my ears, her hips twerk, igniting my brain, and with another pull, come shoots through my cock, spilling into the drain in long streams. A shuddering moan quivers in my stomach, and my knees bend.

"Fuck, Rachel…" I shake my head, fumbling for control. *What am I doing?*

It takes a minute for me to recover, to rebuild the blasted wall I created to keep her out—along with everyone else.

I clean up myself and all evidence of what just happened in the shower. I grab a towel and dry myself before wrapping it around my waist and applying deodorant.

When I'm ready to emerge, I'm back to calm, controlled. I hope they're all good and asleep. The last thing I want is to see her tonight.

I open the door slowly, peeking into the dim hall, when she appears so fast, I almost holler.

"Shit," I hiss, taking a step back as she pushes through the door.

"It's about damn time." Her voice is low and sharp. "I know you're used to having the upstairs to yourself, but all my stuff is in here, too."

"I'm sorry." I step out into the hall, feeling a little shook.

She only slams the door in my face.

Exhaling a breath, I look down at myself standing in the hall in only a towel, still recovering from that orgasm provoked by her. The shower starts, and I almost laugh at my dumb ass.

I totally deserved that. At least I got my deodorant.

I'm in my bedroom several minutes later when the bathroom door opens again. I've pulled on joggers and a long-sleeved tee, but I still need to brush my teeth. Rubbing my palm over my eyes, I want to wait until I'm sure she's settled.

Walking over, I sit on the bed and pick up the book I've been reading.

A soft knock at the door draws my attention, and I look up to see her standing there in sage green sweatpants and a long-sleeved, thin T-shirt. Her hair is down and her face is freshly washed and has a shine like she put some sort-of cream on it.

She looks ready for bed.

She looks really fucking amazing.

"I just wanted to let you know I'm finished in the bathroom." I can't tell if she's apologizing or simply being courteous.

I decide not to go there.

"Thanks." I nod, setting the book aside and standing.

"What are you reading?" She enters my room, and I realize for the first time how much shorter than me she is.

Somehow she always seemed taller at a distance. Here, in my bedroom, her head only comes up to the center of my chest.

"*The Sun Also Rises*," I answer, and her whole face grimaces. I almost laugh. "What?"

"That book is so depressing! Why would you read that?"

"It was on the bookshelf, and I picked it up." I turn it over in my hands, examining the illustrated hardcover. "It's a fancy special edition."

"The hero is impotent."

"The heroine is a nympho." I don't know why I'm defending Jake Barnes.

"She's only with two men in the entire book, and one of them's a bullfighter." Her tone is sharp. "Bullfighters are hot, and she really seems to like him. So she has sex. That doesn't make her a nympho. You could say she's a drunk more than you could say she's a nympho."

"You're right. I'm sorry." I hold up my hands like she has a gun on me.

"No wonder you're always in a bad mood if this is what you're reading."

"I guess you think I should read one of Dylan's romance books instead."

"You should. She has some good ones." She stomps out of the room, and my brow lowers. *What is she doing?*

I don't have to wait long to find out.

"Try this one." She shoves a light blue paperback into my

hands with the words *Archer's Voice* stamped on the front. "It's way more uplifting than that awful slog."

"I actually like Hemingway."

"You'll like this one better. Maybe it'll improve your mood."

I turn the book over, deciding not to argue. A few seconds pass, and she doesn't leave. Setting the book aside, I look at her. She's still frowning, but not like she's annoyed.

"What?"

"You were really good with the kids tonight."

Not what I expected her to say. "What kids?"

"Kimmie and Edward. When they were picking out names for the kitten? You were so good at smoothing things out between them. I was impressed."

"It's no big deal. Kids just want to be heard. They want you to listen."

"It was a different side of you." She tilts her head and smiles up at me.

My throat tightens, and I put my hands on the chair to keep them from touching her. I've wanted to touch her all night.

"I don't have sides."

She laughs low and soft, and my dick responds to the sound. "Everyone has sides, parts of themselves they try to hide for whatever reason."

That.

I use her oblique confession to reestablish my resistance. "What are you trying to hide?"

Her brows shoot up and she blinks quickly. "That's not what I meant."

"I've got to get up early." I step to the door, holding it for her to go. "Tell Eddie to be ready at six a.m. sharp."

"He'll be ready."

She steps into the hall, and I shut the door.

Chapter 6

Rachel

"Hɪs ɴᴀᴍᴇ ᴡᴀs Sʜɪʟᴏʜ." Eᴅᴡᴀʀᴅ ɪs ᴏɴ ʜɪs ʜᴀɴᴅs ᴀɴᴅ ᴋɴᴇᴇs reaching under the deck.

His tone is impatient, and I know he hates it when I ask him twenty questions. But I want to know all about his very first equine therapy experience.

I haven't seen Zane, but I was doing yoga when my brother suddenly appeared and started searching for kittens under the wooden platform where I practice.

"What did you do? Did you ride him? Walk him around? Clean his hooves?"

"He was only getting started for the day, so I didn't clean his hooves." He sits back on his feet, holding up two black kittens. "I think these are the only other males."

"Tell me what you did." I'm doing my best not to get impatient with him right back.

He blinks away from the felines, seeming to remember I'm here. "I brushed him and shoveled the dirty hay out of his stall. Then I walked beside him while a little boy rode."

I frown. That's not what I expected. I thought he'd be doing more riding, not simply being a stable boy. I'm all ready to fuss, but I hesitate. He does seem more relaxed today, which is encouraging after the raucous night we had at the restaurant.

It took me forever to fall asleep, and not just because of all the music and dancing. I tossed and turned in my bed all night trying to forget the sight of Zane Bradford standing in the hall in only a towel with his damp hair around his neck.

His broad shoulders were lean and toned, and he seemed bigger somehow. His muscular chest was dusted with the faintest bit of hair, and I wanted to slide my nose across the planes of his shoulders and lick him. Then maybe bite him.

He seemed on edge, like he might forget he hates me and pull me into his arms. Or maybe it was just what I wished he'd do. He has no right to look so good, and I kind of forgot his order that I stay on my side of the house.

"Miss Gina asked me to identify the male cats so she could have them neutered." Edward cuts right through my lusty thoughts.

It makes me exhale a short laugh. "You're doing a great job with them."

He returns to digging under the deck, and I look up to see Zane stalking in our direction. He's back to scowling and wearing his usual jeans and unbuttoned plaid shirt with a gray tee underneath. But I've seen what's underneath that, and it's yummy.

He's about to walk right past us when I stick out my hand and wave. "Hey!"

Stopping short, his brow furrows. "Hey yourself."

"No..." I look down, exhaling a laugh. "I have something... Miss Gina asked me to ask you to take a look at the sink in the greenhouse. She said it's all wet under there, and it might be a leak."

He hesitates a moment longer, glancing in the direction he was headed before relenting. "Show me."

"Right this way." My voice is soft, and I'm still in my yoga clothes as I walk him down the narrow flagstone path to the green-glass structure where Miss Gina stores her succulents and more delicate flowers during the winter.

It's warm and densely humid when we enter, and I continue to the small sink area in the center of the room.

"Miss Gina and I were trying to figure out where the water was coming from." I open the cabinet doors under the sink to show the pan full of water. "We turned on the faucet, the sprayer, everything. Get down there and watch what happens."

He cuts his eyes to me briefly before squatting down and leaning into the cabinet as I fill a large bowl with water.

"I think it has something to do with the seal around the drain," I explain. "When I pour a big bowl like this down the drain, watch what happens."

I lift the large bowl of water, all ready to pour the entire contents into the sink when it wobbles in my hand. It's heavier than I realized, and with my wet fingers, I don't have a good grip on the sides. All at once, it starts to slide.

"Oh…" I gasp, doing my best to grab it with both hands, but the weight of the water takes over and jerks the bowl to the side. "Oh no!"

The entire quart-sized bowl flips out of my hand, dumping the entire contents of water all over Zane's head.

I can't speak. I've completely lost my breath.

Zane doesn't speak either. He quietly shakes his soaked head like he's not sure what just happened.

"Was this some kind of joke?" The low-burn of fury in his tone sends fire racing up my neck.

"No!" I manage to say through my completely clenched throat. "I'm so sorry!"

He rises slowly to his full height, water dripping from the tips of his hair and sparks flying in his eyes.

"Let me get you a towel." I still can't breathe.

His large hand lands on the top of my shoulder, stopping me. "Leave it. I'll take a look at it tomorrow."

Turning, he starts to storm off, but I race after him. "I have a towel right over here where I was doing yoga!"

"No." It's a growl of fury.

His entire upper body is drenched, and the replay of what just happened, of what I did, flashes through my mind. I press my lips together, and my eyes fill with water. I suck in a breath and hold my nose, but the laughter bursts out anyway.

"I'm so sorry!" I shriek, unable to stop laughing.

That stops him. He turns around and glares at me from across the path, still dripping wet. Both my hands are on my cheeks, and I'm trying so hard not to laugh… and failing.

"You did that on purpose."

"I didn't!"

"Wow, you're really wet." Edward walks up, holding two more kittens, and I lose it.

I bend at the waist, covering my whole face in my hands and trying to stop laughing. When I hear the crunch of boots on gravel, I take off after him again.

"Zane, wait!" I scurry after him, but he doesn't stop.

He's headed to the small bathhouse off the side of the pool, and I wait outside as he goes in to retrieve a towel.

When he comes out, his blue eyes are spitting fire. "Go away, Rachel."

"I'm really sorry." I bite the inside of my lip to keep the smile away. "I-I need a ride home this evening. I rode with Jack this morning, but I don't have a way—"

"What are you doing?"

"Asking for a ride home?" My brow furrows. "Apologizing for throwing water all over you?"

"I asked you to stay away from me."

"I'm doing that!"

"You're not." He takes a step closer as if he might do something.

I'm not sure what, but it sends heat flushing through my

body. He hesitates, then he exhales a growl and starts walking again.

I'm right behind him. He's moving fast, and I almost have to jog to keep up. Then he stops so fast, I almost bounce off his back.

"Oh!"

"What?" It's a sharp question.

I point to the driveway, speaking quietly. "The ride home?"

"Yes. I'll give you a ride home. Now stop following me."

I fall back, watching his fine ass go, doing my best to catch my breath, before turning to the house. Miss Gina wants to do more water aerobics, and I need to cool off in the pool.

"What happened to our fun dance music?" Miss Gina has a pink swim cap on her head with nylon feathers as we do our exercises. "I wore my fancy hat, and now I'm all dressed up with no place to go."

"I'm sorry!" I can't help a laugh. "I had to catch a ride with Jack this morning, and I forgot my Bluetooth speaker in my other bag."

"I don't have a Bluetooth speaker?"

"Not that I could find, but there's not really a reason you should have one. They're sort of a young person's thing."

"Sounds like it's time for me to catch up with the young people." She's playfully pouty. "Get on my account and order me one."

"I will, and I'll be sure mine is always in my bag."

We do a little more bouncing, but she's right. It's not as much fun without my drag queen music. I guide her through a grapevine movement, scissoring our arms back and forth in front of us.

"Why did you ride with Jack this morning? Why didn't you ride with Zane and Edward?"

I glance over to where Mr. Grumpy is spreading mulch in the beds to prepare them for winter. "Zane works at a horse farm in the mornings before he comes here."

"Yes, he does, and that Gloria Fruit keeps trying to steal my best handyman." She lifts her chin defiantly, practically shouting. "She can't have him!"

Her head is turned as if she's speaking to Zane, and I sneak a look to where he's wrapping burlap around her potted rhododendrons. Of course, he glances up at that exact moment, and when our eyes meet, it's a flash all the way to my stomach.

"I'm not leaving you, so you can stop fussing about it." His gruff tone is impatient.

Pressing my lips together, I look away quickly, but my ears are hot. His baseball cap is turned backwards on his head, and he took off his plaid overshirt. The top of his tee is still damp, and I do my best not to grin remembering my accidental attempt to drown him.

"But why was this morning different? Zane does that every day."

We stop going side to side, and now stand in place circling our arms underwater. "Edward started equine therapy at the farm."

"Ah…" She lifts her chin, nodding slowly. "So he had to stay longer today?"

"I think so?" I'm not really sure why they were longer, and Edward doesn't give me any information.

"In that case, I don't mind. What's he doing now?"

"Edward? He checked all the kittens to identify the males. He's not sure about one of the tuxedo ones. You'll have to tell Dr. Moore—"

"Edward's a treasure. I meant Zane. Is he watching us? I bet you're a looker in a bathing suit with all that yoga you do."

"Miss Gina!" My eyes widen at her conspiratorial tone, and I close my mouth. "He's winterizing your garden."

"Ooo, I bet he could handle another garden, if you know what I mean." Her eyebrows waggle, and her voice is too loud.

My face flames hot right along with my core—and in a swimming pool! "I *don't* know what you mean." *I do.* "I'm getting the underwater dumbbells."

"Dumbbells," she says under her breath, and I give her a shocked glare she can't even see.

Taking the foam "weights" off the side of the pool, I hand them to her. "Hold these underwater and move them up and down. Feel that?"

"I do!" Her face lights.

"They're foam, so it's naturally displacing the water for resistance."

"It's amazing. What will they think of next?"

We work out a half-minute in silence, and it's quiet and boring without our tunes. Twisting my lips, I try to think of a conversation that she can't turn into innuendo on me.

"I've honestly never heard of winterizing a garden this far south. I didn't think it got cold enough."

"We get the occasional freeze." That breezy tone is still in her voice, and she's still talking a little too loud for my taste.

I sneak a glance at Zane, who's finishing up with the plants. He's moving her potted fruit trees into the sun, and his biceps flex attractively as he lifts the heavy clay pots.

I chew my lip as I pretend not to watch him with his scowly face, defined arms, and powerful thighs. The muscle in his jaw moves under his scruff, and I try not to remember him in the hall in only a towel with his hair all wet, smelling like masculine body wash.

I've been tempted to use it myself, but I'm afraid he'll catch me and be mad. Not that it would be such a change.

"I'm about done." His deep voice almost makes me yip. "Tomorrow I'll get rid of those mimosa trees."

"Oh, no!" The words jump out before I can stop them.

"What?"

"I like mimosa trees."

"They're weeds." Zane's brow is lowered, and his voice is pure impatience like always.

"But the flowers are so cute. They're like little pink puff balls."

"They're messy, they attract aphids, and they multiply."

Miss Gina continues bouncing in the pool, a smile beaming on her cheeks as she pushes the water weights side to side.

"What do you think?" I ask her.

"I've never seen a mimosa, but I guess we can have one around if it's as cute as you say. It makes me think of pixie dust, like in *Peter Pan*."

"Pixie dust," Zane grumbles.

Miss G only exhales a satisfied hum. "I'm starting to get tired. Maybe I'll head up to my room now, if that's okay?"

"Of course!" I go to her, taking the weights. "Need me to walk with you? Did we overdo it?"

"I'm perfectly fine. I'll see you all tomorrow." She beams at me, leaning closer to stage-whisper. "I wish someone would stay in my guesthouse sometime. I hate being out here all alone, and it's such a lovely space."

I give her the old squint-eye. Not only is she leaving me here in my bathing suit, she's doing whatever she can to get me alone with Zane.

She forgets Edward is also here.

Even if he does have his noise-canceling headphones on pretty much 24-7.

"So you keep saying." I hold her arm as we walk up the wide steps leading out of the pool.

Zane turns away to pack his canvas tool bag. I'm not in my bikini today, because I knew he was going to be here. I'm try-ing not to be *that* girl.

Still, walking around in a one-piece bathing suit makes me feel very exposed in front of him, which is ridiculous.

For starters, we live at the beach, and for seconds, he did see me completely naked in the shower. My ears heat at the memory of waking up with him standing over me, eyes blazing with worry, damp hair hanging over his square jaw.

I do seem to douse him with water a lot. *Angry god.*

I quickly pull an overall-miniskirt over my bathing suit. I feel his eyes on me as I pack up the aerobics supplies, and I search for anything to break the tension.

"I can't believe I forgot the music today, but what's the saying? Imperfect action is better than perfect inaction?" My nose wrinkles and I exhale a laugh. "That can't be right."

"Don't let perfect be the enemy of good." His tone is still grumpy, and I frown.

"That sounds like settling."

"It's the opposite of settling. If you try to make everything perfect, you miss the good right in front of you."

My lips part, and I look up at him. "I like that a lot."

His jaw tightens, and he shifts his stance. "It's time to go."

"I'll find Edward, and we'll meet you at the Jeep."

A quiet smile is on my lips, and a flicker of hope sparks in my chest. He picks up his bag and walks away without another word.

Chapter 7

Zane

Garrett: Jack said you almost punched little Sam Allen in the nuts last night for talking to Rachel.

Zane: WTF?

Jack: Just sitting here.

Garrett: He also said she's sleeping in Dylan's old room. Have you banged her yet?

Zane: What are you? Fifteen?

Garrett: Kissed her?

Zane: No.

Garrett: Asked her on a date???

Hendrix: New phone, who dis?

Garrett: Bruh, nobody says that anymore.

Hendrix: Get off my dick.

Garrett: Grandpaw dick. How are you so old and yet the youngest?

Zane: I'm actually at work.

Garrett: Have Miss G add "Bang Rachel" to your To-Do list.

Logan: I'm in the brothers chat now?!

Garrett: First rule of brothers chat…

Hendrix: Don't fuck it up.

Garrett: Better. Also, nothing said here is repeated.

Zane: And tone down the PDAs with Dylan.

Logan: Are we giving you any ideas?

Garrett: That's my boy—give it to him.

Logan: Rachel's right there, man. What are you waiting for?

Zane Bradford has left the conversation.
Garrett Bradford added Zane Bradford to the conversation.
Zane Bradford has left the conversation.
Garrett Bradford added Zane Bradford to the conversation.

Garrett: I can do this allll day.

Zane: Muting this chat.

Garrett: You can run, but you can't hide.

Zane: This is hell.

Garrett: I bet I know where you can find some heaven…

Hendrix: And you call me a dork.

Walking out to the Jeep, I see Edward is already in the back with his hoodie pulled over his head. Rachel is in the front with her hair down again in those bumpy waves. It was in braids all day tied on her head while she bounced around in the pool with Miss Gina.

She has the shade down, and she's putting something shiny on her full lips. It's not chapstick, but it doesn't have a color. Somehow it makes her mouth even more luscious, and my cock twitches in my pants. *The good right in front of me.*

She looks amazing, and after Garrett's texting all day, now I'm just pissed. I'm not banging Rachel.

Grinding my jaw, I drop my tool bag a little too hard in the back, causing Edward to jump.

"Sorry, buddy," I mutter, and he shifts closer to the other side of the vehicle.

Climbing through the open door roughly, I don't look at her sitting over there taunting me. How does she still smell like honeysuckle after being in a saltwater pool for an hour? And why did I say that about perfect being the enemy of good? I don't supply ammo to be used against me.

"With all the excitement this morning, I didn't get to ask you how it went with Eddie." She shifts around to face me in her seat, and while I don't look, I can still see her glossy lips in my peripheral vision.

Fucking Garrett. I'm not kissing her either.

I crank the Jeep and shove the stick into reverse, turning away from her to look over my shoulder. The sooner we're on the road with the wind blocking out her voice the better.

She only speaks louder, tapping my arm. "How'd it go at the stables?"

I keep my eyes on the road. "He didn't tell you?"

"He told me some, but you know how he is."

"How is he?"

"So far, just like you!" Her voice rises. "How did it go? What did he do?"

"Keep your shirt on." I cut her a glance.

She exhales, and a smile hints at her lips. "Okay. How did it go?"

"He's right here. Just ask him."

"Oh, my lord!" She drops her arms, and I can't help a chuckle.

She's so easy to rile up, and dammit, the angry pixie bit makes me want to fuck her.

"He did good. We started slow, but he liked grooming the horses. He walked Shiloh around the arena."

"You had him mucking stalls."

"We all do that." I take the turn onto the road leading to the house. "We might try riding tomorrow."

Her smile returns, and she puts her hand on my forearm. "Thank you, Zane."

My throat tightens, and I give the Jeep some gas. We're almost home. "Glad to help."

"You are?" Her head tilts. "Why?"

"He's a good kid. I don't like hearing he was bullied at school. I don't like hearing you had to defend him all by yourself. That's not how we do things here."

"I'm learning that." The warmth in her tone makes me itchy.

Thankfully, we're back. I pull into the drive and put the Jeep in park before hopping out and starting for the restaurant without another word.

"Hey, where are you going?" Rachel calls after me. "Zane!"

I hesitate, turning to the side, but not looking back. "Dylan asked me to help her with the Thanksgiving decorations."

"We can help, too! Just give me a minute."

"Don't you need to eat something? You were doing all that exercise." The last thing I want is her fainting again.

"Nope." I look up to see her pop a purple candy into her mouth.

"That works?"

She shoves a hand in her backpack and pulls out a box of

grape Mike and Ike candies. "Yep! I'll just drop off my stuff, and we'll head down."

I wave and continue down the bluff to the restaurant, where I can see people moving around inside. Cooters & Shooters is closed from two to five to get ready for the dinner crowd, but we don't usually have customers until closer to seven.

"Oh, good, you're here." My sister is in her usual cutoffs and logo T-shirt, which is a turtle with crossed pool cues behind it, and flip-flops. "Allie is helping me dig out the November boxes. We've got orange twinkle lights and a few hay bales outside, and the first-grade class made these adorable popsicle-stick turkeys."

"Look at my turkey, Uncle Zee!" Kimmie dances over to me holding up a wooden bird with *Gobble* stamped on its stomach.

"That's actually pretty good." I lift her onto my hip, and she walks the turkey up my shoulder making gobble noises.

"Don't sound so surprised," Dylan mutters.

"Your stuff was always construction paper that fell apart as soon as it got outside in the humidity."

"Kimmie's teacher is very clever when it comes to crafts." Dylan shows me a box full of popsicle-stick turkeys. "The kids will get a kick out of finding their turkeys stashed around the restaurant."

"Smart, and good for business."

"We're giving her a discount all month." My sister winks before heading to the bar with the decorations.

Allie is there putting pilgrim outfits on the condiment holders. "Where's Rachel?"

My jaw tightens, but I don't snap a reply. I don't think the girls are in on the high-pressure campaign.

"She's dropping off her stuff at the house, then she'll walk down with Edward."

Kimmie wiggles, and I put her on her feet. "I'll show him my turkey."

"Oh, good! I was hoping they'd come down and help,"

Dylan calls over her shoulder. "We might actually have this place done before the dinner crowd shows up."

"Folks won't mind if we're finishing up while they're here." Salina Duck, who's been a waitress since she graduated high school walks through. "Hey, Zane."

She says it in a sly voice and even winks, which has my chin pulling back. *What was that?*

Dylan grabs my arm before I have time to process. "Come with me."

I follow her into the storage closet near the exit to the pool tables. We duck and go inside where she has painted pumpkins, corn stalks, and scarecrows in the center of the small space.

"We'll do all the inside stuff. You can start on the porch."

A ladder is folded in the corner, and I lift it onto my shoulder. "Did Gloria say anything to you about a pool tournament the other night?"

"No." Dylan crawls behind a cabinet and drags out a giant cornucopia. "Is this too much?"

"Where would you put it?"

"On the bar?" Her nose wrinkles, and she pushes it behind the cabinet again. "You're right. The dancers would kick it across the room and kill somebody."

I huff a laugh, and she shakes her head. "What's this about a pool tournament?"

"It's still in the planning stages, but I think she'd like to do it after Thanksgiving." I lift a wheel of twinkle lights out of the box and the staple gun. "She wants the kids to be the players and let them go around getting sponsors."

"Do they even know how to play?" She sits back on her heels looking up at me.

"Got me, but I can teach Edward the basics."

"You are so sweet with him." Her head tilts, and her gooey eyes make me ready to go.

"He's a good kid."

"Rachel must be over the moon that you're working with him."

My jaw tightens. "That's not why I did it."

"Oh, I know." She pushes off the floor to stand, picking up the orange streamers before following me out into the dining area. "You always looked out for me…"

"Mom said it was my job as a big brother." I'm only partly teasing—although in Dylan's case, I really let everyone down big time.

"You take care of Kimmie…"

"You help way more with her than I do."

"Well, Jack's all by himself."

When we emerge, Rachel is at the bar with Allie taking the popsicle-stick turkeys out of the crate. She's still wearing that overall-miniskirt thing over her bathing suit, and my eyes slide down her toned legs, all smooth and exposed.

She looks as tempting in a one-piece as she does in a bikini.

Kimmie dances past us twirling her stuffed red turtle, and Edward studies the room with a solemn expression while he holds Smokey in one hand and a pinecone wreath in the other.

The big windows are open, and a cool, salty breeze swirls through the space. I don't stop, heading straight for the porch with the twinkle lights and my equipment in hand.

Dylan follows me, carrying an extension cord and still chattering. "Gloria loves you, Miss Gina loves you…"

I stop at the door, lowering the ladder and leveling my eyes on hers. "Don't say it."

"I just wish you weren't alone all the time."

Shaking my head, I pick up the ladder again. "If only I were alone some of the time."

"Don't be like that. You know what I mean. I just want you to be happy."

"Hold the door." She exhales loudly as I pass her, going onto the porch. "I'm happy. Now let me get this done."

She mutters something about stubborn mules before dropping the extension cord in the corner and going back inside.

I spend the next half hour holding twinkle lights over my head and stapling them to the eaves then moving the ladder and doing it all again.

The girls come in and out placing scarecrows, pumpkins, and corn stalks around the rocking chairs no one ever uses, and I try not to notice how Rachel's skirt rises dangerously high on the back of her thighs when she bends over.

The worst part is when she and Allie hang a garland over the door. I have to turn away from the sight of her full breast swelling out of the side of her bathing suit. I wipe my forehead against my biceps while I staple the last stretch of twinkle lights in place.

I wish it worked to wipe the memory of her bare breasts from my mind. As it is, I have to wait to descend the ladder until they've gone back inside so my damn dick will calm down. Garrett's a pain in the ass, but he's right about one thing. It's been a while since I got laid.

My shoulders and neck are aching by the time we're done, but I'm not saying a word about it.

The brothers' group chat has kept my phone lit up in my pocket. Taking it out, I see more crap about missing my shot and how I'm only getting older.

Garrett takes the opportunity to let me know how at my age I should be worried my dick'll stop working if I don't use it. Hendrix asks if that can really happen, and I reply with the middle finger emoji before shoving the device into my pocket again.

"I noticed you went dark pretty fast." Jack's voice is a low tease behind me as I emerge from the small storage closet where I returned the ladder.

"Thanks for nothing." I cut my eyes at him as I take the beer he's holding out to me.

"For what it's worth, I only answered his questions honestly." Jack crosses his arms, looking at the small crowd filtering into the restaurant. "Rachel *is* a nice girl, and I *do* think she'd be someone you might like. If that's what you want to do."

We're behind the bar near the side patio where the pool tables are located. A few guys are playing a game, and Allie returns from where she apparently just brought them drinks.

"Hey, Jack." Her voice is a little breathless, and she blinks quickly. "How's it going?"

"Doing all right. You?"

"Oh, you know. The same." She waves her hand, and her cheeks turn pinkish.

Speaking of the good right in front of you…

"Austin really likes playing on the team. He says you're a great coach."

"Well, he's a great kid. We're lucky to have him."

"Thanks." The word comes out in a gush, and she hesitates a bit longer before nodding. "Well, I'll see you then."

"See ya, Allie."

My brow furrows, and I look up at him. He takes another sip of beer and looks out the large window at the bay. I've known my brother longer than anybody, and I can tell something's going on in his head. Allie's a pretty girl, and Austin's a good kid.

"I guess we all have our reasons for what we do," I say.

Or don't do.

Clearing his throat, he looks back at me. "Is this about her dad?"

"What?" That pulls me up short.

"Jayden Wells is Rachel's dad. Is that why you've written her off?"

"You know about that?"

"It didn't take much to put the names together. Hell, she practically did the work for us when she got here. She said her dad loved this place, and she was always curious about it. How many Wellses do you know?"

"Still, I didn't expect her to be connected to *him*."

Jack inhales, nodding slowly. "Yeah, Jayden's a real asshole."

"She didn't know anything about what he did." I look down at my feet, and I recall her expression when I told her—first shock then embarrassment then something like resignation.

"Well, it was all pretty long ago. Before Dylan was born."

I think back to that time, when Jack and I weren't the heads of the family. When our actual parents trusted a man who shat all over them.

I remember my dad's shock at Jayden's betrayal. I remember the anger my mom felt when she understood my dad was more hurt over losing a friend than he was at losing a potential business deal.

Sometimes I wished she didn't talk to me so much. Maybe I'd be less protective of their memory.

"If that's what's bothering you, I wouldn't let it." My brother pulls me back to the present.

"You can forgive that?" I know he remembers what happened as well as I do. Hell, possibly better. Jack's two years older than me.

He exhales heavily. "A lot of the boys I coach come from pretty rough situations. Bad parents, no money, crime, drugs, but they're doing what they can to rise above it. They're working hard to stand on their own and have something better the only way they can."

It's not often Jack talks this way about his work, but I know he's right. I remember how it was when I was in high school playing on the team.

"Hell, look at Allie and Austin," he continues. "I'm not going to judge him because his dad's a piece of shit."

Nodding, I turn the bottle in my hand. "I hear you, but giving her a chance feels like letting Jayden off the hook. It feels disloyal to Mom and Dad."

"Things worked out like they were supposed to. I can't imagine Cooters & Shooters any other way, and Rachel's only been honest and helpful."

I'm about to say her dad started off as a friend, too, when

Salina Duck appears. "Howdy, partners." She's chewing gum, and she cocks her hip to one side, sliding her eyes up and down me again.

I straighten, exhaling a low noise. I don't like it. Salina's barely twenty-two, and I remember when she was Kimmie's age, running around here.

"Thomas said he's got extra burgers if y'all are hungry, and Dylan said to make Edward have another one." Just as fast her voice changes and she rolls her eyes. "Of course, *Rachel* made some comment about paying her back."

Jack and I exchange a glance.

"I'll get Kimmie and meet you there." He places his beer in the trash.

Yacht rock is playing softly throughout the restaurant, and Kimmie dances in circles, kicking her leg out behind her as she sings along. She's not as naturally talented as her aunt was at her age, but she makes up for it with enthusiasm.

"Dance with me, Ed!" she cries.

"I'm decorating, Kim." Edward has three small, painted pumpkins in his arms.

"Have you eaten?" I reach out to stop him.

"I had a burger when we got here." He looks down at the gourds. "Austin's mom asked me to put these out by the pool tables."

"Come to the kitchen when you're done."

He nods, and I follow Jack and his little dervish through the double doors. A crowd of friends is gathered around the silver work table when we enter, and Logan's face is beet red.

"It's getting worse!" he groans.

Dylan is right beside him stroking his arm, and Allie is holding a towel over her face, barely hiding her laughter.

Craig rushes to him with a glass of milk. "Drink this."

"It's made with serranos, babe." Dylan's voice is soothing. "They're only one step above jalapeños on Scoville."

"I don't like jalapeños." Logan gulps the milk quickly.

"How do I love this man?" Dylan's hand is on his shoulder, and she's doing her best not to laugh.

I have no idea what happened, but I can guess knowing my little sister. What I can't believe is Logan fell for it again.

"I'll eat it!" Rachel pipes up from his other side, then ducks as if she's embarrassed. "If Logan doesn't want it, I mean."

"Knock yourself out." He slides the plate to her, drinking more milk.

"I feel like I missed something." I'm standing at the end of the table, and Allie waves me over.

"Thomas is experimenting with some new menu items." She puts a plate in front of me. "He's calling it the Melt yo Face burger, and it's made with serrano peppers. I think it's delicious, but Logan, well…"

Her lips twist, and I nod. "Logan's a puss–y cat."

I quickly edit myself when I see my little niece is at his side looking worried.

"I don't think cats like hot peppers either, Uncle Zee." She looks warily at Logan's burger, which Rachel is polishing off in a way that shouldn't be sexy.

She takes a big bite of the thick burger and lets out a groan. "It's so good, Thomas!"

I swallow hard, redirecting my attention to my own plate.

"This one's for you, Peanut." Allie puts a burger with a toothpick bearing a little green flag in front of her. "Green means safe. Red means danger."

"We need to get that to go." Jack's voice is low, and he smooths his hand over his daughter's curly brown head. "School tomorrow."

"Of course." Allie smiles up at him, quickly grabbing paper boxes. "I'll add some fries and a cookie."

"Thanks, Miss Allie!" Kimmie puts her arm around Allie's waist and gives her a hug. "You're the best!"

Jack clears his throat and for the first time, I see the smallest crack in his wall. "Yeah, thanks, Allie."

"It's no problem at all." She smiles brightly, patting his daughter's arms. "You two have a good night."

Edward walks in at that point, and Kimmie skips over to him. "Night, Ed! See you on the flippity flop!"

"Night, Kim. Stay gold."

Rachel puts her hands on her cheeks.

Dylan presses her lips together, and Jack's eyebrow cocks. "See y'all tomorrow."

"We should probably head on back as well." Rachel walks over to where her brother is standing beside me. "Thank you so much for dinner."

"Did Edward get something to eat?" Dylan asks.

"He had a hamburger when we got here this afternoon. Are you hungry?" She looks at her brother.

"Not really." He seems sincere.

"Have a cookie." Allie wraps a large chocolate chip cookie in a napkin. "Have it with some milk, and you'll sleep better."

"There's little scientific evidence that warm milk helps you sleep." Edward takes the cookie from her.

"Still, everyone loves a cookie."

He nods. "Thank you."

We say our goodnights and walk to the house in comfortable silence. My phone vibrates in my pocket, but I'm not about to take it out and see what the brothers are saying at this point. If Logan's adding fuel to the fire, I'm more than ready to call his ass out for being a pussy who can't even eat a spicy burger.

"Bunch of old ladies," I say under my breath.

"What?" Rachel's voice is soft, and she glances up at me.

"Ah… just thinking about something from earlier."

We enter through the kitchen, and I linger as they head upstairs. I'll give them time to get out of the way. Pulling down the box of saltines, I take out a sleeve then grab a bottle of water from the refrigerator.

It seems quiet, and I slowly make my way upstairs. My

shoulders are tight, and I try rolling my head side to side when I get to my bedroom.

Of course, Rachel is lurking around and sees me.

"Did you irritate your back today?" Her voice is soft as she enters my bedroom, and my stomach tightens at the sound of her voice. "I was worried about you when I saw you working on that ladder for so long."

Jack's words are in my ears, and as much as I try to dismiss them, I think my oldest brother is probably right. I don't need him to tell me Rachel's not like her father. I already know she's not.

Now she's standing here in my bedroom. She's dressed in a long-sleeved pink shirt and flowy pants. Her soft blonde hair is brushed out, her face is freshly washed again, and she smells like honeysuckle.

"You don't have to worry about me." My voice is rough, but this time, it's because I'm too tired to fight.

"I know, I know." A smile is in her voice, and she holds out a rolled-up mat. "I have this acupuncture mat you can try lying on."

She unrolls it on top of my bed, and I study the tiny points sticking up all over it. "It looks like a bed of nails."

She laughs softly. "It's supposed to be relaxing."

"Thanks, but I think I'll stick with ibuprofen."

"If you'll let me work on your back, I could get out all those knots."

"Yeah, yeah." I lift my hand to wave her away.

"What's this?" She picks up the saltines. "You eat crackers in bed? What are you, a psycho?"

A damn smile curls my lips at her fake-horror. "I thought I might get hungry."

"No. Just no." She tucks the sleeve under her arm when her eyes land on the book lying facedown on my desk. "You're reading it?"

"I haven't gotten very far."

"What do you think?"

I pick up the pale blue paperback, turning it to the side. "I think she spends a lot of time analyzing every single thing he does."

"He's a mystery to her—and everyone." She quickly adds the last part.

"He's simply doing what any homeowner would do, fixing the steps, mowing the grass."

"You'd be surprised." The way she says it sounds like she's had to pick up the slack on some of those types of chores.

"I'd like to punch that Travis guy in the nuts. Who passes judgment on someone without even knowing them?"

Her lips poke out, and she slides her finger along the edge of the desk, looking down. She doesn't answer, and I'm not stupid. I know what she's thinking.

Still. "I like that she's honest with him," I say.

"Honesty is important." Her voice is quiet.

"It's everything." Mine is firm.

The clock ticks.

The sound of a car passes on the road outside.

With a little nod, she straightens, going to the door. "I'd like to be there when Edward rides a horse for the first time— if that's okay?"

The note of yearning in her tone twists that tightness in my chest. Hell, everything about her hits that wall I've been trying to build with a sledgehammer.

"We leave at six. You're welcome to join us."

Her eyes light, and a smile lifts her cheeks. "I'll be ready."

She skips out the door, leaving the soft scent of flowers in her wake, and I can't help wondering if I'll be ready.

Chapter 8

Rachel

'M STANDING IN THE KITCHEN WITH A GO-MUG OF COFFEE, NIBBLING a strawberry pop-tart before Zane and Edward have even gotten out of bed.

I know those guys. They'll sleep until the very last minute, then roll out of bed, stagger across the hall to brush their teeth, pull on jeans, T-shirts, and in Zane's case, a long-sleeved plaid shirt.

Then they'll both appear, ready to go in less than five minutes. Edward will look like my little brother, while Zane will look like he just stepped off the pages of a men's outdoor magazine.

I, on the other hand, require a bit of prep to look this regular. My hair is twisted up in space buns, and I'm wearing a long-sleeved shirt and the only pair of jeans I own. They're almost 100 percent spandex, because blue jeans are the work of Satan.

I prefer my pants loose and forgiving.

Or skirts.

Still, I figure if I'm going to be hanging around in a barn, I should take my cues from the master and try to mimic his wardrobe. The only problem is I own no plaid, and my sole baseball cap has *Kiss My Grits* patched on the crown.

Gran gave it to me. She thought it was hilarious, but I wasn't old enough to get the reference.

Of course, that launched her into a speech about how all the best shows, movies, music, *everything* are gone, and if she taught a course in college it would be on early 1980s sitcoms and social commentary.

"You're up early." Zane's low voice triggers a hot thrill from my stomach all the way to my toes.

He walks into the kitchen, filling the space with his warm scent of cedar and soap and something comforting all his own.

Kiss my grits.

"I wanted to be sure I was ready, and have some break-fast." I hold up the Pop-Tart I'm eating.

He hesitates, and I swear he almost smiles. "Good call. We don't usually have food out there, and I don't want you to have any problems."

"Don't worry. I always have these." I pull a handful of grape Jolly Ranchers out of my pocket. "Is Edward up?"

As if to answer my question, I hear the sound of the bath-room door closing upstairs.

Zane glances up, and I take a second to admire his strong arms, his broad shoulders, the lines in his neck, his silky dark hair, before his blue eyes land on mine again, stealing my breath.

"Putting on his uniform," I say.

This time he does smile, and his straight white teeth paired with that dimple in his cheek is breathtaking. "He does like that shirt."

I take a sip of coffee to center my thoughts. "I don't think he knows I have three versions of it."

"Where did you find three versions of that shirt?"

"You can find anything on eBay."

He nods, glancing at my mug. "I wouldn't be surprised if he knew. He's a smart guy—and he has a nose."

Pressing my lips together, I give him a half-smile. "I'm not sure middle schoolers will be okay with a kid who wears the same outfit every single day of the week, even if it is clean."

"When I was in school, we had kids with special needs." He speaks slowly, thoughtfully. "It wasn't okay to treat them differently or make fun of them. Or bully them."

"It's never okay on the record. It's when the teachers aren't around that bad things tend to happen. Then it's Edward's fault for being different."

His dark brow furrows, and he looks over his shoulder. "I can only tell you my experience. But it wasn't allowed by my teachers, and we didn't allow it as fellow students."

Shifting my weight to one side, I cross my arms. "What made your school so different?"

"I don't know. I don't know if it was the kids or the parents—or dealing with hurricanes every year."

I lift my chin. "Right. You learned to have each other's backs."

"Either way, we weren't about punching down, and we didn't tolerate kids who did."

The sound of footsteps on the stairs ends our conversation. I take a final sip of coffee as I finish off my breakfast.

When Edward appears around the corner, I hold up the second one from the package. "Are you hungry?"

He steps forward to take it from me. "Strawberry?"

"Always."

He nods, taking a bite before heading to the door.

"What's that?" Zane holds the door as I leave.

"Kellogg's Strawberry Pop-Tarts. The only toaster pastry worth eating."

"Noted."

Shiloh is a gorgeous horse. I don't know how tall he is. I do know horses' heights are measured in hands, but I've never known how it works. All I know is he's tall. My head comes up to the base of his neck. His body is a smooth brown with almost black stockings. A white spot on his head looks like a heart, and he's proud.

He's also extremely gentle, which is unusual for a racehorse.

"We try to get ones that have been gelded for whatever reason," Gloria explains as we walk with her down the hall of the barn past stall after stall of beautiful, shiny horses. "A lot of them are kept for studs, but these old guys weren't just lame, they didn't bring in money. So nobody wanted them."

"They're so beautiful."

"No prizes for beauty in the racing game. It's all about the speed and the endurance—and the money. Above all, the money."

We stop at the arena, and Edward stands beside Shiloh. Zane is with him, and Gloria goes to the horse's other side. My stomach is somehow tight and churning at the same time.

Edward has never done anything like this, but when we got here, he went straight into the stall and started brushing the tall animal without any hesitation.

"Ready to ride?" Zane's tone is upbeat yet calm.

Edward studies the horse in front of him. Shiloh is wearing a traditional western saddle, and he lowers his head before jerking it back up again like he's trying to nod.

"Looks like Shiloh's ready," Gloria's calm voice contains a smile, and she turns to my brother. "What do you think, Edward? It's okay if you want to wait a few more days."

My brother glances at me briefly and seems to make a decision. "I'm ready. The chances of me being seriously injured by a fall from a horse simply walking are very slim."

My breath catches. I wasn't told he could be hurt. I thought you could only get hurt riding a horse if you were running or doing fancy jumps or something professional-level like that.

"You'll be fine. Put one hand on the saddle horn and the other on the back." Zane's low voice is confident, and he helps Edward latch his foot in the stirrup. "If you need the step…"

Before he can finish, Edward lifts himself off the ground and tosses a leg over Shiloh's back. My stomach jumps, but he's sitting with perfect posture on the elegant horse.

He looks like a natural, and my eyes heat. "You did it!"

"Do you want to take a picture?" Sandra is at my side, and I jump.

"Thanks." I huff a laugh, digging out my phone. "I would've completely forgotten."

"We get that a lot." Her voice is warm, and I hold up my phone.

I walk to the front of the horse and take his picture, then I walk to the side again. The only addition to his They Might Be Giants tee and jeans is a riding helmet, but he could be a real horseman for all I know.

"We'd better get moving so we don't run out of time." Zane looks up at Edward. "Ready?"

My brother nods, and they start walking. Gloria's on one side, and Zane's on the other, and they walk at a normal pace into the large arena. Other kids are already there riding with help. A few ride on their own, but all are well-supervised.

I climb the steps to the bleachers and sit on the front row taking a short video as they walk past. Once they're gone, I quickly text it to my grandmother.

> Rachel: Edward's riding a horse!

> Gran: How in the world did he do that?

> Rachel: My coworker also works at a horse farm, and they do equine therapy.

> Gran: What's that?

Rachel: Horses help reduce stress and calm anxiety. Edward really loves it.

Gran: Is it helping him in school?

Rachel: I don't know, but I think it will.

Gran: Is he in school?

My throat tightens, and I don't want to lie to her.

Rachel: I'm starting him in January. I didn't want to drop him in a new place in the middle of the holidays.

Gran: Sometimes that's a good time to start. Less schoolwork, less stress.

Rachel: I think it's exams, but don't worry.

Gran: Your dad asked, and I didn't know what to say.

Anger flashes in my throat, and my jaw tightens.

Rachel: Tell him I'm taking care of it.

Gran: He asked what happened. I don't want to lie to him.

Rachel: Don't tell him anything. He'll only cause trouble.

Gran: I'll do my best, but it is his son.

Rachel: When it's convenient for him.

Gran: I love you, honey. I'd like to see you both.

Rachel: I'll try to bring you here. I don't want to go back there until we're settled.

Gran: Keep me posted.

Rachel: I love you, Gran.

My body is tense, and my muscles are weak from the

adrenaline rush. I don't like knowing my dad is sniffing around trying to cause problems.

"Why does he even care?" I hiss under my breath, and my fingers tremble.

He only shows up when he wants something.

"Everything okay?" Zane's voice draws my attention, and I look up to see him holding the reins with the horse and my brother behind him.

"Yes—all good!" I shove my hand in my pocket, quickly unwrapping a Jolly Rancher and popping it into my mouth. "Gran says hello, Edward, and you look like a real horseman!"

"I like riding horses." He says it like he's reading a menu.

Still, it makes me smile. His face is free of all tension, and it's clear he really does like it.

"I'm so glad I was here to witness your very first ride."

Zane is still watching me like he's worried, which is a switch. "We'd better take Shiloh back. Miss Gina will wonder where we are."

"Don't want her to think we've abandoned her!" I know my voice is overly cheerful, and I'm not helping my *all good* case.

They turn, and I hang out as they slowly walk the horse to the stables. I've got to talk to Dylan and get my shit sorted out now, before something goes wrong.

Chapter 9

Zane

"I've decided I want a Christmas tree this year." Miss Gina's hand is on my forearm as we walk through her Italian-style mansion.

The entire place is beige marble and wrought iron. It's all hard edges and slippery surfaces only softened by the sofas and Persian rugs expertly arranged in each well-appointed room.

You'd think it would be a nightmare for a blind person, but she navigates it with ease having grown up here.

I'm pretty sure it's the most beautiful house I've ever seen. Dylan's been in love with it all her life, and we actually met Miss Gina because my little sister was so obsessed with this place, she insisted we bring whoever lived here some cookies when she was briefly a Girl Scout, before she started dancing twenty-four-seven.

I drove her here, where we met the sunniest, most optimistic blind lady who was thrilled to have the company of "two nice young people with cookies."

Back then, she lived here alone with her elderly gardener

Stephen and a nurse from Birmingham, where her niece lives, but after that day, everything changed. We've been dropping by, visiting, and now caring for her ever since.

"I thought we weren't allowed to move anything." Whenever I tease her about not really being blind, she says she can see it all in her mind—and never, *ever* rearrange the furniture.

I pause, and she continues ahead of me, crossing the massive living room to the twelve-foot windows facing the front of the house.

"We could put it here, so it can be seen from the road." She turns in my direction, sweeping her hand around the vacant space. "I'd like it to be big, and get one that fills the house with scent."

"I'll get you the stinkiest tree on the lot."

"Zane Bradford!" Her horrified cry breaks on a laugh.

A grand piano sits in the corner, and a balcony circles the room above us with bookshelves full of books lining the walls.

Thick beige silk and satin curtains cover the windows, and she slides her hand down a sheer moving it aside.

"Would you like it to be decorated?"

Her lips press together, and her brow furrows. "I don't have Christmas decorations. They always seemed too risky to me."

"I agree."

"Do you think it would be okay to have only lights on the tree? Is that boring?"

"I think it would be beautiful." Rachel's soft voice joins us in the room, and my body tenses. "What made you decide to get a tree?"

My eyes move over her hair hanging long down her back with little pieces curling around her chin and jaw. She's wearing peach-colored wide-legged overalls with a thin, long-sleeved shirt underneath.

She's seemed slightly on edge since we were at the stables yesterday, and she's been very focused on talking to Dylan. My little sister, by contrast, has been slammed getting ready for the Christmas program.

"I'm sure it's old-lady sentimentality, but I feel like I'm missing out on something important." Miss Gina's lips press into a half-smile, and it's the closest I've ever seen her get to unhappiness. "Something the whole world joins in together."

"You're not being left out this year." Rachel steps closer, sliding her hand through the old woman's arm. "We'll make this place look and smell so good, it'll be like Santa's workshop."

"Don't add anything besides a tree, though." Miss Gina's brow furrows.

I take a step closer. "Don't worry. I know the rules."

"Hmm…" She pats her bony finger against her thin lips. "Is Edward in the garden? I think I have a job for him."

"Want me to walk you?" Rachel takes her hand.

"No, no!" Miss Gina lifts it, waving her away. "I can find him. You two stay here and sort out the details."

She scurries away in her long, beige cardigan, and my eyes move to Rachel. She seems almost afraid to look at me, but eventually she tears her eyes away from the direction our employer went.

Her chin dips before she looks up at me through thick lashes. "I think she did that on purpose."

"What would be the purpose?" Her body feels too close, so I take a step away.

"She's an old lady. Old ladies love to play matchmaker." Rachel turns and walks to the wall of mahogany bookshelves. "Just look at these old things. Aren't they amazing?"

She slides out a small, fabric-bound tome, lifting it to her nose before turning it in her hands.

I look up at the skylight far overhead. "No telling what all's on these shelves."

"*Silas Marner*." She opens the cover and reads aloud. "The Weaver of Raveloe. It has handwriting inside. Look."

Excited eyes meet mine, and I relent, walking over to see

what she wants to show me. On the front page in a shaky old cursive, it says Tuesday and Thursday.

"I didn't think you were allowed to write in textbooks."

"I wonder if it's Miss Gina's. Maybe she was homeschooled since she's blind. This could be her tutor's handwriting."

"Maybe." It looks older than that to me.

"Oh, look! *The Black Stallion*." She pulls out another hard-cover edition with gold print and turns it in her hand. "Edward might like to read this."

My eyes drift from the book to the curve of Rachel's cheek. A soft peach color is on the top of them, and I can smell the grape candy in her mouth.

She blinks up at me, and my stomach warms. I take a step back.

"I can't believe my brother rode a horse yesterday." Her lips curl with a smile. "You're helping him so much, opening his world."

"You're giving him books." I nod at the volume she's holding. "They also open his world."

"It's true." Her eyes flash mischievously. "Books are dangerous. They make you think. They give you the idea there's something better out there."

"Or worse."

"I thought you stopped reading *The Sun Also Rises!*" It's a teasing fuss, and I think of something less depressing.

"It was a dark and stormy night?"

"Better." She returns the smaller book to the shelf. "Edward loved *A Wrinkle in Time*."

"Dylan did, too." I walk to the bookshelf, surveying the spines.

"She told me you used to read to her when she was little." Rachel follows me. "I think if I found my little boy reading to my little girl, I'd melt on the spot."

"Readers are leaders," I mimic Edward's tone, and she exhales a laugh.

Reaching up, she slides her finger along the spine of an Emily Dickinson novel. "I used to dream of having a boyfriend like Mr. Darcy."

"Instead, you had boyfriends like…" The words jump out unbidden.

Why am I asking her about past boyfriends? More importantly, why do I feel like I'm hanging off the edge of a cliff waiting for her answer?

"None." She sighs as she says it, and her chin drops to her chest. "I've never had a serious boyfriend."

I don't know how to name the satisfied feeling that flashes in my chest. It's primal, possessive. It's new.

"What's wrong with the guys in Birmingham?" I mean to say it as a joke, but I'm not joking.

She only shrugs, chewing her lip. "They don't like weird little brothers hanging around all the time."

I've got to get a grip on this. Rachel's love life is not my business. Clearing my throat, I take a step down the passage, away from the pull of her gravity.

"Well, I wouldn't worry. You've got plenty of time." The words are bitter on my tongue.

I hate them. I don't want her out there looking for someone. I want to put my hands on her and claim her. I want to make it clear she's mine.

Mine.

What?

"Gran always said that, but I'm almost thirty." She huffs a laugh. "I thought I would've at least kissed someone by now."

Fuck. Me.

"You've never been kissed?" I move towards her.

Her eyes squeeze shut, and she puts both hands over her face. "I know. It's so humiliating. You must think I'm a total loser."

"I don't. I just…" Shaking my head, I look at her. "How is that possible?"

"I mean…" She *pffts* air through her lips. "It's possible. Just look at me."

What does she mean? Is she trying to say she's a dork? She has no game?

"I am looking at you." A woman as sexy and beautiful as Rachel doesn't need game, and being a dork just makes her cuter.

I take a step closer to where she's leaning against the books looking down, cheeks bright red, eyes blinking fast.

"You're like Archer." I lift a finger to slide a piece of hair behind her ear.

She takes a shivering inhale and lifts her chin. Our eyes meet, and our bodies are so close, her warmth radiates against my skin.

"I think maybe I've built it up in my mind so much, I'm afraid for it to happen." Her voice is a rushed whisper.

I put my thumb on her chin. My arm is propped on the bookshelf above her head, and I'm leaning down. She's standing straight against the books, arching her back higher.

Her full breasts rise and fall rapidly with her pants, and I'm not getting away this time. An invisible force pulls me to her, and my fight has left me.

"I could help you with that." My voice is low, and I wonder if I've lost my mind.

What I do know is I've been going out of my mind thinking about her, and here she is, right in front of me, destroying my willpower.

She lifts her chin, green eyes meeting mine as her pink tongue slips out to wet her bottom lip. My dick tightens. Her hand grips the front of my shirt, and she pulls me closer.

"Okay."

It's all I need.

Leaning down, I hold her gaze before blinking down to her parted lips. I cup her cheek in my hand. The other, I move to her waist, sliding it around her lower back to pull her body flush against mine. She feels so good, soft and melting into me, like she belongs in my arms.

On a breath, I seal my lips to hers, and a soft whimper escapes her throat. Her fingers curl against my chest, and one slides higher, to my shoulders and into the side of my hair.

Moving her lips apart, my tongue attempts an invasion, but it's met with an impenetrable force.

Lifting my head, I speak gently. "Open your mouth."

"What?" Her brow furrows, and she starts to blink.

"Your teeth are clenched."

"Oh!" She exhales a laugh, trying to get embarrassed. "I guess I'm nervous. I didn't even—"

Sealing my lips over hers, I try again. This time, her teeth part, and I'm inside the walls. Our tongues curl together, and she makes another soft noise. It registers straight to my cock, and from there, things pick up speed.

She tastes like grape candy. She smells like tantalizing flowers. Her knees bend, and I hold her tighter against my chest, moving her mouth with mine, consuming her, devouring her.

I turn her back against the books, and she rises higher. I pull her lips with mine before kissing her jaw, her cheek, her ear, then making my way back to her delicious mouth once more.

Both her hands are in my hair, and she tugs me closer. She's a fast learner, and now she's nipping my lips, sweeping her tongue with mine and moving her body against me. It's like a dance only the two of us know.

I'm sure she can feel my erection. Her breasts grind against my chest, and I want to slide my hands under her shirt. I want to see her naked again. Her head tilts as our mouths slide, and she moans. Fuck, this feels too good. I've got to stop it. I'm going to fuck her right here in Miss Gina's nice library if I don't.

Slowing my movements, I bring us down. I move my mouth to her temple and inhale deeply the flowery scent of her hair. My eyes close briefly as it imprints on my mind.

She's gripping me and panting, and damn, if the earth didn't tilt for a hot minute.

When I'm pretty sure I've got my bearings, I take a step back.

She's gorgeously mussed. Her lips are swollen, her eyes are dark and lusty, and those tits rise and fall with her pants. Her nipples point at me, and my lips part.

"I didn't build it up," she whispers.

"What?"

"Kissing. I didn't build it up in my mind." She blinks hard, shaking her head. "That was… that was really good."

Moving my tongue around, I realize, I have her Jolly Rancher in my mouth. A silly sense of pride tightens my chest, like I'm back in high school, and we swapped our gum.

And I left my brain in the Jeep.

What the fuck am I doing? I said I wasn't going to kiss her. Now I've kissed her. I said I wasn't going to bang her…

"I've gotta get back to work." I turn, needing to escape.

I've got to get the hell out of here before it's too late.

Who am I kidding? It's already too late.

"Wait!" Her voice cracks on the word. "Where are you going?"

"I never fixed that drain." *Lame.* My jaw clenches, and I struggle to summon my old anger. I've got to rebuild the wall.

"But… But we just…"

"We kissed, Rachel. You're a little late to the party, but that was a kiss. We're both adults. Don't make it more than it was. It was only a kiss."

Wow, I'm an asshole. Twenty points to Slytherin.

But the truth is, I'm doing this for her. I don't need pity, and I don't want help.

I'm better on my own.

Her face flashes, and she pulls her chin back. "It's like I'm having a *deja vu* flashback of all the guys I hated. You really fooled me by being nice to my brother."

"Look, I–"

"No, no…" She holds up a hand. "You're right. We're adults. Thank you for satisfying my curiosity. I'll see you around."

She turns on the ball of her foot and walks out of the room so fast, I'm pretty sure the drapes lift as she passes.

Her Jolly Rancher is between my teeth, and I crunch it, picking up the book she left behind. *The Black Stallion* in black leather with shiny gold print. I return it to its place on the shelf.

My chest is tight and achy, and I put both hands behind my neck, looking up at the skylight. It's so far away.

What the fuck have I done?

I exhale a growl. It wasn't *only a kiss*, and she didn't build it up. Not even a little.

I've kissed girls before, and it was never like that. Hell, that kiss was a full-body experience. It was the kind of kiss where you forget everything around you, the kind of kiss that could go on for hours. The kind of kiss you want to have again and again.

Good thing I know how to push people away. Good thing I know how to break shit. Good thing I'm a fucking *adult*.

That could've gotten serious.

Chapter 10

Rachel

DO NOT CRY. DO NOT CRY.

Dammit, Rachel! I shove the tears off my cheeks roughly as I burst through the door of the small guest bathroom, quickly locking it behind me.

Do. Not. Cry.

The stubborn tears don't listen to me. They continue coating my cheeks, and I press my palm to my chest trying to calm my breathing. Stupid emotional rollercoaster.

I've been so happy with all the good things, like Edward's progress, feeling like we've finally found a community where we have friends and where we can make a home. Seeing Edward sitting tall and proud on the back of that beautiful horse.

Then Gran tells me my dad's snooping around, asking about us, then I act like I have some masochistic death wish by kissing Zane Bradford.

He fooled me with all that talk about my brother and acceptance and not punching down. He turned my head, sharing his favorite books and being all funny and sweet. Why the hell did I tell him I'd never kissed anyone?

"Real smart, Rach." I turn on the cold water, patting it on my hot cheeks.

I got exactly what I wanted.

I wanted him to kiss me, and like the fairytale-believing, hopeless romantic I am, I thought it would change things between us. When has my life ever been a fairytale?

Did I really think he was going to change? Did I think he was going to fall in love with me?

My throat tightens, and I jerk out my phone, tapping the icon for the rideshare app. I know one thing, I'm not riding back to the house with him today.

Searching for an excuse, I check myself in the mirror. My nose is red and my eyes are swollen, and for once, I'm thankful Miss Gina is blind and Edward doesn't care what I look like.

I scoop a handful of water to drink, clearing my throat before opening the door and going to where they're standing outside. Edward is holding a kitten, and she's petting it slowly.

"He's solid black, which is rare." Edward's voice is matter of fact as always. "Black cats typically have some markings."

"What color are his eyes?"

"Yellow."

"Oh!" She puts her hand on her chest. "He sounds gorgeous!"

"Hi, guys." My voice wavers, and I clear it again quickly. "I need to duck out a little early today if that's okay?"

Miss Gina turns to me. "Are you okay?"

"Yes!" I force a smile, taking her cool hand. "It's just that Dylan's been working every evening on the Christmas program, and I've got to talk to her about school stuff. We really can't let another day go by."

"Ah." Miss Gina's lips tighten, and she nods. "Of course."

I can tell she's not quite sure I'm telling the whole truth, but I can't worry about that now. I'm more worried I'm going to bump into Zane before I can get out of here, and I will *not* let him see I've been crying.

"Edward, will you be okay riding back in the Jeep like always?" I don't even want to say his name.

He shrugs. "Sure."

"See you tomorrow." I step forward to give the old woman a squeeze, then wave at my brother. "See you later."

A noise comes from the greenhouse, and I skip a jump at the first sight of his dark head emerging from the glass door.

Our eyes meet, but I turn away fast, dashing to the side gate and down the stone steps to the street where a white car is just pulling up.

"How is it possible I never see you these days?" Dylan pulls me into a hug. "You live in my house!"

We're in the kitchen at Cooters & Shooters, and Thomas is taking out the ingredients for his famous burgers. Craig is in the dining room restocking the condiments for the dinner crowd, and Allie has Kimmie following her around carrying utensil rolls.

I stopped off at the house to fix my makeup and put some powder on my nose before jogging down here. The last thing I need is everyone asking why I'm crying—because I'm *not* crying.

If life has taught me anything, it's how to dust myself off and get back on my feet. I've been taking care of Edward and me for a long time, and I'm getting my head out of the clouds and focusing on what's important—getting Edward in school and keeping my dad out of our lives.

I return her hug. "We're like ships passing in the night."

"At least we're not crashing into each other," she laughs. "I'm lucky if I even get a goodnight kiss from Logan half the time, between helping Jack with Kimmie, teaching, and running this place."

Chewing my lip, I don't say I've heard her and Logan doing more than kissing a few times getting my morning coffee—and run right back upstairs. Why be a wet blanket? She can't help it if their bedroom is right across the hall from the kitchen, and at least somebody's getting love.

"Miss Gina said to tell you her guest house is open whenever you'd like to use it."

"Isn't she the greatest?"

"Yes!" I answer fast.

"And that house is absolutely gorgeous," Dylan sighs. "I might take her up on the offer if only to spend the night there."

"And to get some…" I elbow her, and she snorts. "By the way, you are seriously working the ballerina-core today."

She's dressed in a black leotard with beige joggers and pilates shoes, and her thick dark hair is wrapped in a bun on her head.

"I've got to get back to school." She catches my hand, leading me out of the kitchen. "I spent thirteen years studying ballet, and all I've got to show for it is style—and good posture."

"I think you got a little more than that. You got a class of students who love you, great memories. This guy."

I hook a thumb at Craig as he passes us on his way to the kitchen. "Clint said to tell you he's waiting for you to okay the table bouquets."

"I don't know why he keeps asking me to approve things. I told him I trust him completely," She calls after him.

"He wants it in writing."

She shakes her head, but I know their bickering is never serious.

"How's the wedding planning going?"

"We're on track for June, and I'm trying not to freak out over all the details." She pulls out her phone. "Craig's boyfriend is doing the flowers, and his taste is impeccable. Let me text my okay real quick."

"Show me!"

She turns her phone so I can see the delicate flower

arrangements of what look like pure-white hydrangeas in mason jars filled with tiny lights.

"They're so pretty—I love them." I look up at her frown. "What's wrong?"

"I agree, and he needs to stop sending me all these options. I trust you!" She catches my wrist, pulling me with her. "Nevermind. We've got to help Edward. Can you come with me now? I'll introduce you to Mrs. Laverne. She's the principal, and she'll help you get everything you need to have him ready for spring semester."

"Let's go!"

We take off out of the restaurant, hopping into a sleek, bronze Range Rover. "I usually ride my bike everywhere, but Logan won't mind if we use his car."

"It's so nice." I slide the belt over my lap as I sit in the beige leather seat. "It smells brand new!"

"It's the first time he's owned a car in years. Can you imagine? He said it was more of a hassle than it was worth in New York." She reads the question on my face. "He had a car service."

"Ah." I lift my chin, trying to imagine what it would be like to have that kind of money.

Of course he was a professional football player, but Dylan told me his dad is also a media mogul and never understood why Logan would choose to play professional football. From what she's told me, his dad didn't understand much of anything about his only son.

It's something we all share—difficult backgrounds. Dylan and I bonded immediately over our young-adult losses, although she lost both her mom and her dad.

My dad's still hanging around causing problems.

"Is Edward with you for good now?" She glances at me. "I mean, are you his guardian?"

Nerves twist my stomach. "Not legally. After our mom died, Edward and I went to live with our grandmother in Pine Apple. Then when I got the job with Miss Gina, Gran told me to take it and go, live my life for once. I'd been taking care of him full-time up until then."

"But your parents were still around, weren't they?"

"It's kind of a long story."

"We'll be in this Rover at least ten minutes with all the lights now." She gestures to the traffic signal impatiently.

Tracing my fingernail along the seam of the leather seat, I think of how to say this. "My dad kind of lost interest after Edward's diagnosis, and my mom started drinking all the time."

Her lips pull into a frown, and she reaches over to squeeze my hand. "I'm sorry."

"They might've hired someone to care for him, but they didn't. I could've ignored him, but I didn't." I swallow the ache in my throat. "I played with him and kept him in my room when he was awake. Then when he got older, I took him with me everywhere. He wasn't hard to manage. He was actually pretty easy… just different."

"Sounds like Zane and me." Dylan's voice is thoughtful. "Our mother wanted to spend time with us, but I guess with five kids, it's hard."

"At least she wanted to have a relationship with you."

"But now you and Edward are totally bonded, right?"

I exhale a laugh. "Yeah, and I have no life."

Her nose wrinkles. "That part kind of stinks."

"It was like I had a baby at sixteen, and trust me, the guys weren't interested in my younger brother spouting little-known facts about everything all the time."

"I guess that does put a damper on your social life."

"Yeah," I look down, remembering those days. "I read a lot, and I watched a lot of YouTube videos."

"We all did that," she laughs. "But then you went to college, right?"

"Night school. I worked every day at the nursing home. Not a lot of guys there."

"Wait—are you telling me you've never had a boyfriend?" Her eyes widen, and I feel like I've made a critical error.

"No."

"So you have?"

"No."

"I'm confused."

Waving my hands, I explain fast. "I haven't had a boyfriend, and I'm not looking for one. That's not what I meant. I shouldn't have even said that."

"Oh-kaay, but I heard Sam Allen was hanging around you the other night. He's really nice."

"Dylan, seriously. No. I'm not interested in Sam Allen." The memory of Zane's lips covering mine, tugging and pulling them, our tongues curling together, his strong arms around my waist, my entire lower belly flooding with heat…

She gives me the side-eye. "You're thinking about somebody."

"Edward." My voice is firm. "I'm thinking about Edward and getting him all set up at school." *And keeping my dad off my case.*

Exhaling slowly, I confess, "I can't help feeling like what happened to him at school was partly my fault."

"You can't go to school with him, Rach." She gives me a sympathetic smile.

"I know." My fingers twist, and I study my hands. "But maybe leaving him behind scared him. He's never done anything like that before."

"And you can't get any help from your dad?" Her expression is perplexed, and I figure now's as good a time as any.

"I don't want our dad in our lives. I didn't know what he did to your parents until Zane told me, but now that I do, well, I'm not surprised. I *am* really sorry, though. He's not a good person."

"What do you mean? What did he do?"

"Ditching your parents with the restaurant? Jayden Wells?"

"That was your dad?" Her eyebrows rise.

I nod looking down again, wishing there was some way I could divorce my family.

She doesn't say anything, and I wish I could tell what she's thinking. I hope she'll still be my friend. I hope she'll judge me on my own merits and not by some man she's never met, who happens to be my dad.

I hope she'll still be willing to help us.

"Zane told you all this?"

"Yeah."

"If Zane knows, Jack must know." Her voice is quiet. "But he didn't tell me."

The radio plays softly in the background, and I think about all the high hopes I had when I came here. I think about my dreams of finding a new life, a career, living on my own terms. I think about my silly dreams of falling in love with a handsome man. And I think about how it's played out so far—once again, thanks to my dad.

After a few more minutes of silence, I finally ask her, "What do you think?"

"Well…" She exhales, nodding as if she's made a decision. "It all happened before we were even born. If it mattered today, my brothers would've said something about it. Instead, the restaurant is a big success, Zane's helping Edward, and we're friends. I think we're safe to leave what happened in the past, and we can keep moving forward."

The breath I didn't know I was holding bursts through my lips, and I drop my face into my hands.

My chest aches, and I swallow the knot in my throat. "Thank you."

"Oh, honey." She pulls into a parking space and pulls me into a hug. "It just makes sense. We've all grown so close, and you and Edward are the sweetest things."

"I was so discouraged when Zane told me that story." I blink back more tears. "I've worked so hard to make a better life. I want to be your friend, and I couldn't take another rug being pulled out from under us."

Dylan sits back in her seat, her brown eyes misty like mine, and she tugs the side of my hair. "You've come to the right place. We help each other here. Now let's get in there and see what we can do to help your brother."

Chapter 11

Zane

Jack: Edward said you kissed Rachel.

Garrett: What?

Logan: And now she's avoiding you.

Garrett: What???

Zane: Edward saw us?

I glance over to where he's sitting on the deck reading *The Outsiders*. A black kitten is playing with the string of his hoodie, and it falls back with a little thump before jumping up again.

Garrett: The hell? You kissed Rachel and she's avoiding you? Did you forget how?

Hendrix: Kissing is like riding a bike.

Garrett: Did you give her the stabby tongue? The stiff lip? Slobber all over her?

Hendrix: Burp in her mouth? I almost did that once.

Garrett: Dude.

Zane: I know how to kiss a woman.

Garrett: Did you have bad breath?

Hendrix: Fart?

Zane: Grow up.

Hendrix: Sometimes it can't be stopped.

Garrett: Why is she avoiding you?

Zane: She's not avoiding me.

Jack: She drove my truck to work the past two days.

Garrett: We are never going to get you laid.

Hendrix: Bruh, one time I kissed a girl and she started to cry. Turns out her cat had just died, and it had nothing to do with me.

Garrett: Keep telling yourself that story.

Hendrix: She showed me a picture!

Garrett: I'd cry if I kissed you, Mr. Burpie-Fartybutt

Hendrix: I didn't do any of that with her, and my point is, it might not be him.

Garrett: She's right across the hall. Ask for a do-over.

Logan: It's only fair. You had to listen to Dylan and me kissing.

Zane: You did more than kiss, and her brother's in the house.

Logan: Want us to take him for a long drive?

Zane: No.

Logan: He can go with us to spend the night at Miss Gina's!

It's been two days since I kissed Rachel in the library, and ever since, she's been avoiding me like the jerk I am.

Miss Gina hasn't said a word about it, but I saw Rachel's face before she left that day. I saw her red eyes, and I heard the wobble in her voice. It was a kick in the stomach.

It was only a kiss—and I'm full of shit. That kiss was epic. It was more than I bargained for when she said she'd never done it. I guess that's what they call chemistry.

All I know is I felt myself falling, and I ran.

I honestly thought Edward was oblivious. We've been riding together every day, and he hasn't said a word.

He's getting more skilled at working with the horses, and he seems happy. I hadn't seen any signs of negative behavior, no anger or aggression.

Rachel said he'd gotten in a fight at school, but I'm even more inclined to think he was provoked after spending all this time with him. Now I wonder what he's thinking. Did he see her start to cry?

"How old is Shiloh?" Edward sits in the passenger's side of the Jeep with his hood over his head as we drive to Miss Gina's.

I scratch my thumb under my bottom lip as I think. "Gloria started the farm when I was in high school, almost twenty years ago. Thoroughbreds only race four or five years."

"The average lifespan of a thoroughbred horse is twenty-five to thirty years." His brow furrows. "Due to inbreeding, their life expectancy can be even shorter."

"Gloria has a vet check all the horses every year. I'm sure if there was a problem, he'd have noticed it by now."

"What was the reason Shiloh was retired from racing?"

"Don't know."

"We should talk to Gloria about this."

I reach over and pat his shoulder. "Shiloh's in pretty good shape. I don't expect he's going anywhere for a while."

"It's impossible to know what will happen in the future."

Hell, if anybody knows that lesson, it's our family. Glancing at him sitting straight in the seat, I think about the changes he's had to deal with in his short life. He lost his mom, but I heard Rachel telling Miss Gina he never really knew her.

"Has your sister said anything to you about school?"

His lips tighten, and he nods. "I'm starting at the 7-12 school in January."

"How do you feel about that?"

He shrugs. "Research is mixed on the value of separate middle schools. Many school districts are abandoning the practice entirely."

Not what I meant.

"I went to school here in Newhope." He looks over at me briefly, curious. "When I was there the kids were generally welcoming to newcomers."

"It's a primal facet of human nature to be wary of strangers."

"The good news is they won't be all strangers. Austin will be there, and Allie is the librarian. Dylan teaches dance."

His eyes lower. "I never had friends at school. I'd usually read a book or sit by myself at lunch and recess."

"Things might be different for you here." We pull into the circular drive, and I park the Jeep beside Jack's red truck. "You can always hang out in the library if you just want to read. Allie won't mind."

He nods before climbing out. "She's nice."

"Yep, she is." I reach behind my seat to grab my tools

and the bag of supplies I bought to fix the sink yesterday evening. "Did Gloria tell you about the pool tournament she's planning?"

He nods. "I can't participate."

"How come?" Our shoes crunch on gravel as we walk up to the house.

"I don't know how to play pool."

"Tell you what, next time we're at the restaurant, I'll grab Austin, and we can teach you. Sound good?"

"I'll read up on it."

Exhaling a laugh, I expect that means he'll be a pool shark by the time we have our first lesson.

We go through the gate leading to the back patio, and my stomach warms when I hear the sound of Rachel's voice. "Balsam trees smell really good. You'll love a balsam."

I venture a peek, and I see Miss Gina lying face-down on the massage table. Rachel is sliding her forearms up the old lady's back, which is bare to the waist.

Heat lamps are above them, and Rachel is dressed in short-sleeved beige scrubs. Her hair is twisted up in those two little space buns on the top of her head, and she looks fucking adorable.

Adorable? *Seriously?*

"How big is a balsam tree?" Miss Gina's voice is thoughtful.

"I imagine they come in all sizes." Rachel's brow furrows over her downcast eyes. "We can call around and see who has the biggest."

"A balsam can grow from forty to sixty feet in height." Edward walks over to where they're working, and Rachel jumps at the sound of his voice.

Some kind of atmospheric flute music is playing. It's more noticeable the closer I get, and the smile disappears from her glossy pink lips as soon as she sees me.

She quickly slides a thin sheet over Miss Gina's back before returning to her massage. Miss Gina lets out a loud "Oooh!" and Rachel jumps again.

"I'm sorry!" Her green eyes widen, and she lifts her hands quickly. "Was that too deep?"

"A little." Miss Gina exhales a wobbly laugh. "My shoulders are sore from those water weights."

"I'm so sorry." Rachel slides her palms rapidly over the spot. "Better?"

"Much." She lifts her head slightly. "Zane, you have to let Rachel work on your back. I'm telling you, she has magic hands. I've never felt so relaxed."

Busted. How did she know I was here? I guess Edward gave us away.

Rachel answers without even looking at me. "I'm sure Zane Bradford will be just fine without my help."

"Oh…" Miss Gina lowers her head. "So we're back to that again?"

"I don't know what you mean." Rachel takes a plush robe off a chair and drapes it over the woman's back. "Take your time sitting up. I'll help you off the table."

Miss Gina slides her arms into the robe, rising slowly with her back to us before she stands and ties the belt.

"I heard about a type of massage where one person slides their body all over the other person's. Have you heard of that, Rachel?"

She holds Miss Gina's arm, looking stern. "That's called Nuru massage, and it's not a service I provide."

"It sounds X-rated if you ask me." Miss Gina elbows her side, lowering her voice. "You might learn it in case you meet someone you want to know better."

I glance over to where they're slowly making their way from the massage platform to the house. Rachel's eyes clash with mine, and her face blazes bright red.

She blinks away quickly. "I have no interest in getting to know anyone better. I am interested in getting you changed so we're not late to your hair appointment. Then we're going Christmas tree shopping, remember?"

"Yes," Miss Gina fusses back playfully. "I don't know why you're announcing it for the whole world to hear like we're on the TV or something."

"Because it sounds like you lost track of your schedule." Rachel's voice is a quiet scold. "How do you even know about Nuru massage?"

"I might be blind, but I'm not deaf." Miss Gina waves her hand. "I know about things."

"You're being a pot-stirrer."

"Zane?" The old lady pauses at the patio door.

"Yes, ma'am?" I walk over to where she's staring in my direction while Rachel is looking everywhere but at me.

"The elevator is making a funny noise again. Would you take a look at it, please?"

"I'll look at it again, but I don't know much about elevators." I glance up at the old place. "Who inspects it?"

"Stephen took care of all of that." She presses her lips together. "Maybe you can track down a receipt?"

More like I'll track down her old gardener. "I'll see what I can do."

"Thank you, dear."

The two of them disappear into the house, and I glance over to where Edward is sitting in a chair reading again. Shaking my head, I scoop up my abandoned supplies and return to working on the greenhouse sink.

An hour later, I'm twisted around doing my best to repair this alone, when Edward ventures into the room.

He stands for a few minutes listening to me grunt, before he says, "Do you need help?"

My back is in knots, and I slide out, wondering why I've had my brains in my back pocket. "Yeah, are you free right now?"

"I'm always free." He pushes his long, blond bangs behind his ear studying me curiously.

Because he's only twelve and generally quiet, I tend to forget how smart he is.

"See this?" I show him the rack of handles and curved faucet. "Hold it straight while I tighten the screws."

He nods, and I crawl under the sink again, moving much quicker now that I have an extra pair of hands to hold things steady.

I've just tightened the screws, and I'm testing for leaks as he watches. "How do you know how to do this? Did you watch YouTube?"

"No." I exhale a laugh, as I move to my knees. "Don't get me wrong, you can learn a lot on YouTube."

"I learned to change the battery in Gran's key fob on YouTube."

"That's good." I stack my tools in the bag. "My dad was always handy, and he showed Jack and me a lot of his old tricks."

My thoughts drift briefly to the satisfaction on my dad's face when he'd complete a small job. I smile, feeling the same sense of accomplishment—this drain is repaired.

"I don't know much about my dad." Edward looks down, and I grab a towel to clean the rubber adhesive off my hands.

His dad isn't someone he needs to know, but it's not my place to make that call. "Rachel can talk to you about him."

"You're in love with her." He says it flatly, catching me off guard.

"What?"

"I saw you kissing her." He shrugs. "I'm almost thirteen. I notice things."

My chest tightens, and he's got me stumped again. "What have you noticed?"

"She watches you a lot." He frowns, looking up as if he's sorting through a catalog of facts in his brain, trying to find the best ones to make his case. "You watch her a lot, too, but she looks away fast when your eyes meet. Then her face turns all red, and she starts talking too fast. Or massaging Miss Gina too hard."

I swallow a chuckle. That happened.

"How would you feel about your sister having a boyfriend?"

Not that it would be me, of course. I'm simply curious about what he would say.

"Rachel has always taken care of me." He says it like he's repeating what someone told him, and from what Rachel has said, I expect it was his grandmother. "It's time for her to live her own life."

Walking over, I sit beside him on the deck. "How does that make you feel?"

A tuxedo kitten hops out, holding its little paws up like it'll attack us. Edward reaches over and scoops it up like a giant. *They Might Be Giants.*

He slides his hand down the kitten's head, and the tiny cat submits at once, lowering its ears and snuggling closer to his chest. "It feels like she wants her own family—not a little brother family."

I look down, studying my dirty hands. "Your sister loves you very much. She wants what's best for you all the time, because you'll always be her family."

He pets the black-and-white kitten some more. "You're in love with her."

Clearing my throat, I scrub a hand over my forehead. "I barely know her. It's too soon for anyone to be talking about love."

One side of his nose curls, and he looks up at me. "Mothers say they love their babies the moment they see them."

"That's a little different. Mothers have carried the baby inside their bodies for nine months, and it's their mother."

"My mother didn't feel that way about me." He says

it without emotion, and I am so not prepared for this conversation.

Not any part of it.

I don't like this tightness in my chest or the thought his mother never wanted him.

"I think your sister is smart and pretty. I like her, and I like you, too. I can't speak for mothers—that's something I'll never be, but if yours had gotten to know you, I bet she'd think you're a pretty great kid."

His brow furrows, and he continues stroking the small cat. "I'd like you to be with my sister. You're good."

"Well, thanks." Shaking my head, I walk over to collect my stuff. "Let's head back to the house."

It's after ten when I finish watching the game with Jack and walk back to our house. Logan was at the station providing commentary, and Edward and Rachel left hours ago. I hope they've had enough time to be asleep when I arrive.

My conversation with Edward has been humming in the back of my mind all evening. I think about the few times I've found myself really committed to something.

I think about my little sister Dylan who I loved in a brotherly way. I did my best to take care of her, to protect her, to make sure she had everything she needed.

I went to her dance recitals. I was there when she bought her first pair of pointe shoes. I sat in the chair while the lady helped her tie them around her ankles, and I remember the gleam in her eyes when she went up *en pointe* for the first time.

She was perfect. She was skilled and strong and dedicated, and when she danced, it was really beautiful. It was art.

And I broke it.

I remember my days as a kicker. I remember Dad working

with me in the evenings, holding the ball and giving me point-ers. He would beam with pride saying how I never missed. I hit the same spot every time, and the ball would shoot straight and far.

I remember being the first-round draft pick for the Admirals, their starting kicker. Any time the game was on the line, I'd walk out confidently and seal the win. Every time—until the last time.

The funny thing about being a football star. I thought I didn't care about it. I told myself I only did it because I didn't have anything better to do. It was what Jack did and Garrett did and Hendrix did… It was what Dad told me to do.

I told myself it wasn't part of me. I had other interests—reading, horses, working with my hands.

But when that day came, lying in that hospital bed and lis-tening to the doctor say I'd never play again, I realized I'd been lying. I'd been committed. I'd loved it.

It meant more to me than anything, and it was gone.

The kitchen is quiet as I fill an insulated cup with water before starting up the stairs. These thoughts are heavy on my shoulders, aching in my back. I have every intention of brush-ing my teeth and trying to sleep, when I see the light shining under her door.

Now I'm standing in the hall, staring at that shaft of light, and all I can think about is what a fucking liar I am.

Lifting my hand, I knock softly on the wooden barrier. A rustling sound comes from inside the room, and it takes a few seconds, long enough for me to wonder if she'll do it, before she opens the door a crack and looks up at me.

A thin, twisted towel is on top of her head, and her green eyes are not smiling. "What do you want?" she whispers.

"Can I talk to you for a second?" My voice is quiet as well. I don't want to wake Edward.

She moves away from the door, walking farther into the room, and I step inside, closing it behind me.

Turning to face me, she crosses her arms over the thin shirt, and I can tell she's not wearing a bra. Her cheeks are scrubbed pink, and she's in soft sweatpants. She looks cozy and ready for bed, and I want to pull her to me and run my nose along her cheek and kiss her again.

Clearing the heat from my throat, I fumble for a boner-killer. "I fixed the leak in the greenhouse. The hardware was all dry-rotted and crusted, so I just replaced everything."

She nods. "No more accidental drownings?"

Exhaling a laugh, I remember her dumping an entire bowl of water on my head. "In retrospect, that was pretty funny."

"It was an accident." Her tone is a touch defensive. "The bowl slipped out of my hand."

"I'm sorry."

It feels so good to finally say it, like a weight has lifted off my chest.

I should've said it two days ago.

"You didn't do it." She shakes her head, turning away from me. "I'm the klutz—"

"No, I'm sorry about what I said after... I was a jerk, and I hate that I screwed up the memory of your first kiss."

Her body stills. Her back is to me, and she reaches up to loosen the turban on her head. Long, blonde hair falls down her back in nearly dry waves, and I catch the soft scent of honeysuckle. I watch her fold the towel in her hands, slowly rolling it into a ball.

"It was only a kiss." Her voice is quiet.

"It was more than that." I'm less quiet. "And I'm sorry I ruined it for you."

She still doesn't face me. She continues rolling the thin turban until she finally turns around and slams it with a muted thump on her desk.

"Stop it." Fire simmers in her green eyes, and I take a step back.

"What?"

"I've had it with your emotional roller-coaster. First you act jealous because Sam's talking to me…"

"I wasn't jealous—"

"Then you kiss my face off in the library." She shakes her head, holding out her arm. "Hell, you practically dry-humped me against the women's fiction section, then you say it's nothing."

"I didn't—"

"Now you're here, telling me this." Her eyes are back on mine, and the heat in them burns my stomach. "I've watched you be nice to everyone—Kimmie, Dylan, Thomas, Edward… Why do you only want to hurt me?"

"I don't—"

"Is it because of my dad? Because I'm nothing like him if you cared to look. I can't change what he did, and I'm not going to be ashamed I survived. I escaped that house."

She's so beautiful. Her cheeks are flushed, and her chin is lifted. I love her fight. I love the energy flashing in her eyes. She's a force.

You're in love with her… I can't let that idea take hold.

"I have my reasons, Rachel."

"Give me one."

My stomach clenches, and I won't lie to her. At the same time, she's asking for answers I've never said out loud, not in all the times I've been asked.

"You just have to trust me."

"What does that mean?" She blinks rapidly. "You have reasons to be nice to everyone but me?"

I slide my hand over my aching neck. "That's not what I meant."

Confusion lines her expression, and I know what I'm saying doesn't make sense. It only makes sense when you've lived it. When you've seen me break everything I cared about again and again.

"Tell me what you mean." She steps closer to me.

"It's late, and I'm tired." I turn stiffly for the door. "I just wanted to say I'm sorry. I wish I'd handled it better."

She reaches out to put her hand on mine, to stop me. "I can help you with your pain. I'll set up the table in the morning, and you're going to let me."

"Rachel…" Her name on my tongue is like a soothing balm.

"Don't argue." She moves her hand to my wrist then higher, lightly touching the edge of the tattoo peeking from beneath my shirtsleeve. "It's okay to stop fighting for a little while."

Her touch feels so good, and it's late. It would be so easy to give in to her. Instead, I leave her room before I forget I'm not going to kiss her again.

Chapter 12

Rachel

"I CAN'T DRIVE LOGAN'S ROVER!" I'M STANDING IN THE KITCHEN cringing at the fob while Dylan hands me a travel mug of coffee and opens an overhead cabinet.

"I'd loan you my bike, but it's kind of a haul up to Miss Gina's, and the road's so narrow. It's not safe."

Chewing my lip, I study the silver mug. "But if something happens, I'm in a better position to fix a bike than a Range Rover."

"Nothing's going to happen." She snorts a laugh, pulling down the box of pop-tarts and shaking it. "We're almost out of these, and I know Eddie loves them. Want to walk with me to the restaurant and see what's cooking?"

"Yes!" I do a little hop, and I rush over to grab my bag and yoga mat.

Dylan is in her cutoffs and Cooters & Shooters shirt, but I'm ready for work in my light green scrubs. She slips her bare feet into a pair of flip-flops, and we take off down the hill.

It's a short walk, and she chats about wedding flowers and

the latest batch of bridal bouquets Clint sent for her to approve, but my mind keeps slipping back to Zane Bradford standing in my bedroom last night in all his tortured glory.

I was furious with him, even after he apologized. His apology actually made me madder, because he *can* be kind. I've seen it. Yet there he stood, broad shoulders rising with his breath, that sexy muscle tensing his jaw.

His eyes moved all over my face like he was memorizing everything, letting me say my piece. His gorgeous blue eyes were so tired, and he actually did seem sorry. But why won't he let me help him?

He keeps me at arm's distance, yet he keeps coming back. The intensity in his eyes could burn me to pieces, but he holds the reins so tightly.

He tries to stay aloof and detached, but he's lost so much. I know it has to affect him, but it's almost like he wants to feel the pain for some messed up reason. As nervous as I am about driving Logan's Rover, I need to get to Miss Gina's before he does. Before he has the chance to change his mind.

"What do you think?" Dylan turns her phone to show me a gorgeous bunch of long-stemmed, pure-white lilies tied with a simple, white bow.

"They're breathtaking!" I put my hand on my chest.

"That's what I said last night, and he sent me three more bouquet options this morning! What am I going to do, Rachel?" She wails, resting her head on my shoulder.

"Could it be because of Craig?" Her head pops up, and I explain. "He knows how important you are to each other. He's probably scared he's going to let you down somehow and Craig will be mad."

"Hmm…" She chews her lip, holding the screen door for me to enter the kitchen. "I didn't think about that. But what can I do? I've already told Craig he's driving me crazy."

"I think you just have to put up with it til June."

"No!" she cries, placing both hands on her face. "I can't take any more flower texts!"

"Hey, girls!" Allie skips past. "What are y'all talking about? Yoga? When are we doing it again?"

"Aren't you supposed to be at school?" Dylan straightens. "What are you doing here?"

"I had to take this guy to the doctor, so we're checking in late." Allie slides her phone into the pocket of her khaki pants. "I stopped by for some coffee and one of Thomas's beignets. Oh no!"

She dusts powdered sugar off her beige wrap-sweater. Her dark hair is tied back in a ponytail and little pieces escape around her cheeks. Austin stands beside her looking tired.

"Are you sick, babe?" Dylan reaches up on tiptoes to feel his forehead. "I swear you've grown another foot since school started."

"I'm fine," he grumbles like a typical sixteen-year-old boy. "I couldn't sleep last night."

"I've never heard of a teenage boy not sleeping." Allie crosses her arms, looking up at him worried.

"Sometimes if you grow too fast, it keeps you awake." I wrinkle my nose at his mom. "Growing pains are real, and he's right at the age for it. Try a heating pad."

He nods, walking over to the door. "Mom, I can't miss history class. Our exam is Friday."

"More like, who ever heard of a teenage boy not wanting to miss school?" Dylan mutters.

"Hey," Allie catches my hand. "I was talking to Zane last night, and he suggested I bring Eddie with me to school a few days a week to kind-of get him used to the place, help him find the bathrooms, you know. Is that okay?"

"Really?" My eyes blink wide.

"Yeah, Zane said he loves to read, and I can always use a library aide. He can hang out with me, maybe shelve some books. I'll talk to Ms. Laverne, but I'm sure she won't mind."

"Definitely! Text me what to do. I can bring him by your house, or—"

"Zane said he'd drop him off on the way to Gloria's."

Zane did this.

"Mom!" Austin pushes through the door, and she gives me a quick wave.

"Okay?"

I nod, a grateful smile splitting my cheeks. "Okay! And thank you!"

"Sure thing."

Allie takes off after her son, and when I turn back, Dylan has one hand on her hip and powdered sugar on her lips.

"Can you believe that brother of mine?" She shakes her head, polishing off her beignet. "He acts all stoic and aloof, then he does something so sweet like that."

"Don't forget the horses." My chest burns, and I feel bad for fussing at him the way I did last night in my bedroom. "I'd better get to Miss Gina's. I've got to take care of something."

"Here, take a beignet!" She quickly wraps one of the small yeast donuts in a napkin and shakes powdered sugar all over it.

"I'm not eating this in Logan's car. He'll kill me!"

"Eat it on the walk." She gives me a hug, and I'm out the door, stuffing the delicious, sugary pastry into my mouth.

Driving to Miss Gina's, all the things he's done filter through my head, from the equine therapy to the books to him driving Edward all around…

He broke through the door when he thought I'd fainted in the shower. My cheeks heat when I remember opening my eyes to him staring down at me, soaking wet and worried.

Last night in my bedroom he said it was more than just a kiss.

It certainly was more to me, because I was kissing him. Is it possible he felt the same? How would I ever know with the way he runs from me?

I park in the circle drive and quickly dash up the steps to

Miss Gina's house. I need to check on her and get her all set so I can prepare the massage table.

"Rachel, I'm so glad you're here." She's finishing her breakfast when I enter the dining room. "The nursery called, and they're delivering my Christmas tree today!"

"Oh." I hesitate, looking over my shoulder at the patio. "Did they tell you what time?"

"After lunch, and my niece Alexis called. She's driving down for a visit as well." The old lady holds up both hands. "When it rains it pours!"

"I'll take care of it." I walk over and catch her hands, smiling. "Don't worry about anything."

Her face relaxes, and her eyes narrow. "Something changed. You haven't smiled in three days—and you left early every afternoon."

Chewing my lip, I look around, thinking fast. I'm not about to tell her I'm planning to put my hands all over Zane Bradford and make him fall in love with me today. Not after her Nuru massage comments yesterday—good lord!

"Ah, Allie offered to take Edward with her to the library for the next few weeks—until he starts school in January. She said he could be her aide and get to know the other kids and figure out the campus."

"That's wonderful!" Miss Gina's eyes light, and I've successfully got her off the Zane trail. "Although I'll miss having Eddie Nashville around the house. He knows so much about everything. I felt like I was back in school just talking to him."

"Right…" My voice trails off. "The other kids don't always find it so charming."

"Now don't think yourself out of happiness. Knowledge is power!"

"I know, I know, but middle schoolers aren't known for appreciating things."

"Middle schoolers have self-esteem issues. The sooner he learns that, the better."

She has no idea how difficult that lesson is to learn, especially for twelve-year-old boys.

"I'll try."

"You know, middle schoolers didn't always think little blind girls were charming either." She holds out a hand, and I take it. "Very few, in fact. They didn't like me getting special attention from the teacher, and they especially didn't like how my eyes didn't look in the right direction. For a long time, I wore those heavy, dark glasses to cover them."

"Oh, no…" I lean down, hugging her bony shoulders. "I've never even considered that. You're always so sunny and upbeat. Why are kids such jerks?"

"I don't know, but some are real meanies. You tell my friend Eddie Nashville he's welcome here anytime he needs someone to talk to."

"I love you." I grin, giving her another squeeze. "And I've got some more news—one of us finally convinced Zane Bradford to let me work on his back. Would you mind if I did that for a few hours this morning?"

Her lips form an *O* and her brows rise. "How exciting! You know I worry about my handsome handyman. He carries a lot of weight on those broad shoulders, and now you get to put your hands all over them."

My eyes narrow, and I tilt my head. "You're doing it again."

"Doing what?"

"How does a blind person know Zane Bradford is handsome and has broad shoulders?"

"He does, doesn't he?" She grins mischievously, and I realize I walked right into her trap. "He sounds like he'd have nice muscles, too."

"What does someone with nice muscles sound like?" A slant is in my eyes.

"His voice is clear and strong, and he doesn't wheeze or sound like he gets tired easily. These are all very good signs—means he has great stamina." Her eyebrows waggle.

"Miss G!" My voice rises, and she puts a hand over her mouth as she laughs. "All that might be true, and he does seem to have a nice physique under his clothes—"

"You'll find out this morning."

"It still doesn't mean he's handsome. He could have great stamina and not be good-looking."

"He is, though. I bet he has a square jaw like Mr. Darcy."

"He does." I lean closer. "And dark hair and cool-blue eyes."

She exhales a little squeal. "Go set up the massage table, and take as long as you need! Don't worry about me."

Shaking my head, I make my way to the patio. "I do worry about you. Call me if you need anything."

"I won't need anything. I have a very important audiobook to finish. I'll have headphones on, and I won't hear a thing if you'd like to test out some of that Nuru—"

"Stop!" My voice goes louder. "I can't talk to you about that. It's too weird."

Turning, I head for the glass and wrought-iron patio door as her voice titters behind me.

Every time we get close, Zane Bradford shuts me down, but I'm starting to see a pattern to his behavior. He keeps reaching out, but he pulls back before he can touch the flame.

Only, I felt what he wanted in that kiss. I felt it on my stomach, and I felt it in the strength of his arms around me. He tried to downplay it. He tried to push me away, and he almost had me convinced.

He told me to trust him, but he's going to trust me, too. We've both carried burdens and survived loss. He holds his pain close like a secret, but my job is to relieve pain. He's been doing everything to help me, but now it's my turn to help him.

I know how to survive, and I'm ready to play.

Chapter 13

Zane

> Allie: Rachel thinks your idea is great, and so does Mrs. L. Drop Eddie off at school, and I'll meet you outside.

NODDING, I TAP BACK A QUICK *OKAY* AS EDWARD AND I WALK TO THE Jeep. He's brushing, grooming, saddling, and riding Shiloh all by himself now, and he looks like a real pro doing it.

"Gloria said Shiloh is eighteen," I tell him as we pull onto the highway headed north.

I put the doors on the Jeep again when I realized his hood was so tight over his ears because of the wind. I felt kind-of like an asshole when Gloria pointed it out to me. I've worked around kids like him long enough to know they're more sensitive to their surroundings.

It's different, quieter than I'm used to it being, but he's more relaxed in the passenger's seat.

"She also likes that you care so much about him."

"Did you ask her about inbreeding?"

"I mentioned it." Reaching out, I flick on the radio to Logan's station. At the moment, it's playing classic country music. "She doesn't know for sure, but she thinks he came from a reputable breeder."

He nods, glancing out the window at the passing trees. "He should have at least ten more years then."

"How would you feel about helping Allie at the library today?"

"At school?" His brow furrows, and he turns to me again.

"Yeah, all the kids have to return the books they've checked out before Christmas break starts. She could really use an extra pair of hands."

"I don't know the Dewey Decimal System."

This kid. "I bet she can show you what to do. I told her you're a fast learner."

He looks ahead a few seconds longer, then he nods. "I can help her."

"Great. I'll just run you by on the way. She'll bring you to the restaurant when y'all are done this evening."

His eyes shoot to mine. "What about Rachel?"

"She doesn't mind. Allie's a friend of ours."

Another few seconds of thinking, and he relents. "You'll make sure the kittens are okay?"

"Yep." I nod. "I'll make sure they have enough water and food."

"Let Miss Gina know where I am."

"I'll take care of everything." I turn into the school entrance, and Allie waves from where she's waiting near the office. "Have a fun day. Get to know the place."

His brow furrows as we approach, but he puts his hand on the door. I reach over and give his shoulder a brief pat. "You got this."

Allie greets him with a warm welcome, and my muscles tense as he gets out. I sit in the Jeep, watching as she leads him along the covered walkway and to the building. His hands are in his jeans pockets and his eyes are on his feet as he follows her, shoulders slumped.

Apprehension tightens my lungs as they go. It's unexpected, and the closest I can get to understanding why I feel this way is remembering how Jack said he felt when Kimmie started kindergarten, watching her walk away with Mrs. Patience.

Even though he knew she was safe in school with people we know well, even though he would be just a few blocks away at the high school, he said he wanted to run after her and be sure she knew to call him if she needed anything.

He laughed at himself, telling us about it later at the restaurant, and Allie was practically swooning all over herself. That asshole has a lot of nerve hassling me about Rachel when Allie is right here, clearly in love with him—and his daughter.

I finally start the Jeep again and head out to the highway.

Rachel hasn't left my thoughts since last night. Apologizing was the right thing to do, but so was closing that door.

She's a beautiful, optimistic person with a whole world of possibility in front of her. She doesn't need to be distracted by me. I'll help her as much as I can, but I'm not that selfish.

I am confused when I see Logan's Rover parked in the driveway. The house is empty when I enter, but it usually is. I'm sure I'll find them in the pool or doing yoga or gardening. I need to figure out what to do about that elevator.

Walking to the office, I glance out the window to see Rachel's massage table waiting. She keeps harping on giving me a massage, and I think I agreed to let her last night.

Standing here, in the light of day, I realize that was a big mistake. I don't have time, and I don't have… *time.*

I'm always in control.

When I turn back, Rachel is in front of me with a smile and a tall glass of bright red liquid. I nearly pitch my bag of tools.

"Shit, Rachel. Don't sneak up on me like that."

"I'm not sneaking!" She holds out the glass. "I thought you might like some cool hibiscus tea."

"No, thanks." I start for the stairs, but she hops in front of me.

"I just made it. It's full of antioxidants and vitamins, and it reduces inflammation."

"I prefer sweet tea."

"I can add some sugar."

My shoulders fall, and I give her *The Look*. "You're doing it again."

"Doing what?" She's in those green scrubs, and her hair is pulled up in a high ponytail.

She blinks her bright green eyes, and that sweet smile hits me right in the lower stomach. I exhale a growl and attempt to pass her. "Following me around. I asked you to stop."

"I'm not following you. I made the tea as a thank you for what you did for my brother."

"You don't have to keep thanking me."

"But I do. Allie told me it was your idea for him to be her library aide so he could get used to his new school."

Her eyes are round like she might cry and I glance away fast. I'm not about to see that.

Redirect. "I should've talked to you about it first, I'm sorry."

"Why are you apologizing? I just thanked you!" A light laugh bubbles from her throat. "It was the sweetest thing. And I've got the table warming up for your massage. Miss Gina said they're delivering the Christmas tree after lunch, so we have plenty of time."

"No." I try to pass her again, and again she blocks me.

"You promised."

Our eyes meet, and the energy it sparks strengthens my resolve. I cannot let her put her bare hands on my bare skin. "I didn't promise."

"Are you afraid?"

I shake my head with another frustrated growl. "I'm not afraid. I have to check the elevator. The last thing we need is Miss Gina getting trapped in it."

That damn thing is like a wrought-iron cage, and she doesn't always keep her phone with her.

"Miss Gina isn't using the elevator, because she knows you haven't fixed it." Rachel puts her hand in the crook of my arm. "She asked me to work on your back. She's worried about you."

"What?" This is news.

"She knows you're in pain. In case you haven't been paying attention, she listens to the sound of our voices. It's actually very sweet how she monitors our moods."

"It's creepy, and I'm still not sure she's totally blind."

"She is." Rachel's fingers tighten on my arm, and I realize I'm following her as we talk. "She's also very perceptive. She probably had to be growing up."

"I didn't say I would do this."

"Come on."

Exhaling a heavy sigh, I reluctantly follow her out to the platform I built. Two tall, overhead heating lamps keep the chill at bay, although I haven't noticed Rachel use them when she practices yoga.

Not that I watch her exercising, or stretching in those tight little outfits.

"I usually tell people to strip." She puckers her lips, glancing at my waist. "But you can leave your underwear on if that makes you more comfortable. I can work around it."

Fuck me. "Rachel…" I rub my forehead. "We're coworkers, and this feels like crossing a line."

Especially if I pop a boner while she's stroking my backside, because lord knows I'm not letting her touch my front.

"A bigger line than kissing?" Green eyes slant up at me, but she shakes her head, quickly adding. "We're not actually coworkers. We happen to work for the same person, but we don't work together." She adopts a professional tone. "Miss Gina asked me to work on your back, so it's more a situation where I'm your therapist."

"I didn't do well in therapy."

Her lips twist like she's fighting a smile, like she's not surprised. "*Physical* therapy. I wouldn't even know how to begin to get inside your head."

My stomach is tight, and I study the table. "I'm not getting out of this, am I?"

"Nope." She grins, putting her small hands on both my biceps.

Her gentle push makes me relent. "I'll give you a second to take off your clothes. Then lie on your stomach. I'll peek out to see when you're ready."

I'm never going to be ready, but I'll get this over with so she'll stop pestering me about it.

She walks away, in the direction of the house, although I'm not sure why. I'm not revealing any skin that wouldn't be covered by a bathing suit. I slide my arms out of my shirt and shove my jeans down.

My hands are on my hips as I survey the narrow table, then finally with a short exhale, I lie down on my stomach in only my black boxer briefs.

"Okay!" She appears almost at once, and I wonder if she was watching me the whole time. "I'll just put this sheet over your legs and some music on here."

Atmospheric ocean sounds begin, and I look around at where she's going.

"A bit of lavender aromatherapy for relaxation." Like satellites in space, I'm very aware of her body in relation to mine and the pull of her gravity. "Now we'll get started."

Her voice has turned low and soothing. She rubs her hands together and then leans forward, sliding them over my shoulders. They glide easily over my skin, and I notice she's using some kind of lightly scented oil. Her palms are warm, and she moves them from my shoulders to my neck in long, fluid strokes.

"Is the pressure good?" She leans closer as she asks.

"Yes."

"Let me know if it's too much."

It's not. The tension in my shoulders begins to ease at once. Pain I didn't know I was holding releases like a dam breaking, and an unexpected surge of relief aches in my body. I've never had a response like this to massage.

When I was on the team, we had massage therapists on staff to take care of us, but I wasn't one of the linemen. I wasn't a quarterback or a runner. I had one job, and it didn't require a lot of physical therapy.

Occasionally, I'd overuse a muscle if I didn't warm up properly, but I've never needed this type of work. Of course, I'd also never been hurt so dramatically. Now I understand why the guys were addicted. This is relief I didn't know existed.

"Even though your leg has healed, your body will naturally protect the injured side." Her voice is soothing. "You might not realize you're overworking the uninjured side, which leads to overuse injuries, and Miss Gina has you dragging those heavy trees all over the place…"

"I bend my knees." It's a gentle push-back.

"You still do a lot of heavy lifting all the time. You need regular treatments."

She moves to my lower back circling her fingers firmer and deeper into my muscles. She moves to my ass, but it's not seductive. I'm not popping a boner because she's finding pain I didn't know was there.

I can't hold back a groan as with every stroke, months if not years of stress leave my body.

My brow is tight as I turn my head. "That's it."

"I know." It's a gentle reply. "I can feel it."

So can I. The heat of healing filters into my muscles on every pulse. It's pretty incredible, and I hate to admit it. She's right. This is going to change things.

"How long have you been doing massage?"

"Since college." She gives my lower back a break, leaning closer and running her forearms up my back like rolling pins. "About five years."

Her soft voice is beside my ear. Her soft body is over mine, and this time a surge of heat does tighten my stomach. I think about what Miss Gina said yesterday, and I think of how good it would feel to have her naked, oiled-up body sliding against mine.

The heat in my stomach moves lower to my dick, and I think how easy it would be to roll over and pull her onto my chest, wrap her in my arms and devour her lips.

Clearing my throat I again redirect my thoughts. "Five years?"

I do the math. Rachel is Dylan's age, which puts her right at thirty. If she was only in college five years, that's a gap in her timeline.

"I could only go part time, so I had to spread out my classes. I did all my core requirements at the community college first while I worked. Then I spent the last five years really focusing on my specialty."

With my eyes closed, I think about watching her work. She's so focused, yet so beautiful. She has high cheekbones, and smooth skin. Her full lips purse when she's thinking, and today, she twisted her ponytail into a bun, I assume to keep it out of the way.

"This is a very solid platform. It's well-built and sturdy." She interrupts my musing. "You built it, didn't you?"

"Miss Gina asked me to."

I remember working on it before Rachel arrived, thinking the new nurse would be some aging hippie who didn't shave and ate wheatgrass and smelled like patchouli. Boy was I wrong.

"Have you always been interested in construction?"

Turning my head again, I rest the other cheek on the table. "I wouldn't say that, but I do like building things, fixing things."

"You do very good work." Her voice is quiet, and she moves her fingers along my biceps, fisting her hands and using her knuckles to knead the muscles.

She flattens her palms against my forearms, wrapping her

fingers around them and squeezing. It's like an embrace, and I blink down at her arms resting against mine.

"Thanks."

She's so close I can smell the soft honeysuckle scent of her hair mingling with the lavender aromatherapy.

"You didn't tell the others about my dad." Again, it's a quiet nudge.

"I didn't have to tell Jack."

"You didn't tell Dylan."

"No."

"Thank you."

My brow furrows, and I glance up at her. "For what?"

"Allowing us to be friends first. Letting her get to know me on my own terms."

"You said you didn't know about it."

"I didn't."

"Being your own person matters a lot to you."

She traces the tips of her fingers across the top of my shoulders in a way that feels different now, more affectionate and less therapeutic. "The past seemed to matter a lot to you."

"I talked to Jack, and he helped me see why it didn't need to." I anticipate her next question, so I answer it. "If it had mattered to our parents, they wouldn't have gone ahead with their plans. As it turns out, everything happened the way it was supposed to."

"Like, everything happens for a reason?" A smile is in her voice.

I turn this idea over in my mind. I think about how things would've been different if her father had never left. Would we be different if we'd grown up together? Would our relationship be different?

Would I be lying here on this table thinking about pulling her into my arms and kissing her?

All at once, I push into a sitting position, ready to shut this down.

"What are you doing?" Her eyes blink wider. "We're not done."

"Thanks for the massage, but I can't lie here all day when there's work to do." I start to stand, but I realize I'm only in my underwear.

Her eyes fix on mine, and her cheeks flush. Her chin dips, and she smiles. I can't tell what she's thinking, but she doesn't step back. Instead she steps between my legs, pumping a few drops of oil into her palms and rubbing them together.

"Now *you're* doing it again." Her voice is calm, and she puts her hands on my shoulders, circling her thumbs in the front of my chest.

My brow lowers, and I swallow roughly. What she's doing feels really fucking good, and I don't want her to stop. I like her here, between my legs, sliding her hands over my bare chest and down my arms, sliding her palms flat against mine and threading our fingers.

"What am I doing?" It's almost a groan.

"Running away."

"I'm not—"

"How do you feel?" She lifts her chin, and she must've moved closer.

Her face is so close to mine I could kiss her easily. I slide my gaze along the line of her hair, down the slope of her cheek, to her full lips.

"The truth?"

I haven't felt this good in a long-assed time. I've struggled to keep this above board, but I've tasted her sweet lips. I can't be held responsible for what I want to do sitting here in only my underwear with her breasts rising and falling beneath that thin cotton shirt.

"I always want the truth from you."

Lifting my hands, I put them on her upper arms, gripping her firmly. "I feel like you're playing with fire."

Her eyes flare, and her pink tongue slips out to lick her

bottom lip again. My eyes flicker down to the movement, to the tiniest nip of teeth against plump flesh.

"You could teach me." It's a husky whisper that sends another surge of longing straight to my cock.

"To play?" Fuck, the idea is irresistible.

"You taught me to kiss." Her eyes blink slowly, and she lifts her lips to my jaw. "I trust you."

She can trust me, and looking into her eyes I see something I want. Badly. If I'm brave enough to risk truly caring again. If I take a chance it could break, and I might never recover.

Chapter 14

Rachel

Zane Bradford sits in front of me in all his bare-chested glory. His blue eyes are locked on mine, and that muscle in his sexy square jaw moves as he fights the urge to run.

He grips my upper arms, and I'm practically a puddle from rubbing my hands all over his gorgeous body. He's a work of art from his broad shoulders to his narrow waist. He has the body of an athlete, with smooth skin and lines carving his biceps and triceps, pecs, abs, and those *transversus abdominis* muscles that form that luscious *V* leading into his boxer briefs. *Shivers.*

Now, I slide my hands up his muscled shoulders to the back of his neck, pulling him closer. I blink down to his full lips, remembering how incredible they feel pressed against mine. I've craved their touch since our very first kiss in the library.

It was so much more than a kiss.

He's breathing fast, and I can feel it in the barely restrained heat radiating off him. I'm not letting him go this time.

Sitting on the table, his face is only slightly higher than mine. I lift my chin so our lips are a breath apart.

"Kiss me." It's a mixture of request and supplication to my angry god.

I don't have to ask twice.

With a groan, his mouth covers mine. It's rough, yet careful, and I open my mouth at once to allow him full access. Our tongues curl and chase, and a whimper escapes from my chest on a breath.

My fingers curl in the back of his hair, and my back arches. I press my aching breasts to his firm body, and his hands grip the fabric at my lower back before sliding fully around me.

He lifts one hand to cup the side of my face, tilting my head so he can take control. It's control I willingly give him. My panties flood with heat, and I'm slippery and wet, wanting so much more.

I want everything from him. I want him to take me and teach me. I want him to make me scream and moan and beg for more.

He groans, and he moves his hand down to my waist, but when he reaches the hem of my shirt, he hesitates. I don't want him to hesitate.

Turning my face, my lips are against his cheek. "Touch me."

His fingers fumble with the edge of my shirt, and I decide to make it clear. Leaning back slightly, I grab the bottom and pull it over my head. He hisses, and his eyes narrow, gliding down my neck to my breasts wrapped in thin satin and lace.

He's seen me naked, but it's the first time I've seen him hungry. He's so gorgeous fighting his need in nothing but black boxers.

"Rachel…" he groans. "We can't do this."

Reaching behind me, I unfasten my bra, and it falls away. I'm breathing fast, and my nipples are taut. His eyes darken, and I take his hands, placing them on my body. My eyes close, and I exhale a whimper.

"Fuck," he groans, and his hands flex, lifting and squeezing them, rolling my nipples between his fingers in a way that I feel in my pussy.

"Yes…" I reach for his face and kiss him again.

He kisses me aggressively, and I hold his cheeks, meeting his lips with mine, tangling his tongue with mine. I'm burning alive, and I never want to stop. It feels so good.

His hands slide from my breasts around my back, and he pulls me flush against his bare chest. We groan at the feel of bare skin against skin, and I carefully slide my hand lower, to his stomach.

The muscles jump, and I keep going until I feel it. I lose my breath, and my head is light. He's wearing underwear, but I feel the hard, long cock between his legs. A little explosion goes off in my brain, and I want to hold it in my hand.

"It's so big," I gasp, and he cups my face.

"You're driving me crazy, Rachel."

"I've never done that before." Wonder is in my eyes. "At least, I don't know if I have…"

My fingers curl and slide, and he groans like I really am driving him wild. With another low groan, he grasps the top of my hand, stopping me.

"Do you know what you're doing?" He sounds feral, like an animal.

I'm sure it means something's wrong with me, because it thrills me to my toes. He wants me, and I want him. My stomach trembles, and I can't lie to him.

Shaking my head, I look down at the rod straining his shorts. My mouth waters.

"You'll have to show me," I whisper. "I've never done this before, but I want to learn."

Strong arms surround me, and he pulls me to his chest again with a low groan.

In this crushed position I can't play with his cock like I want to. I'm pinned against his bare body, which is amazing, but I want to move. I want to touch him, kiss him, do everything with him.

I've spent years studying anatomy, learning about the body, giving massages. It's the first time I've ever had the most perfect specimen of male right here wanting me. A man who is fierce and grumpy and caring and helpful… and dark and strong and sexy as fuck.

I squirm, and his arms relax. He places his hands on my upper arms again, moving me back. Then he looks down at my bare breasts again and groans.

"Fuck, you're so pretty." I think he's in real pain when he reaches for the sheet and wraps it over my shoulders. "Get dressed. We can't do this here."

"Zane…" I want to argue with him.

The grown woman inside me who has waited so long for this, who has dreamed of this moment, who spent years taking care of a sibling I love very much, but who is the biggest cock-blocker of all time… I don't want to stop.

"Trust me." His tone is final. "Your first time shouldn't be on a massage table on Miss Gina's patio."

"I don't know." I press my lips into a pout as I hold the sheet over my body. "I think it sounds sexy."

"Sometime maybe, but not your first time." He stands off the table, and he's still erect.

"What about that?" I nod down at him.

"I'm a grown man, Rachel. I can handle an erection."

"Won't you get blue balls or something?"

His brow quirks, and a sexy smile curls his full lips. "I thought you were a healthcare professional."

"I am." However, as I straighten my shoulders, I realize what I'm doing right now is as far from professional as I can get.

"Then you know blue balls are a teenage myth often used for nefarious purposes."

Biting my bottom lip to keep from smiling, I exhale a sigh. "I don't know. I might have blue balls right now."

He chuckles softly, walking to where his clothes are folded neatly on a chair. The muscles in his legs flex, and his ass is toned and firm. How is he so perfect?

"I've got to check on those kittens." He takes the bundle

and heads for the small bathroom behind the greenhouse without looking back. "Thank you, again."

I sigh watching him go, then I look down at my bra and shirt on the floor. "You're welcome."

He's gone, so he doesn't hear my pouty reply.

I fasten my bra and restore my clothing. Miss Gina might have given me permission, but he's right. I'm a professional, and while we're not exactly coworkers, we have a Christmas tree coming and relatives for which to prepare.

But it sounded like he left the door open for a first time *somewhere*, right? I'm certain he did.

"This way!" I hold up my hands as the workers guide the tree on giant hammocks through the doorway. "Careful. Don't hit the walls."

Miss Gina doesn't want the furniture rearranged in her house for obvious reasons, but we had to make a path for the tree to enter.

Zane and I worked together to move everything out of the way, and I put tape on the floor so we could be sure we put every piece back where it originally was. We've been the absolute picture of professionalism since our lapse earlier at the massage table, which isn't to say we haven't exchanged heated glances or covert smiles.

My stomach is a zippy tangle of knots, and I don't know what to think is going to happen next... or when it might happen.

"We're coming around the left side!" The delivery guy waves his hands.

I duck and reach for a tiny ceramic figurine I'm not even sure Miss Gina knows exists. It could've belonged to her parents, and I don't know. Someone might care for it.

Doing my best to protect her things, I fuss at the guys and

make sure they get the twelve-foot tree in front of the window like our dear employer wants.

I'm not sure what got into her head this year to want a tree, but she's sweet to all of us. She gets what she wants.

After what feels like an hour of jumping and ducking—which was probably only twenty minutes—the big, beautiful tree stands proud in the front window.

When we've got the delivery guys safely away, Zane helps me put every bit of furniture in its original position. Then I go and find her.

"Doesn't it smell amazing?" I hold her arm as we carefully enter the living-room-library.

I guess this entire wing is a library, considering how many shelves there are.

"My goodness. It's so fresh!" Her brows rise, and I can tell she's moving cautiously through the familiar space.

"Zane helped me put masking tape on the floor so we'd know where everything belonged after the men left. Not a thing is out of place."

Her wrinkled hand grips the back of a chair, and she nods, smiling. "You did an excellent job."

I glance over at Zane, who's standing back watching. His eyes soften when they meet mine, and I almost forget to breathe. He's never done that before.

Up to now, every time he looks at me, it's been angry or impatient or worse, disinterested. I carefully smile, and the side of his mouth rises. Heat rushes through my veins at the sight.

He smiled at me.

"Tomorrow we can string the lights." Miss Gina's head tilts. "I think that's something I can help you do, isn't it? Since Zane is off on Thursdays."

"Definitely! I'll get the ladder, and you can help me wrap them around the tree."

"I don't like you on a ladder when I'm not here." He uses the stern voice I know so well. "You could get hurt."

"Don't worry, we'll be very careful." I give him a little eye roll.

"I've seen you faint." His tone turns impatient.

"I told you, that never happens! I was in a hurry, and I should've just taken a beat, grabbed some candy—"

"What's this about? Why would you faint, Rachel?" Miss Gina grasps my hand. "Are you ill?"

"It's nothing serious." I slide my hand over the back of hers. "I have hypoglycemia, and if my blood sugar gets too low, I get light-headed. It's *so* not a big deal."

"It's a big deal if you're on a ladder." He is not letting this go, and I make a *stop it* face.

"I've got it under control."

His jaw tightens, and my favorite muscle moves with his annoyance. Good to know some things haven't changed. I've kind of grown to like his sexy grumpy face.

"In that case, I'll be sure we have plenty of sweets and cookies and soda…"

Miss Gina is listing all the sugary items she plans to have when the door opens with a knock. "Hello?"

The voice precedes a woman who would be my mother's age if she were alive. It's a woman I kind of recognize from when I was in high school. Very formal, tweed wool topcoat, St. John suit, and Hermès handbag.

"Claudette?" Miss Gina's brow furrows. "What in the world are you doing here? I thought Alexis was coming."

"Alexis is busy with her children. I made the drive myself." The woman removes her coat, straightening her suit. "My goodness, what is going on here? Who are these people?"

Her tone is sharp, and she sizes up me then Zane like we're robbers holding Miss Gina hostage.

"Mrs. Rosario, it's so good to see you again. I'm Rachel Wells?" The woman frowns at me like I'm a bug, and I continue. "I went to high school with your daughter Alexis in Birmingham."

Her upper lip curls, and her eyes narrow. "That must've been when Alexis had that unfortunate term in public school."

She turns to Miss Gina. "It was your brother's idea. He thought she was losing touch with the common man."

She waves a hand like that's such a ridiculous notion. I haven't seen Alexis in a while, but she seemed nice in school. I hope she hasn't turned into her mother.

"Jameson was such a good brother." Miss Gina smiles thoughtfully. "I miss his laugh."

"I hope your loneliness hasn't led to you making poor choices." She turns suspicious eyes on Zane and me.

That gets my defenses up. "I have a degree in sports medicine from Auburn, and I came here on your daughter's recommendation."

"Is that so?" She seems skeptical. "I'll have to ask if Alexis remembers you."

My jaw drops, and Zane straightens, crossing his arms. From the flinty look in his eye, I'm pretty sure he's as offended by this snobby woman as I am, and I appreciate him ready to spring into action.

"I'm sure Alexis will remember my dear Rachel." Miss Gina's calm voice cuts the tension. "She's an amazing companion, and this is Zane Bradford. He's one of the Newhope Bradfords—a very good family. I've known him most of his life."

Claudette lifts her chin, and her helmet of auburn hair doesn't budge. "And what does this fine young man do here?"

"I'm the new Stephen." His tone is flat, and I bite my bottom lip to keep from laughing.

Claudette Rosario had better not push him.

"I see." She crosses her arms, squaring her stance. "Well, young man, I've come to check on things. My sister-in-law is very kind-hearted and trusting, and I intend to make sure everything is in order and nothing *unusual* is occurring."

"What in the world are you implying, Claudette?" Miss Gina walks to her sister-in-law, and I hold her forearm, helping her reach her goal. I wouldn't say Miss Gina is angry, but an edge is in her voice. "I've been taking care of myself a long time."

"Perhaps we'd better speak about this in private, Gigi." The woman pats our employer's hand. "I'm planning to spend the night, so I'll just get my bag out of the Bentley while you finish up what you were doing."

She turns and stalks out the front door, and I look over at Zane. His expression is difficult to read. He seems concerned, but he doesn't seem angry, which annoys me. For a minute there I'd thought he was defending me.

I'm furious at this rude woman calling my high school "unfortunate," and I don't like her implying we're doing something *unusual* here. I'm about to say as much when our old friend beats me to it.

"Claudette has always been a bit over the top." Miss Gina reaches for my hand, and I pull hers into the crook of my arm. "I suppose you two had better head on out, and I'll take care of getting her settled and easing her mind. Have a lovely evening."

"Are you sure?" I slide my hand over hers. "We didn't get to do any of our exercises today."

"Oh no," she cries, putting a hand over her eyes. "That means I'm going to be extra sore on Saturday!"

"I'll take it easy on you."

Zane steps forward, placing his hand on her shoulder. "I'll see you Friday. Remember what I said about the fainting."

"Don't you worry," Miss Gina nods. "I promise I'll keep an eye on our favorite therapist. She won't faint on my watch."

He shakes his head, and I know he's thinking what I'm thinking. How is a blind lady going to keep her eye on me?

I follow him out the patio door to collect my things. He picks up his tool bag, and we walk down the brick path that leads to the wrought-iron gate at the side of the yard.

"She's got a lot of nerve," I grumble, crossing my arms as we follow the walk around to the circle driveway. "Acting like we're doing something wrong when we're legitimate employees. Acting like we'd take advantage of Miss Gina."

"I don't know." His tone is thoughtful, and my lips part in surprise. "Miss Gina's old. She's blind. She has a lot of money, and she lives in this big old house all by herself. I think it's nice her family checks on her. I was starting to think she was all alone in the world."

"She'll never be all alone in Newhope. Everyone loves her here."

"It's true, but her family doesn't know that." We walk up to where our vehicles are parked. "Logan let you drive his rig?"

"Jack needed his truck. I wasn't there when he left, so I don't know how much Dylan had to do with it."

He chuckles softly, and my cheeks heat. I'm starting to feel like Dylan had everything to do with me being here in Logan's very expensive vehicle.

"You'll ride with me from now on, like before." He says it like there's no room for debate.

"Yes, sir." I tease, and his eyes darken.

Opening his door, he puts his tools in the back seat before taking my arm and escorting me to the Rover. He waits as I fumble to unlock it and stow my things on the passenger's side. When I finally get it started, he steps back and closes the door.

I immediately roll down the window, but he only pats the top of the door. "See you back at the house."

Gazing into the side mirror, I watch his attractive form saunter to his vehicle and climb inside. It's not until I see the engine start that I put it in drive and head out to the street.

Eddie has never been much for sharing his feelings, but I can tell by the light on his face being with Allie today boosted his confidence.

"I've pretty much mastered the Dewey Decimal System." He notes as we brush our teeth before bed. "Apparently a monkey learned it in a matter of hours."

"Is that true?" I squint at him, leaning forward to spit.

When I straighten, he does the same. "It's the most useful method for organizing small collections. Large, academic institutions are more likely to use the Library of Congress system."

"Interesting." I got nothing. "Did you meet any kids today?"

He shakes his head, walking across the hall to his bedroom. "I saw Austin, and Miss Dylan stopped by to say hi. She was dressed in ballet clothes."

"She teaches dance as a PE option." He doesn't respond, and my chest is tight. "Did you like being at school?"

"It was okay." He walks over to his bed and picks up the dog-eared copy of *The Outsiders*, his favorite book.

I chew my bottom lip, because it's his go-to when he's feeling stressed, kind of like my drag queen music. "You're reading *The Outsiders*?"

He turns the book and looks at the cover. "I was thinking about bleaching my hair."

Pressing my lips together, I nod slowly. "In that case, we might get some new shirts... if we're changing things up, I mean?"

"Maybe."

Inhaling slowly, I don't know if this is progress or not. It *feels* like progress, but I've learned to be cautious with my excitement where my brother is concerned. Three steps forward, two steps back.

"Well, don't stay up too late reading, okay?" He nods, and I lean down to touch my lips to his forehead. "Stay gold, Ponyboy."

He exhales a noise like a laugh, and I return to the hall, pulling his door shut. I think I'm making the right decisions for him now. He's an almost-teenage boy, and I have no fucking clue what can of worms puberty will open for us.

But I think I'm doing alright. I press my hand to my chest and swallow the air in my throat. We had a bump in the road, but we managed it. Now we're here in this place of community, and it feels so good. Hope is such a seductive emotion, and it expands so big in my chest, my ribs ache.

It's been a while since I needed a mantra, but the one on my mind at this moment goes, *Have gratitude now, while boldly waiting for what's to come.*

I wrap my arms around my waist and hug myself like I used to do in those days when I had no one else to give me a hug. *Gratitude.*

My eyes blink open, and I see the light under Zane's door. Tiptoeing over, I knock softly. His low voice calls for me to come in, and I open it, stepping inside and quickly shutting it behind me.

He's sitting on the bed in joggers and a tank, and I press my lips together at the sight. Damn those muscles, that sleeve of tattoos. Damn those broad shoulders and that light dusting of dark hair on his chest.

He sits straighter, when he sees me, putting the book aside. "Everything okay?"

He actually sounds concerned, and I almost exhale a laugh-sob. His first impulse is to help me, always. As is Dylan's, as is Allie's, as is Jack's… All of them.

"Yeah, I um…" I look around for an excuse to be here. "I thought I heard a noise."

His brow relaxes, and his lips press into a smirk. "It was probably Logan and Dylan. They can be loud."

"I'm sure you're right." I nod, even though I made it up.

The house is quiet as a church.

His voice turns firm. "I really don't like you climbing ladders when I'm not around, especially to decorate a twelve-foot Christmas tree."

"I told you I'll be fine." I step closer to where he's sitting. "I've been managing my condition since I was a teenager." Looking around, I see the acupressure mat I left him. "Did you try this?"

"Yeah, what kind of sick joke is that?" His voice rises, and I huff the laugh I've been holding. "And you called me a psycho. It's like a torture test."

"It's supposed to be relaxing."

"Are you able to relax on that thing? It's like lying on a cactus."

Chewing my lip, I recognize the book he's holding. "You're still reading it?"

He turns the light-blue paperback over and growls. "Goddamn Archer. Nobody is this fucking perfect. It's like setting every man up to fail."

"You sure are grumpy tonight," I tease.

"Fair warning, I'm not going to notice whether you like folded chips or not." He says it on a snap, but it sets off a kaleidoscope of butterflies in my chest.

"Okay." I take a second to calm my internal squealing. "But you might notice something else?"

His jaw muscle moves, and his blue eyes look past me as if he's thinking. "You really like grape candy."

"Grape is definitely the best candy flavor. I don't know why more people don't recognize it."

"And strawberry Pop-Tarts."

"They're the only ones that don't taste artificial."

I've stepped closer to him. Close enough that I could slide my fingers through his silky, dark-brown hair if I wanted. I could lean down and kiss his lips.

Instead, he rises to stand, and shit. At his full height, he towers over me with me in my bare feet.

I lift my chin, arching my neck to look up at him. "You're so tall."

He puts his hand on the desk beside me, bending lower. "Better?"

"Mm-hm." This time I do reach up and thread my fingers in his hair.

I pull his face to mine and cover his lips with a kiss. He scoops his free arm around me, lifting me higher, closer, and our mouths open. Our tongues chase and curl, and that's all it takes for us to be off to the races.

Our hands are everywhere, touching, grasping. I want to climb him like a tree—I almost do. My fingers curl against the side of his face, and I exhale a noise of pleasure. So much pleasure.

He groans, and it's a deep vibration against my chest. It feels so good.

Lowering me, he stands higher, moving away. "Give me your phone."

Frowning, I take it from my pocket and hand it to him. He taps quickly, and in a second, I notice a buzz on the desk.

"Did you text yourself from my phone?" I arch an eyebrow as if I disapprove.

I don't disapprove. I'm thrilled.

"So I can check on you."

Pressing my lips into a smile, I meet his blue eyes. "I like this protective side."

Large hands grip my waist, and he pulls me to him roughly. "Get used to it."

Leaning down, he starts to kiss me, and I'm on my tiptoes meeting him halfway. Looping my arms around his neck, I press my body fully to his. His hands slide down to grip my ass, and I'm off my feet. Two steps and my back is pressed to the wall.

His waist is between my thighs, and with every rock of our hips, energy surges in my core. I'm hot and wet and needy.

This amazing man, this strong, grumpy man who helps me so much and kisses me like he can't get enough of me. I can't get enough of him.

He tastes like minty toothpaste, and he smells like sandalwood and soap. Moaning, I pull up his shirt, raking my fingernails over his bare skin. His fingers thread in my hair, and he pulls my head back as he devours my neck, teeth scraping my skin.

One large hand finds the hem of my shirt, lifting it to cup my bare breasts, squeezing and kneading.

"Fuck, I love your tits." Leaning down, he covers one with his mouth, and a moan escapes me on a hot breath.

Reaching up, he puts a hand over my mouth before moving to the other side, kissing, sucking, biting. It's all so much, my head spins.

His cock is hard against my stomach, and I rock my pelvis, increasing the friction and heat between our most sensitive parts. Flexing my thighs, I ride him, rising higher on every wave of pleasure.

I've got to be quiet. I'm going to wake Edward, but my mind has tunneled. I want him inside me.

"Dammit." He moves his hand from my breast to my ass, lowering me to my feet and pushing off the wall to get away. "Go to bed, Rachel."

We're both panting, and my brow furrows.

I blink my eyes open to look at him. "What?"

Please say I misunderstood him.

He grips my arm, moving me to the side so he can open the door. "You have to go to bed. Now."

His tone is firm, but I'm dying. "But... But you're... You can't!"

At this point, he's practically lifting me off my feet by my upper arms and placing me in the hallway. "Goodnight." It's a rough growl.

"Goodnight...?" I want to cry, beg, demand. *No!*

He's standing in front of me breathing like the Hulk, and I shake my head, doing my best to use my words after that kiss, that grinding session.

"But what about you?" I nod at the erection straining his pants, my core tingling. "You can't keep doing this. It's not healthy."

"I'm not going to fuck you in my bedroom."

"Ever?"

I reach for him, but he catches my hand, moving it again to my side. "Not tonight."

"Even if I say please?" I force a little smile, blinking up at him.

Another low groan. His fingers close around my hand, and he pulls it to his lips for a brief kiss. "We'd wake the whole house."

"We might not." I want to argue I can be good. I can scream into a pillow.

His eyes travel darkly over my body, lingering on my breasts, my tingling, tight nipples. "When I fuck you, I want to hear your loud moans, your screams. I don't want to be restrained by anything."

Oh.

My knees have officially melted.

"I want that, too."

One last, long glance, and he steps forward, threading his fingers in the side of my hair and pulling my bottom lip with his thumb. "You said you trust me." He leans down to kiss me again, briefly. "Sleep now."

Releasing me, he closes the door, but my entire body is vibrating. Energy zips in my core, and I know for a fact I won't be sleeping tonight.

Chapter 15

Zane

THE SKY IS GRAY, AND THE METALLIC TASTE OF RAIN TOUCHES MY tongue as I drive to the station. The curve of Rachel's breasts is on my mind, the scent of her honeysuckle hair, the feel of her hot pussy grinding against my cock.

All night I tossed and turned, fighting the urge to go to her, break through her door and claim her. It was torture knowing she was right across the hall from me, wanting me as much as I wanted her.

My fingertips hummed with the memory of her soft flesh. My lips pulsed from dragging them all over her sweet skin. The noises, the little whimpers and moans she made when I kissed her almost ripped my control to shreds.

Almost.

I fisted my hard cock, pumping it as I dreamed of her naked body. Her soft, full tits, her round ass. Rocking my hips, I closed my eyes and surrounded myself in the memory of her, thinking of all the things I want to do with her.

It would've been so easy to leave my room and go to her.

She's two steps away every night.

What the fuck held me back?

I care about Rachel Wells—but I don't only care about her. I care about the things she cares about. I care about the things that could cause her pain. I care about her brother, but most of all, I care about the memories she'll have of her first time.

She has plans. She told me she's fought and worked for a better life. I want her time here to be something she remembers with a smile, not something she pushes away with regret.

Sure, it would be easy to get it over with, break the seal, but I want more. From kicking in the bathroom door to make sure she was safe, to sitting on that massage table as she bared her body to me…

Her heated eyes fixed on mine, her parted lips begging for me. My mouth on her breasts, sucking and biting. Orgasm surged through my belly, and I rolled into the pillow, groaning as I finished in the washcloth.

Now, driving to the station, I try to figure out how I'm going to make it happen. I think about stretching her for the first time, feeling her heat and her desire.

She said I taught her to kiss, and I guess that's partly true. She took it to the next level in a way I couldn't teach. It has my mind drifting ahead to how she'll respond to sex.

When Rachel Wells comes on my cock for the first time, it's going to be amazing—for both of us. She's so eager now, and fuck me, she's not the only one. I shift in my seat at the thought, anticipation burning in my stomach.

Garrett: Did you get a do-over or are you still the worst kisser ever?

Logan: Something happened. They're carpooling again.

Jack: I heard massage was involved.

Zane: How the fuck did you hear that?

Jack: Dylan.

Hendrix: Massage? Did you pop
a boner?

Garrett: Did you bone her?

Zane: Bye.

Garrett: I can still draw you a diagram if
you need it.

"What's tonight's Dare Dish?" Oliver Duck sits behind the control board with a headset on watching Logan with what can only be described as disappointment.

My future brother-in-law doesn't seem to notice at all. "Ah, she's making something called Fatalii?"

"Hmph." Oliver flips switches and adjusts the lighting. "Fatalii is pretty tame. It's several steps below the ghost pepper on the Scoville scale."

"Still too hot for me." Logan grins, glancing to where I'm putting my notifications on mute.

I don't need my younger brother diagramming anything. I know very well what I'm doing with Rachel. The only part that's puzzling me is where.

If I'm going to make her first time unforgettable, we're going to need time. We're going to need privacy, and at this point, we don't have either of those things.

As much as I like her brother, he's not very conducive to my plans. Glancing over at Logan, I wonder if I could take him up on that offer to go for a long drive. Taking Jack up on his offer to keep him overnight would be better.

"She's made hot peppers her life's work." My eyes and attention cut back to the teenager currently lecturing us on my little sister's pepper obsession. "She's elevated it to an art form."

Poor Oliver. He's had a massive crush on my little sister for a while now. Too bad he's only sixteen and she's very, *very* taken.

"And you don't even like them." His voice drips with disdain, and all Logan does is laugh.

"It's true." Logan shakes his head, totally oblivious. "But I'll tell you what, Ollie, if it hadn't been for those dang ghost peppers, I'm not sure how I'd have climbed off my high horse and fallen at her feet the way I did."

I swallow a laugh. It's true. Logan's a good guy. I hadn't pictured him being with Dylan when he showed up here with Garrett two summers ago, but now I can't picture it any other way.

"It's Oliver. Not Ollie." The boy gripes.

I grin, taking my seat and pulling on my headphones. "Are you ready to start the show?"

He gives us a point, and we begin.

"Zane Bradford." Logan introduces me. "How's it hanging, my man? What did you think of that Hail Mary save by Simmons against the Buccaneers?"

We launch into our weekly play by play of all the major games of the past week. Logan takes it from the spectator's side, discussing the big hits and the big misses. I take it from more of a coaching side, discussing how teams might take what they've learned into the next weeks' games.

It's a good mix, and our audience is growing fast. We do call-ins, and the phone lines almost can't handle the flood. Logan's dad even made a comment last week on a zoom call that he saw a new celebrity duo in the making.

I've learned from all my years in the business, the best thing to do when people start talking about how awesome you are is to keep your head down and keep working. As soon as you think you've made it, you break.

"How about that new duo of Bradford and Berke for the Pirates?" Logan asks about his old team, Garrett, and his former rival taking his place.

"Ricky Berke is working hard to beat the records you set last year, but I don't see him doing it—at least not yet. He doesn't have your raw talent, and he's too young to have your instincts."

I'm speaking honestly. Blowing smoke up Logan's ass

wouldn't win us any points with the fans. It's true, Logan was possibly the greatest wide receiver of our generation.

"Yeah, but he's got my drive." Logan is impressively generous. "He'll get there. Just give him time."

"Take the compliment." I deadpan, and he laughs, rocking back in his chair.

Did I mention instincts? Logan's got them in spades. We make good sound, but with his looks and charisma, this is good-assed video.

Two hours pass before Logan starts to wrap it. The only drawback is having to sit in this chair so long. My back is tired, and I need to walk around.

Rachel gave me a great massage, and I'm not in anywhere near the pain I was before. Still, a follow-up session would be nice. It leads my mind elsewhere, to something soft and pretty with pixie eyes and an optimistic smile.

> Zane: How did it go today with the tree?

> Rachel: It's really beautiful. You should see it.

A grin relaxes my face, and I can't remember the last time reading a woman's words warmed me from my chest to my stomach.

> Zane: I'll see it tomorrow. What's the word on Claws?

> Rachel: If you're referring to Claudette... good one! She is very claws-out all the time.

> Zane: Is she finding anything unusual?

> Rachel: Not yet, although MG convinced her to attend dare night, so...

> Zane: All bets are off.

I hesitate, studying the screen before I send my next text.

Zane: I'm glad you're okay, no falls.

Rachel: I'll fall for you.

Zane: I'll catch you.

Rachel: It might have already happened.

I exhale a laugh, sliding the device into my pocket again. Looking up, my eyes land on Logan's watching me, and I shift my stance, lowering my brow and doing my best to restore my usual, stoic expression.

Clearing my throat, I act casual. "Just checking my messages."

He chuckles. "The offer still stands. Dylan and I'll be glad to babysit whenever you need it."

I pick up my keys and slide them into the pocket of my denim jacket. "I'll keep that in mind."

Allie dropped Edward by the house after school, and he's really changing. I can see it in his posture, his expression. He's relaxing. He smiles more and quicker. He's making a life here, and it gives me hope.

Rachel texted that she would catch a ride back with Claws and Miss Gina to save me the trip. I almost replied, saying I didn't mind, I'd pick her up, but I didn't. Anticipation is good. Hell, I can't think of anything worse than smothering in a relationship.

Relationship? I slide my hand behind my neck.

Dylan is running around tossing mango cubes and yellow peppers into two large, industrial-sized blenders. She finally broke down and bought a second one as the dare crowd has grown.

"So we're just going to give them citrus salsa, nothing else?" Craig's brow furrows. "That's different."

"It's not really something you eat on a chip," she explains. "It's more something you'd eat with shrimp or chicken… or a hardy vegetable if you don't eat meat."

Dylan's long hair is twisted in a bun, and Logan sits on a stool by Thomas, watching her with an adoring smile from a safe distance. Every now and then she dances over to kiss his lips. He tries to grab her, but she shakes her head.

"Not til I've washed up," she warns. "You know what can happen."

The way he responds to those words makes me believe he knows very well what can happen if pepper oil gets where it shouldn't—we all do.

Looking around, I wonder when Rachel's getting here.

"Two more orders of the special grilled shrimp and one chicken tender special." Salina Duck breezes into the kitchen in her shorts and logo shirt carrying a tray. She stops short when she sees me. "Hi, Zane."

She smiles, approaching me in that flirty manner again.

"Hey, Salina. You doing okay?" I shift, looking over at Edward and deciding it's time for his pool lesson.

"Oh, you know. The same." She shrugs, blinking her dark brown eyes up at me. "I'm doing a lot better now that Craig has stopped messing with the portion sizes."

She cuts her eyes at him briefly, and he immediately protests. "I was helping our customers be healthy. It was a good thing."

"It was messing with my tips." She jerks her chin, adding under her breath. "Egg."

Craig doesn't miss a beat. "Did you just call me *Egg*?"

Salina shrugs, poking out her lips and looking up at me with a smile. "Maybe."

"Is that supposed to be an insult? Like *Egghead*?"

I have no idea what's going on right now, but I'm fighting a laugh.

"Kids used to call me *Egghead* at my old school." Edward

walks up holding Smokey under his chin, a serious expression on his face.

"That's because you're a genius, Eddie" Salina turns fiercely protective on a dime. "Don't ever let those stupid kids make you feel bad for being smart. Okay?"

Edward nods, startled. "Okay."

"Promise me."

"I promise."

"You have a gift." Her voice softens, and she lightly taps her finger on his shoulder.

"Oh, so for him it's a gift, but for me, it's an insult?" Craig waves a hand at her.

"I don't know, *Egg*." Salina picks up the tray of food, turning her body, but never breaking eye-contact with Craig. "Is it?"

His eyes narrow in confused defiance as she disappears through the double doors. "She's one of our best servers, and she just gets weirder."

"She's hilarious!" Allie's loud voice cuts through the noise in the kitchen. "She's totally messing with you, Cray."

Austin follows a few paces behind her. I recognize that saunter from being a teenage boy myself.

"Allie! I'm so glad you're here." Dylan calls from where she's pouring bright orange salsa into a large bowl.

"Don't tell me. You need help serving." She grabs an apron off the rack and wraps it around her waist.

A bowl crashes in the sink, and Edward flinches, still petting the small cat.

I touch his arm. "Let's hit the pool tables. Get away from all this noise."

He nods, and Kimmie is right at our waists, not missing a thing. "I want to learn to play pool! Will you teach me, too, Uncle Zee?"

"I'll teach you, but tonight, I need you to watch." Her shoulders drop, but I lift my chin at Austin. "Come with us. You can help me teach Eddie."

"Sure." He continues past his mom to where we're standing by the double doors leading to the dining room.

"Get me, Aussie!" Kimmie hops up and down, holding her hands over her head.

Austin bends down so she can hop onto his back, and she cheers, swinging her stuffed red turtle over her head.

"Have you seen my cooter, Aussie?" She leans forward, holding his shoulders.

"No." Austin's tone is flat, and he cuts his eyes at Allie.

She and Dylan stand in front of the table with their lips bit between their teeth and their eyes glassy from holding back laughter.

"Look at my cooter!" Kimmie says it louder, waving the stuffed animal at his face.

Allie shrieks, and Dylan's knees bend as she laughs.

Austin exhales a frustrated growl. "Make her stop."

I step over to take my niece off his back. "Come on, troublemaker."

My niece squeals, and Edward walks over to take her hand. "Pool is a serious game, Kim. If you're going to play with us, you have to take it seriously. No goofing off and no talking about cooters. Or you'll have to stay here."

He gives her hand a little shake, and she nods, looking up at him with round eyes. "Okay, Ed."

Edward leads her through the double doors into the dining area, and I glance back at the ladies. Dylan's eyes are wide.

"This should be interesting." Allie has managed to recover enough to hold back her laughter.

Austin waits impatiently beside me, until I hold the door for him, following Edward and his little soldier to the pool area.

The regular Dare night crowd grows as the restaurant quickly fills with customers. When Dylan is ready, the wait staff will march out with whatever new pepper recipe she concocted followed by all the pomp and flare. Allie or Craig will call out the heat warning, then the lights will change and loud music will erupt. The girls will hop on the bar and start dancing *Coyote-Ugly* style, and the whole place will turn into a heat-themed disco.

I'm not sure when the dance-party exploded, but I've learned to go with it. Edward, however, is more sensitive to light shows and loud noises. Being away from the chaos, out on the side patio where the pool tables are, provides a buffer from the noise. At the same time, the screen walls will let me see when Rachel finally arrives.

"Inexperienced players do better with a medium to soft tip." Edward takes one of the shorter pool sticks off the special, children's rack and hands it to Kimmie. "Have you ever played pool before?"

"Daddy taught me how to hold the stick, and he picked me up so I could hit the ball." Kimmie holds the pool cue looking up at him.

She's a little hurricane, but she is very serious about hanging with the big boys and learning pool. It's helpful that someone other than Jack can be firm with her.

"That sounds like the most ineffective way to put a ball in a pocket," he responds.

"It worked!" she argues.

"Let's get started." I nod to the triangle of fifteen balls Austin has racked.

Edward's brow furrows, and he glances down at his stance before surveying the table again. "Feet should be a little wider than shoulder-width apart and at a forty-five degree angle."

He recites the instructions as if reading a manual. Austin and I exchange a glance, and I think we're both curious to see if he's going to be a pool-playing prodigy on his first attempt.

I wouldn't be surprised.

The more he reads about horses, the better he's gotten at the ranch. I half expect him to have Shiloh bowing and doing tricks before it's all over.

"Focus on the spot beyond the object ball." He leans down,

wrapping his index finger over the pool cue and sliding it back and forth a few times. "Shoot straight and with force."

He pulls back and hits the arrangement of balls, sending them flying to the edges of the table. Most of them bounce around, but a solid red and a stripe green each land in a pocket.

"Not bad." I step back to the screened wall, where I have a pretty good view of the dining room. "Pick your pattern."

"Pick the stripey ones, Eddie!" Kimmie Joy bounces on her toes. "Snappy likes the stripey ones best."

"Stripes it is." Edward leans down, sliding his pool cue with a little more confidence this time.

He hits the striped ball, but it doesn't quite make it into the pocket. His brow furrows, and it's like I can see his brain working as Austin steps up to take his turn.

"Go, Aussie!" Kimmie jumps up and down pumping her fists.

Austin has been playing pool here for a few years, and we watch as he expertly guides almost all his remaining solids into the various pockets around the table before faltering on the number six.

"Good work, Austin." I clap his shoulder as he passes me.

Eddie studied his movements the entire time, from the position of his fingers, to his aim, to the variable use of force he used to strike the cue ball.

This time when he gets up to play, he sinks two more balls before missing the next.

"I thought I saw two of my favorite guys out here." I recognize Gloria's voice as she enters the side patio. She's dressed in her usual shorteralls over a flannel shirt and boots. "Who are you hiding from?"

I glance to the dining room where the girls are on the bar dancing to the Buster Poindexter song "Hot Hot Hot," which is kind of fitting for a Caribbean hot sauce. A group of customers has formed a train and are snaking through the hall.

"Not hiding." I tilt my head at my young friend. "It's a little less chaotic here."

She holds up her hands. "Ah, right. I get it." Stepping closer to the table, she watches a few moments as Austin almost sends the eight-ball into the corner pocket.

"So close!" she hisses.

Kimmie jumps up and down. "Your chance to steal it, Eddie!"

Edward's lips are in a line, and he steps up, focused on the balls. Austin, by contrast, is watching the girls on the bar through the screen. He's way less worried about winning than he is wrapping this up and getting out where the action is.

I can't say I blame him. I'd have been more interested in pretty girls dancing on a bar at sixteen than playing pool, too.

My eyes drift to the hall, and when they land on hers, it's a lightning strike. All the feelings swirling in my chest through the night and into the morning surge forward on a tidal wave.

Rachel stands beside a booth where a smiling Miss Gina and an obviously confused Claws sit. Her soft hair sways as she bends her knees, bouncing along to the music and swinging her arms. She's wearing a short, flowered dress with a low-cut front that shows off her luscious breasts.

My stomach tightens with every bounce, and I need to get it together before I have a semi in my jeans. Cheering breaks out behind me, and just before I turn, Rachel's eyes meet mine. She smiles shyly, and a flush of pink rises in her neck.

It's the sexiest thing I've seen all day, and I have to adjust myself covertly before turning around again.

"You did it!" Kimmie yells. "Eddie won!"

"I hope that wasn't beginner's luck, because I fully expect you to win our tournament." Gloria lightly places her hand on his shoulder.

"Beginner's luck is only a supposed phenomenon. It has no basis in fact."

"In that case, you'd better sign up first thing tomorrow morning." Gloria nods, unfazed by his monotone.

"Good game, bro." Austin slaps him on the shoulder as he passes, depositing his pool cue on the rack and heading into the party. "I'll get you next time."

"Will you teach me to play now, Eddie?" Kimmie looks up at him expectantly.

He studies her. "I'll try, but the chances of you becoming proficient at your age are slim."

"Okay!" I huff a laugh, knowing she didn't understand a word of that. "You two have fun. I'm going to speak to Miss Gina."

"Miss Gina's here?" Edward puts his cue on the rack as well. "I haven't seen her all week. Let's have our first lesson tomorrow, Kim."

Kimmie's little lips pout, but I lift her onto my hip. "You know who loves red-bellied cooters?" Her blue eyes cut to mine, a hint of mischief in them. "Miss Gina. Run show her Snappy."

I release her, watching as she runs across the room to where the ladies sit. She's followed closely by Edward, but I hang back a second, sipping my beer by the small bar.

Rachel's eyes find mine again, and she blinks a few times before turning away again. I wonder if I'm the only person who hears a different sort of music playing, when Sam Allen walks up to her table, and the record scratches.

Chapter 16

Rachel

"The restaurant is called Cooters & Shooters?" The way Claudette says it, you'd think it was called Tits & Pussies. "I thought this was supposed to be a family place."

"It's one of my favorite restaurants." Miss Gina's voice is full of laughter, and she's practically bouncing in the passenger's side of her sister-in-law's Bentley.

As for me, I'm doing my best not to be overwhelmed by thick leather seats, glossy wood grain accents, and the general overall richness of the finest car I've ever seen.

A Bentley.

To say this day has been interesting would be the understatement of the year.

I almost never got to sleep last night after Zane's goodnight kiss. I went back to my room and gave my vibrator a workout for a good forty-five minutes, biting my pillow and fantasizing I was coming on Zane's massive cock with every orgasm.

I could barely open my eyes when Dylan called to say she was ready to give me a ride to Miss Gina's. We had a Christmas tree to decorate, and I'm sure Claudette was waiting to see if I'd show up on time or be late.

If I'd be out of order or *unusual.*

The way she said it made me roll my eyes. *What a snob!*

Miss Gina more than made up for it—almost like she was well familiar with Claudette and not bothered by her in the least.

She met me at the door when I arrived, dressed and ready to decorate. "I've got the ladder in place, and I got some tinsel to go with the lights. The clerk said they're like silver rain."

"What are these?" I picked up a box of round, clear ornaments with snowflakes inside and strategically placed, red and green jewels.

"Braille ornaments!" Miss Gina cries, sliding her fingers over the dots. "This one says *Joy to the World.* Isn't it amazing? Claudette found them."

"Alexis found them," the woman corrects her. "She got them from some Internet store and asked me to bring them."

"Why didn't Alexis come with you?" Miss Gina frowns. "I haven't visited with her in ages."

"She has three small children, and as you can imagine, they have school parties just about every day of the week."

"I bet they're adorable." I do my best to join the conversation. "Alexis was always so pretty."

"Yes, well, they're a pretty handful." Claudette pushes at the side of her helmet-hair, but it doesn't move.

"We have the ladder set up by the tree, and I promised Zane I'd keep you safe." Miss Gina gives me a wink, reaching out to me. "We also have all of this on hand for emergencies." I take her hand, allowing her to lead me to a large table at the back of the room where an assortment of Christmas cookies, pastries, and fudge wait.

"You really didn't have to do all of this." I reach into my pocket and take out a grape Jolly Rancher. "I have these."

I press the candy into her palm, and she moves it around, lifting it to her nose to give it a sniff. "Oh, grape candy is the best."

"I knew there was a reason we were besties."

She holds my arm as we return to the tree, and we spend the morning wrapping lights, tossing tinsel and hanging braille ornaments.

"This one says *Peace on Earth*." Miss Gina glides her fingers over the colorful, plastic jewels on the front of the snowflake. "Isn't that thoughtful?"

"People have been saying that for years, Gigi." Claudette carries a tray holding a pot of coffee and cups into the room.

"I was talking about the braille on the Christmas ornaments," Miss Gina breaks into a laugh. "You thought I meant *Peace on Earth* was thoughtful? I hope I'd be able to come up with a better adjective for such a profound sentiment."

I nibble on a ginger snap as my eyes drift from one lady to the other trying to picture them at my age fussing and bickering. They seem to be friends. Or friendly. I'm still not sure what to make of Claudette.

"Now I need to buy Christmas gifts. Will you help me, Rachel?"

"Of course." I go with her to the computer, and she produces a list.

"Go do something else, Claude. You know you can't keep a secret."

"Well, I've never heard such a lie. I am excellent at keeping secrets."

"Like the time I bought Jameson a cloisonné pen, and you told him?"

"I thought that was for your mother. It was a very ornate pen for a man."

"The store clerk said it was unique."

"And he got a big fat commission on that sale. It was Mont Blanc."

"All the same." Miss Gina flicks her fingers. "Out!"

I cover my mouth with my hand, ducking as Claudette pulls her blazer closed in a huff and strides from the room.

"I'm sure she hated that." Miss Gina ducks, and I lean forward.

"She did."

We spend the rest of the day ordering and organizing and eating cookies and really getting into the holiday spirit. It's hard to believe Thanksgiving is a week away.

When it's time to go, Miss Gina decides Claudette should see Cooters & Shooters on a Thursday night, and that's how we ended up here.

Of course, I stopped by the house to change out of my workout clothes and into a pretty dress before returning.

Now I'm straining my eyes for him.

"What's that over there?" Claudette sounds like she's seen a snake. "Are those pool tables?"

"That's the shooters part," I explain.

"Turtles and pool. How very redneck."

Just then Allie gets on the mic to introduce the Dare dish. "Okay, Daredevils, can I have your attention, please? Tonight we have a delicious Fatalii-pepper and mango chutney that should complement the grilled protein selections you have, and by Fatalii, we mean *fatal*, folks. Approach this one with caution…"

She continues explaining the Scoville rating and what to do if you get too hot and start to panic. I know this part by heart— no water, no beer, milk, ice cream, and juice are at the front.

"I will say it's unique." Claudette studies the menu. "How is the quality of the food?"

"Dylan is an excellent cook!" Miss Gina replies before I can, and when the music starts, I step out of the booth to dance.

I'm really standing so I can have a better view. He knows we're here, and after last night, I'd like to think that means he'll be here as well. My stomach twists, and I'm a little sick at the thought he might not.

Bouncing on my toes, I swing my arms doing my best to get rid of the jitters. My dress is thigh-high and low-cut with puffy sleeves and a big flower print.

"They're dancing on the bar!" Claudette seems to be playing the role of Horrified Narrator for the evening.

"I know," Miss Gina cries happily. "I wish I could see them."

I'm still searching, when I hear faint shouts from the pool area. Ice-blue eyes capture mine when I look in that direction, and a soft *Oh!* slips from my throat.

I'm on fire—no Fatalii peppers needed. Heat rushes from my core through my belly into my chest up my neck behind my ears and onto my cheeks.

A shy smile lifts my lips, and I barely hear Miss Gina calling my name over the beating of my heart.

"Sorry, what?" I blink away, stepping closer to the booth.

"What would you like to order, dear?" Miss Gina shouts, and I notice Salina Duck curling her nose at me.

"Oh, hello, Rachel." Her tone is dismissive as usual. "Is it true you became a massage therapist because you couldn't make it as a real therapist?"

"What?" Claudette frowns, looking up at the girl.

"That's two different things," I reply, not in the mood for her jealousy.

Yes, I've seen her batting her eyes, and I know she's got a crush on Zane. She can take a hike.

"I heard it was because you weren't smart enough." Her lips curl into a frown. "Is that true? Or is it because you couldn't take the pressure of other peoples' problems along with your own?"

"I never wanted to be a therapist."

"And yet you are one anyway." She exhales a sigh. "Do you always do what you don't want to do?"

"I'm confused." Claudette looks from her to me.

"Get used to it, with ratchet Rachel around."

My eyes widen, and I'm about to clap back when she walks away without even taking my order. I'm still squinting after her when Gloria joins us.

"Miss G, it's good to see you. Rachel."

"Is that my nemesis Gloria Fruit?" Miss Gina holds out her

hand. "I've decided to forgive you for trying to steal my best handyman."

"Why is that?" Gloria grins, clasping Miss Gina's wrinkled hand in both of hers.

"I hear you're taking good care of my friend Eddie Nashville." Gloria's face tilts, and Miss G explains. "Rachel's younger brother. He's so smart. He already has his *nom de guerre* locked and loaded."

"Ah, Edward!" Gloria laughs. "He's a pool shark in the making all right."

"Fruit?" Claudette arches an eyebrow. "Bunny and Randolf's daughter?"

"Guilty!" Gloria rocks back on the heels of her boots, rubbing the back of her shaved neck.

"I haven't seen them in ages. Do they still have that gorgeous old Victorian home near the polo club?"

"Yes, ma'am, they do!"

"How lovely. Please tell them Claudette Rosario said hello."

"Are you…" Gloria motions between her and Miss Gina. "Sisters?"

"In law," Claudette notes.

I'm chewing my lip, pretending to listen to their conversation, but my eyes are on that side patio. Austin comes out, and the door almost closes… then he steps out.

I can barely breathe with how fast my heart is beating. He's there, just outside the door, but he's not moving this way.

Is he not going to come over here? Is he embarrassed to be seen with me in front of his family and friends? Will I survive that?

He glances this way again, holding a beer to his lips and meeting my eyes. My lips part, and I'm right on the edge when a friendly male voice startles me.

"Rachel, hey! We have to stop bumping into each other this way." Blinking rapidly, I turn to see Sam Allen smiling down at me.

His hands are in his pockets, and he's waiting.

Pressing my lips together, I force my brain to hear what he just said. "What way?"

"Dancing at the Dare night." Exhaling a laugh, he lifts his chin at the bar. "That Craig sure is a fan of Chappell Roan."

Frowning, I tune in to what's playing and recognize the song as "Apple."

"That's Charli xcx."

He shrugs, looking over his shoulder before turning back to me. "I don't pay much attention to music."

"Am I interrupting something?" Zane's low voice sends a wash of heat through my pussy.

He came. My eyes close briefly, and I turn. He's here, standing with one hand in his pocket, his dark hair shining in the disco lights. The muscle in his square jaw moves, and he's frowning as usual.

"Sam doesn't pay attention to music."

"Why not?" His frown deepens, and he glances at the guy.

"Ah…" Sam clears his throat. "I guess because there's so many bands to keep up with these days?"

"Would you like to dance?" Zane takes my hand, and you could knock me over with a feather.

"You dance?"

"I won't step on your toes."

"I'd love to dance with you." I take his hand, following him onto the floor where the driving dance beat fades.

As if he's watching us, Craig follows up with a gentler song.

Zane wraps his arm around my waist, pulling me close, and I rest my nose against the front of his shoulder. I don't know this song, but it's perfect.

Closing my eyes, I'm surrounded by the scent of trees and southern breezes and the ocean. Music floats in a dreamy harmony, and I'm falling, low blood sugar not required.

It's the least scary, the most secure, the happiest thing imaginable.

Warm lips press against my temple, and my eyes flutter open. Zane lifts his head, and I look into his striking, beautiful eyes.

"Sam Allen?" he teases. "Again?"

Exhaling a laugh, I rest my forehead against his chest. His arms are still around me, and I can't believe the comfort of this place. It's the best hug, so safe and warm.

"You came to me." I say the words softly, not expecting him to hear them.

His face lowers again, and he speaks in my ear. "I'll always come to you."

Heat pulses in my veins, and I don't want to leave his embrace. Lifting his head, he studies my eyes, and I think he feels the same way.

But the song ends, and another banger takes its place. It's one of my favorite drag queen songs "Good Life," and the floor fills with enthusiastic dancers. We're surrounded, but he doesn't release my hand.

He leads me in the direction of the smaller bar. We slip through the screen door to the now-dark, empty room where all the pool tables are located.

It's quieter here, secluded from the noise of the main hall, and I think about him being here when we arrived with all the chaos going on out there. Again, he did it for Edward.

My chest warms, and I stop at the first table, tracing my finger along the felt as he lowers the lights, so no one can see us through the screens. A beer sign is still lit, casting everything in an orange-red haze.

"What could we do on this table?" My voice is low, and I hope sultry.

"It wouldn't be comfortable." His is even.

"Not even like this?" I lean forward, arching my back so my butt lifts.

The dress I'm wearing slides higher up my thighs, and he exhales a low groan.

Stepping closer, he puts his hand on the exposed skin of my leg, and my core floods with heat. My eyes close, and I pant as his fingers move higher. My stomach twists, and I wait for him to discover…

"You're not wearing underwear." His fingers slide gently between my legs, and my lips part with a soft *Ahh…*

I'm on fire, and his calloused touch traces the line of my body, lightly entering the top of my pussy. I exhale another noise, not daring to move as he finds my clit. The heat of his body is beside me, and I'm frozen in place as if I'm being stroked by fire.

"Damn, you feel good." It's a low groan.

He takes his hand away, and my inner thighs are slick with my desire. "Come here."

Turning me, he backs me against the wall, stepping in front of me and lowering his face to mine. Our eyes meet, and as he draws closer, I open my mouth, slipping out my tongue to meet his before he pulls it into his mouth.

We're chasing each other's kisses, and once again, his hand is between my legs. This time, he goes straight to my core, stepping closer to circle his fingers lazily around my clit.

"Oh!" I gasp, gripping the front of his shirt.

He's making a tight circle with his hand, applying just the right amount of pressure to lift me onto my toes. I whimper, rotating my hips with his movements.

"You like that?" His voice is a husky groan beside my ear.

I'm nodding before I say the word. "Yes…"

His fingers move faster, circling my clit with focused, determined strokes. My knees bend, and I'm doing my best to kiss him while maintaining contact with his hand.

"Do what I say." His voice is firm, like a command, and I nod.

"Slide your top down." I comply at once, pulling the V-neck apart so my bare breasts spill out.

He hisses, leaning down to suck a hard nipple into his mouth at the same time he slides a finger all the way inside me. I gasp an *Oh!* and he moves it in a slow circle, still focusing the pressure of his thumb on my clit. I hold onto his shirt so I don't collapse. Then he adds another finger, spreading me apart gently.

I cry out, and his fingers thread in my hair, tilting my head back so I can see his eyes. He studies mine as if he's searching for something.

His brow furrows, but his tone is gentle. "You okay?"

Nodding, I reach for him. I have no words for this. I want his body close to mine. I want his lips on mine. I want all of him on all of me.

As if he understands, he wraps an arm around my back, pulling me closer. His fingers are between my legs, stroking my clit and pumping and stretching my insides. Our kisses are ravenous, hungry, driven by pent-up desire.

"Fuck, you're so wet," he groans. "You feel like fucking heaven."

"Don't stop," is all I can gasp.

His erection is against my leg, but I'm fucking his fingers. His delicious thumb has my clit vibrating, near orgasm. It's the focus of my mind until those two fingers inside me curl, and my entire lower half jerks with pleasure.

"Oh!" I cry, thrusting my hips forward.

He curls his fingers again, stroking something deep inside me, and I fly straight off a waterfall cliff. I grip his arm, shivering as my muscles spasm involuntarily. A loud, rippling noise, a cry-filled gasp escapes my lips.

I don't mean to be loud, and thankfully, the dining-hall dance party is raucous enough to cover us. He turns me, wrapping his arm around the front of my shoulders and holding my back to his chest. I can feel his erection, but all I care about is the intense orgasm radiating through my core.

His voice is at my ear. "Tweak your nipples."

Lifting my hands to my exposed breasts, I pinch and pull the hardened peaks. Another surge of electricity shoots through my insides, and my body tries to bow forward.

He holds me firmly against his chest, kissing the side of my neck, my hair, my ear as his two fingers glide in and out. I moan and whimper, stumbling as my knees weaken.

"That's it, baby, ride it out."

I have no choice. I'm having an orgasm I never knew existed. I'm on my toes bucking my hips forward against his hand, and I feel his cheek rise with a smile.

"You're so beautiful." Another kiss to the side of my neck. "It's going to feel so good when I'm inside you."

Oh, God, I believe him. Shivering, the orgasm begins to recede. I'm weak and trembling, and with every final, gentle stroke, another little gasp slips from my lips. Looking down, I see my breasts, nipples erect rising and falling.

He gives me another kiss, another circle of his thumb against my clit, and the pleasure is near pain.

My hand shoots down, and I hold his wrist. "Too much."

A low chuckle, and he moves his palm flat against my lower stomach. His arm releases my upper chest, sliding down to lift and cup my breasts.

"I love these." He kisses me again, sliding his thumbs over the stiff peaks.

My eyes are closed, and I'm glowing and sated. He turns me to face him again, wrapping strong arms around me and holding me securely against his chest. It's the only place I want to be after sharing that extreme experience.

"I've never come like that before."

"You're perfect."

Curling my fingers against his shirt, I exhale the words. "I want you."

His low voice is confident. "I know."

Chapter 17

Zane

"WE COULD TAKE A DETOUR. I'M SURE MISS GINA WOULDN'T MIND if we were a few minutes late." Rachel blinks coy eyes at me from the passenger's side of the Jeep.

When we emerged from the pool area last night at Cooters & Shooters, I was already strategizing how we might find a way to be alone for longer than fifteen minutes.

Her body is so beautiful, and she responds so quickly to my touch. I'm out of patience. I've reached the limit of my control, and as much as I want her to have a memorable first experience, I really want to fuck her.

It doesn't help my resolve that she overtly feels the same way.

Everyone was excited after the dinner dance party last night. Miss Gina and Claws hung around the kitchen "meeting the chef," and Gloria was in full sales-mode, signing everyone up for the pool tournament.

Eddie Nashville is the main attraction, and even if he stayed at a safe distance from the crowd, stroking Smokey the whole time, I think he was pleased.

It was the first time in a long time we all went to bed at the same time, and I fell asleep waiting for the house to get quiet. I had a mind to sneak across the hall for one more hit of Rachel's kisses.

All my carefully laid plans, my resolution that it's better for me to be alone seem to have flown out the window. I was actually considering going back to the house last night after Edward's pool lesson—until Sam Allen showed up.

The sight of her coming on my hand changed all my instincts to primal urges.

"We'd be more than a few minutes late." I glance over at her sitting there in her yoga pants and a hoodie unzipped just enough to give me a teasing glimpse of those perfect tits.

Her blonde hair is in two braids again, and she bites her full lip, doing a little shiver in her seat. I lift the back of her hand to my lips.

Damn this pretty girl sneaking past my walls. She really is a pixie, only now she's sexy as hell.

"Maybe Miss Gina will take a long nap." Her eyes widen as she threads her fingers in mine.

"That just leaves Claws."

A frown curls her upper lip, and she exhales a huff as we approach the large house. We're still holding hands, and I hate to let her go to shift the Jeep.

Once we're parked, I walk around to help her out, and I notice the Bentley has a suitcase in the back.

My brow furrows, and I glance up to see the front door is open. "Maybe we won't have to deal with Claws after all."

"Seriously?" The excitement in her voice forces another grin across my lips.

When was the last time I've smiled this much?

"Oh, you're here." Miss Gina's voice is disappointed. "I tried and tried to catch you before you made the drive."

"What's going on?" Rachel looks from the suitcase in the foyer to Miss Gina to Claws digging in her bag.

"We discussed it last night," the woman explains. "Gigi has agreed to come back with me to Birmingham for Thanksgiving."

"What?" Rachel's voice goes high.

"I know!" Miss Gina holds her hand, making a little frown. "I'm going to miss you all next week, but it has been a while since I've seen Alexis and her family."

I glance at the woman standing behind her. "As if spending the holiday with your real family is so outrageous. You'll be back Saturday."

"I won't miss the pool tournament, will I?"

"The tournament is a week from Sunday, so you should be fine." I step forward and take her suitcase. "I'll check on things while you're gone."

"Of course you will." Miss Gina pats my shoulder. "But do give yourself a holiday and spend time with your family."

She and Rachel follow me as I carry the bag to Claudette's car. She opens the trunk, and I put the suitcase inside.

"I left some cookies for you." Miss Gina gives Rachel a long hug, and just before she lets her go, she speaks in her ear. "Use my guest house as much as you want."

"Oh!" Rachel releases her, and the old woman gives her a wink.

Claudette is already in the vehicle with it running. Miss Gina turns one more time, waving in my direction. "Happy Thanksgiving."

"You too." Rachel steps back, standing in the driveway as they pull away.

She waves as if Miss Gina can see her, and I return to the house slowly, looking around the vast, empty space. The Christmas tree is lit, and it's covered in tinsel and clear, plastic ornaments with red and green beads on them.

Crossing my arms over my chest, I think about what this means.

The door closes softly behind me, and Rachel enters the room. "That was a surprise. I guess we have a week off."

Her voice is quiet, and I feel her presence at my back as an electric charge flows through the air. My chest is tight, and I slide a hand over the hunger in my stomach.

"I still have to fix that elevator." Taking a step away, I turn to face her.

"Okay." Her cheeks are flushed, and she's breathing faster.

Her lips part, and her green eyes are wide and wanting.

Exhaling a rough noise, my hands fist and loosen at my sides. That invisible force strengthens between us, pulling with intense power. It's physically painful to resist.

"I should work…" I try to say, but it's a weak protest.

She blinks once, nodding. "Of course."

I don't move. My jaw clenches, I'm moving as the words slip out on sandpaper. "Fuck it."

In only a few steps I'm on her, colliding with a crash of groans and whimpers. Her hands are in my hair. My hands are on her body, under her hoodie, sliding higher until my fingers find her sports bra.

She steps back, whipping the jacket over her head and removing the bra. I'm doing the same, unbuttoning my shirt as fast as I can, swearing at the tightness of the buttons.

Her hands join mine, helping me, and when it's halfway there, I rip it over my head.

We're together again, skin against skin, mouths united, and another deep groan rumbles from my chest. Our lips part, and our tongues collide, tasting and kissing, mint and water and grape candy.

I lift her off her feet, and her legs wrap around my waist. Miss Gina's guest house is right off the main house. Her pelvis rocks against my erection, and I carry her to the door leading out to the patio. Soft lips trail kisses along my neck, up to my ear, pulling the lobe between her teeth.

"I can't believe it," she gasps. "It's a Thanksgiving miracle."

A laugh vibrates in my chest, and I open the door to the small cottage. It's bright and cheery and cool, with a king-sized bed made up in white linens. Flowers are on the side table, and I place Rachel on her feet while I step into the bathroom for a towel.

When I return, her back is to me. She's standing in front of the dresser, where a plate of cookies sits, and she's holding a note.

"It says, *Enjoy*." Her lips press into a grin, and she glances over her shoulder. "That sly little lady—she planned the whole thing!"

"At least we have her permission." I cross the bedroom, ripping the blankets back and spreading the towel over the mattress. "I've been tested. I'm good, but I'm glad to use a condom—"

"It's okay. I have an implant."

She turns to face me, and when I see her in full, my breath stutters in my chest. My fingers curl, and my cock jumps.

"Damn, Rachel." Hunger thickens my voice. "You're beautiful."

Pink flares in her cheeks, and her bottom lip slips between her teeth. "Nothing you haven't seen before." It's a light tease, and she steps forward, reaching for the waist of my jeans. "My turn to see you. Finally."

I don't move as her slim fingers unfasten my belt, then the top button. She lightly grazes my stomach as she works, and my muscles tense. I'm a live wire, and the air crackles around us.

She lowers the zipper slowly, and as she slides her hands over my hips, pushing the heavy denim down, my cock bobs free, thick and ready.

"Oh, my God!" She wraps her fingers around it.

Her thumb slides over my tip, which is coated in precum. It feels so damn good. Then she smooths her hand down my shaft, and I exhale a groan.

She looks up at me again. "Can I?"

Her voice trails off, and her eyes are fixed on the movement of her hand, gliding up and down, thumb crossing the tip.

"You can do anything you want." I reach for her waist. "We have all day."

Holding my arms, she moves me to sit on the bed. Then she drops to her knees, guiding the tip of my cock to her full lips and parting them. I'm hypnotized watching her pull it into her mouth, keeping her green eyes round and fixed on mine.

My hips rock, and I groan, the muscle in my jaw tensing as I fight the orgasm surging through my pelvis. Reaching out, I thread my fingers in the side of her hair as her head bobs faster.

She leans forward, taking me to the back of her throat, and my ass flexes. "Fuck, Rachel." It's too good, and I've waited too long. "Come here." Reaching for her, I lift her to her feet again.

"Did I do it wrong?" Her eyes are watery, and her lips are glistening red and swollen.

She looks like a fucking wet dream.

"No, baby, you did it exactly right." I grasp the sides of her tight yoga pants, trying to get them off her. "I nearly shot down your throat."

"Let me." She bends down, pushing them off her body and taking her underwear with them.

When she straightens, she's fully naked, and I nearly fall to my knees. Dusty-pink nipples point high on her full breasts. Her stomach is flat, but her ass is round and squeezable. Her pussy is bare, and I reach for her hips, pulling her closer to my mouth.

"I'm going to do what I can to make this less painful." I kiss the place right above her pubic bone, and she sighs a whimper. "It still might hurt."

Her fingers are in my hair, and she curls them against my scalp. "I know." Her tone is ready.

Standing beside her, I lift her gently, placing her in the center of the bed. Her knee bends across her thigh, and she tilts her head to the side, green eyes traveling all over my body.

"My sexy, angry god." A smile curls her lips, and I drop to

one knee, wrapping my arms around her thighs and spreading her wide.

"This is mine." I cover her with my mouth, and her back arches off the bed.

She lets out a loud moan, and I circle my tongue over her clit, sucking and pulling the little bud gently with my lips. Her fingers dive into my hair again, and she squirms closer, pressing her body to my mouth.

I reach up to insert two fingers again, stretching gently, hoping it will help her. Her stomach ripples, and her moans turn to fluttering wails. Her legs stiffen beside me and shake, and I give her two more passes with my tongue before her knees bend, and she comes with a loud cry.

Wetness flows onto my hand, and I reach down to smooth it over the head of my aching cock. Moving higher in the bed, I'm so fucking hard, but I've got to take it slow.

My chest is tight. My whole fucking body is tense.

"Tell me if it's too much." I lean down, but she holds my neck, rising up to kiss me.

"It's not."

Looking down, I grasp my shaft, sliding the tip up and down her wet entrance. When I cross her clit, she moans and arches up to me. I can't hold back any longer. Spreading her thighs wider, I line up and slowly drive into her.

My eyes are fixed on her glistening pink skin clinging and stretching for me. She's tight, but her come makes it easier. I flick my gaze to her face, and her eyes are closed. Her back is arched and her lips are parted as if she's memorizing the sensation.

"Oh, God," she whispers, and I lean down to kiss her full lips.

Her hands move to my cheeks immediately, and she holds my face, curling her tongue with mine as we kiss deeply. The kiss sends need surging through my body, and I push forward more.

She whimpers into my mouth, and I pull back, looking

down to see her virgin body spreading wide, gripping my whole cock almost to the hilt.

"God, Rachel," I groan. "You feel like heaven."

When I'm fully seated, I wait, letting her body adjust to what's happening between us. I'm on my elbows above her, and she lifts her head again, searching for my mouth. I hold her face, covering her lips for another hungry kiss.

"It's so big." She whimpers as she devours my mouth. "I'm so full."

I'm fucking dying with my dick encased in her tight, slippery heat. Everything in me begs to move, but I don't. I let her lead the way.

We kiss and pull each other's lips. I trace my mouth along the side of her jaw to her neck, moving higher into her hair behind her ear. She exhales another soft noise.

Her nipples are hard against my chest, and after a moment, I feel her start to move. I almost cry with relief, and I gently begin to thrust. I slide out and carefully push back in.

"Oh, God," she gasps.

"You okay?" I slide my palm over her forehead.

Her eyes are closed, and her brow furrows. I'm worried it hurts, but she nods quickly. "Do it again."

Fuck me. I don't make her ask twice. Still, I keep it slow, rocking my hips gently despite my primitive urge to jackhammer. No way. Not with my beautiful girl.

"That's it." She gasps, the tension in her forehead starting to relax. "It's there."

Her body moves beneath me, and I realize she's rocking her hips. She's meeting my thrusts, and I loosen the reins a bit.

"Tell me if I need to stop."

She shakes her head, holding my shoulders and bucking her hips. "Don't stop."

My hands are behind her shoulders as I thrust a bit harder, a little deeper, and she gasps. Her arms go around my neck, and our bare bodies fit together perfectly.

Her knees bend, and we rock, thrusting and groaning, moving faster. A bead of sweat traces along my temple, and I'm lost in this place, this sensation, this beautiful woman. It's so much. It's so good. It's never been like this. She's mine.

Pleasure surges up my legs, tightening my ass, jerking through my cock, and I can't hold back anymore.

"I'm coming…" My jaw is tight, and I feel my cock pulsing deep. "Rachel…"

I'm still thrusting and holding, giving her another long stroke as the orgasm shakes my muscles, my stomach, my arms.

She keeps moving, riding my cock until she holds with a little shudder. "Oh!"

Through my own haze of orgasm I shift to the side, slipping my hand between us and stroking the side of my thumb up and down over her clit until she's jerking more and wailing louder.

I give her another deep thrust, and a smile splits her cheeks. "Yes!" She gasps, and I do it again until she starts to giggle. "Stop! It's too much."

A smile splits my cheeks. "That's too much?"

Her eyes are closed, and she's nodding, wrapping her arms around my shoulders and placing her face against my neck. She kisses my skin, tracing her tongue along my throat, and I roll us to the side, pulling her completely to me, cradling her in my arms.

She's amazing, my beautiful girl. This girl who gave me everything. She's mine.

A deep sense of satisfaction washes over me, and I can't believe it. I haven't felt this calm in years.

Chapter 18

Rachel

"**W**HAT DOES IT MEAN TO NOT PAY ATTENTION TO MUSIC?" THE low vibration of Zane's voice tickles my cheek.

I've been dozing a little since he *made me a woman.* A laugh snorts through my nose, both at that ridiculous thought and at his disgusted tone.

"Poor Sam." I lift my head and rest my chin on my hand as I gaze up at this beautiful man.

"Poor Sam?" His brow lowers over his pretty blue eyes. "Sam Allen is an imbecile."

"He is not! Sam is nice."

Those blue eyes fix on mine fiercely. "Are you interested in him?"

"What?" My eyes widen, and I'm about to laugh louder.

Instead, I switch gears.

"Yes." I nod, rolling onto my back and pulling the sheet under my arms. "I was thinking about giving him a call and seeing what he's up to this weekend."

"Just try it." Zane rolls towards me, gripping my waist in both hands and making me scream a laugh.

"Okay! Okay! I was only playing." I laugh some more as he pulls me into his arms.

My back is snug against his chest, and I trace my finger down the line of a tattoo on his forearm. I think about the last time I was in the cocoon of his arms.

"I really like dancing with you."

He leans down, inhaling the top of my head and unfurling warmth through my shoulders. "I can't remember the last time I danced. Prom, maybe?"

"I really like that you saved yourself for me." Squirming around, I want to look at him.

"Me, too." He's over me, smiling down at me now, and my breath catches.

Oh my God, I love him.

Blinking away from his gaze, I lift my arms and pull him down into a hug, hiding my face in his neck while I regain my bearings. While I get my head on straight. Love? Seriously?

Even if he is really, *really* good in bed, how would I even know? He's the first man I've ever been with… or kissed… or followed into his bedroom practically begging for him to take me.

Exhaling a groan, he gives me a little nudge. "What are you thinking?"

"I kind of threw myself at you."

A noise rumbles in his throat, almost like a laugh. "You knew what you wanted."

"Are you laughing?" Leaning back, I cut my eyes up at him. "I said *please*. I stripped naked for you. It was so embarrassing."

"If it makes you feel any better, I was holding on by a thread every time. You have no idea how hard it was to walk away from you. If you hadn't been a virgin—"

"You didn't want to sleep with me because I was a virgin?"

"Correction. I didn't want to fuck you against a wall or on

a massage table because you were a virgin. Now, however, all bets are off."

I exhale a little squeal, which makes him really laugh, which makes me stretch higher in the bed to kiss him. His large hands slide warmly down my back, and I sigh.

"What makes you so good?"

"Hell, Rachel, I'm not good."

"But you are." I trace my nails up his broad shoulders. "Not good like boring. Good like you see someone needing help and you help them. Or you see a boy disturbed by noise or too much wind, and you put the doors back on your Jeep or you take him outside to play pool where it's quieter."

My eyes heat. Of course, I love him. He's sexy and broody and so fucking *good.*

Exhaling heavily, he watches the ceiling fan moving slowly above us as he traces a finger over my arm. "My parents, maybe?"

"Oh, man," I exhale a groan. "My parents did nothing but fight the entire time I lived at home. I don't know when they put down their weapons long enough to create Edward, but from the way my mother acted, it was the worst thing that could've happened to her."

His arms tighten around me. "I'm sorry for that."

"When Edward was diagnosed, people tried to say it was my mother's fault. They never even considered what a jerk my dad was."

"People say a lot of stupid shit."

"My dad was the reason I always dreamed of coming here." My voice gets a little softer, a little more dreamy. "He used to talk about this place like it was heaven. He loved it here."

I can't finish that thought, remembering how much I hung on his words as a little girl. It wasn't until I was older that I knew who he really was—a con man, a fake friend, a deceiver. If there was a way to make a fast dollar in any situation, he was on it.

If the dollar disappeared, so did he.

Zane's hand slides down my back, and I cuddle closer to his side.

In one of her more lucid moments, my mom told me I had the power to make a new path, to break with tradition. She told me I could marry a man who was nothing like my father.

Hell, she said I could marry a woman or not get married at all.

I don't say any of that out loud, but I do think about it. I think about this man, and how he's nothing like my father. From the start, he's only ever taken care of me.

Even after we finished having sex for the first time, he went to the bathroom and came back with a towel to clean me. I took one look at that pure white terry and shook my head no. I skipped to the bathroom and cleaned myself up in the tub.

Five minutes later, we were in bed again, snuggling.

In the beginning, he pushed me away. We fought, he dismissed me, but whenever I needed him, there he was.

"Are you sore?" He traces a finger along the line in the center of my back.

The way he says it tickles my stomach, and I lift my chin to meet his eyes. "I don't think so. What did you have in mind?"

"How long does it take to heat the pool?"

Skinny-dipping in a heated pool with Zane Bradford on a crisp autumn day might be *my* definition of heaven. Second only to being wrapped in his arms. Our naked bodies slide together in the warm water, and the fire in my belly has me kissing him with more urgency.

He holds me close, and I follow his lead, nipping, tasting, devouring his mouth. As much as I love his cock, I might love his tongue a little more. Not only can we make out like ravenous teenagers, he's pretty excellent at going downtown.

I whimper as his fingers slide between my legs, testing my wetness. "If you're not feeling up to it…"

"I feel up to it," I answer quickly, moving my lips to his ear and kissing him.

Lifting his face, he meets my eyes. "You never have to say something because you think I want to hear it."

"Okay." Angry god, slash perfect man.

"I feel like you were holding something back when we were in bed just now."

I swallow air not really believing he picked up on that. "Oh." I exhale a little laugh, shaking my head. "I was only… It wasn't anything."

"What was it?"

We're in the warm pool, naked, our bodies pressed together, the temperature rising. His cock against my stomach, and here comes the truth to deflate everything.

"It was just about what my mom said." I glance down at the water. "She said I didn't have to choose someone like my dad, and at the time I didn't understand. Then you told me what he did, and it ruined everything."

He exhales slowly, lowering his chin to meet my eyes. "Look at me." I blink a few times before complying, meeting his serious blue gaze. "I'm sorry for making you feel responsible for Jayden. I've thought about it, I talked to Jack, and it's not fair to make you pay for his betrayal."

I nod, blinking down again, thinking of him talking to Jack. I remember talking to Dylan. If the two of them don't care… Maybe Garrett and Hendrix won't either? Maybe they'll like me?

"It could be like he brought us together." It's a timid suggestion, me trying to find the positive. Although, where I got my optimistic streak, I'll never know.

"Hmm." He exhales. "I'd like to think something better brought us together."

"Your parents?"

"Miss Gina."

"Of course. It was Miss Gina and this gorgeous old house."

Turning into his chest, I look up at the Italian-style edifice looming over us in this blue-ceramic tile pool. Flowering vines climb the wrought-iron trellises. Twinkle lights adorn the eaves, and as the sun drifts lower, it only grows more magical.

"I wish we could spend the night here," I sigh.

His lips slide along the line of my cheek, and my eyes drift closed.

"I'll talk to Dylan. She and Logan have both offered to watch Edward for us on more than one occasion."

"We could spend the night here?"

"We could sleep in the cottage."

"Miss Gina practically told us to."

Returning my gaze to his beautiful eyes, the blue is hotter, more possessive, and the heat in my stomach turns even hotter. Our mouths meet and part, and his fingers stroke, reawakening the orgasm lingering there.

Floating in this pool, humming with desire, nothing holds us back now, and I want all of him. I wrap my legs around his waist and lean forward to speak in his ear.

"It shouldn't hurt now."

"You want me to fuck you?" A gentle tease is in his tone, and it thrills me to my core.

His hands are on the sides of the pool, and I feel his eagerness. It ricochets heat from my stomach to my toes, and I whimper, leaning closer to his ear.

"What happens if I say please now?"

"Face the wall." His voice is low, and I rotate in his arms.

Placing my hands on the tile, I feel his heat at my back. The soft hairs on his chest brush against my skin, amping the tension, the anticipation.

Strong hands cover my waist, and his voice is low behind my ear. "Hold on."

"Oh, God…" I close my eyes as I feel his tip sliding against my body.

He invades on one hard drive, and my fingers tighten. A cry aches through my parted lips, and I'm so full. He's so big and hot and demanding.

One hand is beside mine holding the wall, and as he thrusts into me from behind, he pins me against him with the other hand circling steadily over my clit.

My eyes roll as I drop my head back against his shoulder. I'm being used in the most thrilling way possible. He's hitting that place inside me that makes me see stars, and I'm going to come so fast. I've lost all sense of place, time…

I shudder a moan. His lips trace my ear, and I can hear him breathing, hot and haggard. Every thrust lifts me higher, and the water in the pool rocks with us. My knuckles are white from gripping the edge. I'm sore, but in a way that somehow makes having sex even better.

We're insatiable. We're ravenous. We're obsessed with each other's bodies, and I'm coming like thunder.

"Don't stop!" I cry, squeezing my eyes.

My ass lifts, trying to take him deeper. He hits me again and again, and all at once, I'm gone, shooting over the ledge, diving off the cliff, flying through space. My stomach flips, and my brain ignites. My legs go rigid then shake with orgasm.

With one more thrust, he holds steady, his own moans shaky in my ear. His stomach quivers at my back, and I feel his cock deep inside me pulsing, releasing, climaxing.

We're breathing hard, and now the water is cool compared to our skin.

The hand on my clit drifts higher to my belly, and he

wraps me up in his arms once more. Leaning my head back, we float away on the most divine bliss.

"You haven't eaten enough." Zane is between my legs.

We're back in the cottage, and I've just ridden his lap to orgasm for the first time. We came in with the idea we'd shower, get cleaned up, but when I bent over to pick up my yoga pants, something about my naked ass in the air led to his mouth on my pussy.

I am not complaining.

"I think I like riding your cock." I've propped my elbows on his shoulders, and he's lifting my breasts, kissing the tops and sliding his tongue around my nipples. It makes me moan. "You're not going to convince me to eat doing that."

"You have perfect breasts. Has anyone ever told you that?"

"No one has ever seen my breasts but you."

A naughty grin slowly curls his lips before he lifts his eyes from my decolletage to my face. "It's a shame no one else ever will. They really are art."

Snorting a laugh, I lean forward to kiss him. "You're crazy."

"And you need to eat. We've been exercising vigorously all day, and you haven't eaten since breakfast." His dark brow arches. "What did you have for breakfast?"

"Yogurt and a half a banana."

"Rachel."

"I didn't know I was going to have a day-long sexcapade! I thought I'd be finishing up decorating, maybe doing light water aerobics."

He lifts me off his lap and slides his legs off the bed. "Don't move. You're not passing out in the shower again."

"Yes, sir." I do a little salute, giggling as he marches out of the cottage completely naked, his toned, muscular ass flexing with every step.

As soon as he's gone, I sink into the fluffy pillows, pulling the blankets to my nose and grinning. I think about my mantras and how I'm supposed to focus on the journey. This is the best journey I've ever taken, and all I want to focus on is him.

My eyes slide closed and I think about his straight, white smile. I think about that dimple that only appears in his cheek when he's really happy. I think about the lines in his strong back and sliding my fingers down them. I think about his powerful thighs, and how he carries me around as if I weigh nothing at all.

I don't even realize I've fallen asleep until he lightly touches my cheek. "Is this a nap or something else?"

"Oh!" I sit up quickly, exhaling a little laugh. "I fell asleep thinking about you."

"Good things, I hope." He kisses my lips lightly before putting a tray on the bed and climbing in beside me.

"So many good things." I kiss the side of his rounded shoulder.

The tray holds what looks like two pastrami sandwiches, two bottles of what I think is lemonade, a plastic container of quartered oranges, a jar of black olives, a sleeve of round wheat crackers, and a hunk of hard, yellow cheese.

"This is a very interesting lunch." I shift in the bed, sitting on my feet. "It's like something out of a Jane Austen novel. I feel like I should be in a field of wildflowers sipping champagne and wearing a hat with one of those chiffon veils."

Zane's brow furrows, and he studies the tray. "I wasn't sure what you liked to eat. I guess I should've paid better attention. I know the fruit and the lemonade are sugary."

"It's the best kind of sugar, too." I lean forward, picking up the plastic bowl. The fresh scent of oranges surrounds us when I open it. "Want some?"

I pop a wedge into my mouth and exhale a hum when the sweet juice splashes over my tongue. "Not bitter at all."

I hold a wedge to his full lips, and after a brief hesitation, he lets me slip it into his mouth. He grins, chewing, and that sexy muscle moves in his square jaw.

My shoulders drop, and I lean back against the pillows. "You are so handsome, Zane Bradford." He exhales a grumpy sound, and I laugh. "I wish we could stay here all week. Wouldn't that be amazing?"

"You'd need a lot more vitamin C if we did that." He gives me a wink, and a thrill flutters in my stomach. "We both would."

He hands me a bottle of lemonade, and I'm not sure how it's possible I want to have sex with him again after four times in one day. I drink the sweet beverage wondering if sex is like this with every man or if you only get one man who makes you feel this horny all the time.

Or maybe I'm a nympho, and I never knew it until now?

"You're doing it again." His voice is low, ominous. "What are you thinking about?"

My eyes widen, and I blink fast as my brain scrambles for something other than I'm a nympho—or I never want to have sex with any man but him ever again.

"We should try Nuru massage." His brow arches, and I chew my lip feeling shy. "Miss Gina kept talking about it, so I watched a video. It's pretty hot."

His eyes darken, and he holds another orange wedge to my lips. "I'm game if you are, but we'll have to wait until tomorrow. It's almost four."

"Oh!" I jump off the bed. "We've got to get back for Edward."

"He knows to walk down to the restaurant if nobody's home."

"I know, but I don't want anyone to think I'm trying to make them babysit."

"Nobody thinks that." He carries the tray to the dresser as I jump in the shower. "I told you, we're a community here."

I'm already in the shower, cleaning up. "I didn't feed the kittens! He's always asking about them, and I forgot!"

"The kittens are fine." Zane peeks into the bathroom, fully dressed in his jeans and T-shirt. "I'll feed Sky, and she'll take care of her babies."

"They're eating solid food now, too!" I step out, grabbing a towel and quickly drying off.

"They're also hunting mice." He changes directions, walking to where I'm pulling on my underwear. "Eddie's almost thirteen. I'm sure he'll be okay a little longer."

Standing up fast, I already recognize that look in his eyes. "As good as that sounds, I'd be worried about him the whole time."

Leaning down, he kisses my lips. "We'll be home in fifteen minutes."

Chapter 19

Zane

WALKING FROM THE HOUSE DOWN TO THE RESTAURANT AFTER stopping off for a quick shower, I notice my universe seems to have shifted. I actually feel different. Garrett would be the first to point out I've had sex for the first time in who knows when, but it's more than that.

My shoulders aren't tense. In fact, all of the tension I've been carrying in my upper back and neck is noticeably absent. It's like I've been released from a cage. My jaw isn't tight, and I have a peculiar urge to smile.

It's weird.

I feel good.

Stopping mid-way, I think about all the Buddhist philosophy I spent so much time studying in the hospital. I breathe deeply. I recall the idea of letting go of control. Is that what's going on?

Lifting my eyes over the silvery tin roof of the restaurant, out to the bay, I study the horizon lit up from the recent disappearance of the sun. It's not completely dark yet. The water remains golden. In fact, the whole sky is a deep, blood-orange, and a lone, brown pelican glides just above the placid surface.

It sends my mind filtering through everything that happened today. The day was a freaking fever dream. Miss Gina drove away in that car, and we passed through a portal. I'm surprised I had the bearings to realize we had to return to the real world.

When we got to the house, as soon as I parked, Rachel had her hand on the door, ready to hop out of the Jeep to find her brother.

She leaned over to give me a quick kiss on the lips, but I caught her face, holding her still for a beat, holding her close for a better kiss, something a little slower, a little warmer. I wasn't ready to let her go just yet. I didn't want the vision to end.

She blinked up at me, and my chest tightened.

Rachel's green eyes shine like the sun rising over the meadow when we take the horses out on a dewy spring morning. When I look into them, I see peace. The battle momentarily stops, and I escape the noise. I see something I've been afraid to allow myself to see.

She's ripping my carefully crafted script to shreds. No attachments, no one gets hurt. It's been my guiding principle since my injury. Don't get too close. Never get too close.

Only, I can't seem to stop myself. If today was any indication, I only want more of her. I don't know what to do with this or what it means for the future. I'm all mixed up inside, because as relaxed and at peace as I am, I can't help looking over my shoulder.

It's the reality I've come to accept as soon as I think all is well.

"I love this kind of sunset." Logan's deep voice draws me out of my turmoil. "I've only ever seen it here."

"It's pretty," I agree.

Although, not as pretty as the pair of green eyes I lost myself in all day long.

"I was thinking about our Thanksgiving show," he continues

as we walk down to the Coot-Shoot. "The Pirates always have a game on Black Friday. We could ask Garrett to drop in and tell us what to expect."

"They're probably not headed to the Playoffs this year." I glance at him, thinking about how the Pirates haven't bounced back since he retired.

I know it weighs on him, but I'm not so sure my younger brother's heart is in the game as much as it used to be either. Logan's retirement seems to have started a chain reaction.

"Yeah, but we always get a bump when we have Garrett on the show. I think listeners like hearing you brothers talk." He holds the door for me. "Maybe we could ask Jack to sit in as well. He's really good on the mic, and I like including the local kids. He fielded a good team this year."

"Jack's good at everything." I grin, thinking about my eldest brother.

The sound of laughter echoes from the kitchen, and Logan nods in that direction. "What do you think is going on in there?"

"I can't even begin to guess." My smile widens, and we head to the double doors. "It could be anything."

"I like seeing you smile, brother." Logan grips my shoulder, giving it a shake. "Feels like the start of something good."

"Yeah, maybe." I can't quite commit to that yet.

Optimism is a tricky bitch. I've dared to go there so many times, only to have it thrown in my face.

The first time was Thanksgiving, twelve years ago. I dared to think we'd survived, that our future was bright, that we'd rounded a corner, and I ended all of that. Hurting Dylan was a wound I couldn't shake, no matter how many times she let me off the hook.

Karma took care of that. Karma is my enemy, I've learned, and I'd do good to remember it. My stomach twists painfully at the thought, and I remember lying in that hospital bed almost two years ago.

When that game started, I sat on the bench watching the

guys play, thinking I'd found my place. I wasn't sure at first, but things were good. I liked where I was, and I could see a promising future.

It was the last game I played.

Logan walks ahead of me into the restaurant, and I consider what experience has taught me. Getting close to Rachel feels like a risk. I can only watch things play out so many times before I start to believe them.

"Hey!" Her sweet voice greets me as I enter the double doors, and my hesitation evaporates.

Good intentions aside, I can't resist Rachel Wells. She's in my blood, and I can't be without her. Hell, I'm thinking long-term thoughts about this girl.

"Hey." My voice is low, and I know that goofy smile is on my face again.

They're all going to see it, but good thing for me, the only big mouths who would give me a hard time are Garrett and Hendrix. And they're not here.

"I was starting to think you'd stay at the house." She's not touching me, but the energy between us is so strong, it might be visible to the naked eye.

She's being very respectful of my space, and I know it's because this is all so new. As much as people have been pushing us together, she won't do anything presumptive. She'll let me take the lead, and it makes me want to wrap both my arms around her and pull her to me.

I want to plant a kiss on her right here in front of everybody.

"I still need dinner." I gaze down at her, lifting my finger to trace a stray lock of hair off her cheek and behind her ear.

Can't she see how important she is to me? Why wouldn't I come down here to see her?

Blinking away, a soft laugh puffs through her lips. Her cheeks flush as if she's embarrassed, and she's so fucking adorable.

"Dylan said Eddie Nashville has been at the pool tables since

Allie dropped him off. He's playing like it's a science experiment, memorizing every move."

"If I know your brother, he's going to wipe the floor with all the other players next Sunday."

Placing her hand over her forehead, she looks up at me. "I think he might!"

"Why would he do something if he's not going to be the best at it?"

"Uncle Zee!" Kimmie Joy dances in front of me holding up her hands, and I automatically reach down to swing her onto my hip. "Ed won't let me play pool. He said I have to wait until after the tournament. He said it's important because it's for the horses."

She puts her little head on my shoulder, and I glance down at her rosebud pout. It's funny how much she looks like Dylan as a little girl, considering she only has half of Jack's genes. Still, it kind of makes me spoil her a little, like she's a second chance.

Second chances… The thought takes hold in my mind.

"Austin could teach you." Even if I want to spoil her, I'd rather spend time with Rachel.

"Aussie said he has to play football. He doesn't have time anymore." She scrubs her face against my shoulder. "He never has time anymore."

I give her a little bounce. "I bet Smokey is lonely now that everybody's playing pool and football. You know he hasn't been away from his family very long."

Her dark, curly head pops up immediately. "I'd better check on him! We can play together!"

She wiggles, and I put her down, watching her take off running in the direction of the kitchen. When I straighten, Rachel's eyebrow is arched, and her arms are crossed.

"What?" I'm not sure I'm ready to hear this.

"You're a real expert when it comes to kids."

"Is that so?" I take a step closer, and she puts her hands on my waist.

"She might be a little spoiled, but you handled that situation. Nice work."

"Are you saying I got out of spending time with my precious niece?"

"Absolutely."

I laugh, ready to lean in and kiss her good, when I hear my sister's voice behind us. "Time to wrap it up, people. We're closing for the night."

"Only my sister would shut down the restaurant at nine p.m. on a Friday," I murmur in her ear.

"To be fair, Thursdays are the big nights here, and everybody's at the high school game." She gives my hand a squeeze. "I'll collect the pool-shark and see you back at the house."

"Did you eat dinner?"

"Yes, Daddy, I had a whole cheeseburger." That sassy little Daddy hits me in a way I don't expect.

Reaching out, I catch her by the waist. "That sounds pretty good. I might have you say that again when I'm inside you."

Her eyes flare, and her cheeks flush red. "Watch what you wish for. It might come true."

Leaning back, I'm still smiling, slowly shaking my head as I watch her walk away, that cute little ass swaying in the direction of the pool tables.

The house is quiet, and I'm lying in my bed doing my best to relax, get some sleep. One thing is on my mind—sneaking across the hall into Rachel's bedroom. One thing is stopping me: Eddie Nashville.

I'm pretty sure if I go to her, we'll wake her brother. I toss and turn a little longer, then I remember Edward sleeps in headphones sometimes.

Sitting up in the bed, I'm ready to make my move when I

hear a soft tap on the door. I'm across the room in an instant, carefully opening the door. When I look down and see her standing in the dark hallway, I open it at once, catching her wrist, and pulling her inside before quickly shutting it again.

"Hey." Her back is against the door, and I'm looking down at her sweet lips.

"Hey." You'd think I'd run a marathon with the way I'm panting.

We're both breathing fast, and without another word, I lean down to kiss her. She exhales one of those soft little noises, and her arms wrap around my neck. In a sweep, I lift her off her feet, opening her mouth with mine, and curling our tongues together.

The semi I've been struggling with is fully hard, and I carry her to the bed, putting a knee on it before lowering her to her back. She's wearing nothing but a thin, long-sleeved tee, and I can see her nipples pointing through the fabric, rising quickly with her breath.

Leaning down, I cover one with my mouth, pulling the stiff peak firmly through the cotton fabric, sliding my teeth over it as she squirms and quietly moans beneath me.

"Zane…" She threads her fingers in my hair, and I rise higher, covering her mouth with mine again, meeting her hungry kisses with my own.

She reaches for the hem of my tee, pulling it higher, and I lean back to whip it over my head. Her eyes darken as they slide down my body, and my cock tents my joggers.

Bending down, I speak in her ear. "I was on my way to you when you appeared."

She cups my jaws in her hands, turning her face to whisper, "You said you'd always come for me."

"I will." I reach down to lift her shirt higher, helping her sit up, so she can remove it completely.

She lies back again, and my breath catches at the sight of her beautiful, naked body in the middle of my bed. A shy smile curls her lips as I study her soft form.

Resting on my elbows, I cup the sides of her breasts, pulling them together so I can suck and nibble them. Her back arches, and she exhales another little moan.

"I made sure Edward was sleeping in his headphones before I came here," she sighs.

It's all I need to know. Moving lower, I catch the sides of her tiny scrap of underwear, yanking them down her legs and tossing them aside. I'm on my knees, and I wrap my arms around her legs, leaning forward and covering her with my mouth.

Her moan is louder now, and I slide my tongue all over her clit, circling with my tongue, giving it a little suck. Her ass bucks in my hands, and her hands are in my hair.

She's riding my face even though she's on her back, and I slide one hand up, reaching higher to pinch and pull her tight nipples. Her body jerks, and her hips begin to quiver.

Soft, undulating noises pant rhythmically from her chest, and I feel when her body starts to break, when her orgasm shocks and shudders in her thighs. Moving my mouth to the crease of her leg, I kiss her skin, and she jumps with another moan.

I shove my pants down, allowing my cock to spring free while she's still glowing.

"Can you take a little more?" We had sex all day, and I don't want to cause her discomfort.

She stretches out both hands, curling her fingers and hissing, "Yes."

It makes me smile, and I move higher, between her thighs, reaching down to align my cock with her entrance.

In one long drive, I'm seated deep inside her. She moans, and her hips move beneath me. Her inner muscles quiver and squeeze my cock, and the feeling of her orgasm fluttering all around me has me shooting to the edge so fast.

"Fuck, Rachel…" I'm like a teenager, rather than a thirty-something-year-old man. "I'm going to come."

Thrusting my hips, I lose myself in the soft warmth of her

body, the slippery heat of her core, and her soft lips at my ear, kissing and biting.

"You feel so good," she whispers, and I realize her hips are rocking with mine.

Sliding my arms under her shoulders, I turn us quickly, so she's on top. Her blonde hair falls all around us, and she leans forward to place her palms on my chest as she rides me.

Her eyes are closed, and her thighs slide up and down my hips. Lifting my hands, I trace my fingers lightly over her ass, and she jumps, moving in a staccato way as her second orgasm surges through her body.

"Oh!" She cries, and I push higher, giving her all of me as her muscles flutter around my cock. "You make me come so hard."

The thread I was hanging onto breaks, and I squeeze my eyes shut as my ass tightens, as the climax I've been holding back rips through me. A roar is in my throat, and I nearly choke, doing my best to keep it quiet.

My cock jerks and pulses into her. My back lifts off the bed, and Rachel exhales another whimpering moan, riding me like I'm a wild horse.

It's so intense, I'm pretty sure I leave my body briefly. Wrapping my arms around her, I hold onto her as my anchor to this world. My eyes are still closed as the air moves in and out of my lungs, as I fall back through space to this room, in my bed, her naked body flush with mine.

Already she feels like home. I could be here forever and die a happy man. All thoughts of risk and rules have left my mind, and all I want is her, Rachel Wells.

She wiggles, and I release my grip on her. Sliding off me, she faces me in the bed, and I roll onto my side to study her flushed cheeks lifted with her grin.

"It keeps getting better," she whispers, and now I'm smiling.

I'm pretty sure I've smiled more today than I have in two years—possibly longer. "Hold that thought."

Hopping out of the bed, I open the door and carefully peek

into the dark hall. It's empty and silent, so I step across into the bathroom, grab a washcloth and hold it under the cool water.

When I return, she hasn't moved, and I go to her, carefully cleaning up our mess. This time she lets me. After our first time, she probably made the right decision to take a quick bath.

Setting the cloth aside, I pull her to me in a hug. I smooth my hand down the line of her back. I inhale the sweet honeysuckle in her hair. She snuggles closer to me the way she did when we were dancing, the way she did when we made love.

She's a perfect fit, and the mad protectiveness twisting in my chest won't let go. I'll never be able to let her go.

We stay wrapped in each other's arms, breathing each other's air until I begin to doze. She's so still, I think she's asleep, but she pulls back.

"I'd better sleep in my room just in case." She moves to the edge of the bed, looking over her shoulder at me.

Her hair hangs long down her back, and when she stands to step into her underwear, I can't help squeezing her cute little ass.

"Zane!" She laughs, skipping away, closer to my desk to pull on her shirt.

It still has one damp spot where I bit and sucked her nipple, and I'm pretty sure she's the best thing I've ever seen.

"You finished the book!" Her eyes are on my desk, and I look down to see she's holding *Archer's Voice*.

"Oh, yeah." I sit up, reaching for my boxer briefs.

"What did you think?"

My brow furrows as I stand, pulling them over my hips. "You know that movie where Bradley Cooper throws the book out of the window?"

"No!" Her cute little angry face makes me laugh.

"Just that one part—Chapter 33? Or was it 34?"

"Oh." Her brow relaxes, and she makes a sorry face. "Yeah, that was scary."

Standing, I walk over to where she's by my desk. "But I liked it. It was pretty good."

"Pretty good?"

"I liked the message about how your actions speak louder than your words."

Nodding, she steps to the door. "It's an oldie, but a goodie."

Watching her tuck the book under her arm, I think about another part I liked, where the hero looked at his girl and imagined the two of them growing old together, and how it would be the ultimate joy. It's how I feel about Rachel, but I don't say it out loud. Not yet.

"Want to read another one?"

"Maybe later." I follow her to the door, stopping behind her when she turns to look up at me.

Leaning down, I give her another kiss, sliding my lips over hers and giving her tongue one more swipe. She exhales a little hum, and it almost has me pulling her to my bed again.

"I could set an alarm," I suggest, and she laughs.

"I'm pretty sure if I got into your bed again, we wouldn't sleep at all tonight."

"That's okay."

Rising on her toes, she gives me another kiss. "Tomorrow. I got some oil to try that therapy."

My brow quirks, and I can't help a grin. "I think it'll be the first time I look forward to a massage."

"I'm not sure how much massaging will happen."

"Even better."

Chapter 20

Rachel

"Jack put Austin in the game last night, and Allie said he threw a touchdown pass!" Dylan holds the pot of coffee over my mug, her eyes lit with excitement.

"Oh!" I smile so big. "I bet Allie was screaming."

"She has no voice." Dylan laughs, and I smile, thinking how great it is to have friends.

I've never had a group like this before, and it's like I'm part of a real family for the first time in my life.

"What will you do now that Miss Gina's in Birmingham for the week? Do you have any plans?"

My lips twist, and I think about what I'd like to do all week. His name is Zane Bradford.

"Oh, I don't know." I shrug, thinking she probably doesn't want to hear about my day-long sex marathon with her older brother.

"You're welcome to hang out with us at the restaurant, but I warn you. I'll probably put you to work."

Sipping my coffee, I wink. "I don't mind that. You have a fun job."

"It'll be pretty dead with people traveling, and we're closed on Thanksgiving day."

"No Dare dish?"

"Not this week, and I'm thankful for that." She exhales a little sigh. "Logan is going to try and work less, so we'll get to spend some time together. Maybe I'll take Miss Gina up on her offer to use the guest cottage."

"You will?" My eyes widen, and I try to remember the state we left it in yesterday in our hurry to get home for Edward. "I'll get it ready for you."

"You don't have to do that!" She presses a hand on my forearm. "I'm perfectly capable of making a bed or airing out the sheets or whatever needs to be done. I wonder how long it's been since anybody's used it."

She might be surprised.

"I don't mind. I've got to run over there today anyway." And practice some sexy massage on her brother.

"I'll go with you!" She smiles big, and my heart stops.

"Oh! Ahh…" I exhale a nervous laugh. "You can't."

"Why not?" Confusion lines her brow, and my brain is scrambling.

"Because, um, Miss Gina…" *Think think…* "Oh! Miss Gina is expecting her Christmas gifts to arrive today, and I'm supposed to organize them for her."

"That's no problem. I can help you!"

"No, you can't!" I shake my head. "She got something for you, and it's supposed to be a surprise."

Dylan's confusion melts into a smile. "Are you serious? She didn't have to do that!"

"I know, but you know she loves the holidays. And she made me promise to organize everything in her Christmas closet."

"Okay." Dylan skips over to the sink, and I nearly pass out with relief.

"I'd better eat something." Lord knows with the things I have planned for today, I don't want to have to stop for a snack.

I only want one snack. The thought almost makes me laugh, and Dylan's watching me again.

"I think you're hiding something." Her brown eyes narrow, and I shake my head.

"Just Christmas things. Being Santa's helper is fun."

"Okay." She grabs her coffee mug off the counter and goes to the door. "If you finish up early, come down to the restaurant. That brother of yours has been playing pool nonstop."

That makes me pause. "Is it okay for him to hang out there today? I can take him with me…"

Please say no… Please say no… Please say no…

"No!" Dylan cries, and I almost faint again. "Eddie Nashville is not a problem. In fact, he's a good helper, and knowing Miss G, she probably got something for him, too."

"Let me know if you need me to come back for any reason."

She waves, making a little *pfft* noise as she heads out the door. "I would like to do yoga with you again if you have time?"

"It's a date! Let's get together this week at the park."

"I'll tell Allie."

"Text me!" She trots out the door, and I stand at the sink, watching her skip down to the restaurant through the kitchen window.

"That was close." The deep male voice behind me sends a thrill straight to my core, and I turn when I feel the heat of his body at my back.

"I didn't really lie. Miss G did order Christmas gifts for everyone. I'm just not sure if they're all coming today."

"I know something that is coming today." He leans down, covering my lips with his, and I sigh, opening my mouth and curling our tongues.

It's warm liquid in my veins and heat in my core. "I'll grab my bag, and we can take off. I'm eager to test out this new massage."

His brow lowers over blue eyes, making my body hum. "Me too."

A palette of blankets and towels are spread on the wooden platform Zane built under the arch, laden with green leaves. It'll be covered in pink bougainvillea again when spring comes, but today, we're surrounded by the scent of cool air and warm woods from the massage oil.

The hush of ocean waves drifts quietly around us from the speakers overhead, and I let the plush robe fall from my shoulders, placing it on the massage table above us.

I'm completely naked, and turning to face him. In this setting, outdoors, with the cool air and the open breeze, it's like we're the only people on Earth.

He sits in front of me on the makeshift bed. He's also naked, and his cock thickens as I move closer. Ice-blue eyes darken, and I tremble with anticipation. I'm so ready, I might come from one touch alone.

"Lie on your stomach." I place a pillow under his head, and he does as I say, placing a hand under his cheek. "First we oil."

Taking the bottle, I pour a liberal amount into my palms before spreading it all over his toned back. His body is so beautiful, long and muscular and athletic. When he's covered, I pour a generous amount of oil over my bare breasts and stomach.

"I'm not using the traditional seaweed gel, but I think the results will be the same." My voice is quiet, and he slides his palm along the side of my calf.

"When you put this body on mine, I'm sure they will." The promise in his voice tickles my core.

"It's also edible, so…"

His groan sends a thrill through my core, making me exhale

a nervous laugh, and I pour more along the back of his legs, his firm ass, then on my thighs and arms.

"Here goes." I lift my leg to straddle his waist, lowering my entire torso onto his, my breasts flattening against his back, my cheek against his shoulder blade.

We both exhale a sigh as our bare skin unites. My eyes close, and my muscles relax. Then I start to move, sliding my front up and down his back. The heat between us grows as the oil allows me to use my weight to massage him.

I slide lower, bending my knees but keeping my breasts in contact with his butt, and I raise my hands up, circling my thumbs in the thick muscles of his shoulders, spreading my fingers from his spine outward following the lines of his physique.

"That feels really good." He groans, eyes closed as his cheek rests on his hand.

"It gets better." A grin touches my lips, and his chest vibrates with a chuckle.

Rising into a sitting position again, I slide forward on his ass to straddle him and rock my hips, grinding my crotch against his lower back. The sensation is instant, sending surges of pleasure radiating into my clit.

My lips part, and I exhale little gasps with every rock. Leaning forward, I grip his forearms, still undulating against him. My breasts press against his shoulder blades as I grind, and my lips are at his ear.

"Fuck, Rachel," he groans.

Sitting up, I carefully turn, so I'm now facing his feet, still massaging his lower back between my thighs. This time when I lean forward, I rub my thumbs down to his calves. My stomach presses on his ass, and I kiss him there.

"Shit," he hisses. "It's getting harder to stay on my stomach."

"One more *effleurage*, and you can turn."

Sitting up, I bring my feet in front of me and slide down so my butt slides up and down the backs of his thighs. "Feel that?"

Another deep groan. "I'm feeling a lot of things right now."

A laugh tickles my stomach, and I slide all the way off before crawling up his side and touching his shoulder. "Roll over now."

He sits up, and his face is even with mine. He hesitates, meeting my gaze with hungry blue eyes, and I blink down to his lips. Our noses are almost touching, and I dip forward, pressing my mouth to his briefly before moving away, straddling his firm abdomen.

He leans back, watching me slide lower with a grin on his lips. His cock is a steel rod extending to his navel. Reaching up, I grip his shoulders as I slide higher, and our mouths meet. His hands are at his sides, but I cup the back of his neck, and this time our tongues curl and circle.

He lifts one hand, smoothing it up to the back of my neck before sliding it down to my ass, tracing his fingers along the line between my legs. A soft moan slips from my lips, and I arch to meet him.

I rest my elbow beside his shoulder, and we're making out as I move my body, as he slides his fingers back and forth over my clit. I'm so hot and shivering with need, but I move away from that source of pleasure. Placing my pussy over his cock, I rock my hips back and forth, massaging his penis with my clit. It's electric.

"Rachel," he groans, dropping his head back as I continue moving up and down his erection.

His back arches higher, and I use my oiled-up hands to squeeze and massage his cock, passing my fingers over his mushroom tip and down his shaft as I rock my hips lower, against his balls.

"I'm going to come in your hands." It's a husky growl, and I feel his orgasm tensing his dick as I work him faster. "Put it inside you."

"That's not part of Nuru," I tease, and he grips my ass in response as if he'll do it himself.

Leaning forward, I rise onto my knees to lick his lips and

slide my tongue with his once more, still holding onto his hard cock before lowering again and guiding it inside me.

"Oh," I sigh as he spears my aching core.

I rock my hips again, and he sits up, gripping my butt in both hands and moving me up and down his length, pressing my clit against his lower belly so I get the right amount of friction on my most sensitive spot.

My head falls back, and his mouth covers my hard nipples, biting and sucking. Loud moans scrape through my throat, and he growls against my skin.

I want his mouth. Straightening, we kiss again, licking and making out. I'm utterly lost in sensation. Riding him, kissing him this way, and as we move faster, as our grinding grows hungrier, my orgasm spins tighter in my lower belly. He lifts me, and I rise onto my knees, whimpering, eyes closed as I chase the gorgeous release just within my grasp.

He moans, chanting my name, and all at once, the earth moves, shattering bliss rockets through my core. My body tenses, and I break into shudders. The orgasm is so hard it ricochets through me, down to the arches of my feet and up to the top of my head.

I'm enveloped in sparkling light, and he groans louder as he comes, jerking and releasing deep inside me. His loud, orgasmic moans thrill me, making me come a little more. I love the way he loses control with me.

We ride out these delicious waves together, wrapped in each other's arms, breathing fast. We rock slower, gently hugging each other as we come down again, relaxed and so satisfied.

Blinking slowly, I lift my face to meet his eyes. They're warm and brimming with affection, it almost makes me want to cry. *How did this happen?*

We didn't even like each other when I arrived. Or maybe we always did, but for some reason we tried to fight it? All I know is in his arms is where I'm supposed to be.

"I've never done anything like that." His voice is gentle.

"I like you touching me that way. It was incredibly hot, but relaxing."

"I guess that's why they call it erotic massage." I tease, sliding my nose along his cheek and kissing him softly.

His brow furrows. "But you did all the work. I have to massage you now."

I'm logy and content, but if he's feeling up to it. "Okay."

"Get on your stomach."

Exhaling a little laugh, I do as he says, stretching out on my stomach on the palette and resting my cheek on the back of my hand.

He lifts the oil bottle, and I sigh as he glides his large palms over my shoulders. It does feel so relaxing and loving the way he touches me. He's not a trained masseuse, but he does a good job circling his thumbs over the muscles in my neck and shoulders.

"That's good." A smile lifts the corner of my mouth.

"Just wait." He slides his hands down to the arch of my back, then lower. "Have I mentioned you have a sexy ass?"

"No," I giggle.

"I love watching you walk away." His thumbs circle my butt cheeks, and the sensation makes me wet. "As long as you come back."

His thumbs move lower, between my legs, and I exhale another moan when he wraps his fingers around my clit, giving it long strokes while his thumb tips into my core. He leans forward, tracing his lips up the line of my back, and surges of electricity follow in his wake.

I just came incredibly hard, but he's fanning the lingering embers, bringing them back to life. He slides his hands to my waist, and I start to shiver.

"Roll onto your back." It's a low command.

Doing as he says, I sit up, meeting his lips before I lie down again. Cupping his cheeks, I hold him to me, inhaling his warm scent mixed with the herbal scents and the oil. He holds my back, leaning forward as he helps me recline.

When he straightens, he studies me a moment before tracing his palms around my breasts. "I love these." Then lightly down my sides and over my hips. "So beautiful," he muses, and I'm floating.

Mimicking my actions, he straddles my body, bracing his weight on his knees. His cock is thick and heavy over me, and I want him so much again. He moves lower, down my legs before sliding his flat tongue up and down my clit. I exhale a moan.

His tongue continues circling, and the heat in my belly bursts into flames. It won't take much after his deliberate strokes, his careful caresses. His palms are on my hips, and when my orgasm breaks, he rises up, kissing me and parting my legs.

Thrusting his hard cock arches my back off the blankets. I rotate my hips, working his cock in my core. His fingers massage my clit, and I'm screaming with pleasure. I'm wetter than I've ever been, and the touch of his hands, the hardness of his cock, the sound of his moans… it's transplendent.

I'm aware of everything, his strength, his bare skin, our movements like we're dancing to our own primitive music. My muscles flutter and spasm, and I whimper as my orgasm vines through my legs and up through my stomach.

He thrusts two more times before holding, eyes closed, body rigid as his cock pulses, again filling me with climax.

Reaching forward, he lifts me in a firm embrace. Strong arms hold me, and our hearts beat loudly as one. It's the most intense experience I've ever had.

Chapter 21

Zane

"**A**RE YOU A BUDDHIST?" RACHEL'S CHEEK RESTS AGAINST MY chest, and she traces her finger along the black and white lines of the Taijitu symbol on my sleeve.

We can't seem to keep our hands off each other. We've had sex in almost every room in Miss Gina's house. We had sex in the pool, on the massage table, in the library against the stacks. She offered to help me work on the elevator and ended up straddling my lap on the bench inside it.

Hanging out at Cooters & Shooters, I caught her making eyes at me from across the kitchen, and we ended up fucking in the bathroom with her bent over the sink. We're like rabbits on steroids.

Tonight, I'm in her bed, and we've set an alarm for early tomorrow morning, Tuesday, before Edward wakes. We're taking him for a horseback ride before I head to Miss Gina's to fix that elevator.

She's not allowed to come to the house today. I have to get

at least one thing done before Miss G returns from visiting her family.

Frowning, I watch her slim finger tracing the circle tattoo on my arm. The taijitu is the yin-yang symbol. It expresses how there's always a drop of dark in the good… but the reverse is also true. In all the darkness, there's still light. She's the light.

She asked if I was a Buddhist.

"A little." I confess.

"How can you be a little Buddhist?" Her nose wrinkles, and she lifts her chin.

Gazing down into her pretty green eyes, I think about those dark days after my accident, how hard I spiraled. "When we lost Mom, then Dad so fast, it was like a hurricane came through, wiping out everything." Her brow furrows, and her eyes fill with concern. "Then when it felt like we'd managed to rebuild, when things were getting better, I hurt Dylan."

"It was an accident," she whispers, circling her fingers around my forearm and giving it a gentle squeeze.

"I ended her career, something she'd worked for all her life." My stomach twists, and I swallow the ache in my throat. "Football was the one thing I could control. I worked hard, I made every goal. I got a million-dollar contract, and I tried to hide from the pain by being the best on the field. Then in one bad play it was all over."

The words settle around us. The soft click of the heating unit breaks the silence. I remember lying in that hospital bed alone.

"You were hurt so badly." Her voice is quiet.

"I'd never felt physical pain like that." My muscles are tight as I show her my truth. "I deserved it." She starts to argue, but I continue. "Karma evened the score, but darkness was still attached to me. I brought tragedy, and I had to understand why and whether I could break it. If all I did was destroy, I had to stay away."

Quiet envelops us, and she continues sliding her fingers over my skin. I see her mind working, thinking, searching for a reply, but I've gone through all the options. I've watched the patterns play out over and over, and I know it's only a matter of time before I break this, too.

"I could sage you."

"You know I don't like that woo-woo shit."

"What you said was pretty woo woo."

"What I said is real. It's not energy or magic. I break things. People get hurt."

She exhales slowly, and I push my emotions down again. I don't talk about this with people, because they want to argue with me. They want to tell me it's in my mind or I'm wrong or get therapy. Then they go on with their lives, and I'm left with the fallout.

Her lips tighten, and she reaches up to slide her thumb along the line of my jaw. "Accidents happen, Zee. Your parents' deaths, your injury, even Dylan's—it wasn't your fault."

"But it was." In my worst nightmares, I still hear Dylan's screams. I still wake up in a sweat feeling the crunch of her delicate bones beneath me.

Clenching my jaw, I force that echo away. "So I studied Buddhism, learned to meditate…"

"To ease your pain." Her fingers trace along my skin, so soothing and loving.

So dangerous.

"It didn't work. I still brace for the tragedy, for the other shoe to drop."

"So you added it to your sleeve?"

I wrap my arms around her small body, pulling her into my chest. Lowering my face, I bury it in her hair. Her arms wrap around me, and she holds me just as tight.

So much comfort is here, so much hope, but my anxiety is fiercely waiting. I think about all the rules I'm breaking with her, daring to get attached.

I try to fight it. I tell myself it's safe. We're only fucking, it's not a relationship. We can still walk away from this. She'll go on and be fine without me. I'll live without her.

Lies. They're all lies, and it scares the hell out of me.

I've got to try and get a handle on this, put things back to where they were, keep her in the safe zone if it's not too late.

Tightening my arms around her body one more time, I memorize the feeling, the scent, the warmth of her in my arms. Then I release her.

"Goodnight." I step out of the bed, tucking the blankets into her side.

"You're leaving?" She holds out her hand as I move away. "Stay with me."

I shake my head. "We're heading out early. Get some rest."

Another pouty noise, but I force my feet to move.

Driving down to Second-Chance Farms, I lower the windows so the cool air can swirl around us. It's not as intense as removing the doors, so Edward should be okay in the back.

I don't want to talk.

Rachel bounced around this morning, making coffee, toasting pop-tarts for her and Edward. I nuked a sausage biscuit.

"I wonder which is worse for you—this or that." She pointed from her crap to mine, and her happy taunting was like nails scratching my conflicted insides.

"One morning, I'll make us a real breakfast." The words came out automatically, and I winced.

My goal was to ease us back to the friend zone, not offer to make her breakfast.

"Just name the day, cowboy. I'll wear my PJs." She sidled

up beside me, and my dick responded at once. "Or nothing at all."

My jaw tightened, and I grunted. *Fuck me.* She wrinkled her nose, held my arm, and kissed my cheek, honeysuckle swirling around us.

Now, pulling up to the barn, we're the only ones here. The therapy kids aren't here this week because of the holiday, and Gloria and Sandra took a little road trip to Orange Beach for a romantic getaway.

"It's been a while since I was on a horse." Rachel walks ahead of us down the center of the barn.

Her ass taunts me in those faded jeans, and she's cute as hell in cowboy boots and a long-sleeved maroon henley. It hugs her curves and enhances her tits in a way that's not helping my resolve.

Shiloh and a few of the other horses hang their heads over the doors of their stalls, watching us with big brown eyes.

"We'd better put her on Nala." Edward nods to the gentle old mare in the last stall.

"Good call." I head to the tack room, with him right behind me.

When we emerge, I notice he's wearing a new plaid shirt over his usual tee. I look down at myself and see we match.

"If I didn't know any better, I'd say you two were a team." Rachel winks, holding the door as Edward enters the stall.

A team. The word tightens my shoulders, and the pressure in my mind increases. If something happened to Edward because of me...

I don't answer, going instead to where Shiloh is waiting and saddling him up. Edward's helping his sister, and I've got two horses ready to go by the time he's giving her a leg-up.

"Nala will follow the other horses, but do you know how to command her just in case?"

"I'm pretty sure I remember." She shakes her head, smiling in wonder. "It's like you've been doing this all your life."

"Horses are easy to work with." Edward walks over to Shiloh, placing his foot in the stirrup and swinging onto the horse's back in one fluid move. "Zane taught me a lot."

She looks over her shoulder giving me a warm smile. "He did."

Shifting on Frodo's back, I look down at the reins in my hand unable to shake this tension.

"Lead the way, Eddie!" Rachel calls, and he gives Shiloh a squeeze and a click.

The sleek, inky horse trots out of the barn, and he's a beauty to watch with those long legs and shiny coat. He might not be able to race anymore, but he's still a work of art.

The three of us take off down the pasture in the direction of the bluffs. Edward leads the way with Rachel between us, spurring the horses from a jolty trot to a gentle lope.

He really is doing great. I've been with him every day over the past several weeks, and still I'm impressed by his progress.

His confidence is through the roof, and I think he's going to fit in seamlessly at his new school. Allie said several of the students already recognize him from the library, and he's getting a reputation for being a pool shark.

Rachel is happy, and her happiness swells my chest with pride. It's what I want to give her more than anything. Her blonde hair lifts in the breeze, and I think of her shining eyes, green as the meadow stretching before us. I want her to have a beautiful life, and after everything she's been through, I'll do whatever I can to make sure it happens.

We make our way to the wide walking path that leads up to the large pier. We turn when we get to the park that continues on the scenic drive north, where we stop to give the horses a rest. Edward slides off Shiloh's back, and Rachel slides down to join him.

"I'm going to call you Roy Rogers."

"Who's that?" Edward frowns.

"He was the king of the cowboys. I'm surprised I know something you don't."

I slide off Frodo and stand beside him, watching as the two of them walk to the water's edge.

"Cowboys herd cattle. I'm not a cowboy." Logical as always.

"I'm still really proud of you." She puts her hand on his shoulder lightly. "You've come a long way since we got here."

He nods, looking out at the water. "I like it here. I wasn't sure at first. It was really hot, and I didn't know anybody. But perfect is the enemy of good."

"That's what Zane says." Rachel glances at me, and I rub my neck, looking down. "I think you've done a really good job here. Zane has taught you a lot, and I'm so grateful for it."

She's looking at me, but I pull myself onto Frodo again. "We need to head on back now."

I've got to get to Miss Gina's, and we'll need to feed and tack the horses. Edward goes immediately to where Shiloh and Nala are standing, waiting to give his sister a leg up.

The ride back is quicker, and when we get to the stables, we each take our horses to their stalls. Edward can help Rachel. It's best if I keep my distance.

I carry my heavy leather saddle to the narrow tack room, and stop short when I see her inside, examining the different bridles and equipment. Without making eye contact, I pass her, dropping the blanket on the ground before sliding the saddle onto its horse.

"I've got this!" Her voice is bright, and she grabs the blanket before I have a chance. "Where does it go?"

Stepping up beside her, I take it. "It'll hang on this rack to dry."

She steps to the door, peeking out, then hops over to me, putting her hands on my chest. "I think he's still in the stall brushing Shiloh."

Rising higher, she goes for a kiss, but I pull back, putting my hands over hers, and moving them down.

"Is something wrong?" The confusion in her eyes twists the pain in my stomach.

"I haven't gotten much work done this week."

"I know." Her voice is naughty, and she waggles her eyebrows.

She reaches for my hand, but I avoid it, going to the shelf and picking up a brush instead. It makes no difference, she follows me into the barn, all the way to Frodo's stall.

"You're limping again." Her voice is upbeat, and my chest is tight. "We need another massage session. The real, sports-medicine kind."

"I'm okay." I open the door and step into the stall, placing my hand on the horse's shoulder.

"You've been doing a lot of hip work. It's only natural your back is tired."

"The pain helps me remember…" I don't finish that sentence.

"Remember what?"

Shit. "You wouldn't understand."

"Who would?"

I don't answer. I rub the brush across and down Frodo's back in a few long moves, then bend down and check his hooves for rocks. Finding none, I start for the door again, where Rachel stands, her arms crossed, green eyes blazing.

I tell myself it's better this way.

"Who do you talk to about your pain?"

"What are you doing, Rachel?" It's a question from our early days of bickering.

"I'm trying to find out who you'll let close to you. If not me, then who? The horses?"

My jaw tightens, and I exhale a growl as I pass her. She's not letting me off the hook.

Taking a breath, she changes her tone to gentle urging. "I

love that you have this connection with the animals. I see how beneficial it is to you and to Edward, but you need more. You need people. You need a person."

She stands in the doorway, blocking my way out of this small room, forcing me to face her.

"We've had a good time, Rachel, but it's time to get back to normal."

"What's normal? Pushing me away? Treating me like I don't matter to you?"

Her words are knives in my chest, but I keep my tone firm. "I told you how it is with me. The pain reminds me not to get too close."

"Are you saying you'll never let me in? After everything we've shared?"

My eyes move from hers to the wooden floor. "It's for the best."

"No, it's not, and if you think you're getting away that easily, you're wrong." Exhaling a huff, she turns on her heel and walks away from me.

I tell myself I know what I'm doing.

I go to where Edward is finishing up feeding the other horses, and I hand him the key to my Jeep. "Give this to Rachel. I'll take the truck up to Miss Gina's."

His brow furrows, and he looks around. "Okay."

"I'll see you later on tonight." Reaching out, I pat him on the shoulder. "Good work today. You make a good trail leader."

He looks up at me, and the confident expression on his face is enough.

Chapter 22

Rachel

T HE WINDOWS ARE UP, MY PHONE IS CONNECTED TO THE JEEP, AND I've cued up my favorite drag queen music. I'm rocking my fiercest moves all the way back to Newhope. I will survive.

Edward's brow furrows as he glances at me from his side of the Jeep. "Nala's a good horse. I'm sure Miss Gloria wouldn't mind if you rode her whenever you need to."

I sing a line to my brother about having a new attitude, and he frowns. "Are you okay?"

"Yes." I shake my finger and keep on singing. "My worries are few."

"Okay." He shifts again. "It's just… you usually play this music when things aren't so good."

"Things are *perfect*." I hit the word hard. "I'm a strong, confident woman, and I'm feeling good from my head to my shoes."

Zane Bradford can't shake my confidence. The first time he pushed me away, I was devastated. This time, he's got another thing coming.

It wasn't just a kiss, and it's not just sex. It's a lot more than that—for both of us. I've seen it in his eyes. I've heard it in his words, and he'd better figure himself out before he loses something really good.

We park the Jeep and hop out, walking down to the restaurant. "Dylan, Allie, and I are going to the park to do yoga. Want to walk over?"

"The tournament is this weekend. Benji Maxwell is coming over to practice."

"Who's Benji Maxwell?" I frown as he continues with purpose.

"One of the kids from Second Chance. He's not very good, but I'm going to coach him. His mother asked if I would, and I said yes."

"His mother asked about you?" Blinking wider, I hold the door for him to enter the large dining hall.

"People have heard of me." He says it so calmly.

We enter, and a stocky woman with short brown hair, rosy cheeks, and a sweet smile stands beside a boy who looks a little younger than Edward.

"Hi, I'm Alice Maxwell." She holds out a hand, and I shake it. "It's so nice of Eddie to help Ben. He really wants to play on Sunday."

Ben is dressed in the usual boy uniform—jeans, T-shirt, and navy hoodie. He looks around the room before looking at Edward. "I've never been this far north."

"We live in Barnwell," Alice explains. "It's such a nice restaurant, and Zane is just wonderful with the kids. He put Eddie and Ben together on Shiloh, and they've done so well together."

I only smile. "I'm Eddie's sister Rachel. It's nice to meet you."

"If it's okay, I'll just walk around downtown and do a little shopping?"

"Of course! They'll be fine here." She thanks us and gives Benji cash. I nod to Edward. "We'll only be gone an hour or two. Text me if you need anything."

Watching him walk away in his flannel shirt and ball cap, with Ben following along like a good little student, my anger at Zane melts into frustration. He does so many good things, helping my brother get ready for school, matching him with kids at the farm. For a whole moment, I consider getting back in the Jeep and driving to Miss Gina's to make him say he loves me.

"Nope." I shake my head, pushing that impulse right back down again.

It's time to be strong for myself. I can't heal Zane Bradford. He has to make that decision on his own, and I've got a date with Dylan and Allie.

"Forward fold…" I lean down to touch my toes. "Hands on the ground and walk out into plank."

Allie and Dylan are in front of me on their mats. We're all dressed in yoga pants and hoodies, and my phone plays a reedy-style of music while we move through the flow.

"Lift your glutes into downward-facing dog, and walk your feet and hands together. Focus on your breathing."

We continue moving through the poses, going down to the mat for abdominal work until Allie starts hollering.

"I'm dying over here!" she cries, and Dylan and I start to laugh. "I thought you said this was going to be gentle yoga. My stomach muscles are screaming."

"We're on our last leg." I quip in a soothing tone as we extend our legs while holding a crunch.

"I'm on my last everything!"

We finish in Lotus position, hands in prayer pose in front of our chests. I guide us through cool-down breathing, and we're done.

"Namaste," I say, squinting up at them.

Dylan's eyes are closed, but Allie falls over onto her side.

"Namaste right here. Send Austin with the wheelbarrow to haul me back."

"Allie!" Dylan snorts, pushing her hip. "It wasn't *that* hard. You really need to move more."

"Sorry we're not all prima ballerinas and yoga… sperts. What's a yoga expert called?"

"A yogini?"

"Mmm… I could go for a martini right now."

"Your vacation mode is definitely activated," Dylan laughs.

"It's true!" I shift onto my knees. "We're all on vacation this week. We should have a girls' night!"

I'm ready to party, not sit in my room right across the hall from Dylan's broody older brother analyzing and obsessing over all his problems until I ultimately break down and bang on his door.

No! I really need to do something.

"The restaurant closes early tomorrow," Dylan offers. "What do you say? Meet at the bar at nine?"

"Is that okay with Eddie?" Allie's nose wrinkles.

"If he's had dinner and is all set, I don't have to be in the house. He's not a baby."

"It's a date, then, and I am so here for it. I've been working my ass off." Dylan groans.

Our mats are rolled, water bottles stowed, and we're walking back to the restaurant along the wide, concrete path.

Tilting my head to the side, I consider this. "You know, I think this might be my very first girls' night."

"Don't tell me that!" Allie holds up her hands. "Girl, that is just too sad. We're going to have to pull out all the stops."

"What are the stops?"

"Shots…" Dylan starts.

"Drinking games…" Allie adds.

"Fuck, marry, kill."

"What's that?" My eyes widen.

"We make up different scenarios, and you have to decide

who falls into which category," Allie explains. "Like Chris Evans, Chris Pine, Chris Hemsworth."

"Wait." I stop walking. "I have to decide which of those I'll fuck, marry, or kill?"

"Easy—kill Pine, fuck Evans, marry Hemsworth." Dylan counts off on her fingers.

"What?" Allie cries. "Marry Evans, fuck Hemsworth."

"You still get to fuck Hemsworth if you're married to him, and just imagine waking up to that every day." Dylan's eyes flutter. "And have you seen his dick?"

"What am I going to do until tomorrow night?" I do a little skip.

I'm so glad I'm not a virgin anymore, even if I'm still mad at Zane. I'm not sure how I'd participate in girls' night never having *done it*. It would be too theoretical.

"Have I mentioned you've been really glowing these last few days?" Dylan narrows her eyes at me, and my cheeks flush.

"I don't know what you're talking about." I'm blinking fast, and I know she knows I'm hiding something.

"Okay… you don't have to talk about it yet." She puts her arm around me. "But just know I approve."

Her words nudge the ache I'm hiding behind my anger. I'd love to break down and talk to Dylan about everything, including what happened today, but what would I say? Her brother, whom I've had sex with a million times over the last five days has suddenly withdrawn over past trauma. Trauma he refuses to talk about.

We're back at the restaurant, and the three of us share a hug.

"I'm headed home. I've got to shower." Allie waves. "I plan to sleep in all day, and maybe I'll get up and do something productive before I come back here to get crunk with you ladies!"

I do a little *Whoo!* cheer.

"You'd better leave those expectations at home." Dylan circles her finger in the air. "We are *not* being ladies tomorrow night!"

With a little happy-clap, I follow her into the restaurant.

"I'll see what Thomas made too much of tonight. It'll be our dinner."

"I'll just grab my brother."

I walk over to the side porch to see what Eddie is doing, and I find him with Kimmie and Austin talking like old friends. Austin is pretty sharp at pool as well, and between the two of them, they're clearing the table fast.

Kimmie bounces on her toes, calling out as each ball sinks into a pocket. "Red number seven!"

"That was actually maroon," Eddie corrects her before lining up to sink the last ball.

"Black number eight!" She throws up both hands, shaking her stuffed red turtle over her head. "Eddie Nashville wins again!"

Austin only chuckles, shaking his head. "I guess I'd better stick to football."

The two of them do a fist bump, and I almost start to cry. We never had this in Birmingham, not even at my grandmother's.

I think about how we left, with everyone up in arms pointing fingers and trying to medicate him. My only choice was to pack his bags and bring him here, keep him with me like I've always done.

Straightening, I turn, and my heart stops in my chest. Zane is behind me quietly watching, a hint of a smile curling his lips. He's so beautiful, distant and clinging to those old wounds. I turn away from him because my emotions are already up.

"You're right." I swallow the ache in my throat. "Things are different here."

He doesn't speak, and I wonder if he'll even answer me. I wonder if I want him to.

Then he says, "Austin's a good kid."

"Kimmie is, too." Defiance is my fallback, and he exhales his assent.

"She's a pistol."

We watch as they put away their pool cues, leave the balls in the pockets, and hang the triangle.

My stomach is tight, but I keep my tone steady. "I met Benji this morning. His mother brought him over for Eddie to coach. She said you put them together."

"Yeah." He straightens, pushing his hands in his pockets. "Eddie's a natural teacher."

The heat between us pulses on every heartbeat, and I don't believe he doesn't feel it. I don't believe his arms don't ache to hold me. The pull between us is so strong, it hurts.

"What are you doing, Zane?" I'm using his words this time.

The muscle moves in his jaw, as he shifts his stance before answering quietly. "Keeping you safe."

My response is equally quiet. "I don't think so. I think you're keeping yourself safe, and you're breaking my heart. And yours."

Ice blue eyes lift to mine, but I have to get away from him now. My stomach is tight, and I'm not hungry anymore.

Placing my hand on the screen door, I enter the game room. The trio looks up at us, with bright eyes and smiles.

"Auntie Rachel!" Kimmie skips over to me, and I'm surprised. She's never called me *auntie* before.

"Hey, cutie." I bend down to give her a hug, looking up at my brother. "I'm headed to the house. Dylan has leftovers for dinner, so be sure and get some."

Eddie nods. "Okay. Thanks."

Straightening, I turn and walk away from Zane, not looking back.

Chapter 23

Zane

ZEN BUDDHISM TEACHES THAT ATTACHMENT IS THE SOURCE OF suffering, and fuck if that isn't the absolute truth. I'm so attached to Rachel, my muscles ache. Every molecule in my being wants her.

Being near her last night, watching Eddie bond with Austin and Kimmie, I wanted to wrap my arms around her like real parents. Our little guy has grown so much.

When the fuck did Edward become *our little guy*?

I'm all fucked up, and I don't know what's right. I wake up in a sweat, my stomach tied up in knots worrying about what might happen to her. I said I'm keeping her safe, but is she right? Am I really running away to protect myself?

"Hey man, you've been looking really good lately." Logan walks out, giving my back a slap. "Did you finally get it together with Rachel?"

We're in the studio to pre-record the show for broadcast to-morrow, Thanksgiving Day. Garrett's lined up to join us on the mic, and Jack is on his way.

Oliver Duck waits to record, watching us with interest. He's still not happy with anything Logan does, but I get the feeling we're good. At least he doesn't give me shit, and his older sister seems to like me—a little too much for my taste.

I don't want to lie to Logan, but I also don't want to talk about it. "I'm ready for the show. Let's do this."

"Okay, then." He turns his back to me, and I notice his thumbs flying over the screen of his phone.

Just as fast, my phone lights up.

Logan: He'll neither confirm nor deny.

Garrett: We finally got you laid!!! High fives all around.

Hendrix: High fiving a million angels. Good work, bro.

I cut my eyes at Logan, who isn't facing me.

Zane: I don't know what you assholes are talking about.

Jack: Rachel's a good girl. Two enthusiastic thumbs up.

Zane: You'd better not be texting and driving.

Jack: I'm at the restaurant, dickhead. Dylan's watching Kimmie.

Garrett: Why are you still grumpy? You're getting hot Rachel pussy.

Zane: Don't ever talk about Rachel like that again.

Hendrix: Fuck me, bro's in love.

Zane: I am not in love.

Lie. I am so fucking in love, I'm running scared.

Garrett: The only time I get pissed when someone talks about a lady is when I love her.

Logan: Rachel's really sweet. It's a good match.

Zane: I'm not in love with Rachel. We're not a match. We're not dating.

Garrett: Why the fuck not?

Jack: What?

Logan: Bruh, did she let you down easy?

Zane: She didn't let me down. We were never together.

Logan: I call bullshit. You totally sexed her up.

Jack: Same.

Hendrix: Many men equate settling down with death.

Garrett: Are you looking in the mirror right now, H?

Hendrix: Again, nothing wrong with staying loose. He's only 33?

Jack: He's 35.

Hendrix: Dang, bro, it's time to get serious.

Garrett: Just be still and let it happen.

Zane: Bye.

Garrett: I'm talking to you in one minute!

Zane: Not about this.

Jack arrives, and I cut my eyes at him and Logan as we pull on our headsets. Logan has a shit-eating grin on his face, and the two of them exhale a laugh at my expense.

I don't engage. "Are we going to talk football or what?"

"Keep your shirt on," Jack chuckles.

Oliver punches a button, and Garrett appears on the screen. Logan counts us in, and we start with the usual introduction, welcome back to football chat, and introducing our guests.

Sitting around the table, it feels good to put all my shit aside and talk about the game.

We discuss the season, last week's games, strategy. Garrett and Logan talk about the Pirates and how that's going, then break down the plays and make predictions. Jack fills us in on which young players to watch out for and where the local seniors are headed.

Football is family. It's comfort. It's sitting around the dinner table with Dad when we were kids, after we'd played hard, and he'd give us pointers on how we could improve our game.

We learned so much from him. I miss him every day, and hell, I could sure use his input right now.

When we're finished recording, I'm restless. I repaired Miss Gina's elevator, the kittens are fed, and without the old lady around finding a hundred little jobs for me to do, I've got an afternoon to kill.

If I go to the house, Rachel will probably be there. Hell, if I go to the restaurant, she'll probably be there.

Jack follows me out, and I catch him. "Would you help me bring the truck back to Gloria's?"

"Sure." He hops into his red Ford step-side, and he follows me down the scenic road, all the way to the big white barn in the middle of a wide-open, grassy field bordered with a long white fence.

The sky is low, and it looks like rain is coming. The weather has been warm, so I expect it'll rain tonight and be frigid tomorrow. I park the truck under the carport, thinking I'd check on the horses.

Jack parks his truck and steps out, walking with me into the barn. He knows what we need to do, and I'm glad I asked him for a ride. He can help me check their feed and make sure the barn is secure against the wind and rain.

Jack's never been a big talker. We could do all of this in companionable silence, but he stops beside me at Shiloh's stall, sliding his hand down the horse's shiny dark-chocolate neck.

"What's eating you, Zee?" He glances over at me.

"I thought y'all had decided I was all good. Ready to settle down."

"I've known you a little longer than them."

I huff a laugh, wondering if two years makes that much of a difference. Maybe it does. Hell, less than an hour ago, I was at the station wishing I could talk to my dad. Jack's always been the next best thing.

"It's not as simple as that for me."

He pats the horse, turning to face me. "It's not simple for anyone, but I will say I haven't seen you so happy in a long time, definitely not since you've been back home."

"It's been a while."

"Is this about her dad?"

"Nah, you were right about that. Rachel's nothing like Jayden."

"So what's the problem?"

My gaze moves to the big, open door, where gray clouds gather like ghosts crowding closer to hide the blue sky.

Saying this out loud is difficult. "I haven't been the same since my injury. I can't shake it."

"Are you in pain?" His dark brow furrows, and I shake my head.

"Not physically." Rachel took care of that. "It's more a sense that good things aren't meant for me. They're for you and Dylan and Rachel…" I exhale heavily. Saying her name makes me miss her. "Not me."

"I get that."

"You do?" I frown up at him.

We turn and walk slowly up the alley to the next stall.

"Sure." He nods, reaching up to pat Frodo's gray neck. "You lost everything in one bad play. You're bound to feel disoriented, lost. Hell, I'm sure there's trauma there."

It's the same thing the therapist said, the few times I talked to him. "Knowing it doesn't make it go away."

After a month of therapy, I couldn't talk about it anymore. Nothing changed.

"Talk therapy didn't work for me."

"Okay, so what if you try something different?" He glances up at me. "What if you work on how you *think* about situations? Everything that happened, that was your path, but everyone has their own path. What if Rachel is here to help you heal?"

Groaning, I turn, clasping my hands behind my neck. "It sounds like wishful thinking."

"It's a real type of therapy, and it works." His tone is firm. "You'll never stop feeling bad if you don't change your mindset. It's called distorted thinking. Sure, a lot of bad shit happened to us. We all lost things, but flip it around. You front-loaded the bad, and now it's time to let good into your life."

My shoulders are tight. My chest is tight, and I know it's going to take more than one conversation to fix what's wrong with me. Still, I'm willing to give anything a try if it'll stop this cycle. "It's a nice idea."

"Practice it. Every time you go dark, actively stop it. Change your mind. Come back."

It feels too simple, but I hear what he's saying. I see the work. "When did you get so wise?"

He reaches out to grip my shoulder. "Things get broken, but you know what happens when a bone breaks? It heals back stronger. You've had a lot of breaks, but you're stronger than you think, brother."

"I think Dylan might take that prize."

"Dylan's a fighter, and so are you. Dylan's path led her to Logan. Let Rachel's path heal your wounds."

The fist is still in my chest. "If I hurt her or let her be hurt, I wouldn't get over it."

"You would." Blue eyes fix on mine. "We're here for you, but you've got to own your strength. It's in you, man. I see it every day. We all do."

His fingers tighten on my shoulder, and he pulls me into a hug. We slap each other's backs, and looking around, I think we're done here. I think I'm ready to get my head out of my ass and track down my angry pixie.

I sure have given her a reason to be pissed at me this time.

Chapter 24

Rachel

"Specially brewed just for you." Allie places a mason jar of iced, bright purple liquid in front of me.

It looks like something out of a circus with a red and white striped paper straw stuck in the center of the gold, screw-top lid.

Allie's wearing ripped, faded jeans with cowboy boots and a long-sleeved black sweater with the sleeves pushed up. Over her shoulder is a bulging cloth bag.

"What is it?" I lift the container, inspecting the drink and unscrewing the lid so I can give it a sniff.

I'm dressed in my black yoga pants and my long-sleeved gray sweater. Edward's been playing pool nonstop to be ready for Sunday. Benji was over for a little while, and I fed them both dinner before the little guy went home.

Zane was at the radio station recording the show all day, and I left before he got back. He's the last person I feel like seeing or even thinking about today. Or any day.

"It's grape Jolly Rancher moonshine!" She lifts both arms overhead in a *V*. "The one constructive thing I did today."

I cough, holding my hand over my nose. "Tastes like… burning!"

"It's supposed to taste like grape." She frowns. "Let me try it."

I pass her the purple jar of death, and she sips. "Holy maracas—grapes on fire!"

"That does it, hand it over." Dylan holds out her hand. She's also in faded jeans with her green Cooters & Shooters tee and flip-flops, and when she takes a sip, her brown eyes bug out. "Jeez Louise! What is that? Everclear?"

"Maybe." Allie jerks her chin, taking the jar from her and sipping again. "It gets better with time. I can taste the grape now."

"Your taste buds are numb," Dylan quips. "If you drink any more, you'll have to spend the night here."

"Austin can pick me up."

"Tell him to bring the wheelbarrow!" Dylan leans forward on the bar laughing. "Okay, for our inaugural girl's night, I made my special goat cheese toasts drizzled with ghost-pepper-infused honey and almond slivers."

She passes her hand, game-show-style over an assortment of food platters on the bar, pausing at the first one.

My eyes widen. "Wow, that is fancy! Although, after the moonshine, I'm not sure my mouth can take any more heat."

"I also have non-spicy honey ones on this tray." She gestures to another platter opposite the hot one.

I grab a slice of toast, popping it into my mouth and immediately groaning. "That is delicious!"

"For the record, I also made cheesy toast this afternoon," Allie holds up a finger, taking another sip of moonshine. "And I ate all of it."

I almost spit my bite laughing, but I catch it with my napkin. "Give back my special drink. You're having too much fun."

She puts the jar in front of me. "I think I'm drunk now."

"I also have an over-the-top hummus platter with feta, olives, prosciutto, corned beef, and lemons. And all this pita." She pulls out a plastic bag of round flatbreads.

"Gimmie." I reach for a cube of feta to pop in my mouth.

"I'm picking up on a goat cheese vibe." Allie circles her hands over the bar of food, before grabbing one of the hot toasts.

"I made Pizza Rolls!" I hold up a bowl full of little tomatoey squares. "Or Mr. Totino made them. I found a box in the freezer, and Thomas said I could take it."

"Garrett must've left those." Allie frowns. "There's no way Craig would eat frozen pizza rolls. Why didn't we invite Craig?"

"As much as I love my bestie, he's still a boy." Dylan takes two more sips of my moonshine and hands it to me again.

I take another long sip and make a sad face. "We killed my special drink."

"Oh, no, there's more!" Allie hops over to her bag and pulls out a plastic milk jug full of bright purple liquid. "Knock yourself out!"

We all cheer, and Dylan hops over to the PA system. "We need music!" She presses buttons, and yacht rock fills the empty dining hall.

"Nope!" Allie is off her stool at once. "As much as I love 'Reminiscing,' tonight is a party night. We need dance tracks."

"Take it away, DJ!" Dylan jogs back to where I'm sitting, grinning from a barstool while Allie fires up Charli xcx.

"Sam Allen thought Chappell Roan was Charli xcx." I am definitely feeling my special moonshine if I'm bringing him up.

"Poor Sam," Dylan leans closer to me on the bar. "How's it going with Zane?"

"Stop!" I hold up my hand, closing my eyes. "No boy talk. Tonight is all about having fun!"

"You're not having fun? But you've been so glowy and smiley, I was going to offer to take Edward for a drive." She waggles her eyebrows.

My lips twist, and she scoops my hand off the bar. "Oh, no! What happened?"

I shrug, not really wanting to talk about Zane. "He shut it all down."

"What?" Allie skips back to where we're sitting. "Why?"

"We were very close." Leaning forward, I meet both their eyes. "All the way close. Then he said everything he touches gets hurt, and he doesn't want to hurt me, and he wants to keep me safe."

"Oh my God, if the choice is a bear in the woods or Zane Bradford, give me Zane!" Allie yells. "He's so good! Have you seen how sweet he is with your brother? And that little Benji kid?"

"Yes, and it's not good at all," I argue. "It sucks!"

"It's a total lie. Zane is completely in love with you." Dylan cuts her eyes at Allie. "And I know who you're completely in love with."

"No!" Allie pinches her arm, which makes Dylan holler.

"Wait, what? Who?" I look from one to the other, and Allie shakes her head.

"I'm not saying his name or the fairies will hear it and it'll never happen."

Wrinkling my nose, I take another sip of grape moonshine. "I've never heard that before. What fairies?"

"It's why you knock on wood," Dylan explains. "So like I could say Allie's in love with Jack..." She raps her knuckles on the top of the bar with every word, "And the fairies didn't hear a thing because I knocked wood."

"You did *not* just say that out loud!" Allie taps on her phone, and "Man on the Moon" by Megan Moroney starts playing.

I count off on my fingers. "First, perfect song, and second, perfect guy for you!"

"Somebody tell him that," Allie pouts, crossing her arms. "Although, to be fair, he is Austin's coach. We work at the same school. It's probably not a good idea."

"If I know my oldest brother, he's doing *all* the math." Dylan pops a hot toast into her mouth. "He's been burned in the past, you both have kids…"

"I know." Allie leans on her hand. "Why does he have to be so damn hot?"

"And if I know my second oldest brother…" Dylan puts her arm around my shoulders, giving me a squeeze. "He'll get his act together. I can't remember the last time I saw Zane smile so much."

"He's got a great smile." My lips twist, and my eyes heat. I blink to my fingers on the bar. "If you're lucky that dimple will appear."

"You got a dimple smile?" Dylan bounces on her toes. "I predict he'll come around sooner than you think."

"Uh-oh." Allie sees my watery eyes. "No tears—it's time for fuck, marry, kill!"

"Yes!" I clap, lifting my chin and shaking the blues away. "How does it work?"

"I have everything…" Dylan digs in her bag, pulling out strips of paper and pens, putting them in front of us. "Everyone gets thirty seconds to write their response."

"Thirty seconds?" Allie cries.

"I want your first impulse." Dylan puts a plastic hourglass timer on the bar. "Some of these could take forever."

I take another sip of moonshine, and I'm feeling no pain. "I have some options, too!"

"Perfect, we'll take turns." Dylan pushes her dark hair off her shoulder. "First is an easy one. Nose piercing, eyebrow piercing, dick piercing?"

Allie is already writing when Dylan flips the little hourglass, but I'm stuck chewing my lip. *What would that feel like?*

The door opens, and my stomach pitches when Logan, Jack, and Zane enter the restaurant like a trio of male models. Zane's eyes immediately land on mine, and his brow lowers. Something different is in his gaze, something hungry, but I tighten my lips, turning away to face the bar.

"No!" Dylan holds up her finger, hopping off her stool. "It's girls' night. Boys are not allowed. I already told Craig—"

"Keep your shirt on, we're not staying." Logan meets his feisty fiancée halfway, putting his hand on her lower back and leaning down to kiss the top of her head.

He's dressed in jeans and a long-sleeved, dark-green sweater. His wavy brown hair is pushed back, and warm blue eyes hold hers.

"We're going to grab some beers and head out to the pool tables. You won't even know we're here."

"Where's Kimmie?" Dylan looks from him to Jack, who's also in jeans and a maroon henley that accentuates his broad shoulders.

Coach Bradford really is hot.

"She's at the house watching YouTube with Edward." Jack goes behind the bar and takes out three Yuengling longnecks.

"What are they watching on YouTube?" Dylan's brow arches.

"Pool Sharks."

"They like that?" I ask.

"Eddie's glued to the screen. I expect Kimmie will be asleep in ten minutes." He hands Zane and Logan their beers.

Zane lingers a moment, and I feel his eyes on me. Shimmers of heat vibrate over my skin, but I won't look at him. He made his bed, and I'm not giving him the satisfaction of seeing how much I want him right now.

I'm fierce.

"Come on." Jack lightly punches his arm. "It's girls' night."

"How'd the show go today?" Allie asks.

Dylan's and my eyes cut to where she's leaning against the bar in Jack's direction. He pauses, blue eyes meeting hers, and a half-smile curls his full lips.

"It went well." He seems like he wants to take a step closer to her, and I can't breathe. "Garrett's always fun, and Logan and Zane are pros."

"He's being modest." Logan grips his shoulder. "Jack fits in like he's done radio all his life, and everybody loves hearing what Coach Bradford has to say."

"I know Austin will be listening tomorrow."

Jack's eyes blink away, and he nods. "He's a good kid."

We're all facing each other, and Luke Bryan is singing about country girls. Tension crackles in the air, but Dylan breaks it with a clap.

"We'll see you all tomorrow. Now get."

Logan huffs a laugh, wrapping his arm around her waist and lifting her off her feet. "Okay, danger girl." He puts her down with a kiss and starts for the screen door that leads to the pool area. Stopping, he reaches for one of the little honey toasts on the bar. "Snacks?"

"Ghost pepper!" Dylan yells, and he tosses it back so fast, we all laugh.

"Been there."

"Let's go." Jack pats his back, and they disappear through the door.

As soon as they're gone, the three of us all turn, giving each other wide eyes. Our heads are together, and we're giddy and laughing, high on grape moonshine.

"He was totally checking you out," I say to Allie.

"Zane was totally checking *you* out!"

Dylan only shakes her head. "Those boys have it bad."

Allie slaps her palm on the bar. "Let's play! What's your answer?"

I look at my blank sheet. "I couldn't decide. You go first."

"Kill the nose, fuck the dick, and marry the eyebrow," Dylan answers like it's so obvious.

"Really?" Allie shakes her head. "We are such opposites. I'd kill the dick, fuck the nose and marry the eyebrow."

"Kill the dick?" I chew my lip. "You wouldn't want to try it?"

"Rachel's kinky." Dylan elbows my side, and my face heats. "It's just a game."

"My turn!" Allie pours us all a fresh round of grape jet fuel.

"I'm not sure I should drink any more."

"Nurse it." She pats my arm. "Ready?"

"I'm ready!" Dylan grabs the timer.

"Paul Mescal, Paul McCartney, Paul Rudd. Go!"

Dylan flips the hourglass down, and Allie has her answers in two seconds. Again, I'm chewing my lip.

"Rachel!" Allie fusses. "What now?"

Leaning closer, I whisper, "Who's Paul Mescal?"

"He was in that *Napoleon* movie with Joaquin Phoenix?"

I shake my head. "Didn't see it."

"*Normal People* on Hulu? About those Irish students who fall in love and have lots of sex?" I shake my head again. "He's got a really big dick."

"Oh my God," Dylan snorts, taking another sip of killer grape. "He does, though."

"Time's up!"

"Wait!" I quickly scribble my answer. "Okay."

"Me first," Allie says. "Fuck Paul Mescal, marry Paul Rudd, kill Paul McCartney."

Dylan gasps, eyes wide. "Evil woman! You'd kill Sir Paul?"

"Please. He's had a good, long life." She motions to me. "Rach?"

"Fuck Paul Rudd, kill Paul Mescal, marry Paul McCartney." I squint my nose. "Just because I don't know who he is."

"Good call." Dylan holds up her hand for a high five. "Paul McCartney could die at any time, and you get all that Beatles money!"

"And *I'm* the evil one?" Allie cries. "You're devious."

"You killed Paul Mescal, too?" I lean over to see Dylan's sheet, but she shakes her head. "I killed Paul Rudd. He's old, and I wanted to try some big Irish dick."

I cackle, holding my hands over my face as I fall back on my stool. "You're right. Can I change my answer?"

"No." Allie scoops up the timer. "You're up, Rach."

"Yay!" I bounce in my seat. "Here goes: Superman, Iron Man, Aquaman."

"Whoa." Dylan's brows rise, and Allie flips the hourglass slowly. "As in Henry Cavill, Robert Downey Jr., Jason Momoa?"

I shrug. "Whatever works for you."

They both sit back frowning, and I write my answers quickly. I'm ready for this one.

"Gah, Rachel, way to shut down the game."

I wiggle my butt back and forth in my chair, humming the melody to Luke Bryan's "Country Girl (Shake It For Me)." That's when I notice a shadow hanging around the screen door separating the bar area from the pool area. I can't tell who it is, but from the way my body's responding, I can make a good guess.

"Time's up!" I call. "Dylan?"

"That was too hard!" she whines.

"That's what she said," Allie snorts, leaning to the side, and I'm pretty sure we've all had enough purple drink.

"Fuck Jason, marry Henry, kill Robert." Her shoulders droop, and Allie shakes her head.

"You disappoint me." She frowns. "It's clearly fuck Henry, marry Robert, kill Jason."

"You'd kill Jason Momoa?" My eyes widen. "But he's so big and hot!"

"That's the problem." Allie curls her nose. "He's too sweaty. I'm thinking he smells like patchouli or BO. Or both."

"He does not!" I cry, offended.

"I guess we know who Rachel's fucking," Dylan yells, laughing.

The screen door opens, and Zane enters the room with his brow lowered. That muscle in his jaw is tight, and he looks like he's ready to rip somebody's head off.

"Zane Bradford!" Dylan yells. "Get out! You are not a girl!"

"I'm getting fresh beers for me and Logan." He slides the refrigerator open and takes out two Yuenglings. "Who are y'all talking about?"

"It's fuck, marry, kill, now get out." Dylan throws a rolled-up napkin at him.

"What does that mean?" He's not leaving.

He's actually acting jealous again, and I'm getting angry.

Allie explains, "We get three options, and we have to sort them."

"Go." Dylan hops off her stool and rounds the bar, catching his arms and pushing him to the door.

"Okay," he exhales, cutting his eyes to me again.

This time our eyes lock, and the hint of a smile on his lips floods my body with lust—followed quickly by anger. Why is he in here snooping around like he's going to do something? It's just like with Sam Allen. He won't let me talk to anyone, then he tells me we can't be together. I bet Sam Allen wouldn't push me into the Friend Zone after the kind of sex Zane and I had.

Reaching out, I grab a handful of Pizza Rolls to eat.

"Goodnight, ladies. Goodnight, Rachel." The low vibration of his voice tickles my stomach, and I consider throwing them at him.

How dare he single me out?

Purple drink clearly makes me feisty, and I've clearly had enough.

Elvis sings "Return to Sender," and I slide off my barstool. "I think I'd better call it a night or I might not make it to Thanksgiving."

Dylan pulls out water bottles, placing one in front of each of us. "Hydrate while we clean up."

Nodding, I open the bottle and take a long drink while eating a few more honey-toasts. "These are really good."

"Thanks! They're so easy to make." Dylan reaches beneath the bar and pulls out a plastic container. "We can put them out as appetizers before lunch tomorrow."

"Do you need help with prep?" Allie polishes off the last of the Pizza Rolls.

"Thomas and I have it covered. He's already got the turkey marinating in the fridge, and I've got the dressing waiting to go in the oven. All you need to do is show up."

"We have to do more than that." I frown, tilting my head.

"You can help with cleanup!" Dylan laughs. "It's my least favorite job."

"Consider it done." I help her stack the plastic containers in the bar fridge, and Allie gives us all hugs.

"I'd better walk home."

"By yourself?" My brow furrows.

The guys filter in from the pool area, and Logan goes to Dylan, tugging her ponytail so he can kiss her forehead.

"Still going?" he asks.

"Girls' night has concluded. We're just cleaning up, and trying to figure out how to get Allie home." Dylan says it looking straight at Jack, and Allie's eyes widen as she glares at our friend.

"I can take you. I've got to drive home."

"Haven't you been drinking?" Allie's voice is flustered.

"I only had one beer. I'm good." Jack smiles, and her cheeks flush. "Just have to grab Kimmie."

She nods, and they start for the door. The food is all packed up, and Logan follows Dylan to the kitchen, where she'll put the platters in the industrial sized dishwasher. My throat tightens, because they all left me here with him.

Zane stands beside the bar facing me, and I'm still buzzy, even though I've drunk an entire bottle of water and eaten one million toasts. I need to get to bed, but what I want more than anything is him. My emotions are all over the place.

I'm mad at him, but it's because I miss him. I want to be wrapped in his strong arms, in that comforting place where I fit like a lost puzzle piece finally found.

"Ready to walk back?" His quiet voice is warm liquid in my veins.

My eyes flutter shut, and I shake my head no. "I'm not walking back with you."

He exhales, looking at the large windows, which are usually open to catch the bay breezes. Tonight they're closed, and raindrops cling to the glass.

"We're going to the same place, Rachel."

"No, we're not." My eyes flash, and that stubborn survival streak rises in my chest. "I'm going to a place where men don't walk away from the good right in front of them because it's not perfect."

"Rachel..."

He takes a step towards me, but I take off for the door. I'm practically running when I push through it, and the rain hits my face in big drops. It's cold rain, and I can feel where it mixes with the hot tears on my cheeks.

Blinking through the moisture, I look for the lights on the ground, lining the path to the house in the darkness. I'm not running, and I hear his voice.

"Rachel..."

"Leave me alone." I pick up the pace.

"I need to talk to you." He reaches for me, trying to pull me into his arms, but I won't let him.

"I don't want to talk to you." I wave my hands, preventing his strong arms from surrounding me. "So many things are broken, but I have to believe I can make them better. I want something better, and I won't let you hurt me again."

"I never want to hurt you—"

"I know, you only want to keep me safe."

"Look at me."

The rain is coming down harder, and I blink up to his tortured blue eyes. "I'm sorry. I'm so sorry, Rachel. I'm sorry for running. I want to make it up to you. I want to give you everything you deserve." Reaching out, he pulls me into his arms, close against his chest. "Let me show you."

My body shudders, and tears warm my cheeks. "What do I deserve?"

"Everything." He kisses away my tears. "You deserve every beautiful thing, my beautiful girl. You're smart and strong and funny and sweet. You take all my pain away, and you help me remember how to play. You make me remember what I was like before the darkness came."

"What are you saying?"

"Don't you see?" He slides the cold rain off my face with his hand. "I love you, Rachel. I've never loved anyone the way I love you. You're my light."

More tears huff through my lips, and my insides melt. "You love me?"

"I love you so much, it terrified me. But I don't want to lose you. I never want to be without you. Will you forgive me for being afraid? For hurting you?"

If he weren't holding me so tight, I'd collapse into a puddle.

"Yes…" I nod as laughter bubbles in my chest. "I never believed you anyway. I knew you loved me, but you had to say it for yourself."

"I'll say it every day." Leaning down, he covers my mouth with his, and I'm lost in his kiss.

Our mouths open, and our tongues curl together. Heat floods my freezing body all the way to my core, and I wiggle my arms out of his tight embrace so I can cup his cheeks.

His lips slide across mine, and he lifts his chin, looking towards the house. "I want to make love to you."

"Go to Miss Gina's!" Dylan yells, and we both jump as she runs past, squealing in the downpour. "I've got Eddie—go!"

"Do it!" Logan slaps Zane on the back, and they keep running to the house.

Zane looks down at me, and I slip out my tongue to lick my bottom lip. Blue eyes heat at the motion, and I feel his body harden against my stomach. Without another word, he turns, gripping my hand in his and leading us in a swift jog to the Jeep.

Chapter 25

Zane

RAIN FALLS OUTSIDE THE SCREENED WINDOWS, AND RACHEL'S SOFT body is above me in the bed. Reaching up, I hold her cheeks, pulling her face to mine as her hot pussy slides up and down my rigid cock.

"I love you," I whisper, moving my lips along the top of her cheek.

"I love you." Her soft voice meets my ears just ahead of her lips.

It's a release unlike any I've ever known. It's freedom and decadence. The first time, it was like being set free from a trap. Now it's like chains falling away. She's always been mine. We only had to find each other.

Her journey has led her to me. Our paths have come together, and it's coming out of the darkness. She's my light guiding me home. She's my companion, holding my hand in the dark.

I'll walk through fire to have her body, and I'll storm the gates of hell to keep her safe.

Her fingers thread in my hair, and my hands move over her shoulders, pulling her to my chest. We kiss and kiss, lips chasing and pulling.

I drag my teeth along the top of her shoulder, and her lips trace the side of my neck. Her tongue touches my skin, and I return to kiss her once more. I can't get enough of touching her, holding her, inhaling her honeysuckle scent, tasting the fresh water I made her drink mixed with salt and sex.

"Oh, God, I'm coming." Her hips move faster, and she grips the top of my shoulders.

Her back arches, and she grinds in a way that erases my mind. Her insides grip and pull my cock, and I exhale a deep groan. I'm not far behind her.

Rolling us to the side, I move my hand between us to massage her clit. One pass over that rigid bud and she jumps, wailing loudly as her body trembles. I'm inside her, the flex of her muscles is all around me, and my cock thickens. My ass tightens, and my balls tingle as I release, thrusting hard before holding, coming deep inside her hot body.

We're breathing fast, still kissing. It's a hunger made ravenous by our separation, reinforced by the promise of always being together.

My forehead rests against hers, and we pant, kissing lightly a few more times before I fall back on the bed and she cuddles against my body. "How are you feeling?"

"Like I've been properly laid." Her cheek is on my chest, and I chuckle, threading my fingers through her damp hair.

She exhales a soft, contented noise that makes me smile. "What are you thinking about?"

Her head lifts and pretty green eyes meet mine. "All you've ever done is help me. You fix things, Miss Gina's house, those kids at equine therapy…"

"They're not broken."

"No, but you help them fix what hurts."

I think about this and nod with assent. "Okay, but why are you saying this?"

Her eyes drift from mine to my chest, where she traces her finger in a circle over my heart. "To thank you."

Cupping her hand in mine, I lift it to my cheek. "You don't have to thank me."

She blinks up to her hand in mine. "I used to be so worried all the time. I was afraid of what might happen, and whether I could handle it on my own. What would happen if I couldn't?"

My brow lowers, and I lift her hand again, kissing her wrist. "I never want you to be afraid of that. You're not alone."

A smile lifts her cheeks, and her eyes meet mine again. "I haven't been afraid once since I met you. Every day, since that first time we were here together in this bed, I've only felt found and safe and home."

Pride warms my chest, and I've given up fighting that stubborn sense of ownership taking root in my heart when it comes to her.

"I wonder what changed," I tease, and a puff of air escapes her lips.

She rises higher, kissing my lips, and when she slides down again, her eyes close. The temperature is falling, but we're warm in bed together. I think she's asleep when she speaks again.

"In Japan they have a technique where they use 14-karat gold to repair broken pottery." Her finger traces my chest again. "They melt the gold and use it to create something new and even more valuable. It's called *Kintsugi*. It means 'golden seams.' Isn't that beautiful?"

"Jack reminded me today when bones break they heal back stronger."

Her head lifts, and she rests her chin on her hand looking into my eyes. "Stronger, like gold."

Leaning down, I press my lips to hers once more. Gold, like the start of a new day. The bright sunlight after being so long in darkness.

"Remind me never to make grape moonshine ever again." Allie sits on the other side of Rachel, holding her glass of iced tea to her cheek.

"You were so sweet to make me a special drink for my first girls' night." Rachel rests her head on her friend's shoulder. "Don't ever do it again."

I chuckle, putting my arm around my girl and pulling her to me. "Eat something. It'll make you feel better."

The rain stopped overnight, but as predicted, the temperature dropped. We're all dressed in sweaters and jeans for the big day.

Gathering at Cooters & Shooters has become our Thanksgiving Day family tradition. It's all decked out for the holiday, and we know to be here at noon.

Once everyone arrives for lunch, we gather for a family prayer led by Jack, then break into serving lines to sample the varieties of turkey Thomas and Jack made—oven baked, fried, and smoked. Dylan made the side dishes, dressing, spicy and non-spicy mac and cheese, fruit salad, cranberry dressing, green bean casserole, corn, and rolls.

As we make our plates, we drift out to the long table situated in the middle of the dining room with Jack at one end and Thomas at the other.

Family and friends filter out of the kitchen and join us as they make their plates.

Allie stabs her scoop of cornbread dressing. "It tastes so good. I just wish the restaurant would stop rocking."

"Oof, I hate that feeling." Logan sits across from us, holding a heaping helping of smoked turkey, dressing, cranberry sauce, rolls, corn, and cheesy pasta.

"Is anything left in the kitchen?" Allie teases, and he tosses a grape at her.

"Not grapes! They're Satan's tiny hand grenades."

"I love grapes," Rachel argues. "It's not their fault you nu-clearized them."

"Is that a word?" Dylan joins us with a plate piled high with cornbread dressing. "I can't believe I made it out of bed this morning. Whose idea was it to have girls' night on the Wednesday before Thanksgiving?"

"I think it was yours." Rachel rests her head on my shoulder, and I kiss it.

"That's all you're having?" I glance at my little sister's plate.

"It's the only thing that doesn't make me feel woozy."

Logan has already finished off half his serving. "We should play a friendly game of football after lunch. Let you sweat out all those toxins."

The girls make horrified faces, and my stomach twists with panic. As soon as it hits, I remind myself of what Jack said at the barn. *Distorted thinking. Change your mindset.* Here goes: Just because we play football as a family on Thanksgiving, doesn't mean something bad will happen.

"I'm down," I say, and Dylan's eyes flicker to mine.

"Really?"

"Sure. Logan's right. Exercise will make you feel better."

"I think it'll make me urp," Allie groans.

"Don't say that word or I will!" Rachel puts a hand over her face.

"Here." I tear off a piece of bread and hand it to her.

She slips it into her mouth, and when I look up three pairs of eyes are watching us. "What?"

"Y'all are so cuuute!" Dylan cries, leaning hard on her elbow and taking a tiny bite of dressing. Her brown eyes are warm as she watches me. "It's been too long since I've seen that smile. I love it."

"It's been too long since I felt like smiling." I rub my hand up and down Rachel's back, and she lifts her chin to kiss my neck.

"Where's Eddie?" Allie asks, leaning her head on her hand.

"Glued to the pool." Dylan nods in the direction of the tables where my brother and Benji are hanging out with Austin. "I made him a plate of turkey and dressing right when we got here, so he's been fed."

"Thanks, Dee. It was sweet of Austin to pick up Benji." Rachel sits up, taking another bite of turkey. "I'm actually starting to feel a little better."

"The water helped," I say, patting her back.

"I'm sure the exercise didn't hurt." Dylan teases. "Did you swallow some of the other white meat last night, Rach?"

"Oh my God," Rachel leans forward with a snort.

"Good one." Allie points at her.

"Dylan." My eyes level on hers. "Spare me."

"Sorry, Grandpaw." She holds up her hands, and the three of them laugh more.

As much as I don't want to talk about my sex life with my little sister, I really like her and Rachel being so close. It bonds us tighter, making us feel more like a foregone conclusion.

"How's the turkey?" Jack walks in carrying two plates of food, followed closely by Kimmie waving a stuffed green turtle over her head.

"Look, Uncle Zee! Uncle Grizz sent me a green cooter!" She waves it, jumping around in a circle before running to the other end of the table. "Look, Baba, it's a river cooter!"

"That's right." Thomas leans back grinning and patting her little back. "Do you know why they call it a cooter, Kimmie Joy?"

"Because it's funny?" Her eyes are wide.

"*Kuta* is the word for *turtle* in Mali and Senegal."

"You're kidding." I turn to Thomas. "I thought some old redneck made that up."

"Nope." Thomas smiles. "They just mispronounced it."

"I have to show Aussie and Eddie and Ben!" She starts for the pool area, but her dad stops her.

"After you eat." Jack's voice is firm, and her path makes an arc back to where her dad is sitting.

She climbs into his lap, and stabs a forkful of dressing. "Mm! Good dressing, Aunt Deedee!" Then she stabs a forkful of turkey. "Mm, good turkey, Daddy! Thank you!"

She kisses his cheek and hops off his lap, running for the pool area. His brow wrinkles, and Dylan leans forward to console him.

"At least she said thank you!"

Jack digs in, and we lean back chatting and talking about the things we're thankful for this year. With family, food, and good health out of the way, Dylan is thankful for her ballet classes. Logan is thankful for the radio station being such a hit. I have to agree.

When we sat around this time last year shooting the shit about football, I didn't really believe him when he said we had a hit show on our hands. Fast-forward a year, and it's not just a radio show, it's a YouTube channel with almost a million followers already.

"I'm thankful for finding all of you." Rachel looks around the table at the warm, smiling faces, before elbowing me in the side. "I'm especially thankful for this grumpy guy who has done so much for me and Eddie."

"I'm thankful for you reminding me how to smile again."

"And on that note, where's the cleanup crew?"

Everyone except Jack, Thomas, and Dylan hops up and starts collecting plates. The girls pack up the leftovers, while Logan and I load the big dishwasher. With so many hands, we're done pretty fast.

"Ready for a friendly game before dessert?" Logan has a football in his hand, and he tosses it in the air.

"You'll have to teach me how to throw a football first," Rachel laughs, shaking her head.

"I'll teach you to throw a ball." I reach out, catching her around the waist, and pulling her to my side.

My insides are churning, but I'm taking it slow, breathing, changing my mindset.

"I'll get Austin." Allie walks into the dining room. "Do you think Eddie will want to play?"

"Ask him." Rachel calls, then looks up at me smiling. "You'll have to teach him to throw a football as well."

"I wonder if Eddie Nashville would like to learn football?" I hook my thumb in the belt loop on her jeans.

"You'll have to ask him."

"We're ready!" Allie's back with Austin and the boys.

We walk as a group down the wide path along the bay to the park. Several people are out walking as well after the big meal, and we speak to old friends as we pass. Logan's tossing the ball, and Austin grabbed one as well, which draws attention.

Folks wander up to the field where we do a little warm up before diving into teams. I pull Rachel to the side to show her how to throw a ball. Austin waits on the other side of the field.

"Spread your fingers out." I hold her small hand. "Put your index finger closest to the point and your middle finger on the first lace…"

I show her how to pull back, shift her weight on her feet, and add a little flick of the wrist as if dunking a basketball, which she points out she also doesn't know how to do.

Her first throw goes straight to the ground, bounces wildly, which makes her yelp and duck, and then rolls off the field.

"I don't think that was right." She looks up at me, and it takes all my strength not to laugh.

Austin is across the field holding his hand over his mouth and bending at the waist.

Eddie stands beside her frowning. "I don't think you lifted your elbow properly."

"I'm never going to get it." She wilts, but I'm not letting her give up.

"Come on. It just takes practice."

We do it a few more times, and she manages to keep it off the ground, although it's wobbling wildly.

"That's good!" I encourage her, and she cuts her eyes at me.

I clarify, "It's good enough for whatever we're doing out here. You don't have to throw it. Just block and run."

Rachel balances one foot on the ball, putting her hands on my waist and grinning into my face before kissing my lips. "Patience is one of your best qualities."

My hands are on her waist, and I grin down at her adorable face. "I'm not feeling very patient right now. I'm ready to wrap up this friendly game and get you alone."

"I wish I'd been a cheerleader at the high school where you played."

My voice lowers. "You definitely wouldn't have been a virgin at thirty."

"If you two are done, we're lining up." Logan jogs over to where we're canoodling.

I give her another quick kiss before lifting her off the ball and jogging with her to the line of scrimmage.

Allie's not playing. Eddie and Ben decide to watch as well, so it's Logan, Dylan, and Austin versus Jack, Rachel, and me. Allie says she'll be the referee slash cheerleader for all, and when we line up, I'm right across from Logan.

"I miss Grizz wisecracking at the lineup." Logan grins. "The brother's chat is going to love hearing about this."

Austin has fallen back, and he counts down to make the snap. We all break, running in different directions. Rachel drives forward to force the pass. I'm on Logan, who I know Austin is looking to be his receiver. I've got him covered too well, so he has to throw it to Dylan, where Jack easily intercepts by plucking it out of the air over her head.

"No fair!" Dylan shoves him, and I start to laugh.

Some things never change.

We all line up ready to go again, and this time it's our ball. Jack is quarterback, and I'm down the field, guarded by Logan. Austin covers Rachel, and Dylan runs at Jack. He puts out a hand, holding her back, and her arms flail as she tries to grab him.

She makes a quick, ballerina twirl, and he's forced to pass it to Rachel. Her eyes widen when she sees the ball headed her way.

"I've got it!" She yells, but my stomach pitches when I see Austin running at her hard.

She jumps, completing the pass, but as she's coming down, he grabs her around the waist, bringing her to the ground. He hops up at once, but Rachel doesn't. She's still lying on the ground not moving. Her arms and legs are spread, and she's gazing blankly at the blue sky as if she's dead.

My knees weaken, and a lead weight smacks me right in the chest.

"No!" I strain, breaking into a run.

Pumping my legs, I cross the park in record time. It's a speed I can't do anymore, and the pain radiates through my back, down my legs. I don't even feel it. I have to get to where she's lying. My vision tunnels as black closes in around me.

It's happening again, just like I knew it would.

She's hurt.

She's broken.

She's not getting up.

I won't get through this if she doesn't get up.

The words swirl in my brain, and I fumble to find my phone to dial 9-1-1. We need help—now. I can't lose her this way. I can't lose another person.

"Rachel…" Her name slips from my mouth like a prayer, when she suddenly sits up smiling broadly.

"I can't believe I caught that ball!" She laughs, looking down at her arms. "It kind of stings, though."

Looking up, her eyes meet mine, and they widen in shock. "Zane? Are you okay?"

I slide to the ground beside her like a runner stealing home, pulling her into my arms. I'm breathing so fast. "Are you hurt?"

"I'm okay!" Her voice is breathless, and she reaches up to place her palms on my cheeks. "I'm okay. I'm not hurt."

"I thought you were injured." I can't seem to catch my

breath. Bending my knee, I rest my forehead on the back of my hand and groan, "You didn't get up."

"I'm so sorry." She moves to her knees, wrapping her arms around my shoulders. "I'm so sorry, I was playing. I was being dramatic. I didn't think—"

"Hey, bro, you all right?" Jack is beside me, leaning down to grip my shoulder.

I lift my chin and meet his eyes, nodding, but I feel like the wind has been knocked out of me. "I'm okay. Rachel's not hurt."

"That was some completion." Pride is in Jack's voice, but I'm a wreck.

"Everything okay, Rach?" Dylan yells from the other end of the park.

"I'm okay!" Rachel yells to her, then she turns to me again, her pretty eyes round with worry. "I'm so sorry, baby, I didn't even think how that would look."

"No, don't." I pull her into a hug. "You were having fun. I overreacted."

"Look at me." She puts her hand on my cheek. "It won't happen again. I love you."

Forcing a smile, I exhale, helping her up as I stand. "Let's finish this game. We're going to win this."

It's a promise to her and to myself.

Chapter 26

Rachel

WE FINALLY CALL THE GAME, ENDING IT WITH A FRIENDLY TIE. The truth is it could've gone on for hours with each side scoring every time they got the ball. For the guys, it was basically passing practice. Dylan and I were useless against them at our heights. The brothers had fun, and Austin was in heaven playing with them.

Walking back to the house, I still feel like shit for re-traumatizing Zane. I'm forming a plan to make it up to him later, when my grandmother's text appears.

Gran: Happy Thanksgiving! Send me a photo of my two favorite grandkids.

I quickly grab my brother around the neck for a selfie and send it to her. In it, I'm smiling, while he's looking away annoyed.

Rachel: Happy Thanksgiving! Did you have a good day? How are you feeling?

Gran: Good. Visited with your aunt Joanne, ate too much.

Rachel: Sounds like the perfect day. Edward is competing in a pool tournament Sunday. He might even win!

Gran: My goodness, he's doing everything down there.

Rachel: He's having the best time, and we've got him enrolled in school. He'll start after the holiday.

Gran: Oh.

Her response makes me frown. I'm about to ask what's up when her next text sends ice through my veins.

Gran: Have you heard from your dad?

Rachel: No. Why?

Gran: He said he wants to pay you a visit.

Rachel: Why would he do that?

Gran: He says he's worried about Edward.

Rachel: Since when?

Anger mixes with the panic beating in my chest. My father lost interest in Edward the minute he turned out to be "different." Only, he used a crueler word, a word that begins with the letter *R*, a word that is completely false.

My fingers fly over my phone.

Rachel: Tell him we're fine. Edward's fine. We don't want him here.

Gran: You'll have to tell him that yourself. You know how he is.

I swallow the fist in my throat. I do know how he is. He'll come in here like a wrecking ball and destroy all the good things we've built. He'll humiliate me, making me ashamed again for what he did to this family who's taken us in and treated us so well.

I need to know how much time I have to prepare.

Rachel: When is he coming, Gran?

Gran: He doesn't tell me much.

Rachel: Thanks for the heads up. I love you

Gran:Love you, honey. I'm sorry.

Pacing my room, I chew the side of my nail, trying to make a plan. I could go to Birmingham and confront him there, but I don't want to miss the pool tournament. Miss Gina's supposed to be back tomorrow, and I'd have to tell Zane.

Sitting on my bed, I put my head in my hands. I don't want to tell Zane. I don't want to tell anyone. I want Jayden to go away and leave us alone. He never cared about us before. Why does he care now?

He's never given us a reason to do anything but hate and hide and resent him. He hurts everyone. I'm not going to let him ruin what Edward and I have here.

The soft tap on my door precedes Zane's entrance. "I sent Dylan and Logan to Miss Gina's. Figured they could check on the kittens, spend the night. Now I'm wondering how we left the place."

A naughty grin curls his full lips, and my stomach aches.

Five minutes ago, I was filtering through all the sexy ways I could make up for what happened in the park earlier. Now all I can think about is the flaming missile headed straight for us.

"How's your grandmother?" He steps closer, and I know he's reading my expression.

"She said my dad is coming here." My room is quiet, and my shoulders tighten with a cringe.

Lifting my eyes carefully, I'm afraid of what he'll say, how he'll react.

His brow lowers, and his shoulders broaden in a protective stance. "What does he want?"

Relief hits me so hard, I'm on my feet reaching for him, and he pulls me into that secure embrace I know so well.

"Gran said he's coming for Edward. I can't imagine what he wants, but I'm sure it will be something hurtful."

"He's not hurting Edward or you." Zane's voice is low, and when our eyes meet again, I know my man means it.

Reaching up I place my palm against his cheek. "I was so afraid of what you would say."

Turning his face, he kisses the inside of my palm. "You belong to me now, Rachel Wells. I hope you're okay with that, because I take care of what's mine."

"I'm okay with that." My heart is beating fast and adrenaline mixes with relief mixes with lust. "Where is Edward now?"

"Last I checked, he was in his room watching pool videos on YouTube."

"Is he wearing headphones?"

"Let me see what our little man is doing."

My lips part, and the breath slips from my chest as he quickly steps into the hall. Blinking after him, affection radiates through my chest with every heartbeat. *Our little man?*

Tears heat my eyes, starting with calling me his and pledging to protect us. Now this?

He returns, and my eyes drink in his tall, athletic form and his soft, dark hair framing his scruffy square jaw.

That rare smile that curls his kissable lips. His broad shoulders stretch the long-sleeved henley he's wearing, the sleeves pushed up to show his muscled forearms, his tattoo reminding him, reminding us to keep going. There's balance, and good is coming.

Loose jeans sit on his narrow waist, hugging his muscular thighs.

"Headphones are on."

Standing, I go to him, reaching for him, and he lifts me off my feet in a consuming kiss. My legs go around his waist, and my mouth opens. Tongues curl together, and I exhale a soft whimper.

Dragging my lips across his cheek to his ear, I whisper, "I wanted to make up for scaring you today, but now I want to thank you for everything."

He steps to the bed, sitting with me straddling his lap. "You never have to thank me for taking care of you. It's my job."

In this position, I feel his erection growing in his jeans, and I rock my body up and down him. "I want to make you feel good. Show me what you like."

Thick fingers slide up the back of my neck, into my hair, pulling gently. "You've been doing pretty good so far."

"It's just what I've seen on porn."

His eyes flash, and his breath is hot on my skin. "My girl's been watching porn?"

Pink flushes from my neck to my ears. "It's how I learned to do the Nuru massage."

"That was intense."

"It takes planning." I slide my core against him again. "Tell me what to do."

"Take off your top."

I quickly unzip my hoodie and pull off my sweater, leaving me in only a thin white undershirt and bra.

I grasp the hem of the shirt, but he stops my hands. "Just the bra."

Reaching beneath my undershirt, I unclasp my bra and slip my arms out of the straps. I pull it away, leaving me in the cotton top that hugs my curves. It's so thin, my areolas are visible through the fabric.

"Hmm…" His low growl makes my panties wet, and I rock against him more.

"You like that?"

"Yes." Cupping my breasts in his hands, he lifts and squeezes, circling my nipples through the fabric.

"I was always self-conscious… I thought they were too big."

"They're perfect. Just like this." He cups me through my jeans, and I whimper. "Take them off."

I stand off his lap, stepping back to give him a show. Unbuttoning the top button, I hook my thumbs in the sides, turning so he can see the top of my lacy thong underwear as I lower them slowly over my ass.

Another low growl vibrates from his chest as he watches me, and I shiver. "What do I do now?"

"Take mine off."

I drop to my knees instinctively, crawling to where he's sitting, dark brow lowered, lusty shadows in his eyes. When I reach him, I sit back on my heels, sliding my hands up his strong thighs to the button of his jeans.

His legs part, and his hands are on my breasts again, fondling and playing. The button is open, and I carefully lower the zipper. He lifts his hips, and I pull the thick denim lower, allowing his hard cock to spring free. It's long and thick, and I want to touch it.

Looking up at him from where I sit, his lips tighten. "Pull your shirt down, and put it between your breasts."

I do as he says, pulling my shirt down so it squeezes thm together, then I lift them, sliding his cock between them and moving it up and down. His eyes narrow, and I feel him thicken.

"Fuck, you're so beautiful." He groans. "I love your tits."

Bouncing on my heels, I lick my lips, I looking up at him, feeling powerful and sexy at the hunger and lust in his eyes. His fingers trace gently along my arms, and he lifts one hand to pull down my bottom lip with his thumb.

I lick it, pulling his thumb into my mouth and sucking, and I feel him start to come on my chest. "Do it to my cock."

Lowering my chin, I pucker my lips around his tip, flicking my tongue all over him. Precum leaks, and I suck it away making him groan deeper.

Grasping my upper arms, he lifts me quickly. "Turn around."

I do as he says, and he catches my hips, guiding his cock into my soaked pussy. His rigid invasion makes me moan, and I lean my head back as his hand goes between my legs to circle my clit.

"That's it… Ride me."

Leaning forward, I place my hands on his knees and bounce my ass up and down on him. It sends him deeper, and I moan as he hits a place that makes the back of my eyes burn. Flashes of pleasure shoot through my core with every hit, and I bounce faster, desperate for more.

His deep moans are at my back, and his fingers lightly trace my ass.

"Oh!" I clasp a hand over my mouth to keep from crying out.

Hot come fills me, and I feel it slipping down my inner thighs as I chase my release, finding that spot again and again until the fluttering starts in my thighs, shooting to the arches of my feet. I keep going, biting my bottom lip hard as I finish, clenching and squeezing him deep inside me.

Strong arms encircle my waist, and he holds me close, his lips at my ear, kissing and pulling the skin of my neck. "You are so beautiful. You're amazing."

My eyes are closed and my arms wrap over his, holding him as I drift back from that state of intense bliss. Turning my face, I kiss his lips, sliding my tongue along his as one large hand cups my cheek.

He lifts me onto the bed, stepping quickly into the bathroom for a washcloth to clean us.

I'm lying on my side watching his gorgeous form as he returns, closing the door. "Pretty sure he didn't hear a thing."

"Thank whoever came up with noise-canceling headphones." He stretches out beside me, handing me the cloth as he kisses my lips once more.

We clean up quickly, and I lie back, threading my fingers in his hair. "I wanted to blow your mind, but I think you only blew mine. Again."

He pulls a blanket over us then lies on his side, tracing his fingers lightly along the top of my cheek into my hair. It's such a gentle caress, and I close my eyes.

"You always blow my mind, Rachel."

Turning into his chest, I inhale deeply his warm scent of sandalwood, soap, and him. "You weren't okay out there today."

"I was not." It's a bitter retort, and I slide my arm around his waist.

"It's what almost drove us apart."

His face lowers, and he kisses the top of my head. "Almost, but not."

"You never told me what changed your mind. Other than the undeniable inevitability of us."

That makes him smile, and he gazes into my eyes. "Jack."

"Him again?"

"Yeah, that brother of mine. He's smarter than he looks."

"You're all too pretty to be so smart. What did he say?"

Zane exhales, scooting around and putting pillows under our heads. "He suggested I work on changing my mindset. Something could always happen, but I won't miss out on the reality of us by obsessing over hypothetical outcomes."

"I'll do a better job next time. I should've thought—"

"I don't want you to stop being you to protect me." He slides his hand over my head. "I'll get there, and our path together leads out of the darkness."

"Our path together is golden."

"My goodness it feels like I've been gone a lifetime!" Miss Gina reaches for my hand, but I pull her into a hug.

"I missed you so much!"

It's the night of the pool tournament, and Miss Gina came straight to the restaurant to witness the event. A tallish woman my age stands beside her. She has bright hazel eyes and straight, strawberry-blonde hair styled in a shoulder-length bob with curtain bangs.

She's dressed in gray slacks and a white shirt unbuttoned at the neck with a matching gray blazer and a bright red scarf. She looks very professional.

"Hi, I'm Rachel Wells." I stretch out my hand. "I'm Miss Gina's nurse."

"Olivia Bankston." She shakes my hand with unexpected vigor. "But you can just call me Liv. Everybody around here does."

"Are you from Newhope?"

"Liv?" Dylan's voice goes high behind me. "Is that you? Lord, I haven't seen you in ages! How are you doing? What are you doing here?"

"Dylan! Oh my gosh!" Liv hops over, bending down to hug Dylan. "Alexis couldn't get away, and you know Mom had that bad fall last month. I don't think she's recovering like she should."

Dylan steps back holding Liv's hands and looking up at her. "You look so good! Supermodel lawyer!"

"No," Liv shakes her head. "Just a lawyer, nothing super."

"I'm sure your mom is glad you're here. I went by and checked on her last week. She should be putting more weight on that leg, so maybe you're right."

"I'll take care of her." Liv smiles, and her eyes travel around the restaurant. "How's Garrett? Is he here?"

"Oh, no." Dylan loops her arm through Olivia's. "Grizz is still playing for the Pirates in New Jersey. He only gets home a few days at Christmas and a month every summer."

"Ah…" Her tone is neutral, but I detect something more. "I know you miss him."

"He is a big space to fill."

"No one ever made me laugh as much as he did."

That's when I see the sadness lining her eyes. Up to now,

I've been chewing my lip, hanging on their every word, trying to figure out who this woman is. Now I feel like I have a little hint.

"Miss Gina!" Dylan cries, running to her and giving her a big hug. "You brought a surprise!"

"It's high time Olivia came home for a visit." Miss Gina pats Dylan's arm, but a twinkle is in her eye.

I've known this old lady long enough to know she's up to something as well.

"They're starting if you ladies want to join us." Zane walks over to take my hand, then hesitates. "Liv, wow—it's been a minute."

He hugs her briefly before stepping back to me.

"Zane Bradford, handsome as always."

"And Miss G, glad you're back safe." He leans down to hug her, and her blind eyes close as she squeezes then rubs his shoulder. "Yep, it worked."

"What are you talking about?" Dylan loops her other arm in Miss Gina's.

"Your brother is very relaxed." She holds out her hand to me. "I hope the guest cottage had something to do with it."

"What guest cottage?" I tease, reaching for his hand. "I think she's onto us."

Zane pulls me closer to his side. "I hope you don't have a policy against people who work for you being in love."

"I wouldn't have it any other way!" Miss Gina smiles, her eyes fluttering to heaven. "I only want to be surrounded by love."

"Well, you came to the right place!" Dylan takes her hand. "Let's get to the tournament!"

"I miss this place." Olivia looks wistfully after the two of them as they go.

"It's pretty special." I give her a friendly smile.

Chapter 27

Zane

GLORIA STANDS IN THE CENTER OF THE POOL ROOM DIRECTING THE kids where to go. They're all pretty rules-oriented anyway, so they're happy to follow her organization.

All of the kids earn money for the ranch by playing, but she has them segregated by age to start. The winners will advance to playing each other until a sole champion emerges.

The longest part of the night will be weeding out the beginners. Still, it's nice to see all the parents here cheering on their kids. I know a handful, since I'm only there in the early mornings.

"Ben had so much fun playing with Eddie!" Alice Maxwell touches my arm. "Thanks for putting them together. I almost wish Ben were going to Newhope next year."

"I'm sure you could put in for a variance if he's not happy at Barnwell." I watch the small boy moving around the table with more confidence than I've ever seen.

Ben is a lot like Eddie. They thrive on structure and accomplishment, and they learn new skills quickly. I do my best not to be angry at a society that would deem them "different" simply because they don't react to stimuli in a "normal" way. These young men have a lot of potential.

They've also started dressing alike in jeans and T-shirts with long-sleeve shirts on top.

After an hour, the tables have condensed. Weaker players have been eliminated, and we have two tables going. At one Eddie Nashville is up against a sixteen-year-old kid I don't know well.

His parents are so nice, I almost feel bad hoping their son loses.

Ben is playing a little girl, who I have to say is killer. Kimmie is enthralled, waving her stuffed turtle over her head and cheering for "pool girlies" in a way that makes me wonder how Jack will ever get her to sleep tonight.

I've had my eye on Olivia and Rachel chatting nonstop. It's curious seeing Liv back in town, but they're hitting it off, talking about Birmingham.

Considering all the shit he's given me, I couldn't resist snapping a photo and sending it to my brother.

Zane: Look who's here.

Garrett: She looks good.

My brows rise, and I've never known him to be so reserved.

Zane: She looks real good. Rachel seems to like her.

Garrett: Does Rachel like you?

Zane: Very much.

Garrett: That's what I'm talking about.

Zane: That's all you get.

Garrett: That's enough. I only want to see you happy, bro.

He doesn't respond, and I count it as a win. After all his harassment, I could do a lot worse, but it's not really my style.

Gloria calls out the winners, and we're down to the last match-up. My brows rise when I see it's Eddie and Ben.

"Oh no!" Rachel hops over to hold my bicep, frowning up at me. "They're best buddies!"

I slide my arm around her waist. "If I know these guys, they'll be very logical about how it all plays out."

Sure enough, the two of them are already talking at the head of the table as they put chalk on their pool cues.

"It only makes sense I'll probably win," Edward speaks low. "It's for charity anyway."

Ben nods, glancing at the table. "It's possible I could win, but the odds are overwhelmingly in your favor."

They walk to opposite sides of the table, and I can't help a grin. I knew as soon as I met Edward, he'd be a good match for Ben. They're only a year apart in age, and they have the same approach to the world.

Edward breaks, and a solid and a stripe go in opposite pockets. He calls solids, and it almost looks like he'll win in a sweep. He only misses one ball, and the crowd gasps, clapping at his skill.

Rachel is at my side, holding my arm. Her green eyes blink

rapidly, and I can't tell if she's on the verge of happy tears or if she's simply excited.

Ben steps up, and for a young beginner, he puts on a good show, sinking three balls in a row before bouncing the fourth off the corner of the pocket.

Edward reaches for his hand, and the two boys shake companionably. The room is silent as everyone holds their breath. I glance around at the amazed faces, and I can't help a smile of pride.

"Is my friend Eddie about to nail it?" Miss Gina's low voice cuts the silence, and a low chuckle ripples across the group.

"I think he is." I answer.

His eyes are focused as he steps up to the table, rubbing the chalk square on the tip of his pool cue. I'm not sure if he's aware, but he's doing a great job building drama.

He steps forward, surveying the table, then leans forward and quickly finishes the game in three plays.

When the eight ball sinks into the corner pocket, the entire place erupts into cheers. Eddie ducks, lifting his shoulders defensively against the noise, and Rachel steps forward to gently hold his arm.

"I'm so proud of you," her voice is quiet, and their eyes meet.

I wasn't there when they were children, when she would go into his room and lift him out of his crib because he was crying. When she was the only one who comforted him. I only know she won't be doing it alone as long as I'm around.

Stepping forward, I put my hand on her back, ready to congratulate them when a scratchy voice cuts through the din.

"That's my boy!" Loud clapping causes the voices to fade, drawing all our attention to a stocky man in a corduroy jacket. His light-hair is streaked with gray. "Another Wells for the win."

Rachel's body stiffens. It's been a long time since I've seen Jayden Wells, and I turn, stepping between him and my girl.

"Jayden." My hands are on my hips, and I'm gratified to be several inches taller than him.

Not to mention a few years younger.

He's a fighter, though. Stepping forward, he squints one eye at me. "You're one of those Bradford boys, aren't you?"

"He is." Jack's voice at my side gives me the backup I need. "I'm Jack Bradford, and this is my brother Zane."

"And I'm Logan Murphy."

My eyes cut to Logan, and I give him a nod before turning to Jayden again. "What do you want here?"

"Well, you sure have grown up. I came to get my son." He's not intimidated by the three of us, which gets my back up more. "Edward, pack your bags. You're coming back to Birmingham with me."

"Eddie's not going anywhere with you." I step forward, arms crossed.

Jayden only laughs, shaking his head and looking down. "I appreciate the welcome wagon." He circles his finger between the three of us. "But he's my son. You can't stop me from taking him, unless you're planning to commit a crime."

"I'll stop you." Rachel steps around from behind me. "I'm taking care of Eddie now. I always have, and you can't come in here and disrupt his life this way."

He shakes his head slowly. "Sorry, daughter, but in fact I can. You see, I've been getting calls from the school for a month wanting to know where he is. It seems you drove up to Birmingham and took him, and now he isn't in school anywhere."

"He's starting school here in January. In the meantime, he's been studying at home."

"Looks like he's been hanging out in a pool hall to me. Gotten pretty good at it, from what I can tell."

"You don't look like my dad anymore." Edward steps forward, still holding his pool cue. "You look old."

He pushes his light brown bangs off his head and frowns up at the man standing at the door of the pool area.

"Don't be stupid, boy." Jayden's tone has my fists clenching. "Of course, I'm your dad."

"Eddie's not stupid!" Kimmie stomps forward, brown curls bouncing around her little shoulders. "He's a genius! He knows about kittens and turtles and giants and pool…"

Jack reaches down to lift his angry tornado onto his hip.

"Yeah, yeah, I know, little lady. He's not stupid. He's just reta—"

"Don't say that word." I fist the neck of his shirt so fast, and my jaw clenches so hard, the muscle cramps.

Lifting him off the ground, I shove him out of the pool area and into the dining hall, away from the crowd, and I'm ready to kick his ass all the way back to Birmingham.

Rachel follows me, along with Jack, Dylan, and Logan. Craig and Allie hang back in the room to distract the crowd and celebrate the winners.

Gloria speaks, and gentle clapping follows whatever she says. Thankfully, it seems the tournament attendees are easily redirected away from what's happening here.

"Hey, okay!" Jayden holds up his hands as he puts space between us.

Protective rage burns in my veins, and I'm sure he sees it in my eyes. "If I ever hear you say that word to him or about him, I'll ram it down your ignorant throat."

A satisfied grin curls Jayden's lips, and it crawls on my skin. I'm starting to realize this is all a game to him, another ploy—but to what end?

"You're not taking Edward." Rachel steps past me. "You don't even want him. You're mean and spiteful and everything you do is only to hurt people. You use people until you get what you want or until they don't live up to your expectations, then you throw them away."

"You sound just like your mother." He huffs a laugh at her. "You're even starting to look like her."

"Mom was a good person until you came along."

"We can debate that another day."

I step up beside Rachel, putting my hand on her shoulder. Rachel knows this man a lot better than I do, but I'm a fast learner. I told her before she wouldn't face him alone ever again, and I want her to know we're here.

"It's time for you to go." Dylan enters the room. "I run this restaurant, and I reserve the right to refuse service to anyone—that includes you."

Jayden steps back, looking around Cooters & Shooters. "You know, I was a part of this place. It looks real good now."

I take another step forward, ready to throw him out the door. "You were never a part of this place. You were supposed to be, but you ghosted when it came time to commit."

"I never had that kind of money."

"Neither did they."

"Give me a break. Your dad had all his football earnings saved up. He was set."

"It was all he had, his life savings. He hadn't played in years, and he had all of us to think about."

"Looks like it turned out all right." Jayden squares off facing us. "Your family is secure. That's all I want for mine. I'm not the bad guy here."

I'm about to argue when Miss Gina enters the room. "Then don't act like the bad guy."

She holds Olivia's arm as the two of them step forward. "Don't do this Jayden. Leave Eddie be. He's happy here with us. He's thriving, and we'll take care of him."

"Miss Gina." He studies the old woman with a calculated eye. "Are you making me an offer?"

Her lips press into a frown, and she shakes her head. "That's all that ever matters to you. One day you'll see there's so much more to life than money."

"Easy to say when you got it." His voice rises, and he levels his eyes on Rachel. "I'll be back in a week to pick up my son. I expect you to have him ready to go."

Turning, he stalks out of the dining room, letting the door slam behind him. My chest is tight, and when I look at Jack, he nods. We've been here before, and we have an idea of what to do.

I think about what he said, what Miss Gina said, the past, and what it all means. He gave us a week, but I'm not wasting a day.

"They tried to take Hendrix and Dylan after our parents died." Jack is standing by the bar holding a beer. "We were able to stop it then."

After the awards were handed out, the tournament crowd slowly dispersed, and Dylan took Eddie with his first place trophy and Kimmie with her cooters back to the house.

Most of the attendees weren't aware of Jayden, and the few who were, didn't understand what was happening. Gloria helped Craig and Allie wrap up the tournament, and we promised to fill them in as they left.

Now it's Jack and Logan, Miss Gina and Olivia, Rachel and me standing at the bar trying to formulate a plan.

"How did you stop it?" Rachel's eyes are wide, and I can hear the desperation in her voice.

"Miss Gina was a big help. She stood beside me before the judge and made sure it didn't happen."

"What did she do?" Rachel looks from him to the old lady whose face is uncharacteristically angry.

"She's got a lot of money and a lot of influence." I put my hands on the tops of Rachel's shoulders.

"I simply knew the town council," Miss Gina interjects. "Nobody wanted to go on record as being the one who broke up the family of our local hero. We all came together and helped them see they were making a mistake."

"It helped that it's a small town," Jack adds.

"We won't have any of that going for us in Birmingham."

Rachel's voice is quiet. "Jayden is no hero, and we don't have influence on anybody."

"No, but you have me." Olivia steps forward. "I know several good family lawyers who will help us. I'll draw up papers, and we'll get him to sign over custody to you."

"He won't do that without some incentive." Disgust is in Rachel's tone. "He must owe somebody money. I'm pretty sure that's the only reason he's back, sniffing around."

I motion to Olivia. "I'll go with you to Birmingham. If you're up for it, we could go tomorrow. If that's okay with you, Miss G? I need to take off for a few days."

"Do what you have to do, Zane." Miss Gina reaches out to grip my arm, determination in her voice. "Protect our Edward."

"Let me check on Mom, and I'll make some calls." Olivia takes Miss Gina's arm as we start for the door. "If I can't get away, I'll find the best person to meet you tomorrow."

We break it up and head back to the house. I've got some packing to do.

Chapter 28

Rachel

"I should go with you." I'm standing in the center of Zane's room, watching him pack. "I'll just be pacing here, not knowing what's going on, waiting to hear something."

Edward's asleep in his bed, and the whole house is quiet. My heart is beating too fast, and I feel panicky.

He pauses, frowning when he sees my expression. Stepping closer, he pulls me to him, wrapping his strong arms around me.

I'm surrounded by comfort, warm woods, and Zane. My eyes slide closed, and I hold him, doing my best to stave off the tears heating my eyes.

"Why won't he leave us alone?" It's a broken whisper.

Zane's arms tighten gently, and he slides his hand up and down my back. "I'll fix this. You won't have to worry about him again."

Releasing me, he steps to the closet for a suit, which he carefully places in his luggage. "We'll FaceTime every day, and you can text me if you're anxious."

"How long will you be gone?" I look up at him, and he smiles, sliding his thumb along my cheek.

"Depends on what Liv is able to do. A week? Maybe less." Leaning down, he kisses me. "Now get in my bed and tell me goodbye properly."

We spend the night together. He makes sweet love to me, easing my mind and helping me sleep, but morning comes too early. I'm back to fidgety standing with him beside Olivia's Lexus, holding his sleeve and not wanting to let him go.

Liv is dressed in a casual red sweater and jeans, but her expression is no-nonsense. "I told Mom we'd be back by the end of the week. I need to see if we can get a judge to see things our way."

When we chatted last night, she told me she's worked as an oil and gas lawyer for eight years in the Steel City, but she's looking to move closer to home now that her mother is getting older.

I learned she and Garrett dated all through high school and were pretty serious, but they broke up when they went to different colleges. Dylan said something about a husband, but she's not wearing a wedding ring. She's really tall, as well as smart and a bit fierce, but a hint of sadness sneaks out on certain words.

She squeezes my hand then walks around to get in her car.

Zane leans down to give me another kiss, sliding his tongue with mine before moving his lips to my temple and inhaling at the side of my head.

My fingers curl in the front of his shirt. "I still wish I was going with you."

"Stay and take care of Eddie and Miss G and the kittens." He kisses me once more. "Let me handle this."

"Okay." Our eyes meet once more, and he gives me one last kiss.

I stand waving as they take off up the road, and when they're out of sight, I do my best to breathe through my anxiety.

It's Monday morning, and everyone's getting ready for school. Dylan has ballet class and Christmas program rehearsals. Edward's going with me to Miss Gina's today, and I walk slowly upstairs to be sure he's awake.

He's in his room, pulling on his *They Might Be Giants* tee, and I prop my hip against the door, watching him. He's growing up. He'll be thirteen before long, and I'm sure he'll want more privacy.

We're supposed to be finding our own place to live, although I kind of lost sight of that task in everything that's happened.

"I was really proud of you last night. First place—wow."

"I don't think the other players practiced as much as I did." He walks across the hall to the bathroom to brush his teeth. "Except Ben."

"Your buddy Ben won second."

He nods and spits, shutting off the water and crossing the hall again. "He'll be first next year."

"You're not planning to play again?"

"I won't be here." He sits on his bed, picking up his dog-eared copy of *The Outsiders*.

My chest aches, and I walk over to stand beside him, placing my hand lightly on his back. "Zane has gone to Birmingham to try and fix this. Don't worry."

He nods, but his expression doesn't change. "This place is magical."

He says it so calmly, I'm curious. "What makes you say that?"

"Everyday I wear this shirt. It's my favorite shirt because it's my favorite band."

"Right…"

I don't know where he encountered They Might Be Giants. I never listened to them, but they're quirky and funny. The shirt is two simple cartoon characters.

"Yet every day when I get up, it's clean again." He frowns looking down. "Yesterday, I got blue chalk on it at the tournament…"

Chewing my lip, I think it's time I come clean, although I'm not sure if he'll be angry or laugh or demand I stop. "What do you think is happening?"

"Miss Dylan talks about fairies, and she says to knock wood so they don't hear you say things." His brow furrows. "I didn't believe her."

"It's not fairies." I sit beside him on the bed. "I bought three shirts just alike, and I've been swapping them out since we've been here."

His lips twist, and his eyes are still on the hem of his tee. "You're the fairy?"

"Zane would say I'm an angry pixie."

"Like Tinkerbell in the Walt Disney movie?"

"I think that's exactly what he meant."

"I can see that." He nods, standing off the bed, and turning to put the book in his pack. "I think he's going to help us."

"He always does."

Zane: Liv knows her stuff. She hooked us up with a family lawyer who's drawn up paperwork for Jay to sign.

Rachel: If he will.

Zane: Leave that part to me.

Rachel: I want to say don't do anything illegal, but I won't mean it.

Zane: I have other means of persuasion.

Rachel: If you give him money, I'll never be able to pay you back.

Zane: Just let me worry about that part. How's Eddie, MG, and the kittens?

Rachel: We all miss you. Me most of all.

Zane: I miss you, too, Pix. I miss your grape kisses.

Rachel: Have to do yoga with MG.
Something for later...

Leaning forward, I pull the middle of my shirt down with my thumb to give him a full shot of my breasts.

Zane: Damn, girl. I can't meet my lawyer with a hard-on.

Rachel: Come home soon, so I can help you with that.

Zane: Working on it, don't worry. I love you.

I exhale a soft laugh, covering my smile with my hand before quickly tapping back my reply.

Rachel: I love you.

Miss Gina's usual smile is absent when I meet her for our gentle yoga class. "Have you heard from Zane?"

"He texted a minute ago. Liv has custody papers all ready, but getting Jayden to sign them is the trick."

"Difficult family members can be so... upsetting." Her face is lined. "I'm sorry you have to deal with this."

"Sadly, it's not the first time I've had to deal with my dad."

We walk out to the vine-covered arch on the wooden platform overlooking the bay. She's dressed in wide-legged linen pants and a long-sleeved shirt. I'm in a similar attire, wide-legged overalls with a long-sleeved tee under it.

I direct her through saluting the sun and waking up our core. Most of what we do is for balance and spatial orientation. We stretch out in warrior pose, but I can tell she's distracted.

It's a short flow, and we finish sitting in lotus pose, focusing on our breathing. Our hands are in the prayer position, and when I peek at her, her lips are twisted.

"Namaste," I say, and she lowers her hands to her lap.

"Is that my friend Eddie?" A genuine smile eases the tension in her face for the first time all day.

"I tried to be quiet." Edward walks to where we're sitting.

He's holding a tuxedo kitten in one hand and a black one in the other. "I think Duke is growing faster than his brothers."

"Show me." She holds out her hands, and he puts the two kittens in her lap, holding them still as she reaches down to pet their little bodies.

I scoot closer, sliding my finger along the top of the solid black one's head. "They're so cute."

"Swiper is the tuxedo?"

"Yes, ma'am." He touches her hand. "He's this one. Duke is here. I think he and Smokey had the same father."

"Duke is definitely bigger than Swiper."

"I thought Smokey was growing faster because they were feeding him scraps at the restaurant, but he's the same size."

Miss Gina reaches out to squeeze my brother's arm. "You take such an interest in things. Gloria said you're an excellent helper with the horses as well."

Eddie's lips pull down, and he pets Swiper. "I'll miss them when I'm gone."

My heart aches, and I want to tell him he's not going anywhere. I want to pull him to me and tell him not to worry. I'll protect him like I always do.

"You'll have to excuse me." Miss Gina stands abruptly. "I just remembered I have an important phone call to make."

She hands Duke to me and leaves us sitting on the platform. Eddie stands, slowly walking to where Skye is stretching in the sun, waking up from a day-long cat nap.

His shoulders are curved, and my throat hurts. I take out my phone again, sliding my finger across the screen to read Zane's last text. *Don't worry. I love you.*

I've been fighting for Edward and me for so long by

myself. No one has ever had my back until now. It's a new experience. Zane said this place is different.

Mom said I have the power to change what fate tries to throw at me and make a new path. I've lived my life believing I could do it, and I have to believe I still can, with the help of our new family.

We've found happiness here, a home, and I'm not going to let anything take that away.

Chapter 29

Zane

“THE CONTRACT TRANSFERS ALL RIGHTS AND RESPONSIBILITIES FOR your son Edward to your daughter Rachel. If anything happens, you will not be held responsible or liable.” Olivia slides the papers across the polished surface of her wooden desk. “All you have to do is sign, and I’ll file it with the court.”

Jayden sits in a beige leather chair, frowning as he takes the document, turning the pages and scanning them quickly. “This means the school won’t bother me anymore?”

“They won’t have any grounds to involve you. Your parental rights will terminate.”

“Terminate.” His nose curls. “I don’t like the sound of that.”

“What don’t you like?” My tone is sharp, and Olivia’s brow lowers.

She very subtly shakes her head *No*, but I’m ready to grab him by the neck and hold him down until he signs on the dotted line.

“It sounds like I’m abandoning my child.” He glares up at me.

My jaw tightens so hard, I'm surprised my teeth don't crack. I want to ask how it's any different from what he already did years ago, but I don't.

I hold myself back and let Olivia do her job.

"This transfer in no way indicates you don't love your child." Her voice is calm. She even smiles. "In fact, it means just the opposite. For many parents like yourself it's the best course of action, and your selflessness demonstrates the greatest love of all."

"Still…" He flops the paper onto the desk. "I think I should be compensated."

"Compensated." My voice is flat, and again, Olivia's lips press together.

"It just seems like everybody's getting something out of this but me."

"You're not having to pay for your freedom. Liv is providing this service *pro bono*."

"Is that like for the band?"

I cut my eyes to Liv, confused.

"*Pro bono* is a Latin term that means *for the good*. It means I'm donating my time to help you."

"It means she's not getting paid. Nobody is." I hit the *nobody* hard.

"Well, that sounds like her business." Jayden exhales, leaning back in his chair again. "It has nothing to do with me. I've got needs."

I'm about to say he *needs* to sign this contract or he's going to *need* emergency medical treatment.

"Why don't you take a day to think about it." Liv stands, walking around her desk. "This is your copy. Take it with you and give it a thorough reading."

She slides her hands down her black pencil skirt, and I notice she's wearing bright red shoes. It reminds me of when she would run around with Garrett all the time in Newhope. She was always wearing something red.

"I'll do that." He takes the papers and walks to the door.

As soon as he's out, she pushes it closed. "That man is a piece of work. How did Rachel turn out so sweet?"

"Getting away early." It comes out a touch above a growl. "I'm ready to take him to court. Let a judge take one look at this two-bit hustler and decide."

"We were able to get a meeting in chambers this week, which is very unusual." She leans back on her desk, crossing her arms. "It can take as long as a month, but they had a sudden opening."

It feels like a good omen. "You can tell him about Edward's equine therapy and how he won the pool tournament. He's making friends and starting school in January. All that has to matter for a kid like him."

"They're all good things, and I'll make the case for the stability and community he has with his sister." Her forehead lines with worry. "But I have to be honest with you, it's nearly impossible to get a judge to revoke parental rights without some form of gross neglect or abuse."

"He essentially abandoned them. Rachel has taken care of Edward since he was a baby."

"Still, she's not his parent. She's a young, single woman, alone in the world with limited income, no permanent housing…"

"She's not alone." Energy is in my chest. "Rachel is my future wife."

It's impulsive, and I'm taking a big risk. But I promised I'd be back with custody papers, and I won't let her down.

"Really?" Olivia straightens, uncrossing her arms and smiling for the first time all day. "Well, congratulations. That definitely helps your case. We can present you as a potential step-guardian. It would be better if you were already married, but it certainly helps."

"I'll arrange a pretrial meeting with Jayden tomorrow morning, and we can see where he stands." She rounds her desk, collecting her laptop and bag. "I doubt it'll make a difference to him, but it might with the judge."

"I think a judge would care that he's only interested in money."

"He can easily deny that." Reaching out, she touches my forearm. "I know it's hard, but let me do the talking."

The next day we meet in a small room outside the judge's chambers. It reminds me of being in the principal's office at school. The walls are plain beige, the desks are scratched-up blond wood, and it smells like chemical cleaning products.

Jayden is back, dressed in jeans and a beat-up corduroy blazer. His beard needs to be shaped up, and his hair could use a comb.

By contrast, I'm shaved and spruced and wearing a Brioni suit from my football days in Baltimore, when I had to get dressed up on occasion for awards ceremonies and special events. Liv is in a gray pinstripe suit as well.

Studying the contrast, I wonder if this will work in our favor or hurt us. Jayden doesn't seem to notice. He still has his eyes on the prize.

"I looked over your contract, and I showed it to my lawyer..." He looks from me to Liv, and I have to bite my tongue to keep from questioning who that might be and where he or she is this morning. "I still say I'm getting a raw deal, and I'm not signing this."

"I'm sorry you feel that way." Liv's tone is patient. "I had hoped we might settle this without having to go before the judge."

"Judges don't scare me, lady. He'll be on my side. I'm the father."

More like the sperm donor. My hands are clenched beside me in the chair.

"Then it sounds like we're finished here." Olivia stands, taking her computer off the table and pulling her bag over her shoulder. "We'll see what the judge has to say."

Jay's eyes widen, and he looks from her to me. "That's it? You're really going through with it?"

"Of course." Olivia smiles sweetly. "That's what you want, isn't it?"

Just as fast, his demeanor changes. His eyes narrow, and he stands, stepping a little too close. "I told you what I want."

"Money is what you want." The sharp female voice draws our attention to the door. "Is that correct, Mr. Wells?"

"Claws?" I take a step back, surveying the stern woman in the St. John suit and helmet of auburn hair. "I mean, *Claudette*, what are you doing here?"

Olivia's brow furrows. "I don't think we've met."

"I'm Claudette Rosario." She extends a hand to Olivia. "President of the Board of the Matrons for the Safeguard of Birmingham's Little Lambs."

"Ah, yes, the Matrons." Olivia tilts her head in my direction to explain. "It's an old, well-established children's charity."

"The Matrons have protected the most vulnerable members of our great city for more than a century." Claws's tone is haughty. "Our endowment is one of the largest in the country. One of our members called me yesterday and said you have a situation needing our attention."

"Who is this woman?" Jayden hooks a thumb at Claws. "What is she talking about?"

I have a feeling I know what she's about to do, and rage burns in my chest. I still want to fight this, to beat his ass for the crap he's pulled on my family and now his own.

As if sensing my rising blood pressure, Olivia touches my arm. "What is your organization proposing, Mrs. Rosario?"

"We'll be happy to provide whatever funds are needed to

ensure Edward Wells's permanent custody is assigned to his sister Rachel. I have a contract drawn up here."

"Funds?" Jayden looks from Olivia to Claws, and the glee in his eyes makes me sick. "What funds are we talking about?"

"Tell me, Mr. Wells, would you agree to turn over your son for the generous sum of twenty thousand dollars?" Claws unsnaps her Hermes bag and removes a long envelope. "I have the check all made out in your name and ready to go."

"Why, yes, ma'am, I most certainly would!" He claps his hands together. "Hot damn, where do I sign?"

Olivia doesn't speak, and her calm makes me wonder if I'm missing something. I'm furious as Claudette lifts her chin, motioning to the papers on the table.

"First sign the contract provided by Ms Bankston. Then you'll sign our contract agreeing to receive the money on a confidential basis..."

"No problem at all!" He scoops up the pen before she finishes speaking.

Olivia opens to the signature page, and he signs quickly. She bends down and signs as well, passing it to me. I take the pages, but it feels like a pyrrhic victory. I don't like him getting paid—especially not such a large amount.

He turns to Claws, pen out, mouth watering.

I growl audibly, but Olivia presses her fingers hard against my forearm.

"Don't be bitter, sonny." Jayden gives me a sarcastic smile. "It takes a special kind of smarts to do what I do."

"Feel free to take a moment to read before you sign." Claws opens her contract to the signature page. "I've taken the liberty of signing for the matrons."

"Gotta tell you, lady," Jayden signs without hesitation. "Y'all might want to reconsider that name. *Matrons* sounds like a bunch of feeble old ladies."

"I'll be sure to bring that up at our next board meeting." She folds the signed contract and hands him the check. Her brows rise, and her expression is light. "Or you can drop your idea for a new name in the suggestion box next time you're in the office."

"I'll let you handle it." Jayden hops back, folding the check and slipping it into the breast pocket of his blazer. "I'm on my way to the Ozarks. Right after I stop by the bank."

"Let me save you a trip." Claws takes out her phone. "Give me your bank information, and I'll send the payment electronically right now."

His eyes widen, and he hops forward again. They exchange information, and I have to walk away from what's happening. As much as I care about Edward, as much as I love Rachel, I don't like seeing this guy walking away with another win.

"Did it go through?" Claws's tone is bright, and I shake my head.

Jayden holds his phone a moment, then waves it in the air. "It went through." He does a little bow. "Thank you, ladies and sucker. Have a nice life."

"Now don't forget, the downtown office opens bright and early at seven a.m." Claws calls after him, turning to tuck the contract into her expensive leather bag.

"Good for you, lady." His hand is on the door when she turns, arms crossed, voice coming down like a hammer.

"You just signed a contract to be the sanitation clerk at our original office building downtown. It's a 100-year-old edifice, and unfortunately, those old sewer lines need constant maintenance and attention or they overflow."

"What's that?" Jayden leans forward, confused.

"The Matrons don't simply dole out money, you silly man. You signed a contract to pay back our generous gift through service to our organization as sanitation clerk for the next twelve months. Our retiring clerk, Mr. Applewhite will be ready to train you bright and early Monday morning."

A laugh explodes through my lips. "It takes a special kind of smarts to be you, Jayden. Have fun cleaning up shit. Excuse me, ladies. *Poop.*"

"You can't do this!" Jayden yells. "I'm not taking your money!"

"You've received the money, and the contract is signed. If you fail to follow through on your end of the agreement, I'll have the judge issue a bench warrant for your arrest." There's the Claws I know and now love. "Give my regards to Rachel and Eddie, and let Gina know the matrons got her call and took care of it."

She walks straight to the door without looking back, and like some kind of uncredited superhero, she's gone.

Adrenaline replaces the acid in my stomach, and I'm ready to run all the way to Newhope.

"She can't do this!" Jayden whines.

"Actually, she just did." Liv's hazel eyes sparkle, and she turns a big smile on me.

I give her a hug, but my arms ache for Rachel. "How soon can we get on the road?"

Olivia steps back, checking her watch, and I can tell she's as amped as I am. "Give me an hour to pack, and I'll pick you up at your hotel."

We leave Jayden in the principal's office still pacing and whining and trying to figure out what went wrong.

Chapter 30

Rachel

"Have you heard anything?" Dylan stands at the large kitchen table mixing her Dare Dish for the night.

It's a blend of Scotch Bonnet peppers with mangos and pineapple.

"We texted this morning. They had a meeting scheduled with the judge this afternoon, but they were also meeting with Jayden first."

"Is that a good thing?" Her nose wrinkles, and I shake my head.

"I don't know. Liv was worried it would be difficult to terminate his parental rights. Can you believe that?" I pick up one of the bright yellow peppers by the stem. "You can ditch your kid for years and years, but you can still come back and make trouble."

"Careful with that little guy." She nods at the pepper in my hand. "You might want to wash your hands with coconut oil before you accidentally touch your eye or nose or anything."

Dropping the fruit, I walk over to the sink to do as she says. If anybody knows the dangers of hot peppers, it's Dylan.

"That's all I've heard, and I've been a little scared to text."

"No news is good news?"

"Something like that."

Dylan stands in front of the blender with her hand on her hip. "Am I in a pepper rut? I've made hot pepper salsa twice now, and both times it's been mixed with mango and pineapple."

"I haven't heard any complaints." I walk back to where she's studying the recipe card. "It's a different pepper, isn't it?"

"What's that face about?" Craig walks over to where we're looking at the menu. "Don't tell me. You're worried Oliver Duck has found himself a new pepper princess."

"Shut up." Dylan bumps him with her hip. "Where's Clint? He hasn't sent me a bouquet selection in weeks."

"He said he's got everything he needs. He's done with you."

My nose wrinkles, and I lean closer on the bar. "Doubtful. It's still your wedding."

"What's the latest on the Edward situation?" Craig walks to the refrigerator.

"Zane told Rachel they were meeting with the judge this afternoon." Dylan carefully dices the Scotch Bonnet "That's all we know."

"You don't know where they are now?" He frowns.

"I've been too scared to bother him." I pull up my phone and open my messenger app. "You're right. He said to text him if I get anxious."

"Yes…" Dylan drops her paring knife and crowds along with Craig around my phone.

My fingers tremble as they move over the face, and I keep making typos. "Y'all are making me nervous."

I'm about to hit send when a low voice almost makes me toss my phone. "What are you three doing?"

I'm running before my eyes even land on him. "Zane!"

He laughs, catching me in his arms and lifting me off my

feet. Our mouths unite, and I don't care that we're in the kitchen in front of God and everybody. Parting my lips, I thread my fingers in his hair, pulling his tongue with mine and wrapping my legs around his waist.

I drop my face to his neck, holding him in a hug. "I missed you so much," I say against his skin.

"I missed you." His fingers are in the back of my hair, and my body is pressed against his.

Lifting my chin, I look around the kitchen from Thomas, staring fixedly at the tiny, black-and-white TV by his grill, to Dylan intensely studying the recipe she's working on, to Craig staring at the ceiling.

"Sorry." I exhale a laugh, then I lift my hand and do a little cheer. "Welcome back!"

Dylan's lips tighten, and she bursts out laughing. "You two are so adorable. I'm so happy my big brother found somebody to love him as much as I do."

She runs over to hug us both, and Craig shakes his head as he slowly joins us.

Moving my tongue around, I realize I have a grape candy in my mouth. "Were you eating a Jolly Rancher?"

"I told you I missed you."

"Stop being so ridiculously cute!" Dylan yells from beside us. "What happened?"

Zane's eyes are fixed on me as he reaches into the breast pocket of the really nice suit he's wearing and hands me a folded document.

Stepping back, I frown as I open the thick tri-fold paper and read the words at the top. *Transfer of Custody*... My eyes widen as they fly down the text. It's a document spelling out how I am officially the legal guardian of Edward. How my dad has relinquished all claims and no longer has the power to make our lives miserable.

It doesn't actually say those words, but that's the gist.

"The judge gave me custody?"

"We never saw the judge. Liv drew up the papers, but Jayden said he wouldn't sign unless we paid him."

Shaking my head in disgust, I return to the signed contract I'm holding. "You paid him for this?"

"Sort of." That dimple is in his cheek, and he takes my hand. "You're not going to believe who showed up at the eleventh hour with a bait and switch."

My eyes widen. "Tell me!"

"Claws."

"What?!" I almost squeal. "How is that possible?"

"Who's Claws?" Dylan jerks on Zane's sleeve. "What happened? Who's Claws?"

"Miss Gina must've called her at some point, and apparently Claws has enough power to command twenty thousand dollars."

"She did not give him twenty thousand dollars." My stomach drops to the ground.

"No, she didn't." Zane drops his head back with a laugh. "She conned the con man."

"I'm still waiting to know who Claws is!" Dylan pushes her brother's arm. "Santa Claus?"

"She might as well be." Zane looks at his sister. "She's Miss Gina's sister-in-law, and she roasted Jayden. He has to pay the money back by working as their sanitation clerk for a year."

"What's a sanitation clerk?"

"Sewage guy."

Biting the hard candy, I shake my head . "I still don't understand."

"She works for this children's charity in Birmingham, and when she said she'd give Jayden twenty thousand dollars, she didn't tell him it would be in exchange for him working for them."

"He fell for it?"

"It was pretty classic the way she rolled it out. He never even saw it coming."

"So it's all done?" My eyes meet his, and his warmth soothes the fear in my chest.

"Almost. You have to sign these, and Liv will file them with the court. Then it's done." Zane pulls me into his arms. "We got Eddie."

"I've never seen anything like this!" Liv stands beside me at the booth, holding a basket of chips and a cup of Scotch Bonnet and mango salsa. "They weren't doing this when I left for college."

Craig is on the bar with the female servers wearing a blond wig and shaking his butt to The Spice Girls.

"Dance with me, Miss G!" Allie skips over to where we're standing, holding out her hands.

I step forward to help Miss Gina out of the booth, and the two of them hold hands as they sway to the music. Miss Gina has surprisingly good rhythm. She twirls her arms in time to the music, and even turns around to shake her booty from side to side.

"Can I get some fries with that shake?" I catcall, laughing and clapping.

We all have our hands up dancing when Liv suddenly lets out a yelp from where she watches us beside the booth.

"Help!" Her eyes are wide and watering, and she's frantically fanning her red face with her hands. "What's happening?"

"Hot pepper alert!" Allie yells, and we both grab her arms, running to the ice cream station beside the smaller bar.

"It's burning all the way down my throat!" Liv bounces up and down on her toes, crying as Allie rips the cardboard lid off the small cup of ice cream. "It's burning my stomach!"

"Don't panic." I pass her the ice cream. "Eat this, quick!"

She puts her entire tongue into the ice cream, tears streaming down her cheeks. "I'm going to be sick!"

Allie runs back with a handful of napkins, holding them for her and rubbing her back. "Hang in there. It'll be over soon. Try to stay calm."

I hand her a spoon, and she dips the ice cream out, swallowing big bites as she sniffs and wipes the tears and snot away.

"It kept getting hotter and hotter. I didn't think it was going to stop." Her wide eyes are on me, and I nod.

"Some of those hot ones can be really scary. You'll get the hang of it."

"I don't know if I want to!"

Allie hands her another cup of ice cream. "I'd better get back to Miss Gina."

"Thanks, Allie!" Liv calls as our friend dives back into the crowd of dancers.

"You okay?" I frown-smile.

She takes another small bite from the new cup. "This helps a lot. I get the whole *Dare* part now."

The music dies down, and I press my lips together. "I can't thank you enough for helping us with Eddie. If there's any way I can ever repay you—"

"Don't mention it." She waves the wooden spoon in front of her. "Glad to help out. That guy was the worst."

"My dad, I know." Shame heats my cheeks, and I study my twisted fingers.

"Don't be embarrassed. We can't always pick the men in our lives." She reaches out to squeeze my hand. "Looks like you're doing better now, though! Zane Bradford is a good man."

"He's the best." I glance past her to the side porch where Eddie is playing pool away from the noise.

"Congratulations on your engagement." My stomach flips, and she shakes her head. "No, that's not right."

"What?" I can barely get the word out for the air whooshing from my lungs.

"It's *best wishes*." She flutters an eye-roll. "You tell the bride-to-be *best wishes*. You tell the groom *congratulations*."

I can't speak, and she studies my face. "Is it a secret? Zane told me in Birmingham y'all are engaged."

Taking a careful step back, I rub my hand over my heart. "I'll be right back."

Energy pulses in my veins, and I go to the screen door, hesitating before I open it.

Eddie is methodically clearing the pool table, while Kimmie holds Smokey, explaining to the struggling feline how kitties don't have to be afraid of turtles.

Zane stands back watching, his strong arms crossed over his chest and a contented smile on his face.

When I told Edward earlier he didn't have to go back to Birmingham, he simply nodded. "Zane fixed it."

It wasn't a question, and I covered his hand with mine. "He did."

"Zane always keeps his word."

Tears heated my eyes as I agreed. "It's true. He does."

"He's like you."

Now, opening the door, I go to him, reaching out to put my hand on his forearm. He uncrosses them, wrapping me in a hug, and I tuck my face against his chest, thinking about this man as my home, my future.

He already decided.

Lips press against my head, and his voice is low. "Everything okay?"

I lift my chin to meet his blue eyes. "Liv just offered best wishes on our engagement."

His brow lowers, and that dimple appears in his cheek. He looks up at Edward and Kimmie playing then back to me.

"I might've said something about you being my future wife." His muscled arm tightens around my back. "What do you think of that?"

Laughter bubbles in my chest, and I reach for his cheeks, pulling him down for a kiss "I think it sounds pretty darn good."

Placing his thumb on my chin, he pulls me to him for another kiss, another shimmering pass of his tongue against mine.

"It's better than good. It's perfect."

Epilogue

Zane

Six Months Later

"I T'S CALLED FOREST BATHING." RACHEL HOLDS MY HAND AS WE WALK along the boardwalk leading through the pitcher plant bog.

I got the book Jack recommended on cognitive behavioral therapy, and when she found it on my nightstand, she was all in with helping me practice mindfulness.

Jack keeps reassuring me it's not woo-woo. Edward was right there with him, explaining PTSD is a real condition that can be caused by any trauma. He'd informed me CBT was a good place to start.

I simply said thanks.

"This isn't technically a forest." I look out at the narrow, vase-shaped carnivorous flowers. "It's more like a swamp."

"Forest bathing is just the term. It can apply to any natural environment where you walk and consciously connect to what's around you."

"Consciously connect?" My eyebrow arches, and she narrows her eyes.

"It's not woo-woo!"

Holding up my hands, I exhale a laugh. "I didn't say it."

"You were thinking it." She reaches for my hand again, and we pause, looking out across the bog full of hundreds of deep magenta and white plants. "They're really pretty, aren't they?"

"They eat bugs."

"Isn't it wonderful? Imagine what it must've been like down here long ago, when they didn't have any sort of pest control."

"Sounds like hell."

"These plants were nature's way of solving the problem. It's so encouraging. There's always a solution."

Lifting her hand to my lips, I kiss it. "It's true."

School finished two days ago, and Eddie's out at the horse farm every day with Ben. Austin started working with them as well after the football season ended.

Our little guy wrapped up a great first semester at his new school. He had the occasional challenge with figuring out the new schedule and finding his classes, but the initial weeks he'd spent with Allie paid off in helping him be comfortable in his new environment.

His grades were a mix of As and Bs, and Rachel cried when she got his final report card. He'd tried to explain that a B was technically not a bad grade, and I had to explain to her brother they were happy tears, which he didn't understand.

Dylan's wedding is coming soon, and we decided to steal away for a little nature walk-slash-forest bath before the boys pull into town.

I'm looking forward to dishing back to Garrett all the hell he gave me, especially since Liv is back in town to be one of Dylan's bridesmaids.

But before all that begins, I have something on my mind.

The boardwalk ends overlooking the bay, and I cage her in my arms as we look out over the dark, rippling water. Frogs sing loudly, and a crane steps carefully among the tall grasses, searching for food.

Leaning down, I kiss the side of her neck, which earns me a little squeal. "Tickles."

"Sorry." I smile, kissing her lips briefly. "When you said forest bathing, I thought we were going skinny dipping."

"Hmm…" She leans her head against my cheek. "As much as I love communing with nature, that would be more fun."

"We should sneak into Miss Gina's pool one night after she's gone to bed."

"I'd rather slip out to the bay behind the restaurant. If we woke Miss Gina, I'd die of embarrassment."

"We've gotten pretty good at being quiet."

We've had to, with Edward right next door, even if he does wear headphones to sleep, we don't like to take any chances.

I've actually located a cute starter home for us on the scenic road north of town, but first things first.

Stepping back, I take her hand, turning her to face me. "I wanted to do this before all the family arrived. We've already talked about it some, but I finally found what I was looking for."

Her brow furrows. "What do you mean?"

Reaching into my pocket, I take out a 24-karat, white-gold ring with a round diamond in the center, surrounded by triangle-shaped baguettes. Her breath catches, and she lightly touches it with her fingertips.

"It's a flower." Green eyes, bright with unshed tears meet mine. "It's so beautiful."

"Eddie said I'm the bee in your bonnet." I can't help a light chuckle.

"You talked to Eddie?" Her forehead wrinkles as she looks up at me, and I slide my thumb over the crystal tear on her cheek.

"Of course. He's a part of our family."

"Oh, Zane." She rests her face against my chest, and I thread my fingers in the back of her hair.

I kiss the top of her head, inhaling honeysuckle. "I read somewhere that life takes courage, and the longer you live, the more courage it requires. It made me think of you and me." Reaching up, I slide a lock of hair behind her ear. "You're smart and beautiful and funny and genuine, and you're brave. I want you beside me holding my hand, because you know how to keep going, you help me be strong, and together we can face anything."

She blinks, and she's so beautiful smiling up at me, eyes shining. "I think our past, the things that have tried to break us, actually helped us fit together perfectly."

"I like that." My smile grows bigger. "Broken things have no walls, no limits, no rules…"

"So a break isn't something to fear?" Her nose wrinkles.

"I'd still rather avoid it, but I'm working on my mindset."

She exhales a little laugh, and I take her hand. "I love you, Rachel Wells. You make me stronger, and I promise to protect you with all my power from anything that might hurt you. Will you marry me?"

She puts her hand on mine, looking up at me. "Yes, Zane Bradford, and you'll always be safe with me. I'll always hold your hand and lead you to the light."

I slide the ring onto her finger before leaning down to cover her lips with mine. Our tongues curl together, and I lift her off her feet, hugging her body close.

We have been broken, we've faced the dark, and together we're stronger.

Together, we're perfect.

Later, at Cooters & Shooters…

"It's a flower!" Dylan cries.

"It's so beautiful," Allie coos.

"Who knew Mr. Grumpy could be so romantic?" Craig lifts his chin, winking at me.

"I knew." Rachel's confident reply warms my chest.

The three women and Craig are huddled around the large silver worktable in the kitchen looking at the ring as Rachel replays everything that happened when I proposed, from what I said to where we were to the position of the sun.

"Good work, bro." Jack grips my shoulder.

"I knew you had it in you," Logan teases.

"I didn't know they were going to dissect everything that happened." Rubbing the back of my neck, I look down. "I'd have planned something more interesting."

"They don't mind." Thomas sits back on his stool, crossing his arms and grinning.

We're all standing back out of the way, holding longnecks and watching them.

"Why aren't you over there?" I glance at Liv, who's standing back with us.

Her strawberry blonde hair is tied up in a ponytail, and she's in jeans and a thin red sweater. She's unusually casual and reserved.

"They don't need me." Her voice is quiet, almost guilty.

It makes me wonder what's really going on with her, and why she's here.

She straightens at once when the door opens, and her face flushes like she's seen a ghost. The loud voice tells me immediately who just joined the party.

"What's all this? Did they find a new pepper in the bog?" Garrett booms, entering the room, and Dylan squeals.

"Garrett!" She runs to him, jumping into his arms for a hug. "I've missed you so much! Did you just get here?"

"Just rolled into town." He lifts her off her feet.

"Don't tell me you drove the whole way again," Logan groans, going to his best friend and grabbing his hand.

"I've gotta have my truck." Garrett pulls him into a rough hug.

"You're going to have a new sister." Dylan holds his hand, dragging him over to where Rachel stands. "Garrett Bradford, meet Rachel Wells, Zane's new fiancée."

Rachel's cheeks are pink, and she looks up at him shyly. "I'm so happy to meet you finally. I've heard so much—"

"Welcome to the family, sis!" He reaches down, engulfing her in a bear hug. "I've heard a lot about you. Where is that brother of mine?"

I walk over to where my oversized younger brother has broken up the group, reaching out to grab his hand.

He pulls me to him, whispering loudly in my ear. "Nice work, old man. She's a fox."

"Old man," I exhale a chuckle. "I've got something for you."

Turning, I'm all ready to present him with Liv, when I see she's gone. My eyes scan from where Thomas is grilling burgers down the hall leading to the back exit, and I see the screen door is cracked. My brow lowers as I realize she ducked out without a word.

"What's that?" Garrett follows my gaze curiously.

"Ah, I'll show you later." I turn back to where everyone is congregated, laughing.

"My man, Cray!" Garrett goes to where Craig is loading plates, and the two of them launch into a discussion of hot music and dance moves for Thursday.

Salina Duck enters the room, glancing at me with a pouty frown. "We still have customers, you know."

"Three orders up," Thomas calls from the grill, and Craig quickly plates them.

Salina cuts a glance to where Rachel stands with Allie, eying her hand curiously, until my future wife catches her.

"Something you want to see?" Rachel walks over, crossing her arms so that her engagement ring is visibly prominent on her bicep. "Something *ratchet*?"

Salina shakes her head, rolling her eyes. "It was a joke, Rachel. Let it go. Like Zane Bradford would ever be with anyone messy."

Rachel's eyes narrow, and she chews the side of her lip. "You've been really sweet to my brother, and I know how it feels to crush on someone as amazing as my future husband."

That sounds better than I expected, even if she is rubbing it in a bit.

Salina's cheeks pink, and she lifts the tray holding the three hamburgers and fries. "Whatever. Zane is clearly in love with you."

Stepping closer, she puts her hand on the girl's arm. "I'd like us to be friends, and maybe, I don't know. I hear Sam Allen's a really nice guy."

Rachel smiles, and Salina eyes her up and down before shrugging. "You might be okay. Edward's the coolest kid I know."

"He really is."

As if summoned, Eddie walks in with Kimmie right behind him, holding Smokey under his chin.

"Uncle Grizzlaaay!" Kimmie yells, breaking into a run to her uncle.

"How's my little peanut?" He swoops her up into a hug, and she crawls around to get on his back. "Did you get your new cooter?"

Exhaling a laugh, I shake my head. He's as bad as she is.

"Everybody loves my cooters!" She waves a hand over her head like she's riding a bull.

Edward stands back, looking up at my brother, who smiles down at him. "You must be Eddie Nashville." Garret reaches out to shake his hand. "I've heard you're a genius."

Eddie shakes his hand. "You're very tall."

"I'm going to be your new big brother."

"You might be a giant."

Garret nods at his shirt. "That's a great band. Named after *Don Quixote*."

Edward's eyes widen, and once again, my brother has made an instant best friend for life.

Rachel walks to me smiling, rising onto her toes to give me a brief kiss. I turn her back to my chest, wrapping my arm around her shoulders so I can hold her as I survey the room.

This place, this kitchen, full of family, strong as ever, unbroken, and pure gold.

Thank you for reading *The Way We Play!*
Be sure to download your **Free Bonus Scene** here:

Up next is *The Way We Score!*

I tried everything to get pregnant, all the way until my asshole
ex-husband cheated, and I left him. I tossed care to the wind
when I decided to get a little crazy with my high school
boyfriend Garrett Bradford after his little sister's wedding.
Six weeks later, I'm staring at a positive pregnancy test and
wondering, *How did this happen???*

Olivia "Liv" and Garrett's small-town, surprise pregnancy,
second-chance sports romance is full of humor, surprises,
angst, heart melting moments and panty melting spice.

Available in ebook, paperback, and on Audio!

Learn about all of my books on TiaLouise.com/Books,
and get your downloadable Reading Guide.

The Way We Score
The Bradford Boys Series

We promised our love was forever. A decade later, two little blue lines might settle the score.

You've heard of those kids who peak in high school?
Meet my love life.
Garrett Bradford was mine from the moment
we saw each other in ninth grade.
Even then, he was a six-foot-four **mountain of muscles with bright blue eyes, a wide grin, and a way with his hands.**
He was the high school football star, and I was
the dance team captain.
We were the storybook cliché… until we weren't.

Now he's the most famous offensive lineman in the league,
and I'm a buttoned-up, ultra-professional lawyer.
My dancing days are over, and **my carefully
controlled life is a mess.**
Infertility killed my marriage, or that's what I told myself.
Infertility and a cheating ex.
And my inability to get over Garrett Bradford.

One reckless night at his little sister's wedding
is **only supposed to be a reunion**, a trip down
memory lane to a time when life was happier.
Six weeks later, I'm staring at **a positive pregnancy test**
wondering, *How did this happen?*

I figure I'm on my own until Garrett overhauls his life,
moves back to our small town, and shows up every
day to massage my feet and hold my hair when I barf
and go with me to all my doctor's appointments.

Our situation has an end date, just
like it did so many years ago.

Unless this little score changes the game and gives
us **the second chance** I thought we'd lost.

(**THE WAY WE SCORE is a small-town, second-chance sports romance with reunited high school sweethearts, close proximity, surprise pregnancy, a protective Daddy Bear, parents to lovers, it's always been you, and found family vibes. No cheating. No cliffhanger. No third-act breakup.**)

Prologue

Garrett

"Y OU'RE STILL READING *FRANKENSTEIN*?" MY LITTLE SISTER DYLAN plops down beside me on the lawn separating the two buildings of our high school. "You've had it a month."

"I thought it would be more interesting, you know, being monsters and all." I groan, turning the skinny paperback in my hands. "It's all thoughts and feelings and boring as hell."

It's spring, although it's still early enough in the year to be cool in the afternoons in south Alabama—meaning it's mid-80s with a light, coastal breeze. I've got my back against a sprawling live oak that's probably one hundred years old, and I look up at the two-story, brick buildings surrounding us.

On the south side are the seventh through ninth grade classes, and on the west are the sophomores through seniors.

Dylan's finishing her freshman year, and she's acting all superior. She's at the top rung of a mid-level holding pen just waiting to move to the bottom again.

I'm at the very top, graduating senior, fielding offers from colleges that will give me a free ride, regardless of my grades, just as long as I join the team and take them to the national championships.

Hell, some are even offering me under the table deals.

None of it matters, I'm going to Tuscaloosa, where I'll be a starting offensive lineman for the Tide.

I glance at the door-stop in her hand. "What's that you're reading?"

"The newest Dragon Lovers book." She does a little shiver, opening the black book covered in gold, swirling letters and elaborate borders to the middle. "It's not boring *at all.*"

I hold my skinny book next to hers, and she's already read two times as much as I have. "Damn, Dee. What makes you such a nerd? If you came at me with that thing, I'd run."

"I'm not a nerd!" She shoves my shoulder as hard as she can, but I don't move.

Dylan is five-foot-four, and with all the ballet dancing she does, she weighs about fifteen pounds soaking wet. I'm clocking in at six-foot-four, 250 pounds if I don't stop eating.

I never stop eating.

"Is *Frankenstein* even 200 pages long?" She squints an eye at me. "Wimp."

"I'm not like you and Zane. I don't like to read."

"I think you haven't found the right book." She gets on her knees getting all excited like she does. "Reading is like movies in your head, only you get to decide how everyone sounds and looks and—"

"Whatever."

She exhales a little laugh. "You're graduating soon. Just DNF it."

"What's that?"

"Did Not Finish."

"What? I'm no quitter. I'm going to finish this thing." I lift the skinny book and slowly read each word on the page. "He's so damn whiny."

Nothing is so painful to the human mind as a great and sudden change...

Shrugging, I guess that's true for some people, but I've always been one to roll with the punches, like the tide.

And our family has been hit with some hard changes, starting with the death of our mom a few years ago. It hurt like hell, but watching her suffer through cancer hurt more.

We held onto each other through that big wave. Then our dad died of a broken heart soon after, although there were pretty clear signs of chronic traumatic encephalopathy or CTE, the football disease. We didn't realize how much Mom had covered for him until she was gone.

He was never officially diagnosed, but our dad spent years as the star quarterback for the Texas Mustangs. He took a lot of hits before he retired and moved his little family to this small town on the coast. My two youngest siblings weren't even born yet.

Losing both of them so fast was like trying to survive a Category 5 hurricane, which we've also done here. Our little community banded around us like they always do, helping our family stay together through the storm surge.

When he was alive, Dad passed his football legacy on to all of his sons, teaching us the game and opening doors for us where he could. Our oldest brother Jack took his place as the star quarterback for Texas.

He's there now, but even two states away, he manages to keep up with his younger siblings back home.

Our second-oldest brother Zane, is being courted by all the big teams, while I'm gearing up for college. My little brother Hendrix is only a year older than Dylan, but he's the most like Dad when it comes to the love of the game.

When Hendrix was a little boy, he'd sleep with his head on a football as a pillow. Now he's a star on our high school team along with me, and I expect he'll be joining me in Tuscaloosa in a few years as well.

Dylan's back is against my side, and she's turning pages twice as fast as I am. I'm about to pull her long brunette ponytail, when I hear the voice that warms my body from my stomach to my toes.

"It came!" Olivia "Liv" Bankston runs up the sidewalk to where we're sitting, waving a large, white envelope over her head.

She skids to a stop, dropping to her knees in front of us, and Dylan jumps up just as fast, leaning in to see what my girlfriend is holding.

Liv's strawberry blonde hair falls over her shoulders in soft waves, and she's wearing a tennis dress in her signature color, cherry-red. You'd think it wouldn't work with her hair and skin so fair, but she looks really hot all the time.

I fell in love with her freshman year, when she came back from drill-team camp four inches taller, curves in all the right places, and legs for days.

Okay, looking back, I fell in lust, I'll admit it. We'd known each other since we were kids, but she'd never looked like that. A little while later, she noticed me, and well, the rest, as they say, is history.

We've been inseparable ever since, sharing everything, all our firsts, all our hopes, all our dreams and fears. Nobody but Liv saw me cry when we lost Mom and Dad. She held me in her arms, kissing my temple and soothing me with her cool hands and her warm body.

Nobody comforts me the way Liv can.

We're the corny, stereotypical football player boyfriend and dance-line captain girlfriend. Hell, I see myself marrying this girl, and I feel fine.

"It's the big envelope." Her hazel eyes are wide. "That's a good sign, right?"

"That's what they say." Dylan is at her shoulder, her brown eyes blinking excitedly. "Open it!"

"What is it?"

"I hope it's my invitation to audition, which essentially means I'm in. I got my college acceptance letter last week."

I scoot forward so her slim body is in the cave of my arms as she tears the top off the envelope. I'm frowning, expecting to see the signature crimson *A* logo. Instead I'm confused to see purple and gold.

The pages are out, and she jumps up so fast, I barely have a chance to register the glossy photo of a girl with long blonde hair on the cover in a white one-piece leotard with a sparkling gold fleur de lis outlined in purple on the front.

"This is it!" She screams, jumping up and down, her face shining with tears. "It's my invitation!"

Dylan is on her feet as well, jumping up and down beside her, holding her arm. Liv is three inches taller as she leans down to hug my sister.

"I have to submit a video audition no longer than one minute…" She's reading the requirements, but I'm confused as hell.

"Switch leap, switch arabesque…" Dylan reads along with her. "I can help you with all of this. Pirouettes are easy."

"Easy for you, Miss Balanchine."

"I don't think there was ever a Miss Balanchine." Dylan's nose wrinkles, and they laugh.

"This is for LSU." My brow furrows, and I feel like a rug has been pulled out from under me. "Why are you auditioning to be a Golden Girl?"

Liv blinks wide eyes up at me. "Because I want to join the Texas professional cheerleaders after college."

"So be a Crimsonette."

"Garrett." Her chin pulls back, and she grimaces like I suggested she go to clown college. "The Golden Girls are the best, most historic precision dance line in the SEC."

My stomach twists as my lips curl in disgust. "But it's *LSU.*"

Dylan gives Liv's hand a squeeze before stepping back

and grabbing her book, and I'm pretty sure she can sense my mood.

She's leaving us alone.

"I've got to meet Craig. We're supposed to be practicing this afternoon. See ya, Liv. See ya, Grizz."

Grizz. Short for *Grizzly*, because I'm a bear. Only, I don't feel like a bear. I feel like a dog who's just been kicked. Hard. I've got the wind knocked out of me, and I'm wondering if I'm the last person to know about this.

"How long have you been planning this?" I hear the confusion, the pain in my voice.

Liv blinks up at me, her pretty hazel eyes wide and pleading. "I applied to all the state schools back in March, but Grizz, you've known what I want to do. It's never been a secret."

Reaching up, I trace my finger across her cheek, moving a lock of soft red hair behind her ear. Her slim palms are on my chest, and I move my hands to her waist, pulling her closer to my body.

"I never knew you wanted to go to Baton Rouge."

"You could come with me. You have your pick of teams."

I almost laugh. "I can't play for the Tigers. I grew up hating those guys."

"You don't have to hate them. It's only football."

It's like I'm in the Twilight Zone. It's like I've spent the last four years believing one thing, and I'm waking up to discover everyone else believed something completely opposite.

Liv has been a given in my life so long, I can't even imagine myself without her.

"What about us?" My voice softens. "Don't you love me?"

I think about every time I've held her in my arms. I think about all the times I've devoured her lips, the taste of cherry lip gloss on my tongue. I think about her long legs straddling my waist, sitting in the driver's seat of my truck, her beautiful hair falling around us as I pulled a hard nipple into my mouth.

I think of the two of us holding each other so tight as she came apart on my cock, and I lost myself deep in her warm body. So many times, I've lost count.

Beyond that, I think of being wrapped in a blanket with her at a bonfire with all our friends, cheering for our home team, prepping for the big games, homecoming, state champs.

I think of her soft lips whispering in my ear, *I love you…*

She's always been my forever.

"Of course, I love you." Her eyes flicker to her hands, and she blinks fast. "It's only four years. If we're really meant to be together, we can make it work long distance."

"But it's the best four years." My voice is soft, pleading. "I don't want to make those memories without you."

Her eyes lift to mine, and it hurts so much. My dream since I was a little boy—or a smaller human, since I was never really little—was to play for the Tide. I grew up in a house of houndstooth and crimson.

Her dream has always been to be a dancer. Not like Dylan's dreams of New York and the American Ballet Company. No, my girl wants to be a show-stopper. She's fierce and sexy.

She's leaving me.

Lifting her hand, she puts a palm against my cheek. "I promise, we can make this work. We just have to believe we can."

I don't want to believe. I don't want to work hard. I want her with me always. I don't want to let her go.

Dropping my chin, I know that makes me sound like a child. "Of course I believe we can. We'll FaceTime and call and text and do what it takes."

"We'll both be so busy, you with practice and games, and me with practice and games." Her lips tremble as she forces a smile, and a crystal tear hits her cheek when she blinks. "You have to believe we can do this, Garret. If you don't believe in us…"

An ache grips my throat, and I slide my hand in the back of her hair, pulling her closer into a tight hug.

"I'll never love anyone the way I love you, Liv." Thickness is in my voice. "If that doesn't mean we can make it, I don't know what does."

"We'll be together when you join Jack and me in Texas. It's only for a little while."

It's only for a little while.

That's what we promised each other…

Get *The Way We Score* today!
Also available on audio.

Acknowledgments

Zane and Rachel (and Edward and Miss G and Claws and the kittens and everyone) consumed so much of my heart, and it was so fun going on this journey with my people, my incredibly supportive team.

Huge thanks and so much love to my husband "Mr. TL" for everything, which includes approving my references to all things legal.

My amazing PA and daughter Kat was invaluable in keeping the wheels turning while I wrote, and my grown-up baby Laura, who made all the illustrations for the cover and the teasers and everything. They're such hard workers, so patient, and my heart is full having them with me.

Thanks so much to the BEST alpha readers on the planet, Jen DeJong, Renee McCleary and Leticia Teixeira. So much LOVE for you ladies.

Huge thanks to my *incredible* betas, Maria Black, Corinne Akers, Amy Reierson, Courtney Anderson, Jennifer Christy, Heather Heaton, and Michelle Mastandrea. Your notes are life.

Thanks to Jaime Ryter for your eagle-eyed edits and to Lori Jackson and Kari March for the incredible cover designs, to my dear Wander for the *perfect* photography, and the amazing Stacy Blake, who helps me make my gorgeous paperback interiors!

Thanks to my dear Starfish, to my Mermaids, and to my Veeps for keeping me sane and organized and helping me spread the word.

I can't begin to put into words how much I appreciate the love and support of all the influencers on BookTok, Instagram, Facebook, and to my author-buds! I love you all so much…

I hope you loved this healing journey, these quirky characters, and all the found-family love! Thank you for helping me do what I do.

Love, football, and spice,

♥ *Tia*

Books by
TIA LOUISE

ROMANCE IN KINDLE UNLIMITED

THE BRADFORD BOYS
The Way We Touch, 2024*
The Way We Play, Oct. 2024*
The Way We Score, Jan. 2025*
The Way We Run, 2025*
The Way We Win, 2025*
(*Available on Audiobook.)

THE BE STILL SERIES
A Little Taste, 2023*
A Little Twist, 2023*
A Little Luck, 2023*
A Little Naughty, 2024*
(*Available on Audiobook.)

THE HAMILTOWN HEAT SERIES
Fearless, 2022*
Filthy, 2022*
For Your Eyes Only, 2022
Forbidden, 2023*
(*Available on Audiobook.)

THE TAKING CHANCES SERIES
*This Much is True**
*Twist of Fate**
*Trouble**
(*Available on Audiobook.)

FIGHT FOR LOVE SERIES
*Wait for Me**
*Boss of Me**
*Here with Me**
*Reckless Kiss**
(*Available on Audiobook.)

BELIEVE IN LOVE SERIES
Make You Mine
*Make Me Yours**
*Stay**
(*Available on Audiobook.)

SOUTHERN HEAT SERIES
When We Touch
When We Kiss

THE ONE TO HOLD SERIES
*One to Hold (#1—Derek & Melissa)**
*One to Keep (#2—Patrick & Elaine)**
*One to Protect (#3—Derek & Melissa)**
One to Love (#4—Kenny & Slayde)
One to Leave (#5—Stuart & Mariska)
*One to Save (#6—Derek & Melissa)**
*One to Chase (#7—Marcus & Amy)**
One to Take (#8—Stuart & Mariska)
(*Available on Audiobook.)

THE DIRTY PLAYERS SERIES
PRINCE (#1)*
PLAYER (#2)*
DEALER (#3)
THIEF (#4)
(*Available on Audiobook.)

THE BRIGHT LIGHTS SERIES
Under the Lights (#1)
Under the Stars (#2)
Hit Girl (#3)

COLLABORATIONS
*The Last Guy**
The Right Stud
*Tangled Up**
(*Available on Audiobook.)

PARANORMAL ROMANCES
One Immortal (vampires)
One Insatiable (shifters)

GET THREE FREE STORIES!
Sign up for my New Release newsletter and never miss a sale
or new release by me!

About the Author

Tia Louise is the *USA Today* and #4 Amazon bestselling author of (*primarily*) small-town, single-parent, second-chance, and military romances set at or near the beach.

From Readers' Choice awards, to *USA Today* "Happily Ever After" nods, to winning Favorite Erotica Author and the "Lady Boner Award" (*lol!*), nothing makes her happier than communicating with fellow Mermaids (*fans*) and creating romances that are smart, sassy, and *very sexy*.

A former journalist and displaced beach bum, Louise lives in the Midwest with her trophy husband, two young-adult geniuses, and one clumsy "grand-cat."

Sign up for her newsletter and never miss a new release or sale—and get a free story collection!

Signed Copies of all books online at:
https://geni.us/SignedPBs

Connect with Tia:
TiaLouise.com
Instagram—@AuthorTLouise
TikTok—@TheTiaLouise